Banker's Draft

Clive Mullis

ISBN:
ISBN-13: 978-1479159819
ISBN-10: 1479159816

DEDICATION

To my wife

ACKNOWLEDGEMENTS

My thanks go to all those who helped me and put up with me not doing what I should have been doing when I was doing this.
Also thanks go to those that read and gave me advice, suggestions and encouragement, namely Lesley, Keith, Dave, Roy, Helen and Sarah.

Not forgetting my long suffering wife and my son — they've had to put up with me.

ABOUT GORNSTOCK

The Twearth is a small bright blue marble of a planet circling its sun in its own unique universe. Other planets frequently come close to it before shooting off back into space with a jaunty wave; all that is except its moon, which is ever-present and stays close to see what happens.

The problem with our universe is that the big bang misfired, and now it's in touch with every other universe that exploded into creation. There's a rift in the fabric of being which allows it to be a peeping tom into all the other universes and the people on Twearth are quick to exploit the anomaly.

On the banks of the Sterkle, a wide flowing river which feeds into the Blue Sea on the Island of Inglion, a poor unfortunate trader was counting down until his last breath sighed from his body; he had been robbed of his cart as well as his stock of leather accessories. The arrow in his side slowly gnawed its way into his internal organs just as a company of Morris men jangled along the same path. Our unfortunate trader could only point to where his cart had disappeared to and stammer feebly, G... G... Gone, S... S... Stock,' before expiring with a grunt. The Morris men nodded sagely, then they buried him in the nearby woods and danced a jig in remembrance — and there the city of Gornstock began to grow.

CHAPTER 1

"'...Where stays the shimmering crystal stream, on light that gazes open seems, Oh what in that which hopeful roams, a guiding light to send you home.'"

Jocelyn Cornwallis III slowly closed the brown frayed leather book with a sigh. The book, whose title "Poetry and Thoughts for Today's Modern Man" scarred black into its dull brown cover, was thoughtlessly cast onto the old oak, once polished desk; on which his boots were presently resting. The tome slid to a halt amidst the dusty paperwork sending motes swirling into the air.

'Yeah, right,' responded Frankie Kandalwick, Cornwallis' friend and employee, grimacing at the tortuous lines. 'So tell me, why do you read such rubbish?'

'Because, my dear Frankie,' answered Cornwallis, casting his eyes around the room and waving a distracted arm, 'it gives one a sense of perspective. This particular poem shows how nature can guide the most wayward, a simple star in the sky, a speck of light, and it can help a weary traveller find home. Those of us who are fortunate enough to be educated recognise the beauty of language.'

Frankie snorted disdainfully. 'Anyway, if that's what you call education, I'll happily stay ignorant.'

Cornwallis slowly shook his head in resignation, he steepled his fingers and then tapped the index fingers against his lips in thought. 'You know, Frankie, I sometimes wonder why I let you work for me.'

'That's 'cause no other bugger's stupid enough.'

'That's about the only sensible thing you've said so far today.' Cornwallis pulled at the neck of his shirt hoping for a draught of air to cool him down, it had been a hot day and there didn't seem to be much air circulating around the room, the window was fully open but the wind decided to go on strike.

Jocelyn Cornwallis III, a tad over six feet tall, lean and clean-shaven, presently sat relaxing in his chair with his feet crossed and planted firmly on his desk. The room, his office, hadn't seen a broom or a duster in months; it was just the way he liked it. He had dark equine features with dark brown shoulder length hair and dressed in a coal black suit which contrasted with the crisp white shirt. He could have a razor sharp mind, but only when he wasn't too distracted. Born to lead a different life, the son of a noble, he suffered the normal upbringing afforded to his class: brought up by a nanny until old enough to attend "School" then destined for a seat in the Assembly. But Cornwallis had other ideas; he decided against following tradition and began a life far removed from that which his father had planned. He decided he wanted to work for a living. On the door to the office, a cardboard sign proclaimed the word *Investigator* in faded lettering.

Frankie had no choice in the matter, a product of the gutter, or if not the gutter, standing precariously on the kerb looking down, a life of lawlessness beckoned. As a youth and a man, he lived up to expectation and forged himself quite a career, until the day Cornwallis and he became reacquainted, and then his life changed; he became honest. It happened suddenly down a back alley with a pocket full of silver jewellery, filched from the house of a dealer in antique curios and novelty items, who had short-changed his brother when he had been trying to offload a stack of lead piping. He couldn't understand how the knife got there, pressed to his throat, but Cornwallis did, he being the one holding the knife. He had seen him leaving by a side window, and negotiations, as they say, continued. His mum used to be a char at Cornwallis' father's city house and they had played together as kids. Built like a brick outhouse with cropped light hair and large calloused hands, few argued with Frankie, and those that did rapidly regretted their decision. The broken nose and puffy ears suggested he sometimes came off second best, but looks could be deceiving, he was a mountain of a man who could move mountains and in their line of work, he was more than useful. He played up to his image of being slow in thought, but many had cause to re-think that assumption, there was more to Frankie than met the eye. He balanced the chair on its two rear legs and reclined against the wall, he sighed and then pitched forward, stood up, and headed over to the dart board — boredom had set in, nothing had happened for days now.

'Triple twenty,' he announced, standing back to the chalk line on the floor.

Cornwallis grinned as he watched.

Frankie screwed up his eye and threw. 'A five. Bugger.'

'Try something easier,' suggested Cornwallis. 'Like the wall.'

'It's these darts of yours, they ain't balanced,' he countered, taking aim again. This time he concentrated harder, he licked his lips but left the pink tip of his tongue hanging out. The dart thumped into the board. 'Single twenty,' he announced, triumphantly. 'Getting closer.'

Cornwallis pulled out half a dollar and slapped it on the desk. 'Next dart, and I'll make it easy for you, sixteen or higher.'

'If you want to throw yer money away, then I'll have it. Yer a loser waiting to lose.' He took his time, concentrating as hard as he could, flexing his arm a few times and then slowly pulling the dart back to his face. His hand shot forward and the dart flew unerringly towards the board, it felt smooth and graceful, a perfect release — the dart hit a seven.

Cornwallis shook his head as Frankie paid up, a nailed on certainty that he would miss. It didn't really seem fair to take the money, but then again… 'Well, Frankie, I don't know about you, but I feel a thirst coming on.'

Frankie didn't need to think. 'So long as you're paying,' he said, as he watched his half-dollar disappear into Cornwallis' pocket.

They made their way down the stairs from the second floor of the four-storey house; Cornwallis had bought the house a few years previously and rented out the ground and first floor whilst keeping the top two floors for himself. The address was in one of the more fashionable areas of the city, Hupplemere Mews, right on the corner with Grantby Street and only a few streets away from the seat of government, so there were always a steady stream of takers for the vacant rooms. At present, a workers agency, a marriage broker and a gentleman's surgical appliance fitter rented the spare rooms and only last week a rather attractive lady who spoke to the dead paid a month's rent in advance; he did think that the surgical supply fitter might have to start reinforcing some of his wares should some of the clientele walk into the wrong room, but that wouldn't be his problem.

Frankie couldn't have been more wrong, something had happened at the offices of Mssrs Critchloe, Flanders, and Goup, Accountants, Greenwalsh Avenue, Gornstock. Miss Eliza Knutt, 51, spinster of the parish, had been found dead in the first floor inner office, and the circumstances were not natural. Miss Knutt had been a cleaner, and she would most definitely not be happy with the state of her former body. The pool of blood surrounding her, and soaking into the richly embroidered deeply piled and very expensive East Pergoland rug began to congeal nicely. Mr Goup, who found Miss Knutt, not a particularly robust man, stared in abject horror at the two paper-knives sticking out of the back of Miss Knutt's neck. He struggled to stop his lunch from making a dramatic re-appearance as it churned in his stomach and then make a short foray up his gullet before deciding whether to go for broke. As Mr Goup stepped back from the door his stomach won the unequal battle and an explosion of half-digested pea and ham pie, together with a half bottle of his favourite Pinket Gregorio wine, came rushing forth.

*

The Black Stoat occupied a corner of a small piazza down Brindlenook Alley, called Cumerbund Square. Tables spewed out from the interior and covered the forefront of the tavern like a rash. It had a diverse clientele to say the least. It wasn't a particularly rough establishment, but it could be described as being a little frayed around the edges as the occasional bout of entertainment did occur, but that only added to the ambience. In the opposite corner stood another tavern, The Duke, and that was chalk to the Stoat's cheese. Only the young and well-heeled frequented The Duke as it considered itself a cut above the rest, serving its drinks in tiny glasses, always with some kind of fruit floating on top. Between the taverns, a variety of premises: a cloth merchant; a candle maker; Fossie's Take Away; a baker's; Ying Pong's noodle shop and an exotic wares merchant.

Cornwallis and Frankie sat themselves down at a table in the piazza not far from the door of the Stoat and caught the eye of Eddie the landlord. Cornwallis held up two fingers and mimed drinking to order a couple of beers. The late afternoon sunshine bathed the piazza in a golden glow which brought folk out to drink and to cool down, the place just starting to fill up. They could see Big George pedalling away in the corner inside the tavern; the brown bear sitting on a geared contraption which, attached to a fan by a large rubber band, gave just enough waft of air to stir the smoke and give a respite from the cloying heat. Outside though, a cooling breeze gently breathed, and Cornwallis eased back into the chair and closed his eyes, enjoying the moment of relaxation and the anticipation of the cooling beer disappearing down his throat — but only for a few seconds.

'Frankie, do you have to do that?' Cornwallis opened one eye and peered at his employee. Frankie had his index finger firmly rammed up his left nostril, a deep excavation taking place. Cornwallis watched in distaste as the finger puggled away until it finally slowly unscrewed from the cavity.

Frankie held up his finger triumphantly before staring at the result with satisfaction, he sniffed, and then deftly flicked the offending article towards the leg of a passing tradesman. 'Technically, no, but I ain't got a hankie.' He sniffed again to check that all was well and grinned back at Cornwallis. 'You could always lend me one of yours.'

'Gods forbid,' replied Cornwallis, aghast, 'I'd have to burn it afterwards. Your snot would just disintegrate my rather expensive silk. No, Frankie, I will not lend you one of mine.'

Their beers appeared and immediately the conversation ceased as the serving girl sashayed her way towards them. She wore a long pale green dress with a golden tasselled braid wrapped around her slim waist, the gentle curves of her hips accentuated by the silkiness of the dress as she moved forward step by seductive step. Long honey-coloured hair hung loose down her back and she had the biggest blue eyes ever. She stood about five foot nine tall and her skin radiated vitality; but the cut of her dress allowed the imagination to run riot as the material struggled to hold everything in place. She arrived at their table and eased forward to put the tray down, and two pairs of eyes watched eagerly, hoping and praying for a wardrobe malfunction.

'Er, you couldn't wipe the table for us, my darling?' asked Frankie, somewhat strained but hopeful all the same, as she positioned the glass in front of him.

The girl stood up slowly and shook her head; piercing blue eyes seared into Frankie's, but then flicked over to Cornwallis'.

'I think you know the answer to that; do I look like I've got a cloth on me?' She held her arms out wide in a stance that said frisk me then, but her eyes said you'd be dead if you tried. Everyone on nearby tables turned eagerly to watch, as if they knew something Cornwallis and Frankie didn't. She smiled sweetly and then picked up the tray; everyone seemed to groan and then turn disappointedly back. 'Eddie just warned me about you two, you know, but for some reason he told me to be gentle.' She wagged a finger of admonishment at them before breaking into a wide smile. 'You two have a lot to learn.' She swished around, and then without another word, headed back inside. Two pairs of eyes followed her intently, and were rewarded when she turned briefly and gave a coy little look over her shoulder before disappearing from view.

Frankie groaned and crossed his legs. 'Where do you think Eddie found her from? She wasn't here a few days ago, it were that Bertha with a limp and she spilled most of the beer before we got it.'

Cornwallis' smile was beatific. 'I don't particularly care where he found her, I'm just thankful that he did. She didn't tell us her name, but I'm sure we'll find that out soon enough. Francis, I think I'm in love.'

As soon as Eddie stepped out of the door, Cornwallis beckoned him over. 'Come on, Eddie, who is she and where did you find her?'

'Looky 'ere, Jack, I can't be 'aving with you chasing after me staff, you know.' Eddie being one of the few people who were well enough acquainted with Cornwallis to use his soubriquet. 'She's 'ere to work and pull in the punters.'

'And I'm sure she's very good at it,' responded Cornwallis, thinking that once word got around this place would be heaving every hour of the day. 'However… Oh, come on, Eddie, tell us.'

The pleading look in Cornwallis' eye was too much for Eddie so he sat down and leant back with a sigh. 'All right then, her name is Primrose, or Rose for short, she's my sister's niece by marriage, meaning, she's *family.*' His emphasis on his last indicated a subtle warning, 'She's come up from Dawling for a time, wants to see the big city, got fed up with a nowhere town and wants to live a little.' He scratched his chin and belched loudly. 'I'm not so sure I done the right thing now, though. Over the last few days I've had more problems than I want to deal with; some of the punters are taking right liberties. She tells me she can handle things, but… I don't know; mebbe I should find another job for her.'

'No, no, no!' Frankie almost screamed in horror. 'You can't do that; she brings a touch of class to the place. No, you keep her on and if you get any trouble then let *me* know and I will personally sort it out for you.' He tapped his chest and sat up straight.

Eddie sighed and stood up. 'I doubt you'd ever be needed: she got taught how to defend herself by a little priest from out east; so far she's broken up three fights and put two people in hospital. She could probably knock seven colours of shit out of the pair of you if she really wanted to.'

Cornwallis' mouth hung open as he stared at Eddie's retreating back.

*

The Police had just arrived at the address of Mssrs Critchloe, Flanders and Goup; a large grey stoned terraced building with two pillars guarding the entrance. Four officers marched in and sealed off the premises. Sergeant Jethro MacGillicudy stood at the door to the inner office and gazed down at Eliza Knutt. He was a big man with a moustache and long side whiskers, his reddish-brown hair flecked with grey and he possessed an air of authority that screamed his rank. Nicknamed the Feelers, the police had been founded by Lord Carstairs Fielding long ago. He had decided enough was enough after being robbed at knifepoint as he took home *his* ill-gotten gains after fleecing the Mayor of several hundred dollars.

'Constable Toopins, if you please.'

'Yes, Sarge.' The youngest recruit elbowed his way to the front to stand next to his sergeant. A skinny creature with a mop of unruly dark hair, he'd already got the nickname of Dewdrop, due to the seemingly permanent droplet of snot hanging from his nose.

'Tell me son, what do you see?' MacGillicudy wrapped an arm around his shoulder and swept the other generously around the room.

'Er... A dead woman, Sarge?' he ventured timidly.

'Yes, yes... and?'

'Er... a lot of blood, Sarge?'

'Well spotted, son, well spotted.' MacGillicudy knew he had to be patient. 'Now, shall we try to be a bit more adventurous in our initial examination of the alleged crime scene?'

Some whispering came from behind him which resulted in a snigger.

'What, Constable Spekes, do you find funny?'

'Sorry, Sarge, but I can't help seeing the alleged knives in 'er neck, and unless she were very inventive, I can't see any alleged alleging at all.'

'Spekes, everything is alleged until we know different. Now get your pencil out and start writing. You can write, can't you?'

'Yes, Sarge.'

The young feelers indulged in some more whispering as MacGillicudy waited. 'Are we ready now, Spekes?'

There was a stamp, a little groan of pain, and then some shuffling. A pencil finally appeared.

'Am now, Sarge, carry on; I'm all ears.'

'Right,' and he rubbed his hands together. 'To the left of the door and in front of the open filing cabinet is lying prone a female body, in her neck appear to be two knives. Blood is on the rug and on the floor. There is a footprint in blood heading to the door. To the right of the door is a desk, and on that desk I can see a lamp, an open ledger, and some papers. Are you getting everything, Spekes?'

'Yes, Sarge.'

'Er... Sarge?'

MacGilliudy emitted a deep sigh. 'What is it Constable Popham?'

'Mr Goup says he wants to throw up, he ain't looking too good, you know.'

'Well, could you ask Mr Goup to kindly go and puke somewhere else, this is a crime scene and I don't want any extras.'

A retching noise entered the sergeant's ears.

'Sorry, Sarge, too late.'

MacGillicudy closed his eyes as the odour wafted beneath his nose. 'Thank you, Popham, I think I can tell that now.'

Some hurried footsteps came up the stairs and a breathless constable stuck his head around the outer office door. 'Message from the Captain, Sarge; he says you ain't to touch or do anything. He wants you to seal up the building and wait for Cornwallis to come. He says he's sorry but the order comes from above.'

'What?' bellowed MacGillicudy, his anger exploding like a volcano. 'What the hell does the Captain mean by handing a perfectly good murder over to someone like Cornwallis?'

'You'll have to speak to the Captain, Sarge; I'm just telling you what he said.' The constable hadn't ventured any further than the door and he could see the three others begin to edge away from the puce looking sergeant as he struggled to contain himself.

*

The eatery and the noodle shop were beginning to do a brisk business as the afternoon moved on to evening. The piazza had filled up and the buzz of conversations echoed around as people began to meet up to eat, drink, and catch up on the day's news. Big George had taken a rest from pedalling and sat with his friend, a panda called Mike, enjoying a cool glass of Bamboo Soda.

Frankie leant back and slid over a piece of paper with an address written in black ink. 'Go 'round there tomorrow, George, he said he might have some work for you. Won't pay much, but if you do a good job, there might be more.'

'Thanks, Mr Kandalwick.' The slow voice had a bass resonance. 'Rats is it?'

'Rats it is. All you can eat and pay to go with it; what more could a bear ask?'

'You're good to me, Mr Kandalwick; I won't let you down. Be 'round there first thing in the morning.'

'That's my bear.'

Frankie turned his attention back to Cornwallis, though Cornwallis' attention was at that moment drawn elsewhere. A man had appeared wearing a black stove pipe hat and a duck arse jacket. Knee breeches and gaiters finished the ensemble.

'Feeler on the prowl, Frankie; now, who do you suppose he's after?' Cornwallis pointed to the little alley off to the side of the Duke; the officer seemed to be studying the little square as though looking for something or someone.

Frankie narrowed his eyes in the dim light as the oil lamps had yet to be lit. 'Looks like old Wiggins to me.'

Wiggins nodded to himself as he spied Cornwallis and Frankie; he shrugged and then strode purposefully over.

'Mr Cornwallis, Frankie,' he said by way of greeting. 'Captain Bough sent me to find yer.' He rummaged in his pocket and brought out a neatly folded piece of paper. 'I've got to give you this.' He handed the note over to Cornwallis and then stood and cast his experienced eyes around the square, looking for anything that might be amiss. He might have been old and well past his prime but he had been a constable for twenty six years and he could smell a wrong 'un from half a mile away.

Cornwallis carefully unfolded the note and began to read. Halfway through he raised an eyebrow and then glanced at Frankie; he smiled a little as he carried on before breaking into a wide grin. He re-folded the note and placed it in the inside pocket of his jacket.

'Well?' enquired Frankie, curious as to what the note said.

'Well, indeed,' smiled a satisfied Cornwallis, 'I am pleased to announce that we now have some gainful employment.' He patted the note in his pocket. 'When you eventually finish that drink of yours, then our friendly neighbourhood constable will guide us to our house of mysteries.'

Frankie drained his glass in one, wiped his arm across his mouth and banged the glass back down on the table. 'Then what are we waiting for? You can tell me all about it on the way.'

*

A crowd had gathered at Greenwalsh Avenue and Constable Wiggins had to force a path through for Cornwallis and Frankie; word had gone around quicker than a fly on acid, and those assembled waited eagerly for any juicy gossip that could be quickly turned into a free pint.

Sergeant MacGillicudy waited on the staircase, far from happy. His flamboyant side whiskers seemed to bristle and his nose twitched as he spoke through clenched teeth. 'Evening to you, Cornwallis. I'm not best pleased about this and I'll have you know I will be speaking to the Captain.' He stood straight as a ramrod and directed his address to just above Cornwallis' head. It took an effort to get the words out, but he felt he put enough contempt into them to make his point.

'Sergeant,' acknowledged Cornwallis, and then grinned. 'I have a note here from your Captain, and he has assured me you will do your utmost to help us with this enquiry. He even says that you yourself are to make yourself available and are now, if fact, to function under my direction. So Sergeant, how do you feel about calling me Sir?' Cornwallis felt that he had evened up the score and now watched MacGillicudy twitch as he digested the information. He actually liked the man, they had even shared a drink or two in the past and he understood how the sergeant felt; to solve the murder would have been a feather in his cap if he could have rooted out the perpetrator: but for some reason Bough had given it over to him, so the question went through his mind, *why*? He knew that MacGillicudy was nobody's fool, and as feelers went, he was one of the best. Given time he would probably solve it, but it had fallen into his lap and he couldn't help thinking that there was more to this than met the eye — and he hadn't even seen the body yet.

Cornwallis stepped over the pile of vomit and then studied the scene from the doorway, allowing all the little details to burn into his memory. Frankie stood behind and peered over his shoulder.

'Hmmm,' contemplated Cornwallis aloud. 'Is that boot print one of yours, Jethro?'

'You know me better than that, Jack,' replied MacGillicudy, insulted. 'No one's been in yet, except maybe Mr Goup. He found her and it's his office. A Miss Knutt, he says, his cleaner.'

'Is he still here?'

'Downstairs, back office. Though he ain't feeling too good at the moment.'

'Frankie, would you go and have a quick word with Mr Goup and see whether he came in and what he did while he was here. I'll come and speak to him when I'm done.'

Frankie turned away and went downstairs; Cornwallis could hear him muttering to himself and grandmother and eggs featured prominently.

'Right, Sergeant,' said Cornwallis, rubbing his hands. 'I want you to get an artist up here and get this lot pictured. A close up of the boot print and the body if you please. Now, let's see what's in the cabinet.' He stepped into the room, and careful to avoid the blood, tip-toed over to the cabinet. He leant over the deceased and looked inside.

If he expected to see anything interesting then at first he felt disappointed. There were files, lots of files, all in alphabetical order, rows and rows of them. The only interesting thing, he supposed, was that someone had left the file open on the letter D. He peered closer and began to read down the list. His first impressions were wrong, some of the names, cross referenced to another number, he supposed to another file, were very interesting indeed. Turning his attention to Miss Knutt, he stepped back and knelt down. The blood had turned a nice deep colour now, having spent too long away from the nice warm insides of the deceased. The knives were quite ornate with ivory handles and he supposed thin blades, making an aesthetically pleasing arrangement with the V of the handles beneath the round grey bun of hair on the back of Miss Knutt's head. He glanced along the length of the body and found nothing out of the ordinary. Standing up, he began to look around the rest of the room, then over to the desk and looked in the ledger, again names, but this time with appointments, a diary in fact. He read down the list for that day.

'Sergeant, would you care to start organising your men. I want that crowd out there spoken to and could you go around all the buildings in the street; see if anyone saw or heard anything, who came in, and who went out. You know the sort of thing we need.' There were just too many people to question; he and Frankie couldn't deal with it all, and he could always go and re-interview should anything of any substance crop up.

MacGillicudy sighed, but though tempted, knew better than to make life difficult. He nodded and then disappeared down the stairs.

Cornwallis tapped his finger against the last name in the diary as he thought. Mr Morris Bezell and it concerned his tax demand. He thought a little more as something niggled there, something not quite right. He tapped again as if the act would force his mind to clarity.

As he thought, Frankie returned from speaking to Mr Goup; he still had a smile on his face as he had seen the melee outside as Sergeant MacGillicudy and his constables got to work. 'He didn't go into the room,' he informed Cornwallis, 'he just puked on the landing and ran. Though he did say that the knives were his and that they had been on the table; used 'em for opening his letters, he said. Miss Knutt had only worked for him for a few days as his normal cleaner had gone off to visit some relative: just a temporary replacement, so he doesn't know much about her. The other partners are dead, so Mr Goup is the only one left.'

Cornwallis looked up as Frankie disturbed his thoughts. 'So we know the boot print must have come from our friend, but why kill an innocent cleaner?'

'Was she innocent though?' replied Frankie, raising his eyebrows in question. 'You can't tell these days; don't you remember Ethel Pinns?'

Cornwallis winced; he did, but thankfully, that case hadn't involved him as the repercussions were widely felt. Ethel Pinns had been secretary of the knitting circle as well as chair of two charities. She had been rich, but nobody thought to wonder how. Unbeknownst to anyone, she ran two brothels, a protection racket, and operated as the biggest loan shark in Gornstock. Eighty three years old and she had been operating beneath the law for sixty two of them. A mass resignation in the Assembly followed her arrest; eighteen members were tied up with Ethel Pinns and her operation. 'Such a trusting fellow you are, Frankie, I bet your mother's proud of you.'

Frankie grinned. 'Of course she is; I'm the only one in the family who never got caught.'

'I caught you.'

'Yes, but you ain't the feelers, so it don't count.'

Cornwallis shook his head slowly in defeat; to Frankie that logic was fool-proof. He turned his attention back to the diary; something still niggled there, but it wouldn't quite click into place. He pulled out a notebook and copied out all the day's appointments, then walked over to the cabinet and listed all the names and references that showed there. He flipped through the files again, and once done, closed his book and slipped it back into his jacket pocket before stepping back and scanning the scene once more. 'I think you might be right, Frankie. Our Miss Knutt had been looking for something, and someone didn't want her to find it. You can see specks of blood on the cabinet and on the inside of the drawer, but not on the files themselves. She had a file open and was reading it when it happened, otherwise there would be blood all over the files. She's lying in front of the cabinet with the knives in the back of the neck, so she must have been bending over the drawer when the assailant struck. I think somebody panicked when they saw her looking at something she shouldn't. Mr Goup has got a few things to tell us; he's an accountant, so one thing's for certain, he's not above bending the law.'

The last of the light began to disappear so Cornwallis lit the oil lamp on the desk; it spluttered as it caught, so he turned the wick down a little as the smoke rose, blackening the glass. A weak illumination filled the room as he pursed his lips in thought; Frankie stood at the door with his hands deep in his pockets, tapping impatiently with his foot.

'You all done now?' asked Frankie, eager to get back to the pub. 'We can have another quick word with the accountant and then get straight back down to the Stoat to chew things over. MacGillicudy can wait for the picture-man.'

Cornwallis suddenly grinned to himself, he hadn't heard a word Frankie had said. 'Mr Morris Bezel, Mr M Bezel. Embezzle! Clever, but no banana.'

Frankie stopped tapping his foot and looked confused. 'Er?'

'The last entry in the diary, Frankie,' explained Cornwallis patiently, 'an appointment with a Mr Morris Bezel. I knew there was something wrong with it. It's someone's little joke, and if we find out whose, then we may have our man. Let's find where the rest of the files are and then go and see if Jethro has come up with anything.'

The main files were easy to find. They were in the back room and stacked in cabinets from floor to ceiling, but there were too many to go through now; they would just have to wait until they had a good few months to spare.

MacGillicudy hadn't had any luck at all. Nobody had seen anything, or more to the point, nobody had seen anything that they were prepared to talk about. He shook his head as he turned to Cornwallis standing at the door. 'Nobody noticed a thing, they say. Look at the street: a coffee shop just over there, a fruit and veg' man over there, a lawyer next door, and a funeral parlour next to that. At the top of the street, there's a tavern, and fancy shops all along the road and they're all telling me they saw nothing, zilch, bugger all. I don't believe them: somebody saw something somewhere.'

'I'm sure someone did,' replied Cornwallis. 'But we both know how things stand. Nobody wants a reputation as a grass and end up like our corpse upstairs. Perhaps a few quiet words might elicit a better response.' It looked like Frankie would have to speak to people and that was going to take time; but at least he could probably persuade someone to talk, as Frankie asked in a way that the feelers couldn't, well, not in front of an audience, that is. 'Is the artist on the way?' he asked, in the hope that something might actually go right.

'Should be here soon,' answered MacGillicudy dejectedly. 'I sent Dewdrop. At least that's something he can do without cocking it up too much. Jack, this force is going to the dogs. Look at what I have to work with nowadays; snot nosed pimply arsed little shits most of 'em, and they still need their mothers to wipe their bottoms for them. The Captain tells me that's the type of recruit we need, young, keen, and no experience, so that we can teach them how to be proper feelers: and I have to put up with the little bastards. Give me someone who has been around the block a few times I say, someone who knows the ways of the world, someone I can turn into a proper feeler.'

'Couldn't agree with you more, Jethro,' replied Cornwallis with a grin, 'but times change, and we have to change with them. You could always come and work for me if it's getting too much for you.'

MacGillicudy narrowed his eyes. 'Jack, you can just stick that idea where the sun don't shine.'

'Always the diplomat, Jethro, always the diplomat.'

Cornwallis and Frankie left MacGillicudy to finish and headed back into the building to speak to Mr Goup. Frankie led the way down the dark passage to the back office where a thin beam of light crept beneath a door. Frankie banged once and flung open the door, and then stared in disbelief. Cornwallis pushed past him and stopped just as abruptly. The room was empty; Mr Goup had gone.

'You sure this is the right room, Frankie?' asked Cornwallis, a little bemused, 'as there seems to be a distinct lack of people in here.'

'The sod's run,' responded Frankie, hurrying over to the still open window. 'The little shit has upped and legged it.'

Cornwallis had to agree. It seemed as if the accountant had

totted up the figures and come to a total he didn't like, that is, all the answers came back to him. 'Your friendly Mr Goup, deciding that discretion being the better part of valour, has vacated the premises. I reckon he was in this right up to his balance sheets. Have a look to see if you can see where he went, but I think he's long gone now.'

Frankie disappeared out of the window and into the dark back yard outside. His eyes hadn't yet adjusted to the change in light as straight away he clattered into the bin. The resultant crash echoing away into the distance as the lid hit the ground and rolled away, which startled the cat, in the process of rooting out rats, which lived amongst the scraps left by the humans. The cat took umbrage and attacked Frankie with sharp razor-like claws, hissing menacingly, as though Frankie had no right to be there amongst all the carnage outside in the dark; it was a feline world and the cat took exception to the interloper trying to take the food from its mouth. Frankie slipped on something soft and squelchy and fell backwards into rubbish stacked against the back wall; he kicked out his leg and connected to the cat which screamed as it flew through the air. Frankie scrambled back to his feet and lashed out again, a box went flying, and the rat, between his foot and the box, exploded in a shower of blood and guts. Frankie's language, which in normality was coarse, rose to a totally new level. The cat crept back and Frankie saw the slit eyes reflecting in the pale moonlight. He reached forward, grabbed the cat around the throat and pulled it towards him. 'Where did he go?' he hissed menacingly. 'We're with the Police.'

'Screw youse,' spat the cat, and then sunk its teeth deep into Frankie's forearm. Frankie yelled and dropped the cat like a hot coal. He swung his foot but failed to connect, and then the cat slunk out of the way again and hissed. 'Youse wants to know where the man went? Well, youse going the wrong way to find out.'

Frankie took a deep breath, trying to control his temper; this wasn't going at all well. 'Okay, Okay. I'm sorry,' he finally muttered. He looked around and saw Cornwallis framed in the window as he leant forward nonchalantly with his elbow on the sill propping up his chin, and he knew, although he couldn't see, that he wore a wicked grin on his face. He turned his attention back to the cat. 'Okay, you win. I want to know where he went.'

'That's better,' rasped the cat, as it slunk back into Frankie's view. It sat down and began to lick its paw. 'That weren't a nice thing youse did just then, mebbe I shouldn't help youse.'

'Look,' said Frankie, becoming exasperated now, 'I've said I'm sorry, what more do you want? If you don't want to help then I'll go get a dog to sniff out the man we're after.'

The cat stopped licking and fixed Frankie with an evil stare. 'Dogs are stupid, they's can't talk and they's unreliable. All they think about is food and humping table legs, and the bitches are even worse.'

Frankie only just kept his temper in check. 'What is it you want?'

'Fish,' came the response. 'A box of fish, fresh from the salty briny. Untainted and ungutted, just as nature intended.'

'No problem,' answered Frankie straight away. 'I can get some sent up tomorrow. What's yer name?' The cat for the first time hesitated. He whispered, and Frankie struggled to hear. 'Didn't catch it, speak louder.'

'I said Fluffy, all right.'

Frankie couldn't help it, he burst into laughter.

'Yeah, yeah, yeah, and before youse start, I've heard all the jokes. It were the kids that named me, but boy, did they regrets it.' He mimed a swipe with his paw, the claws glinting like highly polished daggers.

'Come on,' said Frankie, wiping his eyes, 'I ain't got all night.'

Fluffy jumped up and sat on a box at eye level and Frankie stared into the eyes of a ginger tom, its fighting abilities apparent by the scars. If the cat was human, it would have a spiders web tattoo etched across its face.

'This other 'uman, 'e came from the alley an' crept up to the winda. He tapped, and the 'uman inside opened the winda. They were whispering, so I couldn't hear wot they said, but the inside man climbed out an' then they both hurried down the alley an' got into a coach.'

'Interesting,' remarked Frankie. 'Did you see what the man looked like? I mean the one who knocked on the window. What sort of coach, and which way did it go?'

'Youse want to know a lot, don't you?' answered Fluffy.

'A box of fish can make you very popular with the ladies,' surmised Frankie. 'I suppose how popular depends on what's inside.'

Fluffy regarded Frankie for a moment and then seemed to deflate into a small round ball. 'Youse right; them posh ones down the road won't even look at me, an alley cat they calls me, come back when you've made something of yourself, they says. I reckon a box of lobster, prawns an' halibut would do the trick, don't you?'

'Might well, but how would you get into the Lobster?'

'You'll cook and crack it open for me, won't youse.'

Frankie chuckled. 'I could, but I could also leave it alive. Those claws could give a cat a nasty nip on the nose.'

'Youse wouldn't do that, youse like me, come from the gutter. Like looks after like, ain't that the rools?'

'You ain't looking after me; you're trying to bargain with me. Come on, out with the information or no deal.'

Fluffy sighed and then sat up again. He stretched luxuriously as only cats can and then settled back down. 'It were too dark to see the man, but 'e were dressed in good clothes, no tat, all expensive like; had a cane wiv a silver knob on the end. The coach were dark too, but it had one of them signs on the back, don't ask me wot it said, as cats can't read; oh yeah, and it had yellow writing down the side, but it didn't 'ang around, it rushed off, heading off towards the river.'

'Thanks, Fluffy, I'll send a box 'round tomorrow.' Frankie went to pat the cat on the head, but hesitated; then withdrew his hand thinking better of it.

Fluffy jumped down, disappeared into the yard and within a couple of seconds, a hiss and a crash indicated that hostilities had recommenced; there then followed a few moments of silence. 'Sodding rats,' spat Fluffy.

Frankie grinned then quickly checked the alley but found nothing, so he went to the end and stood looking down the street towards the river. He was in the suburbs and that way led into town as opposed to out of it. The coach could have gone anywhere, but at least it hadn't disappeared into the country. He looked down and saw two steaming piles of horse shit: that won't be there in the morning, he thought fleetingly, I could do with that for my roses.

Frankie climbed back in through the window and found Cornwallis sitting at the desk; he didn't turn around, so Frankie went up and looked over his shoulder at whatever held Cornwallis' attention. It was a blotter, with doodles of a hanging man.

'You reckon that's our Mr Goup?' asked Frankie, pointing a stubby finger at the drawing.

'Reckon so,' replied Cornwallis. 'Seems he may have got a bit of a fright on. I heard what the cat said. Seems the coach was of the hired variety, so we are just going to have to check around. I have a feeling that this case is going to get complicated.' He sat back and rubbed his eyes. 'Come on, I've had enough here. MacGillicudy can keep a guard on the place and we can turn it over tomorrow. Let's get back down the Stoat and you can give me your thoughts.'

CHAPTER 2

Cornwallis took a long slow drink of his beer and then reached into the bowl and pulled out a handful of nuts; suddenly he felt very hungry, having not eaten since morning. He looked around and summoned Eddie over to order a pie and chips. Frankie nodded to make it two, hoping that Cornwallis would pick up the bill. The little piazza was full to bursting and they were lucky to find a table. The lamps had been lit and a comfortable relaxed atmosphere suffused the place with the buzz of talk resounding like a hive of bees. Rose had taken a break and the pair were disappointed that she wasn't going to serve them with their pie. However, they contented themselves with the thought that she would soon be back to work and then they could watch as she floated around the tables, especially theirs.

Frankie flicked a nut into the air and tipped his head back to catch it in his mouth. He gulped, and then broke out into a coughing fit; the nut had hit the back of his tongue and slid down into his windpipe. Cornwallis watched in fascination as Frankie's face went crimson at first, with eyes like mushrooms on stalks as he spluttered and coughed; a pause as breath failed to come, and then he went a bluish tinge as the panic increased. Big George the bear, collecting glasses from nearby tables, altered course and passed by, thumping hard on Frankie's back. The errant nut shot out, pinged off the ashtray and whisked past Cornwallis' ear.

'You finished now, Frankie?' asked Cornwallis with a grin. 'Only if you wish to save me some wages then please carry on.'

'You bastard,' spluttered Frankie. 'You just sat there.'

'Well, not just sat, I was watching as well; and very entertaining it was too. What are you going to do for an encore?'

'You all right now, Mr Kandalwick?' asked George, with a hint of concern.

'Fine thanks, George,' answered Frankie, wiping his snot with his sleeve. 'I appreciate your help, I owe you one.'

'No worries, Mr Kandalwick. It wouldn't look good with the punters dying at the tables. I'll get you another couple of beers.'

'And make sure you put it on that bastard's bill,' replied Frankie, pointing at Cornwallis.

George chuckled to himself as he moved away to finish collecting the glasses, while everyone else, who had stopped talking to look at the hapless Frankie, resumed their conversations.

Cornwallis decided that they had better get down to business and chew over what they had learnt. 'Now that you're fully recovered, perhaps you could spare me some attention,' he began, leaning forward and placing his elbows on the table. 'See what you make of these names.' He passed the notebook with the list of names across the table and Frankie placed a large digit on the book and spun it around to look. He took a swig of his beer as he scrutinised the list.

'Some pretty big names here, are they from the filing cabinet?'

'They are.' Cornwallis lowered his voice to a whisper as he recited them aloud. 'Dacred, Delopole, Dilleyman, Doomcroft, Dopleman, Dunlop, Dunderfield. They're the names that were still there, but someone's missing, I noticed a space between

Dopleman and Dunlop. Now who do you think that could be?'

Frankie screwed up his face in thought and then leant in closer to look at the names again. Cornwallis did likewise, and they both hovered over the book, nose to nose. 'The most likely, looking at who is here, is Dooley, Dumchuck or Dumerby,' ventured Frankie after a few moments thought. 'It would seem Mr Goup had quite a clientele. Are you sure that someone's missing?'

'All big names in the city, all people you wouldn't want to cross, all of them very rich. Yes, I'm sure someone's missing. There was a gap, all the files were clean, no blood. There was blood everywhere else so there should be some on the files, but no. The only answer is that someone took something belonging to one of the three you just mentioned.'

'All of them could do you a lot of harm, I believe,' said a female voice from above their heads.

Cornwallis and Frankie turned and stared up at Rose. She had hold of two steaming round meat puddings in just the wrong position; her chest seemed to be smoking. Cornwallis' trouser department signalled awareness. She put the plates down and leant forward to look at the notebook.

'Pie is off, only puddings left. Uncle Eddie didn't think you'd mind. I know I haven't been in the city long but even I know these names,' she said, indicating the list. 'Are these your suspects?' She saw the perplexed look cross Cornwallis' face so she explained. 'My uncle told me who you are and what you do. I've been standing here for the last few moments listening to every word you said. Are you actually any good?'

Cornwallis recovered quickly. He hadn't noticed her, but he wasn't going to admit that. 'I'm sorry, Rose, but I knew you were there; you cast a very pretty shadow, if I may say so. If we wanted to speak in secret then we would have gone back to my office, as it is, we are just putting the scene together.' It was weak, but it would have to do. He silently castigated himself for being indiscreet; they should have waited until they got back to the office, but it could have been a whole lot worse.'

She smiled, and Cornwallis felt a warm tingling sensation travel down his spine. She heard the scrape of a chair on the cobbles just behind her, so spun around and whipped the seat from the uprising behind of an assistant architect with acne. 'You don't mind do you?' she purred, 'only I've been on my feet all day and just need to sit and rest a little.'

The architect's assistant didn't mind at all; he'd already seen how she nearly decapitated a customer who didn't want to pay his bill.

Rose sat down and leant forward. 'Carry on eating, don't mind me; you can just tell me all about this new case of yours, and how you want me to help,' she said smoothly. 'I've always wanted to investigate a crime.'

Cornwallis nearly choked on his pudding. 'You? Help?'

'Yes, and why not? A girl can go places that men can't, and besides, we have the "intuition". That's always needed in the books I've read, mysterious murder, no clues, smoking dagger kind of thing. Along comes aged spinster sleuth, and before you know it, the perpetrator is banged up in gaol. Easy.'

'Well, yes, maybe in books, but reality is a different thing. It can get quite dangerous because people don't want to get caught—'

Rose reached forward with her hand to Cornwallis' chin and tipped it up so he could look into her eyes. 'They're not going to talk to you, you know,' she said sweetly, pointing a digit to her chest.

Cornwallis desperately wanted to disagree. They were certainly talking, and very loudly at that. He had let his mind and his eyes wander under extreme provocation; the pale green dress she wore pressed them together like two softly inflated satin balloons, they were smooth and silky — they were wonderful. He coughed self-consciously and gave a lopsided grin.

'That's better, now we can have a proper conversation. As I was saying, we have talents of our own and I'm sure you would find me an able pupil; I'm a quick learner you know. You can show me the ropes and I won't expect too much pay to start with. We could even come to some sort of arrangement if it suited you.'

The arrangement that sprang into Cornwallis' mind might not be the one she intended, but oh, what a beautiful image.

Frankie obviously thought along the same lines, as the voice that came out of his mouth resembled a high pitched squeal instead of the deep throaty roar that he normally had. 'I think, Jack, that we should listen to her. I'm sure there would be plenty of advantages for having Rose work with us.'

Rose smiled at Frankie, reached forward and stroked his arm in thanks. He blushed, for the first time ever, he blushed. Under her stare, Frankie turned into some gooey piece of putty and he would have agreed to anything she said just then.

'Well?' she asked hopefully, turning back to Cornwallis.

Cornwallis' thoughts tumbled around inside his head and he tried to get them back into some semblance of order, his fuddled mind eventually came back to a sharp focus and he considered the effect she just had on Frankie. Gods, he wondered, does this girl realise how much devastation she can cause? He shovelled another forkful of pudding into his mouth and chewed slowly as his mind slipped into a higher gear. If she can have this effect on the two of us, he thought, most of the men out there wouldn't stand a chance. Perhaps it might be worth a go, just to see how she performs; and if she can fight as well as Eddie says, then that's just another piece in the armoury. He had only just met her, but he had a feeling that fate had already reared its head and stuck its tongue in his ear. 'Okay, Okay. You win,' he conceded after a while. 'But we'll see how things go, but only as long as Eddie agrees to it. I can't go upsetting my local's landlord.'

Rose beamed, and so did Frankie. She leapt up, wrapped both her arms around Cornwallis' neck and planted a kiss on his head. 'I knew you'd see it my way.'

Her way or not, he didn't care, but everyone else in the piazza probably did as he could feel the envy emanating towards him from every male in the square. For just a brief instant his head had been where any red-blooded male would pay a king's ransom to be, nestled gently between them. He grinned inanely for a moment before dragging his attention back to the pudding. 'I'll speak to Eddie when I've finished this,' he said, feeling pleased with himself.

A little while later Cornwallis cleared it with Eddie and then sat in the bar, chatting to a couple of acquaintances for an hour, the conversation being academic as he had Rose in his direct vision as she pulled the pints. He reflected that he must be looking a bit like a lovelorn teenager, so in the end he reluctantly returned to Frankie, who seemed to be getting on famously with a lady who smelled strongly of fish.

'Lovely girl,' explained Frankie, as she left. 'She guts fish down on the wharf. She's sorting me out a box for the cat and then tomorrow night I'm taking her out on the town.' He rubbed his hands together in glee.

Cornwallis' nose wrinkled at the lingering smell. 'Don't you think she's a bit fragrant?' he asked, wafting the air with his hand. 'Granted she has a few positive features, but odour obviously isn't one of them.'

'She's just come from work; a good scrub and a pint of

perfume and you wouldn't tell what she did. Us poor folk have to stick together, you know, power to the people and all that. To you she may be just a member of the working classes, but to me she has real sole. Hur, hur. See what I did there? Real sole. Hur, hur. Good, eh?'

Cornwallis winced then shook his head; Frankie and jokes went together like a beef and custard sandwich.

The evening drew on and Ying Pong's noodle shop in the corner began to do a brisk trade, judging by the queue, and Fossie's Take Away a few doors down also got into the swing of things; however, the stuff that the few customers were buying only looked appetising when accompanied by copious quantities of alcohol. Cornwallis shuddered at the memory; deep fried whatever and kebabs that walked into the bun all by itself. He'd agreed to have a kebab some weeks ago and the regret was still fresh in his mind: indeterminate slices of meat held together with globules of fat and gristle with a thin cut of onion and cabbage topped with a fiery chilli sauce; perversely he had enjoyed it, until his guts exploded a little while later. The Duke's rich customers, for some reason, seemed to make up the bulk of those indulging. As Cornwallis looked around, he saw MacGillcudy hurrying towards him and he didn't look happy.

'There's been an incident at the scene,' said MacGillicudy, as he eased himself down into a chair. 'This going spare?' he asked, indicating the full pint in front of Frankie.

'You given up resenting us?' asked Cornwallis, an eyebrow raised.

MacGillicudy nodded and then grinned. 'I was pissed off, I admit, but now I'm a bit more philosophical. Weren't your fault you got handed the case.'

'No, it surprised me as well, but carry on, Jethro,' said Cornwallis, though whether he meant the pint or the information was anyone's guess, so MacGillicudy guessed both. It would seem the earlier antipathy had definitely disappeared.

'Someone tried to torch the accountant's office,' he continued, as a stony-faced Frankie watched him down his beer. 'I left Dewdrop guarding the back of the place, but then I heard an almighty kerfuffle. I went through and found a load of oil soaked rags in the doorway. Dewdrop said he went for a leak, so he didn't see who it was, but I found your friendly cat sitting there and he told me what happened. Apparently, as soon as Dewdrop went out the gate some bloke walked in, carrying some rags, he then opened the back door and dumped them inside. The cat decided to stop it when the bloke tried to strike the match; he clawed him, and apparently, the man just turned and ran. I got there just as Dewdrop walked back in and he says he never saw a thing.' He slapped the empty glass on the table and wiped his mouth. 'Ah, that's better. The arsonist left this with the pile of rags; must have dropped it when the cat attacked.' He passed over a book of matches. 'I reckon I'd prefer the bloody cat to join the force, it'd be a darn sight better than the shit I've already got.'

Cornwallis picked up the book of matches and turned it over, looking at the picture on the front, a picture of the House of Assembly, the seat of government. He showed the front to Frankie and then slipped the matches into his pocket. 'Thanks, Jethro. What do you make of all this?'

MacGillicudy took a long breath before replying. 'Make of it all? That's your job now, but if you really want my opinion, then for what it's worth, I think you're playing with the big boys. The murder seems more of an amateur affair, but your accountant disappearing and then this arson attack, well, that's had a bit more thought to it. They picked their moment and went for it. I'd bet my pension there's a great deal of money at the bottom of all this.'

Cornwallis nodded, thinking along the same lines, and this book of matches confirmed it. The matches could only have come from one place; the members bar at the House of Assembly. He saw MacGillicudy sit up straight and then watched as his face contorted into a kind of smile, he then felt a hand rest on his shoulder and knew whom the hand belonged to without even looking around; a warm glow of contentment eased right through him.

'I've pulled my last pint now,' said Rose, sighing in relief. 'I'm now all yours and I can't wait to get started.'

If only, thought Cornwallis, if only that were true. 'Jethro, meet Rose,' he said, with a degree of pride. 'This young lady is now part of my team. Rose, meet Jethro MacGillicudy, a sergeant in the feelers.'

MacGillicudy couldn't stand up fast enough. His chair crashed to the ground as his legs knocked it backwards; he turned, a little sheepishly, and picked it up, placing it back on its four legs. Brushing himself down a little, he leant across awkwardly and offered his hand. 'Pleased to meet you,' he said. 'Did I hear right, you are now working with Cornwallis?'

'I am: as of tonight, I'm the junior member and I'm really looking forward to it. I've always wanted to do something like this; are you part of the team as well?'

'Alas no,' replied Cornwallis interjecting. 'Jethro declined my offer of employment a few hours ago, something about a lack of sunshine; isn't that right, Jethro?'

MacGillicudy to his credit didn't even blink. 'Something like that. You know the force would fall apart if I weren't there to keep it all together, Jack, and besides, what sort of pension would you give me, eh?'

'Perhaps you're right, Jethro. Shame though, I reckon all of us together would make a great team.'

*

Cornwallis woke with a slight ache in his head. The clock on the wall showed it was still early but he couldn't sleep any longer. He turned over and pulled the covers back over his head, blocking out the dawn's early light. After tossing and turning for a while, he checked the clock again; Frankie and Rose were due to meet him here first thing this morning, and he idly wondered if Frankie's head felt the same. They had taken in quite a few pints last night, a good few more than he intended. One pint had led to another and then he very nearly followed Frankie's lead to indulge in one of Fossie's finest — nearly, but not quite. He offered a silent prayer of thanks to whichever God saved him from temptation and his guts from exploding. He reluctantly swung his legs out of bed and stood up, tentatively rubbing his temple. The ache, now he was upright, turned into a pile driver smashing rocks in his brain. He caught his reflection in the full length mirror hanging on the wall and stared: not too bad really, he thought, as he took in the apparition. Red eyed and dishevelled but still human. He breathed in and tensed the muscles in his stomach alleviating the paunch. He let the breath out and the paunch reappeared. He'd been fit when he first started being an investigator: five years ago now, and then he had a washboard stomach, a six pack, each muscle honed to perfection. He'd had nothing else to do except keep the girls on his father's estate, and those he met in the city, happy. Gods, he'd had to be fit to keep up with it all. He had everything: money, power, influence, and the inevitable seat in the Assembly to go with it. He still had the seat, but being an unwilling member, he'd sent in a proxy. He had tried to get out of it, but once elected only death or disgrace could displace him. He still sometimes wondered why he didn't take up the option of a life at ease; the reason, he reminded himself, were the so-called friends and hangers-on: slack-jawed imbeciles, nothing between their ears, rich and with time on their hands; their only goal in life, their only ambition, being to have fun. All well and good up to a point, but as time wore on the point became stretched; and then people began to get hurt. The last straw was a game of Battleball. There were about thirty of them, and they used the streets as a pitch. Thirty young fit men rampaged through the city annihilating anything that got in their path, and Cornwallis watched from the side-lines as a young mother with a baby in her arms got caught up in the melee. It must have been fate that prevented him from taking part that day, because he would never have been able to live with himself if he had. The young men said it was just a game so the authorities put it down to high spirits; the mother's family called it murder. Cornwallis found he had a conscience and vowed to distance himself from his so called friends.

Being qualified to do nothing didn't lend him much in the way of a career though, but he knew he had a sharp mind. He'd been intrigued by the investigative work of the feelers, but joining the force was out of the question; his background wouldn't allow him to do a low paid job like that: but he could set himself up as a private investigator.

Most of the work in the first couple of years had been mundane stuff, like following adulterous spouses, but it paid well and he managed to cultivate a network of informers for when the more exciting work did come in. Eventually even the feelers were putting work his way and his reputation slowly grew.

He finished dressing and walked downstairs to the office. The coffee steamed on the stove and Frankie sat there with a smile on his face; the smell of the coffee battling against the strong odour of fish that hung all over the place.

'For God's sake open a window,' whined Cornwallis, biting back the nausea. 'It reeks in here.'

'Ah, that'll be the cats reward; picked it up on my way over. Do you know what time they start over on the wharf?'

'Early, I would guess. Couldn't you sleep?'

'Slept like a baby, boss, nothing like a good nights' drinking to set you up for the day. You look a little bleary eyed if you ask me; are we a little delicate this morning?'

'Let's just say I've felt better. Did I do anything stupid? I can vaguely remember MacGillicudy beating a hasty retreat after refusing to join you in a kebab, but after that it's a blur.'

'Ah,' replied Frankie, with a knowing leer.

'That "Ah" seems to be loaded,' groaned Cornwallis, picking up the coffee pot and pouring two steaming mugs. 'You'd better tell me now; I don't want you to surprise me later.' He handed one to Frankie and slurped at the other as he sunk down into the chair behind his desk.

Frankie had a grin from ear to ear; he intended to savour this moment like a fine wine, swirling it around the glass and sniffing the bouquet, drawing out the pleasure in anticipation of a beautiful outcome. 'Are you sure you want to know?'

Cornwallis grimaced. He rubbed his head and then shut his eyes as the sun rose above the window sill, the light seeming to act like a dagger searing into his brain. 'Yes, let's get it over with.'

'Well,' began Frankie, rubbing his hands. 'You know old One Eyed Monty?'

'The beggar?'

'The same. Well, we were walking down Goshead lane when you decided you needed a leak, so you just turned into the doorway and flopped it out; me on one side o'you, Rose on the other.'

'Oh Gods.'

'Yep, you could say Old One Eye got one in the one eye courtesy of your one eye; he was having a quiet sleep in the corner. I will add that Rose declined your kind invitation though.'

Cornwallis buried his head in his hands. 'What did I say, or do I want to know?'

Frankie chuckled. 'Let's just say that you invited her to help, which is more than old Monty will do the next time he sees you. She helped the old boy back to the Stoat to dry off, which judging by the length of time you took, would've taken quite a while.'

'Gods!' Cornwallis' head hit the desk and he covered it with his arms. If only the floor would open up and swallow him whole. It got worse then as the footsteps on the stairs indicated the imminent arrival of their new colleague, Rose.

Frankie was enjoying himself immensely, an embarrassed Cornwallis was not an everyday occurrence and he vowed to make the most of it while it lasted; in fact he felt certain that he could get a good few weeks entertainment out of this, and he intended to drag it out for as long as he could. The footsteps stopped just outside the door and the handle turned slowly, the door began to swing back on its hinges and Rose breezed in. She stopped dead at the sight of Cornwallis cowering under his arms and Frankie sitting there with the biggest grin on a face that she had ever seen.

'I take it he's remembered what happened?' she observed dryly.

Frankie's feet, which had been on the table, crashed to the floor. She had decided to forego the pale green low-cut dress of the night before and had replaced it with an outfit not unlike

Cornwallis himself. White shirt, tight black trousers and jacket, black boots, and her hair tied behind in a ponytail. Needless to say, she looked far better than Cornwallis did. 'Good morning, Rose,' he said, her outfit having an interesting effect on him. 'I can safely say that he is now aware of what happened, though he says that he can't remember.'

'I'm not surprised he can't remember. Does he normally drink like that?'

'Only on days that end with a "Y".'

She laughed, which made Frankie beam in delight. She went over and pulled up a chair to sit opposite Cornwallis, who still had his head in his arms. She slipped off her jacket and hung it over the back of the chair before sitting down. She winked at Frankie before holding up her left hand, and then waited for Cornwallis to look up. When two bloodshot eyes eventually did, she leant forward and waggled her little finger teasingly under his nose. Frankie roared with laughter; Cornwallis just groaned again and then reburied his face.

'Okay, I behaved like a pillock,' said the muffled voice. 'I'm sorry, now can we leave it at that?'

Rose patted his arm and leant back. 'Of course we can — for now at any rate,' she added mischievously.

Frankie wiped his eyes and finally managed to control himself, but it took a lot of effort. Rose's nose finally got the better of her and it twitched in distaste. 'What's that smell?' she asked, looking around. 'It seems like fish, but from the state of this place, it could be anything.'

Cornwallis raised his head and tried to shake off the pounding between his ears, they had work to do, so the hangover would have to wait. 'The smell is Frankie's fish,' he explained, his voice quiet so as not to disturb his head. 'He picked up a box on the way here. I don't know why he couldn't have waited, but we are lumbered with it for the moment.'

'A whole sentence; well done. You must be starting to feel better. I hope you haven't got me here to clean this place up; look at the state of it.'

All three looked around the office, but Cornwallis and Frankie couldn't see anything amiss. Everything was where it should be; all the files were there, all the books, a couple of empty mugs. Granted there may be a little dust here and there, but it was a place of business, not a parlour.

'What do your clients think when they come in?' Rose asked, standing up and beginning to inspect the room. 'It doesn't create a very good impression. Where are all your records?'

Cornwallis shuffled uncomfortably. He then pointed to the groaning shelf opposite, where files teetered on the brink, and stacks of rolled parchments oozed along its length. There were books scattered throughout to add to the weight and made the whole shelf bend like a broad grin. Rose wasn't impressed.

'So much for client confidentiality,' she observed. 'All that should be locked away neat and tidy. If you want me to work for you then you're going to have to change your ways. You need a secretary to get all this in order; but before you say anything, it's not going to be me. You can advertise for one, or if you'd prefer it, I can sort you out a nice efficient lady who will get this place organised in no time.'

The hangover prevented Cornwallis from arguing at the moment, he just wanted a couple of hour's peace so he could suffer in silence and die quietly. A secretary and a discussion about it was the last thing he wanted at the moment. 'We'll talk about it later,' he said, rubbing his eyes. 'In the meantime you and Frankie will go to the accountant's and get all the paperwork in the building safe and secure somewhere. The arsonist must have thought that there's something still there, so we need to find out what it is. You also need to speak to all the people again, Frankie, see if you can get them to talk this time. You can then follow up on this hire-carriage that took Roland Goup away, see if you can find out where it came from and who hired it.'

'Right, boss,' replied Frankie crisply, 'and what will you be doing while we're doing all the work?'

'While you pair are doing that I will need to follow up on this book of matches, and also to get Rose an Investigator's license; that is when I've finished sawing my head off.'

Frankie smashed his hand down on the table and stood up; he looked pleased with himself as he saw Cornwallis wince as the sound reverberated around the office. 'Come little lady,' said Frankie, offering his hand to Rose. 'Time to show you how a real detective works; we shall leave his highness to his misery and venture forth into the great outdoors, and once there, we will go and kick arse.'

Rose stood up and accepted Frankie's hand, giving a little play-curtsy at the same time. 'Thank you kind sir, it makes such difference to meet a real gentleman.'

'For God's sake,' screamed Cornwallis. 'Will the pair of you just sod off.'

A grinning Frankie picked up his box of fish and then stomped over to the door and wrenched it open. Rose whipped her jacket off the chair and quickly followed after. Cornwallis opened one eye to watch them leave; hangover or not, she really did have a very shapely bottom.

Once outside, Frankie adjusted his grip on the box and began to stride down Grantby Street, with Rose falling into step beside him. The sun had climbed higher now and bathed the city in a warm comfortable glow. People emerged from their houses, filling the streets with early morning conversation as they made their way to work or to the shops for the day's supplies. An argument raged, as a dray and a cart tried to negotiate the crossroads further down. Gornstock was coming alive.

'The first rule of investigating...' began Frankie, as they passed the two drivers arguing, '...is to never investigate on an empty stomach.'

They watched as one threw a punch and drew a copious amount of claret from the nose of the other. The horses seemed oblivious to the fight raging in front of them and just stared off into the distance as a crowd began to form. Straight away bets were changing hands as the onlookers sized up the combatants. The victim got up, wiped his nose with his sleeve, and then aimed a vicious kick to the groin of the other. There came a sickening soft squelchy sound as the kick went home, the recipient doubling up in pain and falling to his knees.

'Around the corner is one of the best places in all Gornstock to get a proper bacon sarnie,' continued Frankie.

Nose-bleed was just about to lash out again with his foot, into the undefended head of his adversary, when the groaning man lunged headfirst into the belly of nose-bleed. They both tumbled to the ground and rolled around flailing punches as the onlookers cheered them on.

'Shouldn't someone stop them?' asked Rose, raising an eyebrow.

'Gods no, that will totally spoil their fun,' replied Frankie, peering into the dray and whipping two bottles away and into the pocket of his coat. 'They're at it most mornings. They both try and get the timing right and cut each other up. It's been going on for years. You can't stop them, goes against the city charter, freedom of expression and all that. They'll finish soon and will chalk up who's won fer today.'

The fighting men rolled under the rear of the dray's horse,

and sure enough, the equine took the opportunity to express its opinion. A great dollop of steaming shit splattered onto the heads of the two drivers, followed up by a great roar of approval coming from the watching crowd. A ripple of applause began at the entertainment, and the two horseshit-covered men spluttered to a stop. The applause continued, and like well-seasoned actors, the men rose from beneath the horse and bowed to the crowd. The cart's driver tried to jab a last sneaky elbow into the face of the other but the cart's horse, seemingly acting as referee, lurched forward and ran the wheel over its owner's foot. The man screamed and hopped around in agony, swearing at everything in general, and horses in particular.

'Come on,' said Frankie, 'I'm hungry.'

Rose and Frankie continued on their way down Grantby Street until they came to a little alley, they turned into it and Frankie indicated that they should keep to the overhang. Shortly Rose saw why as a splash of something relating to night-time relief hit the ground and formed into a gooey puddle. At the end, they entered into a wide thoroughfare called The Trand, where opposite stood the House of Assembly, a gigantic imposing edifice built from the red granite quarries of Scleep far to the north. It backed onto a bend in the river, by which the stones came down some two hundred years ago by hundreds of barges.

'Aren't we going the wrong way?' asked Rose, a little confused. 'Isn't the accountant's on the edge of town?'

'It is,' replied Frankie. 'But first things first, breakfast and then work. We'll grab a lift when we're done.'

They walked along The Trand a short way to a street stall nestling in the corner, a banner held up on two poles above it proclaimed "Sal's Sizzler". Nobody with a sense of smell could pass by; the aroma grabbed the nostrils in a headlock and refused to let go. There was already a throng of customers crowded around, but Frankie elbowed his way through and Rose followed in his wake. They were now in effect at the back of the house, where a team of servers were struggling to cope with the demand. Frankie grabbed a couple of crates and sat down, indicating that Rose should too. A small thin reed of a woman with wild grey hair marched over and clipped Frankie around the ear.

'That's for not visiting your mother yesterday like you promised,' she berated angrily. 'How can a mother's son treat her so badly? A poor weak woman in the autumn of her life and you don't go and see her regular like. You should be ashamed of yourself, young Francis.' Her eyes opened wide as she saw Rose sitting next to him. She clipped him again. 'And you haven't even introduced me to your young lady.'

'Aw, mum, don't do that. What's people going to think?'

'They'll think that my son is a lazy good for nothing who can't be bothered to go and see his old mother, that's what they'll think.' She folded her arms across her chest and tapped her foot waiting for a reply. Frankie looked up into a sea of faces all agreeing with his mother.

'That's not fair, mum. We got a job and were tied up all last night.' He shuffled his backside around on the crate trying to regain some dignity. 'You know I can't make it sometimes, but I promise I'll make it up to you; and anyway, this is Rose and she's just started working with us.' He flicked his eyes to Rose and grinned inanely. 'This is my mum, if you haven't already guessed.'

Rose stood up and offered her hand. 'Nice to meet you, Mrs Kandalwick, Frankie was just telling me what a wonderful mother he had.' She shot Frankie a reassuring smile.

'The name's Sal dear, nobody calls me missus nowadays, not

since the son of a bitch that was Frankie's father ran off with that tart of a tailor's pattern cutter.' She spat the last in contempt, but then regained her composure. 'You're not his young lady then?' she asked, still hopeful. Rose shook her head. 'Shame, a mother is never fulfilled until she gets her grandkids. About time he got his finger out, you listening, Frankie? Grandkids, I want grandkids. You must know what yer little dangler's for.'

'Yes, mum,' answered Frankie, resolved now that his mother was determined to embarrass him, whatever the circumstances. 'Anyway, you already got grandkids, loads of 'em.'

'Not from you, I ain't, I expect all of you to do your bit. Look at Justine, she got four of 'em, and another on the way. Barney has got two, admittedly not from the same mother, but he's doing his bit, and Jason's got one'

'All right, mum.' Frankie held up his hand in defeat. 'I get yer point. I'll see what I can do.'

'Good, you get right on to it. Now, what are you going to have?'

Frankie felt that the tirade had now come to an end and he could relax at long last. 'Special please, mum; we got a long day ahead of us.'

'Right you are son; and you, young lady?'

'I'll have the same please, Sal.'

Both Frankie and his mum stared at Rose for a moment, but then they broke into a grin.

'Two specials over here,' shouted Sal, to no one in particular. 'And hurry, my boy's got work to do.'

As if by magic, two enormous great rolls appeared, both the size of dinner plates, and each had a napkin that just about covered a small corner. Sal gave one to Frankie and the other to

Rose, and then stood back to watch them eat. Rose stared for a moment as she held hers in both hands. She lifted up the lid to see what was inside and saw what amounted to half a pig and an array of eggs, all covered with a brown sauce.

'Are you sure you're going to manage all that?' asked Frankie, already tucking into his.

'You watch me, tiger,' replied Rose, attacking the roll with gusto.

CHAPTER 3

Rose's stomach, stretched to the limit and complaining severely, threatened to explode as they sat on the back of the blacksmith's cart as it rocked down the road. She had never eaten so much in her life, but pride had got hold of her and she had no intention of giving in until she'd forced every last morsel down her throat. Sal had scrutinised every mouthful, and had nodded with pleasure as the special finally disappeared. She now felt like one of those toys which wobbled but couldn't be knocked down, and the motion of the cart and the smell of the fish compounded the issue. She desperately tried to listen to Frankie as he told her about how he came to work with Cornwallis.

'We came from The Warren, one of the worst places in the city. We were poor and mum struggled to bring us all up. Like all kids around there, we started nicking a few bits to sell. Mum didn't exactly encourage us, but she were grateful to 'ave a few luxuries every now and again. She used to work at Cornwallis' house but got in the family way again and had to leave. When she started the stall, we were all so used to the thievery that we couldn't stop, two of me brothers got caught and got banged up inside, and it weren't long after that that Cornwallis came across me again, skipping away from a house with a pocketful of silver. We used to play together as kids when me mum took me to work, so he knew what mum would think if another of the family went inside. He then offered me this job, and with a knife pressed up against me throat, I could hardly say no, could I?'

Rose nodded her agreement; just then, she couldn't trust herself to speak in case the special made a comeback.

'We make a good team, me and Cornwallis. As he comes from the nobs, we just about cover all bases. If I'd known being honest could be this much fun, I would never have started nicking stuff in the first place.'

The cart trundled its way through the city centre and out into the suburbs. Frankie's voice droned on and on, and Rose began to feel a little better. By the time they came to decamp from the cart, she only felt full, and not full to bursting.

'Morning, Constable Popham,' cried Frankie, as the toe of his boot nudged into the reposing policeman's wedding tackle. 'Sleeping on the job again, eh? The bloody front door isn't even locked and here's you away with the fairies.' His hobnails began to grind down on something soft and squelchy.

Constable Popham awoke suddenly with a feeling of dread and discomfort, the pressure on his nether regions being of a different type to that which he had been dreaming; a pressure that teetered on the edge of being intense pain. 'What the f...?' His hands pushed out and connected with the rock solidity of Frankie's boot. He scrambled back and managed to sit up, rubbing the offended area with an intensity that was sure to make him go blind. Popham then saw Rose standing next to Frankie and his world collapsed into a crimson void as his arm movements slowed to a halt.

'Now, that's not a nice thing to do, Popham, in the presence of a lady,' said Frankie, with a smirk. 'If I happened to be a policeman I'd have you arrested. Sergeant MacGillicudy will be so impressed that you were doing the one arm shuffle and sleeping on the job.'

'I wasn't,' spluttered Popham. 'I might have had a few

49

minutes doze, but I wasn't having a wa…' He stopped himself just in time.

Rose tried her best not to laugh.

'We been on double shifts, Frankie, honest. Everybody else gets to go home, but we has to stay here. I only shut me eyes for a few minutes, honest.' Popham clambered to his feet and went to adjust himself, but then thought better of it. 'You won't tell the sergeant, will you?' he added pleadingly.

Rose stepped forward and placed a gentle hand on his arm. 'I'm sure I can persuade Frankie to keep quiet, Mr Popham, a double shift must be very tiring, even for a young fit man like you.'

Popham's eight stone six pound seemed to swell to nearly nine stone as he stood up straight, trying desperately to look like the man who would have a girl like this on his arm. He gave what he thought was a winning smile, but it came out more of a leer.

Frankie gave him a cuff around the head. 'And you can stop that as well or I *will* be telling MacGillicudy what you've been up to while his back is turned. Now, who's upstairs?'

'Spekes, Frankie,' replied Popham, now shrinking back to his normal size. 'There's just me, Spekes and Dewdrop. Nothing's happened all night, been as quiet as a flea's fart.'

'Just as well then, 'cause you lot couldn't catch a cold. So Dewdrop is out back then? Well let's hope he's more alert than you were.'

Frankie and Rose turned to go through, and she gave Popham a wink that would keep him occupied for weeks to come.

Dewdrop had been dozing too, but the sound of Frankie waking Popham up, stirred him from his slumbers. So when Frankie and Rose got to the back of the building, he stood ramrod straight with eyes as bright as they could be.

'Oh my,' exclaimed Rose, 'If it isn't Lord Cecil Toopins.' She put her hand to her mouth in astonishment. 'And here you are working as a policeman.'

'Ohmegodohmegod.' Dewdrop's face drained of colour as Frankie fixed him with a beady stare, he tried a grin but it didn't work; Frankie's eyes just bored into him and squeezed his brain in a vice-like grip.

'A Lord working as a feeler,' continued Rose aghast, her hand against her mouth. 'I think that is wonderful. Your family must be very proud of you giving something back to society like this.'

Dewdrop's attempted grin turned to a grimace. 'I... I... I think I just heard Popham calling for me, I... I'll just see what he wants.' He wrenched open the backdoor and took a couple of steps before he stopped, stood back, slammed it shut, and then rushed off the other way, past Rose and Frankie and down the connecting corridor. 'Wrong way,' he croaked as he disappeared.

Frankie stood looking at Rose for a few seconds. 'Lord Cecil Toopins?' he asked, incredulously.

Rose smiled sweetly and began to chuckle. 'He's been down the Stoat the last few nights trying to impress the girls. Don't worry, he didn't convince anyone, but we all let him think he did.'

'I'll Lord Cecil him when I get my hands 'round his scrawny little neck.'

'Leave him be, Frankie, a boy's got to dream sometimes, and I think that in these circumstances the less said the better.'

'Yes, but a Lord?' Frankie shook his head, as if Dewdrop could pass himself off as part of the nobility; it defied description. 'Oh well, if that's the way you want it. But you won't stop me having a little bit of fun at his expense though, will yer?'

'Only if he doesn't get hurt.'

'He, he, he,' he chuckled. 'Don't worry, he won't. But just you wait 'til Jack hears about this, it'll make his day.'

Frankie flung open the back door and, still laughing, wandered into the yard. Under his arm, he had the box of fish and he laid it down on top of the stack of rubbish at the back. 'Here puss, puss, puss. Here kitty, kitty,' he called lightly. 'Lots of luverley fish for yer. Come and get it. Come on, pussy.'

Rose began to look amongst all the junk while Frankie called. The oil soaked rags were still there, but pushed into a corner. She got a stick and started poking around, turning it over to see if she could dislodge anything wrapped up within the folds. She sighed disappointedly as if she hoped there would be a card or something with a name and address that would save them all this trouble; but she did notice that the rags weren't exactly rags. They were good cloth, not cheap and nasty like most of the people wore. She poked the pile some more and then noticed a little tag on what was once a shirt. Leaning closer she could just about read the label. "Biggins and Shute, Cavel Row." 'Frankie, come and look at this,' she called. 'I think I've found a clue.'

'What's that then, my darling?' asked Frankie, sauntering over. He squatted down beside her and took a look.

'There's posh for you. Biggins and Shute, eh? Cavel Row. Same place Cornwallis gets his from; if these are someone's rags then I can't imagine what the good stuff looks like. Well done, your first morning on the job and you score a point. You just learnt the second rule of investigating; notice everything.'

'Is that what you do?'

'Oh yes, eyes always peeled and ready.' They were too, as he had noticed that Rose had the top two buttons of her blouse undone and the third, at that moment, strained at the leash, but he managed to drag his eyes away and stood up. 'Better find a sack to put all this stuff in,' he said, becoming business like again. 'Jack will want to see all this.'

'Wants to see what?' asked the cat.

Frankie's head span around. The cat sat next to the box of fish, and despite all the junk, had managed to get up there silently. The tongue licked the paw with a kind of relish, as if there was a delicate morsel still attached. 'These rags,' replied Frankie. 'The ones that were going to be set alight. I hear you stopped it all happening.'

'Youse hear right. Used to be a nice quiet area it did until youse lot came stomping along. I suppose youse going to want to know what happened.'

'We do.'

The cat held out its paw and pinged the claws out one by one. 'That's what happened,' it said, swiping the air. 'Got the man good and proper; he won't be bothering any feline in a hurry again, I can tells youse.'

'Yeah, well done. But what actually happened?'

The cat jumped down and came to sit in front of Frankie and Rose. 'It were all quiet like, when one o'those feelers sneaked out the back gate. Being a bit curious, I took a peek, and I's wished that I hadn't. He went right down the end and he must've had a blockage by the sounds of it. It were then that my attention got diverted by the man sneaking in; the same one that were 'ere earlier.'

'You mean the one that helped the accountant get out?'

'That's the kitten. He went right up to the door and dumped that lot inside. I wondered what he were doing, but when I saws him get those matches out, well, I fought, that's enough for me, so I's sort of 'ad a word wiv him. "Oi, what you doing wiv that lot?" I spits. And do you know what, he near shat himself there and then. I reckon he didn't know some cats could talk.'

'Most people don't,' answered Frankie. 'I just chanced me arm when I spoke to you. What happened then?'

'Well, I spits some more and then I jumps right at him, unsheathing me claws in mid-air. Youse should have seen it, would have made my daddy proud it would. Before he could move I swipes him wiv the right, and before I hit the floor, I swipes him wiv the left. Beautiful move; got him both sides of the face. He couldn't take no more so 'e just turned and ran.'

Rose squatted down again and began to fuss the cat. Frankie watched with a certain degree of jealousy as her hand began to stroke and fondle it. It didn't take long before the purring started, and Frankie could have sworn he felt the ground tremble with the vibrations.

'What else?'

The cat waited for a couple of minutes until Rose stopped. 'Youse can keep doing that as much as you like sweetheart, I may be a cat but I knows a good looking 'uman when I sees one.'

'I think that's enough, Fluffy. What else happened?'

'Aw, just under the chin, sweetheart, go on, just a little longer.' The cat waited for just a few more seconds and then sighed. 'Nothing else happened. The feeler who took a dump came rushing back in just as that sergeant came storming out. However, when I's went to look where the man went... ere, follow me.' The cat tore itself away from Rose and walked out into the alley, he turned towards the street where the hired coach had waited the night before and sat down next to a bloody handkerchief. 'Here, 'e dropped this. Just shows what a good job I done on him.'

Frankie leant down and picked it up. Blood covered the once white silk handkerchief, but in the corner, he could see a little embroidered "K". 'We're picking up clues left, right and centre today,' he said, pocketing the article. 'Carries on like this and we'll have the murderer bang to rights before dinners on the table.'

'And talking about dinner,' said Fluffy. 'Can youse take the lid off me box of fish?'

'I reckon that's the least you deserve,' answered Rose, patting his head. 'Just show us where you want it.'

The cat's grin spread from ear to ear. 'Down here, I'll shows youse.' Fluffy sauntered back down the alley with his tail high in the air. He passed the gate to the accountants and went a couple of houses further down; he turned into an even smaller alley and then into a small fenced off yard. 'This 'ere's where I have's me resting place, just bung it in the corner.'

Frankie had shot back in to pick up the box and hurried after Rose and the cat. 'You sure?' he asked, when he caught them up. 'Looks a bit risky to leave stuff around here.'

'My domain,' answered Fluffy. 'If youse ever needs me again youse will always find me here, or if I'm not here, then the cat that is will be waiting just for me, if youse get my drift. Hur hur.'

MacGillicudy waited for them with a fresh bunch of feelers when they returned, having now dismissed the night-watch. He stood in the front hall, leaning nonchalantly with his back against the wall.

'Morning Frankie, Rose.'

'And a good morning to you as well, Jethro,' replied Frankie, and then got straight down to business. 'Cornwallis wants all the paperwork taken away and put somewhere safe, we need to keep it in some sort of order so that we can go through it all later. Do you think your lot are capable of doing that?'

'Got two wagons outside already waiting. Do you think I'm a complete idiot?'

Frankie turned to Rose and smiled. 'Do you think I should answer that?'

Rose looked sympathetically at MacGillicudy, but replied to Frankie. 'I think it would be safer if you didn't. Aren't you going to show me the scene of the crime?'

'Body's already gone to the morgue,' interjected MacGillicudy. 'And I've got someone looking for the relatives. This is Roland Goup's home address. I've already been around there and the housekeeper hasn't seen him. Dewdrop said the artist will drop the pictures off at your office later today, and I think Rose is right, Frankie, don't answer.'

Frankie grinned and patted the sergeant on the shoulder before pocketing the address. 'I wouldn't dream of it. C'mon, Rose, let's take a look upstairs.'

Thankfully, someone had cleaned the puke from the landing, but the office was just as he and Cornwallis had left it last night, with the only missing entity being the late Miss Knutt. The blood had dried nicely now, so Frankie didn't worry too much about where he stepped. He went over to the desk and looked at the ledger, tapping his finger on the last entry, the Mr Morris Bezel. He showed Rose and then sauntered over to the filing cabinet. Cornwallis had already gone through it, so it wasn't open on the letter "D", instead, the letter "C" stared back at him. Frankie turned away, then a thought occurred to him. He stepped back, flicked the file and then gave a low whistle, looking at the name of Jocelyn Cornwallis. Rose came and stood next to him, and both were silent as they looked at the file.

'What do you think it means?' she asked quietly.

'Means? It means our friend and employer knows a little bit more about this than he's told us,' replied Frankie, equally sotto voce. He felt betrayed and an overwhelming sense of disappointment washed over him. His boss knew Roland Goup,

56

had probably sat in this very office talking finance with him, so why hadn't he said anything?'

'I don't know about that,' answered Rose sadly. 'But I assume that the reference number leads to another file, so perhaps we should take a look.'

'There're hundreds of files in the back room so it's probably in there,' replied Frankie, his anger beginning to rise. 'C'mon, let's find out what the little bastard's been up to.'

Frankie snatched Cornwallis' file out the cabinet and then marched next door with Rose hot on his tail. The great wall of filing cabinets looked daunting at first until Rose deciphered the reference number.

'83, 7, 16. Looking at this I should think it means cabinet number 83, the rest should become apparent when we open it.' She walked along until she came to the right cabinet and opened the door. Inside there appeared to be around a dozen boxes, each with a number on it. She withdrew box 7 and laid it on the table behind her.

They hesitated now, neither of them wanting to open the box. Frankie's initial burst of anger had subsided and he was scared of what they might find inside. Rose decided to take the initiative and untied the piece of string holding the lid on. She found file number 16 and slid it out, placing it on the table.

'Okay, here we go.' She opened it and began to read. Frankie, in a last semblance of respect for his boss, turned his head away. 'How old would you say Jack is?' she asked, after a few moments reading.

'How old? About thirty four, I think, why?'

'Well, if he is, then he had meetings with Roland Goup when he was about two years old. This is his father, you twonk.'

Frankie whipped his head back around and stared at the file. 'I knew that,' he said eventually, 'I just wanted to see if you were on the ball.'

'Frankie,' admonished Rose. 'No, you didn't; so don't try that one on me. Look at the amount of money listed here.'

'Shit,' exclaimed Frankie, looking at the totals. 'I've never seen so many noughts on the end of a number, and that's just the amount filed for his tax; there must be oodles and oodles more that he hasn't declared.'

'And is Jack going to inherit the lot?'

'He sure is. Gods, in that case he can give me a pay rise. 'Ere, are you thinking that you might want to get to know him a little bit better, so to speak?'

'Frankie,' exclaimed Rose, 'What a thing to say, I hardly know him.'

He grinned and then winked. 'Well, sorry. It just came into my head looking at all that money. I'll tell you one thing though,' and he tapped his finger on his chest. 'For all those noughts, I'd bloody shag him!'

Back downstairs and now in a much better mood, Frankie and Rose joined MacGillicudy, who patiently waited for the office to become available so he could shift all the paperwork down to the station. He figured that the only safe place would be in one of the spare cells, where at least he could keep it under lock and key. Frankie agreed. The only thing left to do here now was to go and bang on a few doors and see if he could shake out a few memories.

The next couple of hours were a pretty fruitless exercise as nobody had seen anything untoward. Frankie became frustrated and it began to show. Rose had quickly picked up that there were various ways in which to question people and that Frankie's methods were not necessarily conducive to getting results. After Frankie had pinned a smart-arse costermonger up against the wall by his throat, Rose had gently suggested that perhaps she should have a go instead.

Rose found it interesting that she hadn't found Frankie's methods distasteful. People did find him intimidating, and he used that to his utmost advantage, but now knowing him a little, she realised that a lot of it was for show. True he could be menacing and she had no doubt that he wouldn't flinch from ripping someone's head off, should the need arise, but then again, neither would she.

Her problems had begun quite early in life. The village of Dawling may have been a backwater but it had all the elements of a large town with all the undesirable features. The fact that she had matured early brought about a serious amount of unwanted attention. The young boys she could handle, but when some of the older men started taking an interest, then it became a lot more serious. There were a couple of very big reasons why, and she started to hide those reasons under as much cloth as she could. Apart from family, she felt safe with only one person, an old priest who lived in an old tumbledown barn just outside the village. She didn't know where he came from, but as he had almond shaped eyes, she surmised that he came from somewhere out east. He would come into Dawling to her parent's shop for supplies every few weeks and would always stop to talk to her. During one of these chats, her life took a new turn. Some older lads were trying to look big amongst their peers, so began to tease her as she talked to the priest; but the teasing changed as the lads goaded each other on, the comments became nasty, and the gestures that went with them left no doubt in the mind as to what they referred. The priest watched, listened and then finally stepped forward, warning them to stop. Being small and thin, the lads thought he posed no threat to them whatsoever, so they laughed at him and then began to push him around too. Rose pleaded with the lads to stop, but they just ignored her and carried on. However, within a few frantic seconds the five lads had changed their minds, the priest had floored every one of them in a lightening blur of intense activity.

Rose had stood open-mouthed in astonishment as the priest's arms and legs whirled about with a deadly grace; a kind of poetry in the movement, balanced and coordinated, every punch, every kick, timed to perfection. It was effortless, and she could have sworn that she saw sparks flying: the dance mesmerised her. She made a decision.

When he'd finished he just turned to her, and with a gentle bow of his head, smiled shyly. Not a grin of victory, but a gentle smile, full of warmth and humility; and he wasn't even out of breath.

'Thank you,' she had said, and he inclined his head in acknowledgement. 'Could you teach me to do that?' she had asked hopefully.

He had taken a deep breath before replying, as though all the woes of the world were upon his shoulders. 'There is much that I can teach you, should you be an able pupil. I can give you an inner peace; enlightenment; a sense of being; an affinity with the world; a feeling of contentment; the certainty of knowing.'

'Bugger that,' she had replied. 'Couldn't you just teach me how to kick their gonads into their necks?'

For the next three years, she spent all her spare moments at the tumbledown barn with the priest. He taught her everything he had promised, and she felt a spiritual peace that she couldn't explain. She felt at one with the world; she was seventeen, but had the mind and the wisdom of a person far far older. But, most importantly of all, he had taught her not only how to kick the lads' gonads up into their necks, but to go way further and blast them out their ears.

The priest had disappeared the day after he had told her that she had now learnt enough. She now had to make her way in the world, but armed with the skills he had taught her, he said that she would always know the right thing to do. And she had too. She stayed at Dawling for a few more years and despite a couple of instances where she had to utilise her skills, she earned a new respect. The men learnt to keep their distance, excepting, of course, the one or two that she decided were not too troublesome, and she found that everybody wanted to be her friend.

At twenty three, she decided that the time had come to leave home. Her uncle had a pub in Gornstock and her family suggested that she should see life before life passed her by.

Primrose Morant packed her bags and headed off to the big city.

It may have said "Coffee Shop" on the outside of the establishment, but the inside told a different story. Little old ladies taking afternoon cream cakes and biscuits were now a thing of the past, they had been forced out, and in return, this coffee shop had become a drug dealers' paradise. When they entered the establishment, Frankie had to look twice, as he thought all these types of places were consigned to the slums; to have something like this in the posh bit of the city was a shock to the system. Smoke rose thickly to the ceiling with the pungent aroma of coffee intermingling with the even more pungent aroma of undiluted gaseous expulsions. Rose took it all in her stride as they stood at the entrance and waited until the buzz of conversation died in the throats of the patrons. There were around thirty or so men and youths sat around the bare wooden tables, and they all looked up at the new arrivals with varying degrees of distrust and hostility.

Frankie cleared his throat to speak, but Rose laid a hand on his sleeve and gave a brief shake of her head. 'This is mine, don't forget,' she whispered into his ear.

'Okay,' he replied quietly, 'but if it turns nasty then it's going to be mine.'

Rose nodded her agreement and then scanned the sea of faces again. 'An incident across the road yesterday afternoon, at the accountant's,' she called out to everyone there, 'resulted in the death of a cleaner; does anyone here know anything about it, who went in, who came out?'

The silence following her question went on for a few seconds, then one or two began to chuckle, and before long, all of them were laughing, until a voice from the back bellowed across it all. 'You is taking the piss little lady, come on, yer not really one o'them feelers are ya, darling? Yer one o'them strip-a-thingy's, aren't ya? Come on, get yer jugs out. I'm a'ready and a'waiting for ya.'

The laughter increased to a level that threatened to raise the roof. Frankie's face set as hard as stone as he fought with his temper. Rose gently touched his arm. 'Mine, remember,' she said into his ear to remind him.

Rose smiled, and then flicked off the band that held her hair in a tail behind her head. She shook her head to let the tresses fall languorously around her shoulders before undoing a couple of buttons on her shirt. She slowly walked forward, emphasising a wiggle as she made her way through the cacophony of crudity the like of which made even Frankie wince. She eased her way to the back of the room where the speaker sat, holding court with three other men. A greasy looking specimen in his forties, he had a large gut pushed up hard against the table, stinking of stale sweat and halitosis. He wore a brown stained shirt with a loose neck tie and his flesh appeared ingrained with dirt. Rose sauntered up to him in a most suggestive manner, smiling all the while. She caressed his arm then eased behind him, and then rested her hand on his shoulder.

'I told ya lads, she's one o'them strip-a-thingy's. Come on, who bought 'er fer me?'

The laughter continued as everyone waited for something to happen, and then Rose made sure something did. She gripped the man's neck tie and swung it around, tightening the knot and deftly tying the ends to the back of the chair just as his hands came up to protect his throat. His face quickly turned the colour of beetroot and he spluttered from the lack of air. The coffee shop fell silent as they all watched the grease-ball frantically struggle for breath. One of the man's friends jumped up from the table and Rose kicked out, sending him crashing to the floor, another got up, and Rose spun around with her arm and rendered him instantly unconscious, a third got up and Rose kicked him hard in the unmentionables; the man's eyes bulged just for a moment before he collapsed, groaning in agony. Frankie, meanwhile, had grabbed another and proceeded to use his head as a punch-ball. The silence of the room then erupted in a cacophony of noise as the rest of the clientele scrambled for the door in a sudden mass exodus. Shortly, everyone had gone, all except for Frankie and Rose and their victims. Frankie continued to punch his man, with a distinct thunk-tap-thunk-tap-thunk-tap noise, the tap-tap-tap being the back of the head bouncing off the wall with every punch.

'I can't hear you,' yelled Frankie, into the face.

'Freddie the Weasel,' spluttered the reply. 'I saw Freddie the Weasel.'

'That's more like it, my friend. Now don't you feel better for telling me that?'

As Frankie let go, the informant slumped to the floor in an

untidy heap. He turned away and grinned at Rose. 'Now, that's what I call a proper interrogation.'

The only noise left now came from the back table where a gentle snoring emanated from the unconscious man, and a panicky whine came from the other, moaning that he couldn't feel his leg. The grease-ball could only utter an increasingly demented 'N, n, n, nnngh,' as the stricture continued to bite into his neck.

'You going to let him loose, Rose? Jeez, but you're quick. I've never seen anyone move so fast. Jack is going to be chuffed to bits when he hears about this.'

'He's got about another half hour before he expires,' she replied, quite calmly. 'I think that maybe he would like the time to reflect on his manners, especially where women are concerned.'

The door crashed open and Sergeant MacGillicudy strode in. He quickly took in the situation and grinned broadly. 'Well, well, well, Frankie, what have we got here? I saw everybody running out, and I thought, hello, Frankie and Rose have just gone inside there.' He took a quick look at Frankie's punch-bag and gave a brief tut-tut, before moving over to Rose to take a look at her victims. 'Oh, oh, oh. Look at who it is; I've been looking for this one,' he cried triumphantly. 'As I live and breathe, it's Samuel Snodgrass; but if I'm not mistaken, *you* might not be breathing for much longer.'

'I've heard the name,' responded Frankie, taking a renewed interest. 'But I never had the pleasure. What's he doing around these parts, Jethro?'

'Been forced out, Frankie. Dealers like him are the scum of the city; they all scarpered when the feelers came down hard on the trade. He's wanted as three kids died after buying some gear off him. He cut the good stuff with cleaning fluid and they burnt away from the inside out. Didn't know he set up here, but I do now.'

'Bonus time then, Jethro. You'll have to speak nicely to Rose though, as she's the one who's sort of tied him up.'

'He's a lucky fella then… Sorry, Rose, force of habit,' he added quickly.

'Not to worry, Sergeant. I'll leave him in your capable hands; I assume you want these others as well?'

'Oh yes, It's like having all my birthdays rolled into one.'

The police wagons bounced along the road with Frankie and Rose sitting in the back, together with all the files and paperwork removed from Roland Goup's office. Up ahead, another wagon had more paperwork, but also five prisoners trussed up like turkeys. They were both feeling pleased with the morning's work, and Frankie eagerly anticipated having a word with Freddie the Weasel. The informer had informed them that Freddie had gone into the accountant's, coming out a little while later. He waited for a time in the coffee shop, and then when Mr Goup went out, Freddie went back again.

He knew Freddie from long ago, a nasty little sneak thief who came from the Brews, a slum area south of the river near the docks. If the poor people lived in the Warren, then those who lived in the Brews could only aspire to live in the Warren. It was the lowest of the low, the cesspit of Gornstock, a broken lawless society with a ramshackle collection of tenements and small cottages and deep dark alleys. Sometimes, even its inhabitants feared to tread its streets.

'So you think this Freddie is our murderer?' asked Rose, leaning back.

'Seems likely. I reckon someone paid him to lift some stuff, so he went in first to case the joint as the Mr M Bezel; he probably thought it was funny. When the accountant went out, he went back in, but hadn't thought there would be a cleaner cleaning; he must have panicked when he thought he might get caught, and so exit one cleaner. Anyway, we'll soon find out.'

Frankie gave a cheery wave to the driver as they hopped off and headed off down the street towards the bridge. They passed the Guilds Hall where the heads of all the guilds met to manipulate the city's prices, and then on through the park and out, down one street and across another, which led to the Gornstock Bridge. They turned right when they crossed over then down the embankment to a dense grey monstrosity of dilapidated buildings that were already crumbling away. There should have had a warning sign, saying "STOP. DO NOT PASS." They had arrived at the Brews and hell on twearth.

'Looks a nice place,' observed Rose, with a shiver running up her spine.

'I take it you have not been here before then?' replied Frankie. 'Well, stick close to me and you won't go wrong. There are little pockets of sanity in here and we'll mainly stick close to those areas. Stick yer nose in where it's not wanted and yer liable to have it cut off.'

'Oooh, I can't wait.'

She didn't have to. Frankie stepped into the narrow alley without another thought and Rose dutifully followed behind. Even though the sun shone brightly, the buildings leant over above them, seeming to touch, cutting off the light and making the place dark and dingy. Underfoot, the cobbles were slimy and the smell reeked of something long long dead. Already an interest had developed in the newcomers, as what passed for curtains here twitched to allow for viewing. The heavy silence seemed doom filled as they continued to go deeper into the slum.

'This place might interest you,' said Frankie, sounding very much like a tour guide. 'A little old lady runs this shop, has done for more years than I can remember.'

Rose peered in through the dirty cobwebbed window and saw axes and swords and picks and shovels and all things mine-like. 'What's this then?' she asked.

'Look next door.'

She did, and a great brick arch had a sign saying "Oxhead Street Underground"

'What's the underground then?'

'Dwarfs is what it is. They mine, and this is one of their entrances. There are quite a few dotted here and there all over the city. The Assembly gives them contracts for the ore; though only the Gods know what they do with the money. Mind you, if someone got their finger out they could have a nice little transportation service down there. This is one of the shops that supplies them. Mostly they stay underground, but more and more often nowadays you'll see them on the surface, mostly to drink mind, and boy can they drink. They like spending time in the pubs, but I suppose you know that, seeing that you've been working in a pub. Generally, I think they're nasty little bastards who thankfully keep well out of my way.'

'Frankie. That's not nice. I think they're rather sweet. Short, but sweet.' She waited, but the joke sailed over Frankie's head and splattered against the wall.

'Come on, we've got a bit further to go before we come to the weasel's abode.'

They carried on deeper into the Brews and passed a few more of the slum's establishments. Rose swore blind that some of the meat on sale would have barked or purred in an earlier form of life, and some of it would definitely have squeaked. One place in particular intrigued her though; it had a sign saying

"Colliderscope" and showed an old weather beaten board painted with stars and other astrological symbols. She looked in through the window and saw a couple of people staring into little glass screens.

'I'm going to have to ask, Frankie; what are they doing?'

Frankie stopped walking and turned back to join her at the window. 'Well, you know the Universal Collider just outside the city?'

She nodded, everyone knew about that. In the Collider, the universes touched. If you had enough money you could see what would have happened if you had taken a different direction in life, by tuning in to a parallel universe. That was the cheaper option, but still astronomically expensive. The other option used the theory that if you looked through the universes in the right direction, it could create a time loop, and then you might be able to see what could happen in the future. But if the prices they charged for the cheaper option was astronomical, then for this option, they were mind blowing. Only the very rich could afford to even think about using it.

'The people that run this place say that they have managed to get a link to it, although you can't choose what to see, you can have a look at what is happening somewhere else. So what they're doing is hoping against hope that they will see something they can use to their advantage. The thing is; all they're doing is staring at themselves staring at themselves, so to speak, because their other selves in the parallel universes are doing exactly the same thing as themselves. But it keeps them off the streets.'

'Er, I think I know what you mean. So if I went in there and had a look in the glass, I would just see me staring back.'

Frankie nodded. 'If you paid the ten dollars they're asking for the pleasure.'

'Ah.' The penny dropped. 'But couldn't I be just staring at a mirror? I mean, how would I know that I was looking at another universe?'

He looked at her knowingly. 'What do you think?'

'I think that someone is making a lot of money by conning people with a couple of mirrors.'

'Yes, but how would you *know*, eh? Tell me that?'

Rose hesitated as she thought, but then Frankie supplied the answer.

'This is the Brews, Rose; hope doesn't come cheap.'

They moved on, and soon they were staring up at a dilapidated four storey building which lurched rather than stood. The mortar holding the bricks together had crumbled away, leaving holes everywhere. Most of the windows were boarded up, with the front door, half off its hinges.

'Here we are. The Weasel's lair. And, typical of the people we want to speak to, he's on the top floor. Be careful where you tread, most of the floorboards are rotten.'

Frankie led the way inside to what was once an imposing vestibule but now a hall full of rubbish. A couple of people lay in the corner, sleeping off their indulgences and unaware of their presence. The stairs led up on the right and Frankie gingerly started to climb. Rose followed, being careful to place her feet exactly where Frankie put his.

'Smells of wee,' she said, sniffing distastefully.

They continued up to the top floor where a labyrinth of passages led off into distant corners of the house. The boarded up window let in a little dull light through rents in the wood, which vanished after they took the first bend. Frankie fished out a match and sparked it to life. The faint glow showed a couple of doors on either side of them, but he led the way past and turned into another passage. A door blocked the way, and Frankie took a slow breath and hammered on the flaking paintwork.

There was no reply, so after a couple of minutes he tried again.

'Right, that's it, time to kick the door in.'

'He might be out,' reasoned Rose.

'He might,' responded Frankie, with a grin. 'But let's find out.' The match in his hand burned down to his fingers and he let out a curse as he flapped his hand to cool it down. Despite being plunged into darkness, Rose chuckled behind him.

'Why don't you just try the door knob?' she suggested, as he struck another match.

'Yeah, well. I was just gonna do that.'

He did, and the door clicked and swung open a couple of inches. He turned to Rose and flashed another grin before pushing the door further. It groaned and rasped as it unwillingly opened up enough to let them in. A grubby window in the back wall let in a little grubby light, which matched the very grubby looking room. Frankie spun around to take stock of all he could see and very quickly wished he hadn't.

'Oooooh. That's nasty.'

Rose turned to where he stared and she too wished she hadn't. 'Oh, bollocky, bollocky, bollocks,' she moaned. She'd seen corpses, loads of times and they didn't hold much fear for her; but all the ones she had seen had been lying down, agreed not necessarily flat, but she had never seen one standing up before. Admittedly, he wouldn't have been standing had it not been for the ten inch nails hammered through his wrists, and his thighs, and if it wasn't for the one that stuck out of his mouth, and for the one protruding from his forehead. She fought down the bile that rose to her throat and took a few moments to settle herself down. 'I take it that's our Mr Weasel?' she ventured, when she felt she could speak at last.

Frankie nodded slowly as he stood in front of the corpse.

'And I take it that's not one of his party tricks?'

Frankie raised a laconic eyebrow.

'Sorry, nerves,' she explained contritely. 'I'll tell you one thing though; I wouldn't want them to put up *my* shelves, he's not even straight.'

Frankie raised the other eyebrow and stared at Rose for a few moments. 'Just for that you can take off his boots,' he said eventually.

'What? Why?'

'Because someone left a boot-print at the scene, it's either that or you can turn this place over. Your choice.'

Rose looked around again; the place was a mess. The fug of stale tobacco and body odour assailed her nostrils and she doubted that the window had ever been opened, but underneath that, another smell lurked, indicating that something really unpleasant hid beneath the detritus, and one look at the stained threadbare mattress lying on the floor was enough to make her come to a decision. The boots were the better option.

She crouched down, being careful not to let her knees touch the dirty wooden floor. A little blood pooled beneath the body, but far less than she would've thought. Behind her Frankie continuously swore as he fought with the junk. Rose had her own problems though: with Freddie's thighs nailed to the wall, it made removing his boots somewhat difficult. She untied the laces and sort of twisted his lower legs to slide them off and recoiled as the whiff from his sockless feet hit her nostrils. With that problem successfully negotiated, she took a moment to recover then eased back, looking at what he wore. The trousers were ill fitting but of a good quality and relatively clean, the shirt was cheap and thin and couldn't be described as anywhere near clean. The two didn't quite go together.

'Is there a black jacket amongst that lot?' she asked, turning her head.

Frankie grunted as a reply before tossing over a matching black jacket. She picked it up and started to examine it. It too was clean and she smiled to herself when she saw the label, the same as the one on the oily shirt: Biggins and Shute of Cavel Row.

'Where do you think he could have got a posh suit from?'

Frankie turned over a pile of soiled linen and a stack of unwashed plates and quickly wished he hadn't. 'Jeez,' he exclaimed. 'The bastard. There's a string of dead rats here, and when I say a string, I mean a string; he's threaded the whole lot.'

Rose stood up and peered over his shoulder, catching the overpowering nauseating smell, the same underlying smell that she had sensed only a few minutes earlier, and now here she had it in its full undiluted form. 'Why has he done that?' she asked, as another bout of nausea churned her stomach.

'He's been selling 'em to the butchers down the road, I reckon, maybe he gets more money if they're a little high. You just asked me something?'

She coughed and swallowed to calm her stomach down. 'Yes, where would he get a posh suit from? This comes from the same place as the oily shirt back at the accountant's.'

'Oh, does it now? Well, he could have nicked it, but maybe that's stretching coincidence a little too far. What about the trousers?'

'The same place, I'm sure. I haven't looked, but I'm a girl, I can tell these things.'

'You'd better have a nosey just in case; anyway, there might be a name or sommat on it.'

The look she gave Frankie would have killed a lesser man, but he just grinned and winked at her.

'I'm sure the Weasel won't mind.'

'He might not, but what about me?'

'Experience, Rose, life's all about experience. Anyway, you wanted to deal with him, look at the shit that I'm sorting.'

'All right, all right,' she said, holding up a placating hand. 'I'll take a look if it keeps you happy.'

Rose stood with her hands on her hips looking at Freddie the Weasel and wondering how she could get at the back of his trousers with the minimum of interference. It was going to be difficult whatever way she chose. With him nailed to the wall, the only way she could think of was to undo the fly buttons and drag the back of the trousers around to the side, with luck, she should then be able to see the label, job done. She took a deep breath and crouched down again, hesitating for only a moment before getting down to the unpleasant task. If Freddie had been alive, he wouldn't have believed his luck as Rose began to untie the string around his waist and then undo the fly. Frankie went very quiet as he watched.

Rose's eyes widened in shock as the trousers slid down to rest on the nails in his legs. 'The little shit is not wearing underpants,' she yelled in surprise.

Frankie moved in a little closer. 'Jeez,' he exclaimed. 'Will you look at that. They should have called him Freddie the Horse. He's lucky they didn't nail *that* to the floor.'

Rose whipped her head around. 'Frankie,' she admonished. 'The poor bastard's dead.'

'Yeah, isn't he just; but a little runt like that! Where's the justice.'

Rose shook her head and pulled the back of the trousers around into view. Biggins and Shute, Cavel Row, nothing else. 'There, satisfied?'

'I was, but now I'm not so sure... Oh, you mean the label.' He flashed her a grin. 'Yeah, Biggins and Shute it is. Now when you pull 'em back up don't forget to fold it all back in again, can't have any of that hanging out. If it's any consolation, I don't think we'll bother bringing the trousers back with us. Oh, hang on a minute. You ever seen a white eared elephant?'

Rose shook her head, but then felt that she should have said yes.

Frankie leant over and pulled out the pockets of Freddie's trousers, then pulled them up, leaving a certain thing hanging out. 'There,' he said triumphantly. 'Good, innit?'

'Frankie, I'm going to give you fair warning. I'm going to remember this.'

Frankie grinned, a genuine grin. 'Rose, you have the makings of a great investigator. You're developing just the right amount of cynicism, and it's still only your first day on the job.'

Rose couldn't help it; she had to smile.

When Freddie the Weasel regained his modesty, Frankie announced that they'd spent enough time there. They would have a word with a feeler to let them know about Freddie's demise, but Frankie doubted if the corpse would be still there by the time they got around to dealing with it. The Brews scavengers would be waiting to pounce, and besides, the room would probably be rented out again by nightfall. They still had to visit the carriage-hire firms and it was already well into the afternoon.

'We'll dump this lot back at the office first,' said Frankie, referring to the boots and jacket; MacGillicudy had the oiled soaked shirt back at the station, and he had the handkerchief stuffed into his own pocket. 'I've got to go see my mum today and then I have a date with a lady. If we shake a leg we can get the carriage firms done with time to spare.'

'Are there many carriage firms in the city?' asked Rose, taking a gulp of fresh air.

'Oh yes, but only four that we need to worry about. Most of 'em hire cheap open carts, but we're looking for a covered coach, which means expensive. Don't worry; this is going to be a piece of piss.'

CHAPTER 4

Cornwallis lifted his head from the desk and realised that he had been asleep for the last hour or so. He rubbed the back of his neck, pleased to note that the headache had now gone. He'd been a fool to drink so much, and he winced when he remembered what Frankie had said; he resolved to find One Eyed Monty and drop him a couple of dollars in recompense. The coffee was still warming on the stove so he poured himself a mug and gulped it down. He looked at the door where he had last seen Rose, remembering the sight of her bottom as she disappeared through. He regretted that he had sent her out with Frankie, but he knew he couldn't have her with him when he went to the House of Assembly; women were only allowed in to make the tea and clean the privies and he doubted if could have passed her off as a woman who does. Those hallowed corridors were a bastion of all things male, it would cause apoplexy among the older members should Rose appear with all her attributes. Still, he'd try and make up for it later.

Before he went to the Assembly, he would have to go and see Captain Bough at the police station; he needed to know why the case had dropped into his lap and who had ordered it. Someone had, that was for certain. He couldn't imagine Bough relinquishing his grip on a murder without a serious degree of pressure; he had plenty of resources to deal with it, maybe not as professional as himself, but resources nonetheless.

Scooters Yard Police Station was a large dreary grey building that exuded gloom and despondency. A few steps led up to the big double doors that led in to the reception and Cornwallis bounded up and entered. Bare wooden benches lined the walls and there were three doors; the one to the right meant that if a visitor went through he would be unlikely to see daylight for a very long time, the one to the left meant that the police wanted to speak to you but you had a good chance of going out again, the one in the back wall meant you were safe. A lectern with steps accessed from behind, dominated and loomed over the back wall, so high up that you had to crane your neck to talk to the officer who occupied it. People milled around the busy open area, most with a feeler attached, waiting to hear their fate. The sergeant presiding dealt with it all in a detached manner, indicating with a flick of the wrist which door needed to be opened. Cornwallis barged his way through to the lectern and waited until Sergeant Grinde had finished with the young boy in front.

'Youse been found with a screwdriver in your pocket, my lad, to me that's carrying with intent,' bellowed the sergeant.

The youngster looked panicky. 'It's me dad's, he sent me for to fetch it like. He's doing sum work and t'other one broke. Send someone to ask him. Honest, I ain't dun nuffing.'

'Youse were seen running away, my lad, from what we're yet to find out, but youse was running with a screwdriver in yer pocket. A spot o'leisure will loosen yer tongue.' He flipped his hand and the door to the right swung open.

The feeler accompanying the youngster grabbed hold of his collar and lifted him up. The lad started screaming and tears ran down his face as he struggled to loosen the grip on the back of his jacket.

'I ain't dun nuffing. Honest. Just asks me dad — please.'

The door slammed shut and the protests were abruptly cut

off.

'Next,' yelled the sergeant. 'Oh, it's you, Cornwallis.'

'Good morning, Sergeant Grinde,' replied Cornwallis, as he looked up into the big bearded face with rosy red cheeks. He looked like everyone's favourite uncle, but Cornwallis knew him as an evil malicious bastard. 'I'd like to see Captain Bough as a matter of some urgency if you please.'

'Captain Bough, you say? And why would you want to see our Captain?'

'I think it's enough that I want to see him, Sergeant. As to the reason, I will let the Captain tell you should he wish you to know.'

Sergeant Grinde looked as though he sucked on a lemon as he struggled to find a reason to refuse Cornwallis. Everyone had heard the request; and what if the Captain got to hear that he had turned Cornwallis away?

'I'll just wait here then, shall I?' prompted Cornwallis, as he moved to the door beneath the lectern.

Grinde finally gave a curt nod and flicked his hand. The door swung open and Cornwallis stepped through, thanking the constable on the other side. He looked up to his left and saw Grinde looking down at him. Cornwallis just smiled, one day Grinde would overstep the mark; he just hoped he would be there to see it. Grinde turned his attention back to the miscreants and continued to do what he enjoyed most: spreading misery and injustice in equal measures.

The young constable led Cornwallis down a short corridor then up a flight of stairs; they went along another corridor then the constable tapped on an office door on the left, he paused a while, and then a strained voice bid him to enter.

'Mr Cornwallis to see you, Captain,' said the feeler, before scampering back to wait on Grinde's judgements.

'Ah, thank you. Morning Cornwallis, what can I do for you?'

Cornwallis stepped into the office and looked at the pile of paperwork on Captain Bough's desk. There seemed to be an inordinate amount, with more on the floor, covering any clear space. Bough fidgeted and appeared distracted as he struggled to bring it all under control.

'Just need a little information,' replied Cornwallis, negotiating a stack of papers that had "Felonious Assaults" written on the top in large script.

'Be careful with that lot,' screamed Bough, with a serious look of panic on his face. 'I've just spent four hours going through it all.'

'Gods, what an exciting life you lead. Life at the top can't get much better than this.'

Bough shot Cornwallis a venomous look, staring in silence for a few seconds, before the shoulders collapsed and he seemed to shrink to half his size. 'At this moment, Cornwallis, I'd give anything to become a feeler on the beat again, anything.'

Cornwallis pulled at the back of a chair and a cascade of files slid to the floor. 'Oops. Sorry.'

Bough sighed. 'I haven't touched that lot yet, so you're lucky. If I had then you would be a corpse by now.'

Cornwallis sat down and regarded Captain Bough; mid-fifties with grey hair thinning on top, a ruddy clean shaven face with sharp features and a physique which resembled a pipe cleaner. 'Having problems then?' he asked, noticing the bags under the captain's eyes.

'Problems are the least of my problems,' grumbled Bough, running his fingers through the thin strands of his hair. 'I haven't been home since yesterday... no, the day before yesterday; and I won't get home until all this has been done. The only plus is that I've got out of a visit to the wife's mother, but the downside is that she has now come to us instead. A snap audit from the department and they want all the figures for the last five years. I tell you, Cornwallis, I'm seriously thinking of packing it all in. The only thing stopping me is that Grinde is the senior sergeant, so would become acting captain in my place. Just imagine the damage he would do.'

'Grinde as Captain?' Cornwallis shuddered at the thought. 'They wouldn't, would they?'

'Radstock, the Secretary to the Minister, said only yesterday, and I quote. "Sergeant Grinde is the epitome of good policing. Conscientious, thorough and impartial. A credit to the force." Yes Cornwallis, they would.'

'Gods, that doesn't bear thinking about. I take it you're staying then?'

Bough nodded. 'I can't even think of retiring while he's still here.'

'In that case I wish you a long and happy life. What's Radstock doing here anyway? The likes of him don't normally run the risk of rubbing shoulders with the mere mortals.'

'No, surprised me as well. He just turned up and began issuing orders. He didn't say why he wanted the figures; just that he did. I can't argue with him, as you know, so here I am. He ordered me to hand the murder over to you, said I had much more important work to do and that this takes precedence over everything else. He seemed pretty angry to start with though, kept asking if it was a murder or a theft; he calmed down in the end, and that's when your name came up. I take it the murder is why you're here?'

Cornwallis nodded, 'I'm just curious as to why I got handed it, but if you're so busy that would explain it. Wonder why he was so angry?'

'He didn't say, and he wouldn't answer me even if I asked.

To be honest, I didn't want to hand the job over to you, a good investigation like that sets the men up for the rest of the year. I put MacGillicudy onto it straight away, but then Radstock shoved his nose in. I take it MacGillicudy is being cooperative?'

Cornwallis nodded again. 'He's being most helpful.'

'Good. I know you're doing the investigating, but you might need all the help you can get.'

You mean you want to keep a finger in the pie, despite Radstock, thought Cornwallis.

'If he was senior sergeant I would definitely pack it in. Did you see the shower of shit he had with him? I've even had recruitment taken out of my hands, all done centrally now at the ministry. If I didn't know better I'd swear they were trying to destabilise the force.'

A knock at the door interrupted them and a constable came in with a sheath of papers under his arm. 'Sorry, Captain, but custody has asked if you could sign these release documents. It's getting a bit full down there.'

Bough groaned. 'Let's have a look at what our sergeant has done now.' He took the proffered sheets and began to study them. 'Charge: Dangerous driving and causing an obstruction: cart driver swerved to avoid oncoming vehicle and overturned, covering street with molasses. Charge: Causing a breach of the peace: barrow boy ran over foot of arrestee, who looked at said barrow boy in a threatening manner. Charge: Wanton destruction: apprehended when burning wood in a brazier on the docks. Charge: Aggravated burglary; why's he letting this one go?'

'He forgot his key, Captain; it was his own house. Been here since yesterday keeping Psycho Pete company.'

Bough shut his eyes in despair for a few moments. 'Is he still intact?'

'Yes, sir, but he's gibbering a bit.'

Bough picked up his pencil. 'Here you are. I'll just sign the bloody lot and hope that there's not too much damage done.'

'Plenty more later, I'm afraid, sir; custody officer is tearing his hair out.'

'He's not the only one, Constable. All right, keep me informed.'

'Yes, sir.'

Bough turned back to Cornwallis. 'See, it never ends.'

'So it would appear. What's Pete done this time?'

'You wouldn't believe it. He said he had a visitation from the god Aumadorn who told him he had to clean up the mines. So he went down Steeple Road Underground armed with a toothbrush and a cloth; an hour later he came up bound hand and foot. Grimwald Stormcraker, one of the mining engineers, said they found him polishing the quartz. In the end, it took five of them to get him to stop. Apparently, it was a good seam too. Three of the dwarfs are out of action for a couple of weeks; a toothbrush can be a dangerous weapon in the wrong hands.'

Cornwallis chuckled as the imagined scene played out in his mind, then he reached into his inner pocket of his jacket and pulled out a form. 'If you could sign this, I would be grateful. I have a new investigator, just started this morning.' He passed it over and let Bough scrutinise it.

'Female? Not like you, Cornwallis. I thought you only worked with Kandalwick.'

'Times change, Bough; got to get modern. It won't be long and the women will get the vote too.'

Bough looked aghast. 'Don't say things like that, Cornwallis. Can't imagine what it would be like if I had to employ them. Gods, one at home is enough.' He scribbled on the form and handed it back. 'Your life, but you'll rue the day you asked me to sign this, you mark my words.'

The form safely back in his pocket Cornwallis stood up and went to leave. 'Maybe, we'll see. I might even thank you in the end.'

Cornwallis closed the door and headed back down. The reception had thinned out a little and he managed to get out without Grinde seeing him, being too busy berating a lady of negotiable virtue to notice. Once outside, he took a deep breath of the morning air and stared up at the cloudless sky. Life felt good, he thought, as he jauntily set off, leaving Scooters Yard behind him.

The conversation with Bough re-ran through his mind as he walked. Radstock wielded a lot of power in the corridors of the Assembly and used his influence like a sledgehammer. Why, he asked himself, did the secretary become angry when he'd heard that a murder had been committed? He'd queried it, asked if it wasn't just a theft. Why? Roland Goup's accountancy practise dealt with a lot of rich men, including his father, as he'd found out yesterday, so a serious crime there could have serious repercussions. Goup's disappearance seemed to indicate the accountant knowing too much, someone didn't want him to talk, and someone obviously didn't want anyone to go through the files, hence the arson attempt. Did that implicate Radstock? He'd prevented the feelers from investigating, which didn't sit right; he would have had total control over any investigation if he left it in Bough's hands, and the explanation as to why he got handed it, was very thin. He couldn't blame Bough for trying to keep a hold on things by giving him MacGillicudy; he would have probably done the same, had he been in the same position. The jigsaw had only just been tipped out of the box, and it looked as if it would be a bugger to put together.

Cornwallis wondered how Frankie and Rose were doing. He

checked his pocket watch and saw that it was nearly mid-day, they should be finished at Goup's place by now and he briefly thought to call in at the office to see if they had returned. His distracted walking had taken him towards the Assembly, so he decided to wait until later to catch up with them.

The Assembly opened for business at mid-day, although the members would have been there since morning. They would go straight to the members bar ready for a liquid lunch, and continue until well into the afternoon. He might even be able to catch Radstock, to see what he had to say for himself.

Tradition had a lot to answer for, he thought, as he wandered up to the red granite monstrosity that was the House of Assembly. A crowd had gathered as they did every day at this time for the opening of the house. The Jig that began the official day was about to commence, so Cornwallis stood at the back of the crowd while he waited for the show to finish.

The Morris Guard took up their places and waited for the melodeon player to begin. Twelve men faced each other, six on each side of the door. They were dressed in dark waistcoats and trousers with white shirts, each had a wide brimmed black hat with little golden bells. Tied around their legs were more bells, and fancy handkerchiefs were looped around their belts. All of them carried thick sticks of about three feet in length. The melodeon groaned into life and the crowd drew in a collective breath of anticipation.

The Jig began.

First, they hopped on one leg, **jingle, jingle, jingle,** then the other leg, **jangle, jangle, jangle,** and then alternate legs, **jingle, jangle, jingle, jangle,** and then the sticks came into play as they arced over towards their opposite dancer's head and the defender raised his stick for protection. **Clack**. Then the reverse. **Jingle, clack, jangle, clack, jingle, jangle, clack, clack,**

clack. Gods was it tedious. Then they began to dance around each other and the noise really began to grate on his nerves. He knew it wasn't going to last long but he still wished he had timed his arrival better. The sticks were being thrown with some venom now, the result being that the jig became ragged. Cornwallis knew that when the Jig finished, and the Morris Guard withdrew, one or two of them would regret the breach in discipline; it would be straight around the back of the barracks and the sticks would be used for another purpose. Eventually the Jig ground to halt with a loud and final **CLACK**. There followed a pause, and the dancers parted to take up their original positions. The door to the Assembly opened and the Squire of the Morris marched out. He walked between his men, shooting them a withering glance; he'd noticed the raggedness of the display and was going to make sure that someone would pay. He came to stand on the top of the steps and cried out that the Assembly was now open for that day's business. He turned smartly and strode back through the door, then his men turned, not quite as smartly, and marched after him, leaving two to guard the door. The formal opening had ended, and the crowd, now satisfied, began to disperse.

Cornwallis mounted the steps and entered into the foyer of the Assembly. The wizened old porter sitting behind the desk welcomed him formally and politely. Behind him were the Guards ready to throw out anyone the Porter didn't like.

'Ah, the Hon. Mr Cornwallis, sir. I trust you're keeping well?'

'Very well, thank you, Perkins; and you?'

'Mustn't grumble, sir, mustn't grumble. What brings you to the House today, sir? If I may be so bold; we don't normally see you in this hallowed hall.'

'Just a little business, Perkins,' replied Cornwallis, tapping his nose and winking conspiratorially. 'Hopefully, it won't take long. Tell me, has my father come in yet?'

'Oh, right you are, sir,' responded Perkins, puffing himself up and returning the wink. He now believed himself to be privy to some secret information, and that was currency in the House. 'He has indeed, sir, not half an hour ago was I chatting to your good father, great man he is, always got time for us servants of the House.'

'And rightly so, Perkins, you're the mortar that holds the place together. I don't know what we'd do without you.'

Perkins beamed in pride. 'Why thank you, Mr Cornwallis, sir, chip off the old block you are, sir, if you don't mind me saying so, sir, chip off the old block.'

Cornwallis muttered his thanks and turned to go through the filigreed doors to the lobby; another porter pulled on the brass handle and let him through with a brief dip of his head. Cornwallis strode into the cavern like interior with a feeling of dismay. Through the accident of his birth, with no other talent or aptitude involved, membership of this house and the traditions to go with it came to him through just his father's ability to put his wedding tackle in the right place. He needed nothing else to be a pillar of the establishment. What an archaic system it was.

The vast lobby spread out before him: the green marble floor stretched out ahead with four rows of tall white pillars rising thirty foot into the air, the roof above ornately painted, from which hung several huge chandeliers, an enormous expanse of decadence, and all for show. Used firstly as a walk through for the members, but secondly as a meeting place for those who were not members. Already reporters from the press hunted in packs: The Gornstock Examiner, The Gornstock Times, The Daily Moonshine, The Tribune and Herald; Cornwallis ignored them to a man. He marched straight across to the far side where a small door led to an antechamber. Here a wide staircase rose up to the floors above, while the corner housed the elevator, a box-like construction which had a chain attached to its roof; the chain rising up to the rafters and back down again to a large room next door, where the mechanism for lifting resided. There were two big wheels, one for going up, the other for going down, and each powered by a bear who would walk for miles without getting anywhere. Inside the elevator, a flunkey fussed and fawned over anyone prepared to risk it. Cornwallis didn't trust the contraption, so he used the stairs instead.

Up on the third floor, Cornwallis walked down the long corridor to his office, one of hundreds that filled this area of the House; it overlooked the river, so at least it had a view. He rapped on the door out of politeness before twisting the handle and swinging the door open. Conrad Speckleby sat at the desk going through a small pile of papers; he looked up at the intrusion, and then jumped up in welcome.

'Jocelyn, it's good to see you. It's been a long time since you were last here,' a worried frown crept onto his face. 'Oh, I haven't done anything wrong, have I?'

Cornwallis gave his proxy a brief smile and shook his head. 'No, nothing wrong. I'm only here to see a couple of people and thought I'd better see how you're doing. Everything okay?'

'Oh, rather,' he exclaimed, relaxing again. 'It's been such fun. Voting here, voting there, never a dull moment.'

'Good, good. Glad you're enjoying yourself.' Cornwallis smiled again and a long pause ensued, he had never really managed a long conversation with Conrad, who was a product of the same education system as himself; he knew his manners and which spoon to use for the soup, which summed up his total list of qualifications. Cornwallis considered him naive, but harmless; which was why he chose him to be his understudy. He'd known him from school, but Conrad had no title, a definite disadvantage for someone who had no discernible talent. He looked as innocent as a new born puppy and acted like one too. Cornwallis coughed gently and thought he'd better at least try to show some interest. 'What are you up to at the moment?'

'Oh, well, lots of things really,' Conrad chirruped. 'We have a major vote concerning the Gornstock Bank this afternoon, I did wonder if you'd come here because of that; and the other day we had a vote granting a loaf of bread a week to the elderly and infirm: they're to get one each, free.'

'Wonderful idea,' replied Cornwallis cynically. How the elderly and infirm could survive on just a loaf of bread a week was beyond him; the normal government policy was to give them as little as possible in the hope that they would die off quicker. 'And what is the bank vote for?'

'Well, it's to lend it some money. Apparently, it hasn't got much for some reason or other so it has asked the Assembly to help out a bit.'

Cornwallis looked confused. 'Hang on,' he said, holding up his hand. 'Let's go through that again. You just said the bank has got no money?'

Conrad nodded. 'That's what they say. I'm doing as you said and following the lead from your father. Apparently, we're voting against it, but it will probably still go through. It's jolly exciting all this you know.'

'I'm sure it is.' A kernel of concern lodged itself into his mind, but Conrad would know nothing, so it would be a waste of time trying to talk to him about it; he would just have to speak to his father. 'Oh, well, I'd better leave you to it then.'

'Right you are, Jocelyn,'

Cornwallis frowned in thought as he made his way back

down the corridor. He couldn't fathom how the bank could have run out of money; that was what it was there for. He felt sure that Conrad had got it wrong, that it was really the other way around and the bank had to lend the government money, the normal way of doing things. He knew his father would be in the bar by now and so headed downstairs to the first floor.

The bar bustled with activity; he walked through the door and it seemed as if every member of the Assembly had made an appearance. Cornwallis threaded his way through the throng, nodding a greeting every now and then, recognising some and having not a clue as to who some of the others were. He forced his way to the counter where some bar staff were taking orders and waited until he caught the eye of one. He popped a couple of olives into his mouth and looked around for the pork scratchings, but there were none there, the greedy bastards had already emptied the pots. He fished out the book of matches that MacGillicudy found at the scene last night and compared it to the ones on the counter. The pictures were different.

'Yes, sir?' The bartender interrupted his thoughts.

'Ah, yes. A pint of splodge please,' answered Cornwallis, remembering that splodge was the general term in here for best bitter. Within seconds a foaming pint appeared and Cornwallis thought that they must have a few already drawn, sitting there, waiting beneath the counter.

'I'll put it on your tab, sir.'

'Thank you. I'm Cornwallis, but you can put it on my father's. Before you go could you take a look at this for me?' Cornwallis handed over the little book of matches and waited while the barman twisted and turned it in his hands.

'It's a matchbook, sir.'

'Yes, I know that,' he replied patiently. He wanted to say more, but knew he couldn't, not if he wanted another drink, that is. 'It's different to these others; do you know why?'

'Oh, yes, sir. These ones are for the members,' he said, indicating the pile on the counter, 'and this one comes from the Inner Ring's bar, sir. They like to be a little different to everyone else, sir,' he added in a lower voice.

'The Inner Ring? Oh, yes, of course, silly me; must have picked up the wrong one.'

The bartender smiled sympathetically, obviously used to the eccentricities of Assembly members and now he would just add another one to the list. Cornwallis eased himself away and went to look for his father; he would undoubtedly be here somewhere.

The only people allowed in the Inner Ring bar were the inner circle of government who hammered out all the major policies. That meant, the head of the government, also known as The Warden, and his Inner Ring colleagues, plus the secretariat of the various departments.

Cornwallis ticked off in his head the names of those who could use the Inner Ring Bar when he saw Radstock over on the far side talking to a couple of men who he didn't know, he watched the secretary for a few seconds, but then a group came and stood right in front of him, blocking out his view. When he got to peer around the group, Radstock had gone. 'Bugger,' he said quietly. He took another mouthful of beer and had a moment where he remembered how drunk he'd been last night and how he meant to cut back, but then he decided to cut back tomorrow and took another pull. His eyes scanned the bar as he walked around and eventually spotted his father holding court with three of his cronies. He walked over and his father stopped mid-flow as he caught sight of his son.

'Gods, a visitation. Given up the day job, my boy?' bantered Cornwallis senior, the Earl of Bantwich.

Cornwallis smiled back. He was looking at himself in thirty years' time, the only difference being that his father had grey hair and dressed with more panache; light green suit with a gold waistcoat, and wearing a frilly cravat at the neck, which really looked more like a waterfall under his chin. 'Not yet, but don't worry, when I stick the silver spoon back up my arse, you'll be the first to know.'

'Hope for you yet then my boy,' replied the earl with a smile. 'What brings you to this den of iniquity then?'

'A little enquiry, that's all.' He got on well with his father which was unusual amongst the peerage; probably because they moved in different circles so had no need to compete. 'I just saw Conrad; he tells me there's a vote this afternoon on the bank, apparently, it's run out of money. What's it all about?'

'You started to become interested in politics, then?' asked the earl with a raised questioning eyebrow.

'No worries there, I'm afraid, it's just that it sounded a bit strange.'

'Not so strange when you think about it. The bank is as greedy as ever but it's over-reached itself this time. I think we need to give it a kick in the old whatsits and stop the loan it's asking for. But it will go through; a lot of people here will lose a lot of money if it doesn't.'

'But you won't?'

The earl grinned. 'Let's get it right, *we* won't.' He apologised to his cronies and steered Cornwallis away. 'I'll explain, but we don't want everybody to know our business.' He caught hold of a steward, ordered two pints of splodge and then indicated an alcove where they could speak in private. Once they had settled on the plush red velvet seating, the earl began. 'We have a good accountant, my boy, very dextrous with figures he is.'

Cornwallis nodded in understanding. 'Roland Goup you

mean?'

'The very same, how did you know that? Never mind, probably told you at some time. Well, Roland is the best accountant in the city and has managed to move most of our money away; he's put it into hard currency, gold, silver, diamonds, etc, and of course the odd bond or two, some of it here, and some of it abroad. The result is that we keep only a small percentage in the bank over here and that's what he declares for our income. It's a bit underhand, I know, but it's not exactly illegal. The upshot is that we may lose a little should the bank collapse, but most of it is safe.'

'And that's what everybody else has done is it, moved their money out?'

'Oh no, only the more prudent of us, that's why the vote will go through. You may not notice, but most of the people here are panicking like mad. The bank has got them by the short and curlies. I don't doubt that there has been some under-the-counter dealing in all this, it's probably buying the votes of half the people here.'

'And what will happen to the people out there?' Cornwallis indicated with his hand the general populace of Gornstock.

'I'm afraid that it's going to be bad for them; they don't know it yet, but they will soon, whatever happens. The problem for them is that they lose either way. If the bank collapses, then their money goes too, if the Assembly loans the bank the money it needs, then the Assembly will need to claw it all back, and that income will come from the taxes. Where the bank has leant money, it will demand it back, probably at a very high rate of interest. In either case the general public will pay. It's hard I know, but that's their lot in life. They've got to have something to be miserable about, it keeps them happy.'

'That's a bit harsh isn't it?'

'Of course it is, but the point is...' and he waved his arm around the bar '... is that this lot doesn't have to pay.'

Cornwallis slowly shook his head at the injustice. 'So why has the bank got into this state anyway?'

'Good question, my boy. It invested the money badly, speculated too much, and when it came to pull it all back there wasn't anything there. It neglected to put the money in safe areas like gold, etc, and instead put it into a paper chase, relying on the success of large businesses here and abroad. Basically it played the market and lost.'

'And we have to pick up the pieces.'

'*We* don't.'

'I understand now. So Roland Goup has protected *our* money then.'

'He has, clever man that.'

'And if I told you that at present, I'm investigating the murder of Roland Goup's cleaner at his office, and that the said Roland Goup has disappeared, and that whoever murdered the cleaner also got away with some files, what would you say?'

The earl stared at his son in dismay; he went pale as the blood drained from his face. 'Tell me you're not.'

'I am, and Radstock knows about it too.'

The steward returned with two pints, took one look at the earl and beat a hasty retreat. He didn't want to have to deal with another corpse; these old members have got into the habit of dropping dead in the bar, and he was buggered if he was going to deal with another one.

'Radstock?' The earl had taken a large gulp of splodge which had the effect of restoring a little colour to his cheeks. 'What's he got to do with it all?'

Cornwallis explained how Bough had given him the investigation on the behest of the Secretary to the Department of Justice. He outlined what Bough had told him and where he'd got to so far in the investigation. He showed him the matchbook and told him how Roland Goup had disappeared. In fact, he told him everything. He had no concerns that his father would tell anyone, and it might be just as well that there would be someone in the Assembly able to keep their eyes and ears open. A dropped word here, a whisper there, might be enough to lead him to the person behind it all.

'Well, this is all a bit of a shock, I can tell you.' The earl drained his pint and clicked his fingers at another steward. Two more pints were shortly on the way. 'I'm going to have to think this one through. The good news is that I have all the documents so that our money is still safe. It is a bit inconvenient, but it should pose no problem. But you don't know whose file went missing?'

'No, could be a choice of three, I think: Dooley, Dumchuck or Dumerby. Do you know any of Goup's clients?'

'God's no, I have my suspicions who some may be, but we tend to keep it all quiet. It's not the done thing to talk about personal finances here. Those names are interesting though. As you know, Dooley is a member of the Inner Ring as Chief of the Treasury, and Dumchuck is president of the Gornstock Bank. Dumerby retired as head of the Stock Market last year. If you are going to rattle any of them, I would step very carefully.'

'I know; I will have to be very certain before doing anything. I'll speak to Radstock first though.'

'No, don't. Leave him to me. I have a little leverage I can use,' and he winked conspiratorially.

Cornwallis would have liked to have asked more, but he knew his father wouldn't tell him what the leverage might be. He would just have to trust him.

'Come up to us in the next few days, your mother thinks

you've left the country.'

Cornwallis agreed, and they passed the next half hour in pleasant conversation with the accompaniment of a couple more pints. Finally, the bell went for the members to take their place for the vote and the bar began to empty.

*

Cornwallis chewed the cud as he walked down the street. He had his hands thrust deep in his pockets, and jangled the money as he walked, totting up how much he found. It came to eight dollars and forty three cents. He'd been hungry when he left his father, so he'd grabbed one of Sal's sausages from across the road. He hadn't been expecting that she would launch into him in that way and it had taken him a little by surprise.

'Do you think you should be taking on a young slip of a girl like that in your line o'work? She 'as too many bits and pieces if you asks me,' she had said, doing a pretty good job of indicating Rose's figure. 'At her age she should be at 'ome pumping out the kids, not gallivanting around the streets looking like that. Me stall got rammed with people, an' I couldn't serve the half of them as they kept looking at 'er and whimpering; and they wouldn't move away. She ain't going to blend in the background like you and Frankie can, you know. People are going to *notice* her. And anyway's, you need to get a haircut if you intend trying to do what I think you're intending trying to do. No, on second thoughts, don't think it, just do it; ask her out, show her the sights, be romantic. You can manage romantic, can't you?'

'Yes, Sal,' he replied meekly. Was he really that transparent? Perhaps she had a point; he hadn't had a haircut for a while now. A bit of male grooming might give the right impression, smarten himself up a little, and you never know what might happen. He'd tried to convince himself that he had taken her on for all the right reasons, but in reality, he had taken her on for all the wrong reasons, and he suspected that Rose knew this too. Perhaps he shouldn't have a haircut after all.

The little bell gave a tinny sounding ting as he pushed open the door. The shop was empty, so he sat down and picked up yesterday's paper while he waited; the drapes over the internal door were pulled shut, so he thumbed through the broadsheet, just scanning all the gloom and doom headlines. An Aardvark had eaten its owner, a ghost had been arrested for burglary; but the police had difficulty in keeping the handcuffs on. The woodcut print on page three looked interesting, but he really wasn't bothered that Chardonay from Appleridge thought the new government policy of a loaf of bread a week was generous and showed how much they really cared; it was more to the point, that with her, there really were a couple of points where you could hang your hat. He flipped through the pages some more and then finally laid it down, destined to be cut into pieces and hung on a nail on the privy wall, a fitting end to a gutter press rag, poor Chardonay, he thought, he wondered if she knew.

'Oh, Meester Cornwallis, welcome welcome. It's bin' a long long time since we 'a seen you. Come through, come through.' Alphonse gave a big beaming smile and put his hands together as if in prayer.

Cornwallis winced at the sight of the colours; a yellow flecked coiffure with a bright red shirt and yellow trousers, but worst of all, he wore sandals. But he stood up anyway and followed Alphonse through, trying not to look at the ensemble.

He stepped through the heavy drapes to another room with a tiled floor where three chairs faced the wall with a mirror in front of each. It was empty apart from a meerkat who had a roll-up stuck in the corner of its mouth and wore a tartan flat cap, sweeping up the hair cuttings with a tiny broom. Alphonse clapped his hands and shortly a young girl came out.

'Look who's a 'ere, Sophie, it's a Meester Cornwallis.'

'Good afternoon, Mr Cornwallis, what can we do for you? Wash, cut and blow-dry?' Sophie affected the irritating hairdressers' chirpiness as she led him to a chair.

'Just a trim please,' muttered Cornwallis awkwardly.

She sat him down and quickly wrapped a large sheet around him and tucked it into his collar. She then ran her fingers through his hair which caught on the tangles. 'Oh no, this will not do. It's going to have to be the full works. It's lank, got no body and split ends are everywhere.'

Before he could protest, Cornwallis felt the chair spinning around, she reached forward and pulled a handle over the sink and hot water gushed out. The chair tipped back and before he knew it, Sophie dumped some shampoo and began to wash his hair.

'Tut-tut, you should take better care, Mr Cornwallis,' she admonished, as she lathered up. 'A man in your position must always look the part. People like smart, and the smarter the better. Of course there are always your lady friends too, they like to feel that you take the trouble with your appearance, it makes them think that you care.'

She droned on and on and Cornwallis managed to blank most of it out; he shut his eyes and began to relax, finding it really quite pleasant as she massaged his scalp. He just got to the point of drifting off when the chair sprang forward and she wrapped a towel around his head. The chair spun around again and Sophie began to rub vigorously to dry the excess moisture. 'Now, let's see what we can do for you,' she said, as the scissors began to snip.

Cornwallis stared at his reflection as the hair parted company with his head; down below, he could hear the muttering of the meerkat as the rain of hair fell onto its cap. A tiny corkscrew of smoke rose up from its roll-up as he swept the cuttings away.

'That's better.' Sophie seemed pleased with the result as she flicked the comb and moulded it into some form of shape. 'Just the air-drier now.' She looked down and gave the meerkat a tap with her shoe. 'Jeremy, time for the drier, please.'

The meerkat pulled a face and flung the little broom down. 'Bloody humans,' it exclaimed. 'As if I ain't got enough to do.' It walked to a small door under the sink and yanked it open. A pipe led from the stove at the back of the shop to a seat with two pedals, another pipe led out from this and he gave this end to Sophie before climbing up on to the seat; he then began to pedal away furiously.

'Won't be long now, Mr Cornwallis,' said Sophie, as she teased his hair with a brush, the end of the nozzle pumping out hot air in an ever increasing amount as the meerkat gathered pace.

Cornwallis groaned inwardly as the brush did its work; she twisted it into curls down his neck and coaxed waves into the top, but embarrassment prevented him from saying anything, just wanting to get the whole thing over.

'Oh, much better now, don't you think?' she said at the last flourish of the brush.

Cornwallis nodded and gave her a brief smile. 'Thank you, Sophie, very nice.'

She smiled in gratification. 'Now then, Mr Cornwallis, something for the weekend, perhaps? We have large, extra-large, and who's a lucky boy.' She looked down into his lap and grinned flirtatiously. 'I should think you're the latter.'

Cornwallis blushed. 'Er, no thanks, just the haircut. I'll settle up with Alphonse, if that's okay.' He did wonder for a few seconds why they didn't do small and medium, but then he realised, nobody would admit to being small.

He ripped the sheet away and hurried from the chair, his eye caught the sight of Jeremy as he slumped exhausted over the support bars of the drier, the rollie dangling forlornly from his lips; he did feel a brief moment of sympathy.

Alphonse appeared at the inner door and stood aside as Cornwallis brushed past, he waved at Sophie to stay in the shop and then turned and followed Cornwallis through with a flourish. Once the door closed, Cornwallis slumped into an armchair and sighed. 'Did you tell her to do this on purpose?' he asked, with a steely glint in his eye.

Alphonse raised an eyebrow in question and then grinned. 'Your own bloody fault, you let her do what she wanted.' The voice had changed, the mannerisms had changed, and Alphonse became Algernon again. 'So what did you expect?'

'I expected a haircut, not...' he struggled to find the words as his hand wafted around his head, '... not *this*. Hang on, that rain butt still outside?'

Alphonse/Algernon nodded.

'Right then.' Cornwallis leapt up and wrenched open the back door that led to the little yard. He took a second to look around and then marched the couple of steps over to the butt. He flung off the lid, and thankful to see it full, grabbed hold off the sides and plunged his head deep into the water. It was cold, but he didn't care; when he surfaced, the curls had gone. He shook his head to rid himself of the water and felt much better again. He turned and marched straight back in with his normal confidence restored. 'I need you to ask around, Al. There's been a murder.'

Algernon poured a coffee for them both and handed one to Cornwallis before sitting down. 'In this town? There's a surprise,' he said ironically.

Cornwallis had come across Algernon a year ago whilst following a suspicious husband's wife. The husband suspected her of having an affair and he employed Cornwallis to find out who with. It came as a bit of a shock to find out that she liked to spread her favours around, being fruity with not just one, but five; she had been one very busy lady. Algernon happened to be one of them, but he didn't know he was a confirmed heterosexual conman posing as a hairdresser. She had wanted to see if she could "convert" him, and it didn't take long before she thought she had. Pleased with her success she began to give him money and then set him up in this very place to keep his head above water, which had been Algernon's plan all along; he planned to sell it without her knowledge and then disappear with all the money. Enquiries soon exposed the truth, and Cornwallis took advantage of the situation by threatening to reveal all to the husbands of the other two women who were at that time enjoying his company. Cornwallis expanded his little group of informants by one, and seeing an opportunity, bought the hairdressing business from the woman and kept Algernon on to feed him all the gossip divulged by the customers. He couldn't believe the information that came out from the bored women who came for a simple cut; who was having an affair with who, what their husbands were up to, legal and illegal, all manner of secrets were whispered into Alphonse's ears. There was also the fifty per cent income from the shop, which came in very handy.

'Up Greenwalsh Avenue, the accountants. Roland Goup. His cleaner got killed and I need to know all the whispers, all the rumours. Dig around a bit, pull in a few favours.'

'I will, but you need to do me a favour too. I can't carry on with this any longer, you have to give me a break,' pleaded Algernon. 'I mean, it was all right at the start, but I can't keep this pretence up. It's getting to the point where I'm Alphonse even when I'm at bloody home.'

Cornwallis had little sympathy. 'You started this lark, and let's face it, you're doing all right in money terms, and you're still popular with the ladies. The girls do all the work, so all you have to do is stride around the place.'

'Yeah, but even my mates are beginning to think I'm really like Alphonse.'

Cornwallis held his hands up. 'Okay, Okay. I'll think about it. Once you've found out what you can about this murder, that is.'

Algernon sighed in relief. 'Thank you, Mr Cornwallis. I'll do what I can. But just get me out of here — please.'

Cornwallis left by the back door, not wanting Sophie to see how he'd destroyed all her hard work. The dunking had turned his hair into just a shorter version of the hair he had before going in, and he felt it wouldn't elicit too many snide comments from Frankie later on. He decided it was time to head back to the office. Frankie and Rose should be back by now and they could then decide what to do next. He remembered that Frankie had a date tonight with the fish girl, so if he played it right then he could spend a nice few hours relaxing with Rose. Life wasn't so bad after all.

He bounded up the stairs to the office, anticipating a successful conclusion to the evening he had planned. On the way back from Alpnonse's he had called in at a nice little restaurant and had booked a table, subdued lighting, a quiet corner, flowers on the table sort of place. It would make amends for the embarrassment of last night, show him to be a man of refinement, show her that he knew how a girl should be treated.

Afterwards perhaps a slow stroll back through the theatre district where he knew there would be some street entertainment, and then back for "coffee".

He flung open the door expecting two faces to be looking back at him; instead, a dozen gilt framed paintings confronted him, all lining the wall, all depicting in gruesome detail the demise of Miss Knutt. Cornwallis stood dumbstruck at the size of the things, each painting a six by three foot representation in exquisite detail. They were enormous. So too was the bill stuck to the corner of the one showing a close up of the knives in the back of the neck. Cornwallis then remembered that MacGillicudy had sent Dewdrop to get the artist; and he had only gone to the foremost painter in Gornstock, Mikel An' Jello — and he'd put sodding cherubs on every one.

Cornwallis closed his eyes and shook his head. Perhaps when he opened them again they would be gone and a proper set of police paintings would be in their place. But no, when he opened them again they were still there, in all their magnificent glory. Mikel An' Jello. Just a miniature would cost a small fortune, let alone a dozen full scale, full size, masterpieces. The size of the bill made his legs turn to jelly and he had to sit down. One thing for certain, MacGillicudy and the feelers were going to pay.

He leant back in his chair still staring with shock at the paintings when he noticed a note on his desk in Frankie's spider-like scrawl, telling him that they had found the murderer, but now he too had been murdered. Freddie the Weasel had a reputation in the underworld, but only as a thief and a chancer; details were sparse, so Cornwallis knew he would get the whole story later. The bag in the corner contained the evidence, and the note ended with the information that he and Rose were off to check the coach-hire companies and should be back before late afternoon. Cornwallis checked his watch; it told him it was now five thirty so he settled himself down to wait. Anytime now, Rose and Frankie would walk through the door, and then shortly after he could wave Frankie off to his evening of fishing. That would just leave him and Rose. It would be bliss, if it wasn't for the paintings.

CHAPTER 5

Frankie held the door open for Rose as they left Brownlow and Son, the second carriage-hire firm they'd visited so far; the first had been as this one, just two carriages and neither had been out; besides, they had the wrong colour of livery; silver, and they were looking for yellow.

'Where now?' asked Rose, falling into step alongside Frankie.

'Loxley and Jennings. They're just around the corner. Might have more luck there as it's bigger and they have yellow writing. The fourth has yellow too, so one of them should come up trumps.'

'Then why bother with the first two?'

'Because Cornwallis would go mad if we hadn't checked, it was easier to get them out of the way first.'

Rose nodded, but she wasn't happy. 'Didn't you find him a bit jumpy?'

'Who? Brownlow?'

'Yes, his eyes kept moving and he swallowed a lot. Didn't you notice?'

'Well, now you come to mention it, maybe he did look a bit edgy. I noticed something else too; he didn't seem to see you. I mean he looked at you, but he didn't seem aware of you; to him, you were just another person, and not a…a…a girl.' Rose had had an effect on nearly every man they'd come across during the day, and even some of the women; giving rise to some seriously involved imaginings from Frankie, needing a cold shower to dispel. 'Perhaps we had better not write this one off just yet, then.'

They crossed the yard and walked out through the gate, and if they had bothered to turn around, they might have seen a curtain twitch in the upstairs window. Instead, they headed off down the road, oblivious to the unsavoury character who had just watched them depart.

'Very well done, Brownlow,' said the man without a name, as he walked back in holding a very large and very sharp knife towards the anxious individual. 'They didn't suspect a thing. You make sure it stays that way. The people I work for would look very badly on someone who opens their mouth when they didn't want them to.'

Brownlow looked at the man, and then at the knife, and then back to the man again. He swallowed nervously. 'I have no intention of doing that whatsoever. I just want it all finished.'

'Ah, might be a problem there. You see, you owe too much money, and until it's all paid back, with a little interest of course, then I'm afraid you will do everything we ask. It's a lesson for you, Mr Brownlow; never overreach yourself. My employers love to take on bad debts because they find people can be so accommodating, given the right incentive.'

Brownlow buried his face in his hands. He'd taken a loan out from the bank to keep the business he'd inherited from his father afloat, but a lull in the carriage-hire market meant that he couldn't keep up with the payments. The bank sold off his debt to the highest bidder, a finance house which had recently acquired an awful lot of money; and now he knew why.

The man sat down and reached forward to spin the picture on the desk around. He tapped the end of the knife against the frame and smiled at Brownlow who looked back, horrified. 'Nice twin girls you have there, Brownlow, the missus don't look too bad neither. Good market out there, you know. The girls would get a pretty penny and I should think your wife might get a bob or two as well. Saw them the other day, lovely family you got there. You must be very proud of them.'

Brownlow's face paled, he hadn't been expecting this turn of events. 'You leave my family out of it; it's got nothing to do with them.'

'Oh, but it has, Brownlow. Be very assured, it has. One little lapse on your side and you'll find out it will have a lot to do with them.'

*

'Well, that was a lot of good, a big fat zero.' Rose sighed with frustration as they left the last of the hire companies. 'But I still think Brownlow was nervous, shall we go back and have another word?'

'Naw, I reckon we can wait until tomorrow, besides, Jack will probably be waiting, and don't forget I've got to see my mum or there will be hell to pay.'

Rose laughed, 'Well, you're the boss, Frankie.'

They walked along the street with the late afternoon sun beating down, heating up the horse shit and all the other effluence that either lay in the street or ran through the open sewers. The city dwellers got used to the smell; and some people actually deemed it unhealthy to breathe fresh clean air, Workers had begun to make their way home and a steady trickle of people headed towards the suburbs; Frankie and Rose went against the flow and headed in towards the hub.

'Fancy a doughnut and a coffee?' enquired Frankie. 'Just a

quick one mind, it's been a busy day and I reckon we deserve it.'

'Why not,' responded Rose. 'I take it you're paying?'

'You're a quick learner. Yes, I'll pay.' He grinned; he hadn't had such a fun day for a long time.

The coffee shop had a few seats outside in a little cordoned off area; there were a couple of large plants in pots and an awning that gave a little shade. Frankie and Rose sat down and gave their order, keeping their thoughts to themselves for a few moments. After a few minutes, their refreshment arrived; neither of them realised just how hungry they were and the doughnuts disappeared rapidly.

Rose licked the sugar off her lips, which to Frankie made it a wholly different experience, and sat back contented. 'Just think. Last night I was pulling pints and today I've been hunting murderers. What's tomorrow going to bring?'

Frankie's thoughts were somewhere else at that moment. Most of the day he had managed to keep his mind on the job, with only a couple of slips here and there; but watching Rose eat a doughnut. 'Hmmm? What did you say?' he replied, coming back to the real world.

'I said, last night I was pulling pints and now I've been hunting murderers. I just wondered what'll happen tomorrow,' she replied, unaware of where Frankie's thoughts had been.

'Much the same I expect, unless Jack has already solved it.' He fidgeted in his seat and then took a slurp of coffee. 'Don't worry, he won't have,' he added, seeing her look of concern. 'Hopefully, he's picked up a couple of clues as well, so what we'll have to do is put them all together and see where it takes us.'

'And we do that tomorrow?'

'We do, unless you and Jack decide to do it tonight. I can't as I'm out with a lady.' He sat back and the smirk on his face indicated his expectation of the outcome.

'Frankie, I thought you were a gentleman.'

'That's just an illusion; I'm the same as the next man.' The smirk continued. 'Anyway, Sadie knows what's what. She ain't exactly loose, but she cuts enough slack to those that know her, if you gets my drift.'

'And Jack? Who does *he* know?'

'Ah. And why would you want to know that, little lady?'

'Just curious.'

'Yeah, right. It wouldn't have anything to do with all those noughts we saw earlier, then?' he asked, leaning back triumphantly.

'As it happens, no,' she said in all seriousness. 'I just happen to want to know a little more about my employer. I know he's rich, and last night I found out he can be a twonk like all men, but there are degrees of twonkiness, and I want to know where on the scale he is.' She rested her arms on the table and dabbed her finger around the plate picking up all the leftover sugar. She then licked it off slowly and luxuriously with her tongue. Frankie thought that his luck was just about to change for the better when he realised that she wasn't looking at him at all, but just over his shoulder.

A noise like "Neaughhh Neaughhh" came from behind, closely followed by a loud crash and a cry of anguish. Frankie spun around, startled. The middle aged man behind had dropped the hot cup of steaming chocolate he had hold of, with the super-heated liquid taking the path of least resistance and pouring into his lap; unfortunately, allowing him the certain knowledge of what boil-in-the-bag really means. In panic he grabbed hold of the napkin and stood up, trying to dab himself down, and in the process knocked over the table. A waitress appeared and righted the table, but as she began to help with the clean-up, he shooed her off in embarrassment. The good citizens of Gornstock showed their sympathy with a loud cheer and a round of applause. He quickly paid up and hurriedly left the cafe, keeping his eyes firmly rooted to the ground whilst walking like a demented chicken; the brown stain on the front of his trousers was going to take quite some shifting, and the red raw knadgers some explaining.

'Did you do that?' asked Frankie in amazement, as the noise died down.

Rose smiled and winked. 'A bit of unwelcome attention, considering I'm with someone; I thought it quite rude.' She reached forward and tapped his arm. 'You were telling me about Jack, where on the scale he is.'

Frankie smiled and shook his head. 'Rose, you are interested, aren't you? Well, I won't have a bad word said against him. Yes, he's rich, and he owns a few businesses around the city, but he don't like bullies and cheats. He's normal, Rose, so I suppose on your scale, he's about half way.' He wondered whether to tell her how interested Jack was in her, but he had the feeling she already knew, and besides, a love-struck Cornwallis was always entertaining.

'I can live with that, just general curiosity though. I like to know what I'm getting myself into.'

They finished up and Frankie tossed a few coins onto the table as they left. The initial rush of people had dwindled and now only a trickle were left on the streets, so it wasn't hard work pushing their way through. Frankie, feeling lazy, wangled them a lift into the centre of town on the back of a cooper's cart. Strangely, very few refused a request from Frankie when he was after a lift, maybe it had something to do with the way he stepped out in front of them and grabbed the bridle, and possibly with the way he continued holding on while the one way conversation continued, and it might be to do with the way he wouldn't let go until the driver agreed to go to wherever Frankie wanted to go, in this case, close to the Assembly would do.

By the time they reached Hupplemere Mews, the light began to fade as dusk settled in. The marriage broker on the first floor nodded a greeting to Frankie as he closed up for the day and Frankie did wonder what damage he had done, as he seemed to be very pleased with himself. The general fee was ten per cent of all money that changed hands, so he supposed that there must be at least two families who'd lost a fair amount that day. He couldn't figure out why some people had to resort to his services, but then he thought that perhaps, unless they bought a partner, no other bugger would have them.

Cornwallis dozed with his feet on the desk when they came through the door; he hadn't even lit the lanterns so the place was in semi-darkness. Frankie banging the door startled him into wakefulness; shiny leather chair plus a smooth suit equalled a sliding investigator; Cornwallis' arse hit the floor with a loud thump.

'Sleeping on the job again, boss?' cackled Frankie, as Cornwallis scrambled to his feet. 'There's us doing all the bloody work while you lord it up. Worked our fingers to the bone, we 'ave, not to mention the wear and tear on our boot leather. Ain't that right, Rose?' Then he added in a softer voice to her. 'I reckon that's about a seven on your scale.'

Rose managed to stifle a laugh by biting down hard on her bottom lip.

'What's that you said?' asked a flustered Cornwallis, regaining his seat. 'I didn't quite hear that.'

'Not important, boss,' replied Frankie, flicking a match and lighting the lantern on the desk. He pinched out the match and then turned around and saw the pictures lining the wall. 'Jeez, they weren't here earlier. Will you look at the size o' them.'

Cornwallis only had eyes for Rose for a few seconds and smiled a greeting as his mind went through the arrangements he'd made for the evening. Restaurant booked? Check. Witty conversation rehearsed? Check. Drinks cupboard full? Check. Etchings to be seen? Check. Bed tidy and made? Check. Everything sorted, just need now to get Frankie out of the way. He dragged his mind and attention back to what Frankie had just said. 'Aren't they just. Never trust a feeler to do anything right. That Dewdrop only went to Mikel An' Jello; MacGillicudy is going to have one hell of a shock when I give him the bill.' He flicked his eyes back to Rose and smiled again. 'I gather you've had an eventful day,' and he waved the note they had left earlier. 'You had better fill me in on all the details.'

'We will. Nice cut you've had there by the way, is there a special reason?'

'No, no. Just thought I'd kill two birds with one stone.'

'Algie,' piped up Frankie. 'You've set him ferreting around, ain't ya?' Cornwallis nodded, agreeing that he had. 'Algie,' he explained, turning to Rose, 'is one of our erstwhile employer's informants. He runs a haircutting business and is privy to some really interesting information, viz a viz, who's knobbing who, etc. He…' and he flicked a thumb to Cornwallis, '…owns the place, so Algie hasn't got an option really. He can be quite useful, or at least, up 'til now he has.'

For the next hour or so, they exchanged information, with Frankie extolling Rose's virtues and revelling in the way that she'd handled Sam Snodgrass. Rose underplayed her contribution to events, but even so, Cornwallis listened with undisguised admiration; Eddie had got it spot on, Rose knew how to handle herself. The manner of Freddie the Weasel's demise indicated some kind of retribution; but they would have to find out whether he had overstepped the mark within his own patch or somewhere else, and for that, they would have to speak to Gerald. Gerald, the undisputed King of The Brews, the all-knowing, all-seeing, ruler of the slum, knew everything that happened within his domain. Perhaps it was just as well that they had to go and see him, because should Rose stay an investigator, she might have to go into the Brews on her own one day, and she would need to be safe. Cornwallis wrote everything down in his little notebook, and as he revealed his day's activities, he noted them down as well. A lot of the information needed to be sifted, of course, then they had to find a way to link it all together, and there were gaps, but gaps were there to be filled. All in all, a pretty interesting first day of an investigation, he decided.

Cornwallis presented Rose with her brand new investigators licence while Frankie applauded; she picked it up and smiled as she read the words. It was official now, and he had put it in an official looking wallet too. She practised flicking it open a few times before slipping it into her pocket, still smiling.

'Well, that's that, then,' said Frankie, as he got up and rummaged in the sack of clues they had brought back. 'We had better make sure we're right and Freddie did kill the cleaner.' He pulled out a boot and went to check it against the painting. Rose and Cornwallis joined him as he laid the painting on the floor. 'Cherubs? I don't remember any cherubs being there.'

'I believe Mr An' Jello is rather fond of them,' answered Cornwallis with a frown. 'It's what you call his trademark.'

'They're very sweet though,' observed Rose, 'and cute. Look, it's even got a little bow.'

Frankie grunted and then lined up the boot against the canvas. All three knelt, with Cornwallis and Frankie either side of Rose. They were looking keenly with their heads all close together and their arses high in the air to see if the boot-print in the painting matched the boot-print in their hand, it did, even down to the little notches in the heel.

'Well, he may be expensive, but you have to admit, he's a bloody good artist. He hasn't missed a thing,' observed Cornwallis, laying the boot over the picture one last time. 'Exact size as well.'

The door flew open and in strode Cornwallis senior. He stopped short and stared at the three arses raised into the air. 'Well, well, what have we here? If I was in the Assembly, I'd say you three were after promotion.'

Three heads turned as one.

'Oh, I say, Jocelyn. You never described the beauty of your new assistant.' The earl's face lit up in sheer unadulterated pleasure. 'I do apologise my dear, just my little joke. Mind, if they let women into the house, just let me say that you would go a long long way.'

Rose had the decency to blush a little which shocked Cornwallis as he thought her impervious to embarrassment.

'Get up my girl and let an old man dream again. God's you are something special, are you not.' He had a definite glint in his eye as he took hold of Rose's hand as she climbed to her feet. He kissed it tenderly and then laid his other hand on top. 'I'm Jocelyn's father, and I take it you are the delightful Rose.'

'I am.' She left her hand in his and smiled shyly. 'Pleased to meet you, er, sir.'

'Sir? My gods, girl, don't be so formal, call me Jocelyn please, everybody does.'

'No they don't,' echoed Cornwallis and Frankie together.

The earl grinned. 'All right, they don't. But Rose can. You don't, Frankie, because you are a peasant, a pleasant peasant granted, but you wouldn't be happy being anything else.'

'I could think of a few things to call you, if you want,' said Frankie, climbing to his feet.

'Surely you wouldn't in the presence of a beautiful lady?' He cast his gaze on Rose again. 'When he really wants to wind me up he calls me dad, seeing that his mother used to work for me.'

Rose giggled.

Cornwallis' jaw had dropped. Where did this Rose come from? Up until now, she had looked people right in the eye and told them their fortune straight. This one acted like a demure little schoolgirl doing her best to please the master. What did his father have that he didn't? She was like putty in his hands, and he had only just walked through the door. Frankie mumbled something which sounded to Cornwallis very much like "Noughts".

'Isn't mother expecting you home tonight?' asked Cornwallis in desperation.

'Oh, no, no, no. She's at one of her committee meetings again. No, I'm at a loose end right now, just popped over to tell you about that little thing we discussed earlier.' He released Rose's hand reluctantly and led his son over to the corner to speak to him quietly.

Cornwallis turned and saw that something amused Frankie, he whispered something into Rose's ear and got rewarded with a kick to the shin; he then just burst out laughing. Must be a private joke between the two of them, he thought jealously.

The earl bent close to Cornwallis' ear. 'Radstock is worried,' he said seriously. 'He wouldn't open up at first, but I squeezed him a little, and then he wouldn't stop. He prevented the police from investigating because he thought that they would have pressure put on them to come up with an easy answer. You, however, would be a totally different proposition.'

Cornwallis concentrated fully on his father. 'Go on.'

'Apparently, someone put the wrong figures over to Roland Goup, so someone else decided to get them back. I should think it all went horribly wrong.'

'Surely Radstock knows who's involved?'

'If he does, he's certainly not saying. I had to put an awful lot of pressure on him to get what I did.'

Cornwallis mentally filed away the information for future perusal. 'Anything else?'

'Only the normal sort of thing; a member is getting a few others to invest heavily in his company, not unusual, but some are placing their life savings with him. I suppose after the bank's problems they are going to try and make their money elsewhere.'

'It had better be a good company, then. Who is it?'

'Kinterbsbury, Pelegrew Kintersbury. He asked me, but I declined the option. The vote went through by the way; the Assembly will be lending the bank the money it needs.'

'That's not surprising. Anyway, we know who killed the cleaner, a petty thief from the Brews. But when Frankie and Rose caught up with him, someone had got to him first. They found him dead.' Cornwallis then told him the grizzly details.

'Oh that's nasty,' exclaimed the earl, and then looked over to Rose. 'The poor girl, her first day, too.' The earl thought for a moment. 'You know, I think you had better be careful with this one.'

'I think you might be right. We have clothing from Cavel Row, which equals money, and we have a silk handkerchief with the initial K, which equals more money. Money seems to be dripping off this one.'

Just then, MacGillicudy came in; he took one look at the Earl of Bantwich and raised an eyebrow. 'Milord,' he greeted, doffing a pretend cap. 'Am I intruding at all?'

'Not at all, Sergeant, I was just about to leave.'

'Me too,' said Frankie. 'My mum'll be mad at me, as it is, and I 'ave to squeeze Sadie in somewhere.'

MacGillicudy sniffed his armpits. 'I had a wash this morning as well.'

'Don't take it personally, Sergeant,' laughed the earl. 'Now, I should think you want to speak to my son, so I will leave you be; but as I'm a little hungry now,' he turned his head to look at Rose. 'I would be delighted if this young lady can come and keep me company, there's a cosy little restaurant just around the corner.'

'I would be honoured,' replied Rose, stepping over and wrapping her arm around his. 'Do you know, I have never been taken out to dinner before, none of my old boyfriends were ever interested in eating, and since I've been here, nobody has asked.'

'Never been taken out to dinner before? My Gods, what is the world coming to. Well, let me be the first and we'll make it a night to remember.'

Cornwallis stood speechless, his mouth opened and closed, but he just couldn't get the words out. To make matters worse, Rose waved, and then blew him a kiss, as she marched out with his father, all his plans — ruined.

'What's the matter with you then, Jack?' asked MacGillicudy, handing over Freddie's trousers before sitting himself down. 'You look like the world's just dropped out of your arse.'

Cornwallis shot him a look. 'It has, Jethro.' He grimaced and then sighed. 'Upstaged by my father. Oh well, it could have been worse. I had planned on taking Rose out to dinner but I didn't get around to asking, then along comes my father, and... well, she's off and I'm stuck here with you.'

MacGillicudy chuckled. 'And I expect you were after afters?'

'Hoping, Jethro, just hoping. Dinner, a stroll, then... you know.'

'Nightcap?'

Cornwallis shrugged his shoulders. 'In my dreams. Ah well, every cloud and all that.' He dug deep but found a smile from somewhere. 'Look around you, Jethro, what do you see?'

MacGillicudy did and gave a low whistle. 'Looks expensive to me.' The penny, as it were, dropped. 'Oh, no. That's not Dewdrop's work, is it? Tell me it's not. Please, tell me it's not.'

'Mikel An' Jello, police artist extraordinaire.' Cornwallis sat down and pushed the bill across with his forefinger. 'There you go; all yours. I think Bough will go apoplectic when he sees all them; what do you think?'

MacGillicudy went pale.

'What's wrong, Jethro? You look as if the world's just dropped out of your arse.'

'I'm going to strangle the little runt.'

Cornwallis suddenly felt a lot better about Rose now; there's nothing like spreading a little joy around to give you a nice warm feeling inside, and if MacGillicudy would only stop crying, it would make it a whole lot warmer — and drier.

When the sergeant eventually managed to control himself, which took some time as he kept pulling the bill out and looking to see if the decimal point had magically moved about three places to the left, he managed to get to the reason why he had come to see Cornwallis in the first place. Snodgrass decided to be highly co-operative, and doing everything in his power to avoid the rope necklace that was destined to be his future. It would seem that all the money he'd made from the drug deals since moving to Greenwalsh Avenue went through the offices of Mssrs Critchloe, Flanders, and Goup. Snodgrass would give weekly deposits to the accountant as per his instructions, and the day after he would go to a warehouse on the docks to pick up his supply for the next week, together with his earnings. It had all been going on for some time now and was a pretty lucrative little enterprise. He never saw who controlled him, as all meetings were held in the disused warehouse, and the man involved always managed to hide himself in the shadows to avoid revealing his identity. The same unknown man who had arranged for him to take on the coffee shop in the first place.

'You been to this warehouse, Jethro?' asked Cornwallis.

MacGillicudy nodded. 'Been derelict for the last five years; used to belong to the Great East Company until they went bust: nothing there now apart from a few dusty old bags of tea.'

This is all getting very murky, thought Cornwallis, rubbing his face with his hands. What else was going to come to light? Highly placed members of the Assembly screwing money out of the system, a murder, no, make that two murders, and now drugs and money laundering. It would seem a lot of fingers were stuck in a lot of pies. He would have to think about all this. Goup appeared to be central to the whole thing; maybe he should put all his efforts into finding out where he went.

'Come on, Jethro, I can't think straight at the moment, a couple of pints might help.'

They decided to drown their sorrows at the Policeman's Truncheon, the favourite haunt of the off duty police officer, just around the corner from Scooters Yard. The sign, above the tavern, the subject of adulteration over the years, turning the truncheon into one massive phallus held up by a smiling policeman. For some reason, the feelers took a great deal of pride in the place.

The snug was quite full, but they found a table right at the back which offered a degree of privacy, which MacGillicudy indicated might be required if they intended to chew the cud. A noisy boisterous place sometimes made for better thinking anyway. They ordered two pints from a pretty young serving girl, who risked her life, and her wobbly bits, every time she moved amongst fifty or sixty randy young feelers, and settled down.

'Freddie was a mess,' began MacGillicudy, squirming to get comfortable. 'I went up there with a few lads once the news had filtered down. Took a proper artist with me too; you should have the pictures soon. There are some evil bastards around.'

'So Frankie and Rose said,' answered Cornwallis. 'What did you make of it?'

'Execution, definitely. Reckon they stopped him talking before he said something he shouldn't, didn't trust him, see, hence the nail in the mouth. Looked like ships nails to me, and they were a rare old bugger to get out, I can tell you. Pliers and a claw hammer didn't cut the mustard, ended up smashing the wall down with a sledgehammer. When we finally got him free, the bastard was stiff as a board. Have you ever tried getting a star shaped corpse out of a tenement?'

Cornwallis pictured the scene in his mind then grinned. 'No, can't say I have.'

'Well, I tell you, if you were there you wouldn't have found it funny. At one point we had to make him do a cartwheel along the bloody corridor.'

Cornwallis stifled the laugh building up inside him.

'And then we had the stairs: Gods, what a farce that was. He couldn't go down flat on his back, and when you turned him sideways you had a leg and an arm out of reach.'

'What did you do?' asked Cornwallis, straining to hold it all in.

'In the end, after he got wedged at the first turn, I sent a lad out for a washing pole. We strapped the top arm and leg to it and hoisted him like a litter, had to slide it out at every turn of the stairs and spin him like a dancer, and then slide the pole back in. I left them to it in the end and went to wait in the cart, it took them nearly an hour to get him down.'

Cornwallis eyes began to water from the sheer effort of trying not to burst out laughing, but in the end he lost the battle and creased up hysterically.

'Glad you find it so funny, Jack; next time you can sort the sodding corpse out yourself.'

Cornwallis was so grateful to MacGillicudy for lightening his mood that he paid for all the beer over the next two hours. The place had become rammed with feelers, leaving hardly any room to get a truncheon out, let alone swing it, but then the pub song started up so Cornwallis decided it was time to leave. He forced his way out to the strains of "A Policeman's truncheon is a wondrous thing, grab it by the handle and watch it swing, hold the end so good and tight, hold it up for the girls delight…"

The refrain followed him down the street, but after a couple of turns, he could barely hear it at all. There were a few people out and about; a couple of drunks lurching from side to side until they eventually knocked into one another and collapsed in a fit of giggles, a few couples arm in arm, smiling and talking in low voices. He did feel a little pang of jealousy, as he would have been hoping to do the same — had his bloody father not got in the way. However, it didn't dampen his mood too much, and he chuckled to himself as he walked, thinking of the problems that MacGillicudy had had. Traffic was light: there were a few Traps clipping along Broad Street, a couple of carts, the late-night rubbish collectors, and one or two lone horsemen. He kept to the pavement and managed to filter most of it out of his mind. The problem of the case seemed to force its way back into his head, and he wrestled with the thought of what he had to do tomorrow; then a sharp crack of a whip intruded into his reverie.

He hadn't really been paying much attention to what was going on around him, which turned out to be a bit of a mistake, because the driver of the coach thundering towards him, was.

Cornwallis looked up as a twin-horsed low-slung sports coach came hammering towards him. He noticed that it was the type favoured by the rich young arse-wipes who were becoming the bane of the city, earning big money in the finance and technology areas and spending vast sums on all the latest gizmos. He also noticed that the lanterns had been extinguished and that the wheels had been especially widened to give more stability around corners. He noticed that it had been painted black with blacked out windows, and that the driver sat in a lowered seat. He noticed all this in the brief half-second it took to realise that the cart was aiming for him.

The coach slewed across the street and mounted the pavement; Cornwallis couldn't help but notice the four nostrils of the jet black stallions steaming with effort. A whip cracked above them as they thundered onwards and he stared transfixed at the ensemble as his life flashed through his mind, the regrets, the mistakes; why is it, he thought, that when your life is about to end, it's always the bad things that come to mind? Never the good stuff, like when he took a turn in the broom cupboard with that young scullery maid called Gilly, or that time he played strip poker with the three girls from that travelling fair and won. Or that time when he got pissed up to the eyeballs and bet a hundred dollars on the spin of a wheel and his number came up at odds of forty to one. His brain worked in quick motion while the world slowed down. The coach seemed to take an age to reach him, and he felt as if he could've had a quick cup of tea and a ham sandwich while he waited. He heard another crack of the whip, and the horses soon loomed above him; they were snorting with snot flying out in torrents, a fleck splattering into his face just as he willed his legs to move. He flung himself sideways just as the overhanging lantern clipped his shoulder, spinning him like a top through the air. The coach lurched onto two wheels as the driver dragged the thing back onto the road, then it sped away down the street and screamed around the corner. Cornwallis landed and bounced to a stop hard up against the billboard advertising "Gumpy's Special Cyder, like mother used to make." He groaned, his shoulder felt on fire, his head swam, but pain was good in these circumstances, because that meant you were still alive.

The few people around rushed to his side, the women hovering at the back of the crowd, not wanting to see just at that moment in case his head had gone missing; but the groaning soon convinced them that at least that part of him still functioned normally, and they pushed their way to the front.

'Somebody should run and get an ambulance, there's a depot just around the corner,' said one.

'Shouldn't we move him?' asked another.

'No,' answered a man who thought he knew what to do. 'His head might fall off, and besides, he's lying on a dollop of dog shit.'

Someone sniffed loudly. 'I thought that were him; you sure he ain't cacked himself?'

'Well, I ain't gonna check.'

A horseman galloped off to call the ambulance while Cornwallis listened to all the advice and observations; his shoulder stung like mad, but his head now began to clear. He rolled over onto his back and stared up at the sea of faces.

'Did anyone see the coach?' he asked hopefully. 'Did it have a name or something on it?'

'No, mate,' answered a male voice. 'It was unmarked, nice coach though. Looked like a custom build based on a Truly and

Hope sling-back, them wheels must have cost a fortune. Good turn o'speed, them, especially when it's got two horse power like that one. It had a lovely paint job.'

'Thanks, I must remember to get one.'

Cornwallis sat up and tried to move his shoulder, it creaked a bit but it still moved as it should; he sniffed, and noticed a dog turd hanging from his sleeve. He flicked it off to the annoyance of a bloke who stood at his side.

'That's nice, trying to help you and you're chucking shit at me. Sod you mate, I'm off.'

Good riddance to you too, thought Cornwallis, next time I'll make sure I get you between the eyes. He managed to get himself to his feet and then tried a few unsteady steps; nobody helped him as they were watching to see if he would drop down dead or something equally entertaining. When it became clear that he was going to survive, and there wasn't too much damage done, people began to drift away, much to Cornwallis' relief.

He stretched to ease the aches and then just started to dust himself down when from the distance he heard a *Dingalinga*, *Dingalinga*, *Dingalinga*, getting gradually louder. Then a single-horsed wagon came around the corner with a big red cross painted on the side. *Dingalinga*, *Dingalinga*, *Dingalinga*, it went. Cornwallis turned around to see nothing else on the road. He shook his head in bewilderment; somebody obviously liked playing with his bell.

The wagon skidded to a stop right next to him and the driver called down. 'You seen an accident, mate? Someone said one 'appened right here.'

'There was,' replied Cornwallis, 'but it's all done with now.'

'Bugger,' exclaimed the driver. 'Not done anything the last three nights and just as you put the kettle on you gets a shout. Drop everything you do and rush out, and when you gets there, everyone has buggered off. That's people for yer.'

'Yeah, very unreliable,' agreed Cornwallis.

'Come on, Smudge,' said the driver to his mate, 'let's go back and *you* can make the tea this time. I've made the last twelve cups, 'bout time you done something.'

Cornwallis watched the ambulance turn around and slowly make its way back down the road, thankful that he wasn't going with it. He finished dusting himself down and then started to walk back home. He wanted to dismiss the incident when it occurred to him that the coach must have been waiting for him; it was the only street on the way back that you could get up a good turn of speed, which meant that it must have known that he had to walk down there, which in turn meant that it knew he'd been in the Truncheon and that he had to come back this way, which also meant that it or somebody must have followed him from the office in the first place. Frankie and Rose had left just before him; did they have someone tailing them as well? He broke into a run. His shoulder hurt like hell, but that didn't matter. Frankie could look after himself, but Rose was with his father and they were a different matter entirely.

*

Roland Goup rested; he had no real choice in the matter as the room had just a chair, a table, and a flea ridden mattress lying on the floor. It didn't have a window, and the light, if you could call it light, came from a cheap tallow candle that sat high on a ledge where he couldn't reach. The candle had been replaced a few times via a little hatch just behind it, but no one had spoken to him; the only noise being the metallic scrape as the little hinged door slid up and a new candle took its place. They had been generous enough to give him a crust of bread and a little water, which had come through another little hatch in the door, but it could hardly be described as a feast. He had nothing to occupy his mind so he had difficulty in judging how long he'd been there, as all he could do was either just sit there, or walk around and around the little room. He'd slept, but it had disorientated him, and he had no idea whether it was day or night. The big problem was that he had time to think, and he didn't want to think, he had done too much thinking, especially when they first approached him. Just a little false accounting, they had said; hide a little bit of money here and there, which wasn't a problem for a good accountant and, even if he said so himself, he happened to be a very good accountant, one used to hiding money in figures that could just be considered legal under scrutiny. But this now had grown too big and the money he had recently been hiding definitely erred on the illegal side. Now all that had come to an end with Miss Knutt's murder, and it brought home to him just how serious his situation had become.

When he got into that carriage and that brute tied him up and put that bag over his head, he realised that perhaps he wouldn't be going to the accountant's seminar after all. He tried to think where it went wrong, what he had done. The thought came back to that man over the road who had given him a bag of cash a week; he knew that it was illegal money, but he enjoyed the challenge, and he'd hidden it so well. His mind drifted and then settled on something else, the receipts and invoices handed in by a gentleman's wife last week, together with a Gold Bond issued by the Gornstock Bank. That had been an enormous amount, but not so unusual. So which one was it? Only one person could tell him, and then he might be able to find a way of making it right again. He must have upset someone, unless Miss Knutt, had upset someone, but he couldn't for his life think how. She was just a temporary cleaner, so her demise wouldn't really affect anyone.

He thought he had been his friend. Roland Goup laughed to himself; a bad mistake where money was concerned. When he came to the office after that thug of an investigator had questioned him, he thought he was safe. He could hide away for a while, and then maybe set up again in another city. It didn't matter where, he just wanted to play at the figures; it gave his life meaning. Accountancy made him feel alive, it got all his juices flowing, giving him a buzz like nothing else. Some people needed to live dangerously, like hurling themselves off of a bridge, some people needed war and conflict, and some needed to risk all they had for a turn of a card. He just needed a double-entry ledger and a tax return. It was sexy, it was exciting, it was nearly as good as... No, he couldn't think about her in here, it wouldn't be right.

*

Bertram Radstock felt very tense; it had been a long day in the House as the business kept going on and on and on. There had been a debate on expenses and it was in his best interest to make sure that nothing changed. Though the debate really only payed lip service to the general public, there were a few naive radicals who thought that everything should be open, transparent, and above board. It wouldn't do to look too closely at most members' claims, as like his, they were more often than not to do with "incidentals". Fortunately, the radicals lost in a most gratifying manner and most of the members could relax again. He checked his watch; it had gone nine, but he didn't want to go home just yet. He had a little victory to celebrate and he wanted to use the expense account on something very close to his heart. He left the House and walked down the Trand, at first quite casually as if out just for a stroll, but then he quickly dipped down a side street with a quick furtive look over his shoulder. He didn't have far to go, though the closer he got to his destination the quicker his pace became. Another couple of side streets and he came out into a crescent of grand houses fronted by a small park, a neat row of four-story red brick houses with small flowered gardens enclosed by ornate iron railings. He took another quick look over his shoulder and then lifted a latch on one of the gates; he then skipped up the small flight of steps and rattled the knocker on the door. After a few moments, the door opened and a smiling face appeared.

'Oh, Mr Radstock. You're late tonight; busy day?'

'Yes, Mrs Fitchley, I'm afraid things seemed to go on forever.'

'Well, never mind, come through, and would you like a nice cup of tea while you wait?'

He thanked Mrs Fitchley and followed her in, his tension departing as soon as the door closed behind him. He followed the housekeeper into the parlour and sat down in the green velvet armchair that he always used. He cast his eyes around the room, pleased to see that things were just the same as always. Mrs Fitchley excused herself and scuttled off to make the tea while Radstock picked up the paper and pretended to read.

The housekeeper returned a short while later with the cup of tea and a plate of biscuits. She set them down on the table and handed the cup to Radstock.

'I made these myself, Mr Radstock,' she said, proffering the plate. 'Proper dunking biscuits that won't collapse.'

'Thank you, Mrs Fitchley, you're very kind.' He reached forward to take one and tried it out. 'Oh superb, Mrs Fitchley, they don't even wobble. How do you do it?'

'That's a trade secret, Mr Radstock, must keep some things

to ourselves, you know.' She smiled, pleased at the reaction.

Radstock smiled back and dunked the other half of biscuit.

Mrs Fitchley, thought Radstock, as he looked at her, always very efficient, but that came with age and wisdom; a handsome woman, mature and sensible, not like some of them young flighty ones. He had thought to offer her a position at his house, should her situation change. Always soberly dressed, always neat and tidy, always prim and proper; he liked that in a woman servant. He supposed that she had never indulged in too much of anything, as her clear, smooth complexion showed, though her hands did have a few signs of work on them. Her hair, a dark nut brown, could do with a little attention but she was what she was and he felt that that's how it should be.

He finished his tea and she took the empty cup, placing it back on the tray. 'I should think things should be ready for you now, Mr Radstock. I'll show you through.'

He got up and followed her back out into the hall. She led the way, taking him further into the house and into a back sitting room, not quite as posh as the parlour, with a small door on the side wall. Mrs Fitchley smiled as she opened it.

'Down you go, Mr Radstock, and don't forget to be careful of the bottom step; needs a little work as it's a bit loose.'

'Thank you, I will'

Radstock descended the stairs, hopped over the bottom step, and then hesitated in front of the door to the den. The door above him had closed and now he stood in the dark, all alone. He sighed deeply and felt that all was well in the world.

He looked longingly at the faint outline of the door into the den for a few seconds before grabbing the handle and going in.

As soon as he got inside, he turned his attention to the row of silver ornaments spread out over the table. He walked over, picked up the cloth, and began to gently rub a small figurine. It didn't take long to get the shine he wanted, so a couple of minutes later, with that one done, he turned to another.

'Did I tell you to start?' asked a stern female voice from behind him. The door had opened silently and he started at the sound of her voice. 'Don't move,' she ordered. 'You know the punishment for not doing as you're told?'

'Yes, mistress,' said Radstock meekly. He replaced the ornament and the cloth and turned around.

'And keep your eyes to the floor.'

'Yes, mistress,' he replied, sighing deeply in remorse, before proceeding to strip off his clothes.

She gave him permission to look up once he had removed his clothes and Radstock gave an involuntary shudder of excitement. Miss Lena stood there in all her glory: long thigh-high black leather boots with thin high heels and wearing long black leather gloves, her head covered in a black leather mask with just holes for her eyes and mouth. Her long shiny black hair hung down her back but she wore little else apart from a couple of strategically placed strips of leather. She looked magnificent.

She held a riding crop in her hand and as she stepped forward, she pointed it towards him. 'What do you call that? A hamster has more to offer than you. Clean.'

'Yes, mistress.'

And Radstock did, and he was as happy as a pig in shit.

Mrs Fitchley laid out the tea and Radstock again sat in the chair. He felt particularly satisfied tonight and he loved the way she had tied his hands behind his back when he had to lick the bowl on the floor. The clatter of the tea cup brought his reverie to a close and he took the empty cup with his hand still shaking.

'The mistress seems very happy tonight, Mr Radstock; very pleased with you, I think.'

'Thank you, Mrs Fitchley; one must do one's best you know.' He put the cup down and counted out the money before handing it over.

She smiled and put the money into her pocket. 'She's not always happy with the gentleman, you know; you must be very precious to her. And how has business been going, if I may ask?'

'Good and bad, Mrs Fitchley. I seem to recall telling you that there are a few greedy people around the House, well I understand now that someone got killed because of it.'

Mrs Fitchley's hands flew to her mouth. 'Oh my, how awful; what happened?'

'Well, it would seem a cleaner got killed when she got in the way of a burglar. It happened up at Greenwalsh Avenue the other day; at an accountant's.'

'The poor woman, what is this city coming to?'

'Don't worry, Mrs Fitchley; it's not something that should concern you.'

'No, no. I'm sure you're right,' she replied, pouring the tea. 'It's just that people have no respect nowadays, always out for something and they don't care when someone gets in their way.'

'Exactly, Mrs Fitchley, my opinion precisely,' answered Radstock. 'We are getting too soft, we should have more discipline, let them feel the whip end occasionally.'

Mrs Fitchley smiled. 'I'm sure the mistress would appreciate your sentiments, Mr Radstock.'

Radstock just realised what he had said and coughed to cover his embarrassment. He finished his tea and got up to leave, thanking Mrs Fitchley warmly and asking her to thank the mistress for him. He shortly found himself back out on The Crescent and grinned inanely, it had been a wonderful night and to make things even better, no one was around to see him make his way home.

CHAPTER 6

Cornwallis woke up and stared at the ceiling, hoping against hope that last night didn't happen. He moved his arm and winced as the shoulder complained, yep, it certainly happened.

Last night he'd run as fast as he could to the restaurant where his father had taken Rose; when he got there and enquired, he found that they had left there some while before. Cornwallis didn't know where to look next. He panicked for a moment but then reason took hold, he decided to go to the Stoat and see if they were there. He ran again through the streets, but two sprints in short succession might not be a good idea for someone whose general idea of exercise was to walk slowly to the pub. He puffed his way towards the Stoat with his chest heaving and his shoulder screaming. When he got there, he had to take a few minutes rest to get his breath back, just around the corner so that nobody could see him. When he recovered enough, he walked around nonchalantly, as if he'd just arrived for a pint, but he couldn't see any sign of either his father or of Rose. Eddie was still hard at work, so Cornwallis asked him whether Rose had returned.

'Oh yes, came back an hour ago with your father, right fine style apparently. Dropped her off in the coach out back, then they had a little nightcap and then Rose went off to her room.'

'She still there?' asked Cornwallis, relieved. 'Nothing untoward happened to her?'

Eddie laughed. 'Jack, you're talking about your father there.'

'I know, I know. I just got a little worried, that's all; could you go and ask if she's still all right?'

'What's going on, Jack? This is not like you,' responded Eddie, a little concerned. 'Has it got anything to do with working with you?' he added, suspiciously.

Cornwallis laughed. 'Come on, Eddie, it's not as if I would get her to do anything even remotely risky. No, she didn't say if she would be back tomorrow, you know, first day, new job. She might have changed her mind, that's all.'

Eddie shook his head and grinned. 'I don't know, Jack; what are you coming to, eh? I'll just send one of the girls up to ask her, if that will make you rest easier.'

He did, and he also poured him a glass of Glockcombers Special Reserve, whisky distilled by the dwarfs down in the mine, one hundred and sixty percent proof and it had a kick worse than a mule with toothache. Eddie gave it on the house, so Cornwallis downed it in one.

'Hey, steady, Jack. You don't want steam coming out of your ears again.'

Cornwallis felt it hit the mark and he gasped, then his eyes began to bulge as the heat radiated quickly through his veins, cooking him from the inside out. His mouth opened silently in a mute display of pleading, and then the alcohol hit his brain like a sledgehammer. A volcano erupted behind his eyes, threatening to take the top of his head clean off, with the molten larva dribbling down his face, chest and towards his feet. He sighed as the feeling subsided, leaving behind a warm glow of exquisite pain; strangely, his shoulder had stopped hurting now.

Eddie screwed the top back on the bottle. 'I reckon one's enough for you.'

Cornwallis still couldn't trust himself to speak, so he just nodded in agreement, another one might just finish him off at the moment.

After a few minutes, Cornwallis couldn't decide whether he felt better, or worse, but at least he'd found his voice again. 'How do they make it, Eddie? And how come the glass doesn't melt?'

'Beats me, I just sells it. Those little buggers can drink it like water but it don't affect them 'til the second bottle.'

The girl came back from her errand with a wide grin on her face. She looked at Eddie first, and then flicked her eyes to Cornwallis. 'She says, and I don't think she was too happy about me waking her up, that of course she's bloody all right and if he's going to be coming around here to check that I'm all right then he'll find out that he won't be all right because I'll make sure that he isn't all right. All right? And tell him I'll see him in the bloody morning if that's all right. Er, that was her talking and not me, if you understand.'

'That sounds like Rose,' observed Eddie, grinning.

Cornwallis breathed a sigh of relief, yep, that certainly sounded like Rose talking, he could rest easily now. 'Thanks for that,' he said a little sheepishly. 'Hope she won't give you any grief in the morning. I'll go back now, got a lot to sort out.'

He'd tried Frankie's place on the way back too, but he knew he planned to be somewhere else, so it wasn't a surprise when he didn't get an answer. He'd just have to wait and be patient.

He climbed out of bed and looked at the bruising on the shoulder in the mirror, a delightful purple and orange colour with just a hint of yellow. It felt stiff, but he could still move it. He dressed slowly and then went downstairs to the office, hoping that Frankie had already arrived. The peace and quiet indicated that Frankie had not yet turned up. He had had no idea where to look for Frankie last night; he just clung to the hope that if anything had happened he could at least look after himself. He fired up the embers in the stove and put the coffee on ready for when Rose and Frankie arrived, and then sat down, waiting for footsteps on the stairs.

It felt uncomfortable knowing that out there, someone wanted him dead. Just two days into the investigation and things were starting to happen. It meant that he had got close to someone, closer than he realised. Now who? The coach had probably been stolen, by the sound of the description; nobody in their right mind would use their own to run someone down like that, but if they could find it, there might still be a clue. He rubbed his hand over his chin, which reminded him that he hadn't shaved; it could wait, he decided, there were more important things to do. The names he had to play with were Goup, Radstock and Freddie the Weasel; he supposed he could add Eliza Knutt to the list, but she and Freddie were dead. Goup had disappeared, so that just left Radstock, and of course, Samuel Snodgrass, who had conveniently been in the cafe opposite Goup; so possibly even drugs are involved too. Who was "K" who had dropped the handkerchief? Another name was Brownlow, and both Rose and Frankie had thought him nervous. Anyone else? He wracked his brain, but couldn't come up with anything more, apart from the attempted murder last night.

At last, he heard footsteps coming up the stairs and he stiffened slightly. Relax, he told himself, nobody would come here to murder him. The handle twisted and the door slowly opened and in came Rose, looking as if she could spit feathers.

'What on twearth were you playing at last night?' She stormed over to him and leant forward, bracing her hands on the desk. 'What did you think was going to happen, eh? I was with your father you twonk, we had dinner… '

'Rose,' he said quietly, trying to interrupt.

'…and then he took me around the west end and we watched some of the street entertainment. Then he took me home. Nothing…'

'Rose,' he tried again.

'…did, or was, going to happen. What are you, some sort of stalker?'

'Have you finished now?'

'Finished? I've hardly started!'

'Rose, last night someone tried to kill me.'

'Turning up in the dead of night and waking me up… What did you just say?' she asked, stopping mid flow.

'I said, Rose, last night someone tried to kill me. I was scared that someone had gone after you too, but I didn't want Eddie worried.'

She stared at him, horrified. 'When? How? Are you all right? What about Frankie?'

'Look, sit down and I'll get you a coffee.'

She slumped down heavily just as he got up and went over to the stove; he poured two mugs and brought them back over while she watched his every step. He gave a wry grin, slipped his arm out of his jacket and shirt, and showed her his shoulder. 'A coach tried to run me down when I walked up Broad Street after coming out the Truncheon. Not a runaway, deliberate. I just managed to jump out of the way in time, but it caught me a glancing blow. Someone must have followed me, so I thought someone must have followed you and Frankie too. I haven't heard from Frankie yet, and I don't know where he is. He wasn't home last night when I tried.'

'Oh Gods,' she exclaimed. 'And I just let rip at you. I'm sorry, Jack.'

He slipped his shirt and jacket back on and sat down. 'Forget it, I should have thought. What's important at the moment is that Frankie walks through that door.' He pointed and stabbed his finger in emphasis.

They sat in silence for a few minutes and stared at the door.

'Does it hurt?' asked Rose, after a while. She tried a soft smile and pointed to his shoulder.

'Just aches a little,' he replied, with a twitch of his mouth. 'But I'll live.'

The minutes ticked by in more silence; it wasn't that they were awkward with each other; they were just both getting increasingly worried. Cornwallis knew that Frankie would normally be in by now and Rose picked up on his anxiety. She wanted to ask him more about the attempt on his life, but she felt that he wasn't in the right frame of mind to answer properly. He began to tap his finger on the desk, a sure sign of agitation; then he stopped suddenly and listened intently. There were footsteps on the stairs.

'Morning all,' cried Frankie, as he breezed into the office, throwing the door wide and letting it crash against the wall. He stopped dead in his tracks. 'Blimey, look at you two, somebody died?'

'Very nearly, Frankie, very nearly,' replied Cornwallis with a sigh of relief. 'And I thought you might have as well.'

'What? What the hell are you on about? Rose, what you been doing to him?'

'I'll let him explain,' she said, getting up and walking over to him, 'but I'm glad you're here.' She planted a kiss on his cheek and patted his arm.

'I don't know what it is you're up to, but carry on if you're going to do that again.' He touched his cheek, which still had a mild sensation of moist warmth from Rose.

'Right, we can all breathe easier now,' said Cornwallis, clapping his hands. 'Frankie, you can fill the coffee mugs, and then we have a lot to talk about.'

'Yeah, right, okay,' replied Frankie, scratching his head in confusion.

It didn't take long to bring Frankie up to speed with the events of last night. He was as shocked as Rose, and no, unless you counted exhaustion, there hadn't been an attempt on his life either. The coach sounded interesting though, not the average runabout, that's for sure. A few enquiries were bound to come up with something. A Truly and Hope sling-back was a classic anyway, and customised, well, not many of them about.

Cornwallis decided to let Frankie search for the coach, as he seemed to be interested in that sort of thing anyway, but first he could inform MacGillicudy of the attempt on his life before hunting for the coach, and besides, perhaps the feelers had already been notified of a stolen vehicle.

Which meant that Cornwallis could spend the day in the company of Rose, and it would give him the opportunity to play on his shoulder, and his near death experience, to elicit some more sympathy. Together they would go and see Brownlow again and see what would happen when they squeezed him a little. They agreed that from now on, all of them would keep in regular contact, no off-the-cuff inquiries were to be made, each must know where and what the others were doing. After every task, return to the office and leave a note with the time, findings, and next line of enquiry. It might be a little inconvenient at times, but if a little accident did occur, then at least there would be a starting point for the others.

Understandably, Cornwallis felt a degree of nervousness when he and Rose ventured out into the big wide world; he knew that one failed attempt, meant invariably that a second could be waiting around the corner. He made sure that Rose stayed on the inside of the pavement, so if anything should happen, he could at least offer some protection. He was concerned with being followed, ordinarily not a problem, but walking with Rose, he soon found that she sort of stood out. The streets were busy with people and traffic but they stopped regularly and looked in windows trying to spot anyone looking suspicious.

Rose went over her and Frankie's interview with Brownlow again as they walked. Cornwallis contented himself with talking business rather than anything else, even though he desperately wanted to know what she and his father had talked about last night. He struggled to keep his mind fully on the job as they walked, his concentration kept wavering and he constantly reminded himself of the priorities.

Cornwallis began to relax when they finally got to the quiet streets. It would be difficult for anyone to stay out of sight when there were only a few people around, and a few quick checks confirmed that indeed they were on their own. Brownlow's was not too far now, just a couple more streets and they would be there.

'Let's wait around a bit first,' suggested Cornwallis as the carriage yard loomed into sight. 'See if anyone comes or goes.'

'I may be new to this, Jack, but two people standing on the pavement staring at a yard is not exactly inconspicuous.'

'True, which is why we are not going to do that. You are, however, going to be very interested in buying some clothes. I assume you're happy to try on everything in the shop? Looks like they do a bespoke service too, so you can get measured for that as well; a good hour and a half I reckon. As your companion, I will be bored to death by it all and will feel the need to stare mindlessly out of the window.' He grinned. 'That's how it goes, isn't it?'

'Not exactly, you have to feign interest and tell me how I look. And, if I'm trying on everything, there has to be a reason. The assistants will want to know where I'm going, what it's for, and all that kind of stuff.'

'I'm sure you can come up with something; you're a girl, you're used to this sort of thing.'

Rose took a large intake of breath when they walked through the door; she had never seen so many racks of clothes. It seemed as if they catered for every style, taste, colour and occasion, but as they weren't buying, she didn't worry about looking at the prices. Cornwallis did though, just for curiosities sake, and he winced at the amount they were charging for just a little strip of cloth. He should have realised as it said boutique at the front entrance and not ladies apparel; that in itself put a nought on the end of a dollar. He looked up and saw Rose getting stuck in; he smiled to himself as she rummaged through the rails, for all intents and purposes a serious shopper. The two pretty assistants were buzzing around her like flies on a fillet of steak.

He cast his eyes out of the window and over to the carriage yard, where he could see a little movement, but it seemed to be just a couple of lads dipping in and out of the sheds. He heard an "Oooh," from behind and he turned around, finding the two assistants grinning at him. He furrowed his brow for a moment and then thought Rose must have said something, so he just grinned back inanely before continuing his observation. The chatter from the back of the shop increased, and so did the rummaging.

The minutes passed, and then more minutes passed. Rose was good at this, he thought as he stared at the yard. He realised it had been quiet for quite a while, so turned his head briefly to look; one of the girls stood next to a rail, adjusting it, but Rose and the other girl were out of sight. When he turned his head back, he saw the gate of the yard opening and a heavy set man with a mean countenance walk out. He dressed smartly with an expensive suit, but Cornwallis saw through him immediately, he was a thug. You could dress a turd up as much as you like, but it was still a turd underneath. The man appeared to be waiting for something.

A polite cough from behind disturbed him and he turned his head to see Rose standing there. He gawped; he just stood and gawped. He felt his chin hit the floor as he stared at her, the thug outside all but forgotten. The colour was purple and it was a dress, he knew that much, but he just didn't know how it fitted like that. It seemed to be fluid, it seemed to mould itself to her; it seemed to show everything but nothing. Oh Gods, he thought, this isn't fair.

'Do you like it?' asked Rose, twirling around. 'The clingy bits move with you, but I can't wear anything under as it shows the outline otherwise. I'm wondering if it's too tight around here.' She turned to present her back and indicated her bottom area. 'What do you think?'

Cornwallis ran his hand over his mouth just to check that saliva hadn't leaked out and found to his relief that it hadn't. 'It's very nice,' he croaked eventually.

The assistant huffed. 'Very nice? Is that all you can say? I would say she looks beautiful in it. Don't you agree?'

Cornwallis nodded, not trusting his voice.

'I think he likes it really,' ventured the assistant to Rose. 'Quiet type is he? Well, never mind, let's try the next one.'

Rose and the assistant disappeared from view again and Cornwallis just stared at the empty space she left, trying to imprint all the details in his mind before it left him forever.

Eventually he remembered why they were there and he turned back to look out of the window again. The thug was still there, waiting. He paced up and down and then stopped for a moment to light a cigar, flicking the match carelessly away. A coach appeared a few seconds later and the thug seemed to relax, it drew up outside the yard and he climbed in. The driver snapped the reins and the coach sped off. Cornwallis had seen the livery and he smiled to himself; if Brownlow is involved, then he now had another clue.

'Coffee, sir?' asked an assistant, who had come up silently behind him. 'Only your betrothed said that you might want a cup, seeing as she might be here a while. A complete going away ensemble will take some time to put together, you know, especially when you haven't told her where you're going.'

Betrothed? thought Cornwallis, she had told them we were getting married? He felt quite pleased. 'Yes, thank you. Er, no, it's a surprise.' He looked at the girl and smiled as he thought he should. She handed the mug over and smiled back; she had pretty little features with a sort of luminescence in her skin, she then ran her fingers through her long dark hair to reveal slightly pointed ears. She's an Elf, he thought, then that would explain the dress.

'Half Elf,' she said, as if reading his mind. 'We get used to the look, you know, the sort of double take, the slight twitch of the eyebrows as if you can't quite believe it. We don't mind, my sister and me, but it does get boring when people go on about magic rings and things.'

'I should think it would. Your sister?' and he indicated the other assistant.

'Yes, this place is all ours, you know, make everything ourselves.'

She hurried away and began to fuss after Rose again, who

now wore fitted trousers with a loose blouse; he supposed she didn't like it as she hadn't asked his opinion. More garments came off the rails and the process of trying on and parading continued; he felt he was beginning to get the hang of this now and he looked forward to seeing what came out of the changing room next.

She looked good, no, better than good, in everything, but nothing could compare to that first dress she wore. They huddled around the lingerie bits now and even though he hoped, his hopes didn't materialise. He heard the giggling and could only imagine what they were talking about. There weren't many elves in Gornstock and those he had met tended to be aloof; these two were like a breath of fresh air, and he supposed it had to do with the half that wasn't elf.

He checked his pocket watch. It was a shame but they had been there long enough, and had seen enough. Rose appeared to be enjoying herself, but work pressed. He mined the indication that they should go and Rose quickly got the message. She made her excuses to the two girls and went to change back into her normal clothes.

One of the girls came over to Cornwallis and stood beside him. 'His name is Maxwell, by the way.'

Cornwallis was startled. 'Maxwell?'

'Yes, the man you were staring at.' She indicated her ears. 'We have very good hearing, and we notice things like the investigators licence that fell out of your "betrothed's" pocket. The driver of the coach called him Mr Maxwell.'

'Oh.' He didn't know where to look. 'Thank you. Er, sorry. You don't mind, do you?'

'No, gives us something to do, and anyway, it's nice to fit someone like her. You should see some of the women who come in here; they want us to perform miracles, but it would take more than a miracle to get them to look anywhere near how they want to look.' She grinned mischievously, 'Unlike your "betrothed."'

Cornwallis grinned back, they had been rumbled, and he felt that he should pay for some of the time they'd spent with Rose. He pulled out his notebook and wrote down a figure; the girl looked at it and nodded. He scribbled some more and then ripped the page out and handed it over.

'Oh well, it was fun while it lasted,' groaned Rose, once they were outside. 'I thought I was doing ever so well too.'

'You were, and I saw what I wanted. It doesn't matter that they found out; Elves appreciate secrets and they said they won't say anything, so all in all, a successful start to the morning's work. Out of interest, what were you all giggling about?'

'Girls union I'm afraid. If I told you, I would have to kill you; but you wouldn't want to know anyway.'

Cornwallis thought that actually he rather did want to know. He suspected that it had been rude and suggestive and that it had involved him, which was a good enough reason, considering his thoughts were rude and suggestive and involved her. However, he didn't push the point but just replied with a smile.

As they crossed the road, he described what he'd seen from the window while she tried on the clothes and they both came to the conclusion that they might be seeing rather a lot of Mr Maxwell in the coming days.

Rose pushed the gate open and they walked through into the yard; there were a few coils of rope and a trough for the horses, but very little else. The stables were over to the right and the sheds to the left. The route to the offices took them past the sheds with a half open door. As they approached, Cornwallis looked in, and saw to his amazement a partly dismembered coach. He nudged Rose and indicated that she should look too;

he saw a Truly and Hope sling-back, probably the one that tried to run him down last night.

They stopped and peered closer; there didn't appear to be anyone about, so they quickly went inside. The coach was in the process of being stripped down, panel by panel, and there were a number of large crates close by, some of which were already full.

'I think we've hit the jackpot,' ventured Cornwallis. 'Let's see if Brownlow can get himself out of this.'

'Oi! What're you doing?' A lad came into the shed obviously not expecting someone to be there. 'Sorry, but customers ain't allowed in the sheds, could be bad for yer 'elf.'

'My elf?' queried Cornwallis. 'She isn't an elf, she's a girl.'

'I sees that mister, hur hur. But I's mean yer 'elf,' replied the spotty youth.

His overalls were covered in grease and Cornwallis thought that if they had to grab hold of him he would just spit out of their hands like a bar of soap.

'I think he means health,' suggested Rose, smiling.

'Yeah, 'course I do, that's what I said, 'elf. You taking the piss? We got sum o'them others over t'road, youse know. Keep's well clear o'them, I can tell you. They's keep going off to the woods to do secret fings and such; I could tells youse sum stories, I could.'

Cornwallis shook his head, trying to understand the yoof... he shook his head again, youth, was nigh on impossible nowadays; they had a language all to themselves. He just hoped it wasn't catching.

'What sort of stories?' asked Rose, biting her lip to stop herself laughing. 'I'm intrigued.'

'Well, I don'ts know if I's should say really, not fer girls, if youse unnerstands me.' He winked at Cornwallis. 'I reckons he's got a good idea what I mean's.'

'No, I don't,' replied Cornwallis in all seriousness.

The youth's eyes widened. 'You must do mister. You know's, they dance around in the nuddy and all that, do sum magic stuff and the next fing you see is that they 'ave some bloke with 'em,' he mined something in the trouser region. 'They's gets up to all sorts of fings down there, they do.'

'You've seen this?'

'Well, not me. But a mate's mate o'mine 'as, an 'e only just got out alive.'

Rose didn't have to bite her lip now to stop herself laughing; the youth's rantings were so far off the scale of reason that any humour had disappeared into the ether, she was aghast. She knew why elves went to the woodlands; they went for peace and tranquillity, to get away from the noise and the hubbub of the city for a few short hours. They were part of nature. 'I suppose your mate has told you that dwarfs eat babies, and that fairies steal your valuables as well, eh?'

'Er, no, don't be daft,' he said affronted. 'Me dad told me that.'

Rose knew she would be hitting her head against the wall trying to get this lad to see reason, she only hoped that he would one day come to realise just how stupid he sounded. 'Well, thank you for your advice and your concern for our health. I think we will leave you now to get on with your work.'

'Yeah, right, got to get this fing stripped by this afternoon.'

They left the shed and walked over to the office.

'You sure that's the one?' asked Rose.

'Oh yes,' answered Cornwallis, rubbing his hands with anticipation. 'Now, let's see what Brownlow has to say on the subject.'

Rose nodded her thanks as Cornwallis opened the door for her; she took a half jump in and then headed to her left across the lobby and in through another door into the empty reception area. With a quick look at Cornwallis, she pushed open the wicker gate and went through. Brownlow's office was at the back and the door was ajar. From inside they heard a man sobbing, quietly, but with a degree of desperation and despair. Rose and Cornwallis exchanged a look and then he flung the door wide open.

Brownlow sat at his desk leaning forward with his head buried in his arms; the sobbing sounded quite pitiful in its way, but Cornwallis' recent experience with the coach in the shed had taken away any sympathy he might have had. Brownlow looked up through red-rimmed eyes, took one look at Rose and reburied his head.

'Go away, I've nothing to say to you,' he whimpered.

Cornwallis noticed he sobbed onto a small picture, so he reached forward and went to pull it away. Brownlow reacted with hostility and smacked down hard on Cornwallis' hand.

'Don't touch that,' he screamed.

Cornwallis jumped back and rubbed his hand. 'Bit tetchy, aren't we? Has that got something to do with being implicated in murder, per chance, Mr Brownlow?'

Brownlow howled. 'What do you mean? Murder? I haven't done anything like that.'

'Gods, I can't put up with this shit much longer,' groaned Cornwallis to Rose. 'Doesn't he realise we might be able to help him?'

'Mr Brownlow,' tried Rose more gently. 'What's happened to make you like this? Mr Cornwallis and I need to ask you some questions, and I think by the way you are going on, you might have some answers.' She went around to the other side of the desk and put a comforting arm around his shoulders. 'Come on now, take a deep breath and tell us what's happened.'

Brownlow's sobs began to lessen and he leant into Rose.

'Hey, steady,' yelled Cornwallis.

Rose hushed Cornwallis with a finger to her lips. 'There, there, Mr Brownlow. Just tell us what's happened.'

Brownlow began to get some control back and reached into his pocket and brought out a handkerchief, he blew his nose and wiped his eyes before shoving it back. 'They said they are going to sell my family if I don't do what they want. They'll pack them up and send them out east, and then sell them to the highest bidder. I have to do as they say or they'll end up as slaves.'

'Who are *they*, Brownlow?' asked Cornwallis.

Brownlow looked up at Cornwallis. 'The finance people,' he wailed.

'Finance people?' he murmured to Rose, with a look of confusion.

Rose shrugged her shoulders. 'We don't understand, Mr Brownlow, you had better explain.'

Brownlow struggled to get hold of himself again; he sighed and then shivered. 'The bank sold my loan to a finance company when I couldn't keep up with the payments,' he explained. 'Now they are telling me I should help them out with some favours in lieu of the instalments. I just wanted to keep my business afloat, and now all this.'

'What sort of favours?' asked Cornwallis, as if he didn't know.

'I had to use one of my coaches the other night to pick someone up, and then I have to use my yard to dismantle another coach.'

'Do you mean Greenwalsh Avenue?'

Brownlow nodded. 'Yes, I had to take two men there and pick up a third; then I had to take the two of them back again later. They put some sticky paper on the side of my coach so it didn't look like one of mine. They say they have a few more little jobs for me, but they haven't said what. It's all last minute stuff.'

Cornwallis nodded; they were getting somewhere now. 'And where did you take the third man you picked up?'

'The docks, an old warehouse that used to belong to the Great East Company.'

Cornwallis wanted to jump in the air and whoop; they had found where Goup went. Instead, he kept his face neutral. 'The coach you're dismantling in the yard, how did that get here?'

'It came during the night; they have a key to the yard. They just told me to take it apart and pack it up. They're going to pick it up later this afternoon.'

'Are they now,' cried Cornwallis. He reckoned a few pieces of the jigsaw were now in place, the corners and most of the edges. 'What time?'

'About four they said.'

'And what is the name of the finance company?' asked Rose.

Brownlow turned his head to look at her. 'I've told you everything, haven't I? Oh Gods, what's going to happen? My wife, my girls!' He began to panic and leapt out of the chair.

'Don't worry, Mr Brownlow,' replied Rose, clinging onto him and calming him down. 'We can make sure they're safe.' She mimed a "can we do that?" to Cornwallis, and he nodded. 'Now, the name of the finance company, please.'

Brownlow settled back down; he began to sob a little, but not as bad as before. 'The Gornstock Trust and Holdings,' he said in the end.

'The man I saw leaving here an hour ago, Maxwell, is he from the company?' asked Cornwallis.

'Maxwell? Is that his name? I never knew it; he's just the man who tells me what to do. You said something about murder earlier?'

'Two people have been killed, Brownlow, and not very nicely. I suspect that won't be the end of it, either.'

Brownlow stared in open-mouthed horror, and then began to wail.

Cornwallis grabbed a piece of paper off his desk and hastily scrawled a doodle, and then ripping it in half, handed one piece over to Brownlow. 'Whoever has this half,' and he held up his bit of paper, 'you are to go with, as you'll know they will have come from me. Do you understand?'

Brownlow nodded and then wailed again.

*

Frankie was not in the best of moods as he waited for Sergeant MacGillicudy. He'd just run the gauntlet of Sergeant Grinde and still seethed at the way the odious sergeant kept him waiting. The thoughts that were currently going through his mind were evil, immoral, and definitely illegal; they would probably get him a five to ten stretch, but hey, the satisfaction.

He looked up at Grinde and aimed an imaginary crossbow when a tap on the shoulder distracted him. 'Watch it, you'll spoil my aim.'

MacGillicudy chuckled. 'You'll have to go to the back of the queue, Frankie; you do for him and hundreds will want to do for you for getting in first. Popular man is our Sergeant Grinde.'

'Yeah, well; one day.'

A rookie feeler watched him with big wide eyes of astonishment; Frankie noticed and then lowered his crossbow to aim right at him. 'Yer sandwiches or yer life, sonny boy, what's it to be?'

The feeler wasn't sure whether he should grin or run, so he

did both, darting to the other side of the room in order to find something to do.

'Don't do that to the sprogs, Frankie, their mums won't like it.'

Frankie grinned at MacGillicudy. 'You're getting soft, Jethro; you used to be first in the queue when it came to initiating the youngsters.'

'Times change, Frankie, we have to be correct nowadays.' His mind strayed wistfully to days gone past when he had got hosed down in the middle of winter and roped to the A frame, only to have the canteen slops tipped down his trousers. 'No, those days have long gone.'

'Ain't they just,' agreed Frankie. 'Jethro,' he said, changing the subject and becoming serious, 'I need you to check the crime reports from last night. I'm looking for a stolen coach, so it could even be in the last couple o' days.'

'I can have a look, why?'

'Someone tried to run Jack down last night, and very nearly succeeded.'

'Last night? I was with him last night.'

'I know. It happened just after he left you as he walked down Broad Street. A Truly and Hope sling-back, customised. Blacked out windows, wide wheels, low-slung seat. He was lucky, just came away with a bruised shoulder.'

MacGillicudy gave a low whistle and shook his head. 'Just as well he didn't have Rose with him then.'

'Rose? What's she got to do with the price of carrots?'

MacGillicudy gave a thin smile. 'Jack planned to take her out last night, but his father got in the way. Booked the restaurant and all he had.'

'Did he now? The randy little sod.'

They walked over to the crime book with MacGillicudy

detailing Cornwallis' plans for last night. They were gossiping like two old women over the garden fence and they received one or two strange looks from the feelers hanging about. Frankie seemed far more interested in Cornwallis' plans than looking for a stolen coach and only reluctantly dragged his attention back to the job in hand. MacGillicudy flicked open the book and turned a few pages to get to last night when a booming voice bellowed down from above.

'Civilians are not allowed to scrutinise official police documents, Sergeant.'

Both MacGillicudy and Frankie looked up and saw Sergeant Grinde looking down.

'Youse know the rules, Sergeant MacGillicudy. I don't wish to report one of my fellow sergeants, but I will if I have to. Got to set an example to all our young hofficers.'

'Grinde, you can just sod off,' steamed MacGillicudy. 'If you wish to speak to me then get off your fat arse and come down here; if not then get back to what you do best, and that is being the worst bloody feeler in the history of the force.'

Frankie, a little surprised with the vehemence of MacGillicudy's reply, could only agree with the sentiments, but MacGillicudy was normally more tactful than that.

Grinde's face went puce; he didn't know what to do. Someone speaking to the senior sergeant like that, when he was only doing his duty, went far beyond his comprehension. 'What d'you say, Sergeant MacGillicudy? Would you mind repeating that, as I'm not sure if everybody 'eard.'

'I said, Grinde. Get your fat arse down here. Are you sodding deaf as well?'

Grinde slapped down his pencil and began to climb down the ten steps that led up to his domain, shivering with indignation. Frankie looked from one to the other and then cast his eyes around the area. There appeared to be eleven feelers who were unsure if they had heard correctly, their faces registered dumb shock, but then one or two began to grin with anticipation.

'Think about this, Jethro,' Frankie said quietly. 'Time and place and all that.'

'Don't worry, Frankie, I am thinking.'

Grinde reached ground level and then drew himself up to his full height of five foot four; his beard bristled like the hackles of a dog and he stabbed a finger into MacGillicudy's face, jutting his head forward at the same time. 'Sergeant, do I have to repeat that civilians are not allow... OH... OW!'

Sergeant Jethro MacGillicudy did what everybody else had been longing to do for years. He grabbed the jabbing finger in one hand and bent the digit back whilst at the same time bunched up a fist and let fly, straight into the face of Sergeant Grinde. A sort of schmock sound reverberated, reminiscent of a sock full of wet horseshit being slapped against the wall and Sergeant Grinde's face erupted with a spray of blood. The digit still pointed, but not in the right direction, as the sergeant slumped to the floor.

'See, Frankie, I told you I was thinking.' For some reason, years of pent up frustration and animosity had erupted as Grinde had called down, the red mist descended and it triggered a primal reflex that MacGillicudy could not deny; it said slap the bastard.

A silence, so complete, fell on those witnessing the event, so much so, that you could've heard a feather land on a fresh pile of snow and it seemed to go on forever, until someone started to clap his hands. Very quickly, everybody else joined in, and Frankie wondered if there was to be an encore. Grinde started to come around and the applause cut off just as quickly as it began. Frankie caught a blur of movement from behind him, and he supposed that somebody had gone off to tell Captain Bough.

'There goes my pension.' observed MacGillicudy solemnly. 'Right, Frankie, let's have a look at the crime reports, it's probably going to be my last chance.'

They did, and found that a coach fitting the description had been stolen yesterday from across the river. Frankie scribbled the address down just as Grinde pulled himself to his feet.

'Youse, MacGillicudy, are history. I'm going to 'ave you for that, in front o'witnesses too. You'll be drummed out of the force,' he spluttered through loosened teeth. 'Drummed out of the force!' Suddenly, Grinde grabbed his hand as the pain hit and he cried out; it was a little delayed as it must have taken a wrong turn somewhere, but eventually it found the spot. Frankie grinned at his discomfort.

'What's going on?' yelled an authoritative voice. All eyes turned as one. Captain Bough, having been fetched by a young feeler, came in; he had been talking to Constable Wiggins in the corridor and was there in moments. He looked at the face of Grinde and groaned, but then he saw the finger and winced in sympathy. From what the feeler had told him, and what he saw, he had a fair idea of what had happened and thought quickly. 'Everyone, back to your duties. Grinde, get that finger sorted out and then report to me. Wiggins, you are now acting Sergeant, get up there and start processing that lot,' he pointed to the reception on the other side of the wall. 'Sergeant MacGillicudy, I think I'd better have a word with you.'

Bough turned and marched out, closely followed by MacGillicudy. They went down the corridor and up to his office, where Bough collapsed into his chair with a sigh of resignation.

'Okay, Jethro, close the door and tell me what happened.'

MacGillicudy slammed the door shut and stood to attention

right in front of the desk. 'Accident, sir. Sergeant Grinde did annoy me, I admit to that, but then he came down from his lectern and started pointing his finger at me. I took exception to that, sir, and grabbed hold of it; but then he seemed to stumble, sir, so I reached out quickly to stop him falling, and, I'm sorry, sir, him being a short arse and all, I missed and connected with his face. Pure accident, sir.'

Bough stared at MacGillicudy for a few moments and then wiped his face with his hand. 'Jethro, if that's going to be your official response, then fair enough, you will write a report and hand it to me this morning, but we have known each other for years, so please, don't take the piss. Now give me the unofficial version.'

'Unofficial, sir?' asked MacGillicudy innocently, staring fixedly into space.

'Sit down, Jethro, and yes, I want the unofficial.'

MacGillicudy flicked his eyes to Bough and then hesitated for a few moments, as if weighing up his Captain. He came to a decision and then let his shoulders sag before slumping down into the chair. 'All right, Harold. The bastard had it coming to him; you know that. I just decided that the time had come. I was just going through the crime reports with Frankie Kandalwick when he started to shove his nose in. I saw red, and thought bollocks to him. He stood in front of me, his finger wagging, and I just wanted to ram my fist down his throat — so I did.'

Bough grinned. 'You and everybody else.' He picked up his pencil and began to tap out a rhythm on the desk, thinking quickly. 'So,' he said eventually. 'He provoked you?'

MacGillicudy's eyes lit up. 'Oh yes, a great provocation, it was; he was breathing, ain't that enough?'

'Jethro, I'm going to have to interview everyone who saw it; if anyone tells me the truth then I'm not sure I will be able to do too much about it. Tell Frankie Kandalwick not to leave, I'll need to speak to him too. Why were you going through the crime reports with Frankie anyway?'

'Someone tried to run Cornwallis down last night, nearly succeeded by all accounts.'

Bough looked shocked. 'Really? Well I never.'

Frankie sat at a desk playing at flicking little paper balls around the room when MacGillicudy came back in. Another feeler followed behind him and began to line up all the witnesses to the "occurrence" to drag them off to see the Captain.

'Well?' asked Frankie, raising his eyebrows as MacGillicudy sat down.

'Who knows? He wants to see you too, and you ain't allowed to leave until he does.'

'Oh bollocks. I've got to look for that stolen coach and all; I can't be sitting here all day.'

'Sorry, Frankie, I shouldn't have tapped him.' MacGillicudy smiled ruefully.

Frankie flicked another ball of paper and got rewarded by an 'Oi, stop that,' when he came to a decision. 'Can I borrow one of your better youngsters to get a message to Jack that I'm tied up here?'

'I suppose I still have the authority. Write it down and I'll get it sorted.'

Grinde came back in with his finger in a splint; he shot Frankie and MacGillicudy an evil look and then mimed a rude gesture with his good hand.

Frankie laughed and called out. 'You get a lot of practise doing that, don't you, Grinde?'

There were a few sniggers, but Grinde ignored them all and carried on walking through. He intended to have his say now, and when he got back, the whole lot of them were going to find out pretty quickly that they couldn't mess with him and get away with it.

CHAPTER 7

'Gentlemen, we must call this meeting to order. Are we all present?'

A murmur of agreement came from all those assembled. They were sitting around the table in the boardroom at the Gornstock Bank, drinking coffee and nibbling on a selection of biscuits and small fancy cakes. Mr Abraham Dumchuck rattled his small hammer on the table and everybody looked up.

Dumchuck would have described himself as portly; everyone else would have said fat. In his fifties, years of over indulgence had taken its toll. Jowly with little piggy eyes and just a few strands of thin hair covering his pate, he thought he cut an elegant figure in society. He dressed finely, as only the rich can, to hide his ever expanding waistband.

'We have this morning received into our possession the loan kindly given to us by the Gornstock Assembly. It is a substantial sum and it will allow us some degree of freedom to resolve our obligations. It is my intention that we use this money wisely. There are many diverse investment opportunities which I'm sure will yield a substantial profit, and allow us to continue to be the lifeblood of the city. It is unfortunate that circumstances have dictated that we required a loan in the first place, but world markets have fluctuated, and in some cases ceased altogether. We also were too free with depositors' money when it came to small personal and business loans, but steps have been taken to resolve these unfortunate dealings by offering them to certain financial institutions. Any questions so far?'

'Yes, we're out of ginger crunchies at this end. Could someone pass the plate please? Oh I say, are they cupcakes? We didn't have any of those up here.'

Dumchuck waited patiently while the required confections slid along the table; when they settled again, he continued. 'We have to decide now what constitutes our most urgent requirements, seeing as we now have money in the bank, ha, ha, ha.' He waited for a response to his joke, but it died as it left his lips and he could already hear the gravediggers shovel. He coughed to hide his embarrassment and carried on. 'So, gentlemen, your suggestions please.'

'I suggest that we bring in the wine, if we are going to be here all day. Is there going to be lunch supplied? I have a dickey tummy and I have to eat regularly, don't you know. Little and often is what my doctor tells me, little and often.'

'Yes, Mr Bloomtit,' answered Dumchuck, 'so you have told us, on numerous occasions. I'm hopeful that we can conclude our business this morning though, if that's any help.'

'No lunch then? No wine?'

'No to both, Mr Bloomtit.'

'Bugger.'

'It is, isn't it, Mr Bloomtit. However I'm sure you can manage for just a short while.'

'What about our bonus?' asked Mr Jacobson. 'We're bankers, and we've put a lot of work into all this over the last few weeks.'

Dumchuck smiled benevolently. 'I heartily agree, Mr Jacobson, we have indeed. It has been tough work too, lots of stress in making all these decisions, and it is not our fault that it all went wrong. I suggest that we should pay the full bonus that we are due; and perhaps a little extra for the anguish we've all suffered. Do we agree?'

The 'here here's' were plentiful, with laughter, lots of foot stamping and banging of the table, the motion carried unanimously. Dumchuck wrote it down in his book.

'Now gentlemen, there has been a request from one of the financial institutions that I spoke of, for a small loan of liquid capital. The Gornstock Trust and Holdings have generously bought some of our worst debtors off us, but they have now run into a little difficulty. It is my opinion that we agree to this request, as the rate of return that they are willing to pay is two per cent above rate, which constitutes a good return for our investment. Are we agreed?'

The bankers in the boardroom were still congratulating themselves on passing the motion for the bonus payments and were hardly listening to Dumchuck as he spoke; however, thinking that perhaps he was asking for only a small amount, they all agreed without another thought. Dumchuck wrote it down in his book.

'Thank you, gentlemen. I will prepare a draft for them, a Banker's Draft,' he waited, but the shovel came out again. 'Anyway,' he hurriedly continued, 'that now concludes the main business of the morning, so it's just the little sundry items to deal with now.'

Dumchuck conducted everything else to his satisfaction; there were no dissenters as they were all still pleased with the bonus payments. More tea and cakes came in which pleased a few, but within a couple of hours they had finished the business, agreeing that from there on in they should be frugal with the bank's money.

He closed the door as the last one left and smiled to himself, rubbed his hands in glee and then began a little jig. It had all gone so easily that he felt just a touch guilty; good old Mr

Jacobson, he needed to get them in a good mood and bringing up the bonus payments worked perfectly. He thought he might have struggled to get the loan through to Gornstock Trust and Holdings, but it went through on the nod: all in all an excellent morning's work.

The door opened and Pelegrew Kintersbury, Secretary to the Treasury, member of the Assembly, and co-conspirator, came in. A tall thin man with a generous amount of light wavy hair, the same age as Dumchuck, had sharp pinched features and a jutting chin. At the moment, his distinguishing marks were some nasty looking scratches on both cheeks of his face.

'How did it go, Abraham?' he asked, as he sat himself down.

'Like a dream, old boy, like a dream.' He looked at Kintersbury's face and his eyes widened. 'What happened to you?' he asked, looking at the scratches.

'That's good,' he replied, ignoring the question for the moment. He helped himself to one of the few cakes left over from the meeting and chewed it slowly. 'However, not everything has gone as well, I'm afraid.'

Dumchuck stared hard at Kintersbury. 'What do you mean?'

'I mean that your little mistake has led to the demise of Roland Goup's cleaner. If you hadn't let your wife send all the paperwork to Goup, then we wouldn't be in this situation. We've had to make Goup disappear as he is not the most robust of men if it came to an interrogation; I have him safe somewhere at the moment.' He indicated his face with a slight wave of his hand. 'I got this at his office; a cat seemed to take exception to me being there when I tried to burn the building.'

'Oh Gods.' Dumchuck looked horrified. 'We only had to ask Goup for the paperwork back and then nothing like this would have happened.'

'No, no, no. We couldn't, as he had already sent in the

return to the department. He would have been audited and it would have been found "missing". We had to do the burglary to dispose of your mistake fully and completely,' he explained. 'I have already suggested that there were errors with the return, and thankfully, my Minister believes me. Dooley wanted to send in the dogs with the amount of money in that return, this way there is no evidence at all, and we can blame the police for their shortcomings. Unfortunately, Radstock happened to be at Scooters Yard for some reason and has put Cornwallis on to it, which could be a little problematic. However, we are tying up the loose ends; the burglar we used has already had his association with us ended,' he smiled to show his meaning, 'and we are hopeful that everything else can be resolved just as easily.'

'Oh, I do hope so,' said Dumchuck. 'We can't afford to let things go wrong now.'

*

Cornwallis waited in the office hoping that Frankie would return. He couldn't give him very long as they needed to be back at Brownlow's pretty sharpish. He'd had the message that Frankie had sent and he returned one of his own, suggesting that he untangle himself from the mess at Scooters Yard quickly. Cornwallis really did need him, and it was sod's law that MacGillicudy had chosen this day of all days to land one on Grinde.

Rose had gone to get the cat from the back of Goup's office; they had thought long and hard on the way back from Brownlow's as to how they would follow Maxwell; the chances of being able to follow on foot were remote, especially if the cart got up some speed. Two people running through Gornstock would elicit some worried looks, as anybody running in this city would be doing it to get away from the person holding a meat cleaver, who would invariably be chasing. He also considered the fact that he didn't think he could run further than a few hundred yards without having to stop to draw breath, which would be seriously embarrassing, especially if Rose could. It was about time he got himself some hooves and wheels he thought, in the meantime, he would grab a cab, then try and get the cat on the back of Maxwell's cart.

He paced the office as the clock ticked on, waiting for the footsteps on the stairs. He wasn't happy about letting Rose go, but the options were somewhat limited; someone had to stop at the office in case the cat couldn't be found in time and he didn't want her to have to go and follow the cart on her own. He couldn't give her much longer now, he had to go, and soon.

There were some footsteps on the stairs and Cornwallis breathed a sigh of relief, but then he noticed that unless Rose had put on an awful lot of weight in the last hour or so then the footsteps weren't hers, they were far too heavy and slow for a girl of Rose's proportions.

'Good job you sent that note back, Jack,' said Frankie, as he breezed into the room. 'Managed to show it to Bough and he let me go. Poor old MacGillicudy is right in the shit now, but jeez, did he catch him a good 'un.' He mimed the punch that Grinde had received. 'Best straight right I've seen for a long time. Here, where's Rose?'

Cornwallis returned the grin. 'Gone to find your friend, the cat. She should have been back by now but we can't wait any longer, you got here just in time, we need to go.' He explained briefly what had gone on. 'I'll leave a note for her to meet us at Brownlow's and hope that she's not too far behind. You can tell me all the details of your incarceration later as you will need to make a slight detour first. I want you to go and see Gerald.

Brownlow's family could be in deep trouble and we need to get them safe.'

'Bloody hell, you mean I ain't got time for a coffee?'

'You haven't got time to fart, Frankie. Here's the sign I've agreed with Brownlow, half a doodled note. He has the other half and this is the address. It will tell him to trust the bearer of this piece and to do what they say. Ask Gerald to hide the family somewhere and I'll square it with him later.'

'So where do I catch up with you?'

'Maxwell will pick the coach up at four or thereabouts, so I should be in a cab just down the street. If I'm not there then you're too late, just come back here and wait.'

'Don't like the sound of that, we ain't gonna know where you are; I'd better get a move on then, ain't I.'

Frankie hurried out and hailed a cab. He had to get south of the river into the Brews and back north in space of just an hour and a bit; he just hoped the traffic would be kind to him.

Cornwallis finished the note to Rose and left it on the desk; he dropped a few coins next to it so she could pay her fare, and left. He just hoped she wouldn't be far behind.

*

He had a good view of Brownlow's from where he waited, just up the road on a bend and he told the driver to look as though he was having a break. The driver relished the opportunity of a chase into the unknown; he'd been hoping that something would happen to brighten his normally dull day.

'Well, guvnor, whenever yer ready, just give me the word,' said the driver, munching on a cheese sandwich. 'Ain't nobody in this 'ere town can get away from me.' This was his proud boast and Cornwallis had heard it before.

'I never doubt you, Coggs, but we don't need to go hell for leather all the way through the city. All we need to do is to follow at a discreet distance.'

'But that ain't no fun, Mr Cornwallis,' replied Coggs with an air of disappointment. 'This 'ere 'orse goes like the clappers when it's got a mind to. Two wheel cornering's are no trouble to this 'un, I even got it to do a four wheel drift once; shit, you should 'ave seen that. Beautiful it was, beautiful.'

'I'm sure it was, but let's keep to the sedate, this time.'

Coggs happened to be one of Cornwallis' ever increasing circle of contacts; he'd used him quite regularly as he had proved that he could keep his mouth shut when the need arose. This was one of those times, and Cornwallis breathed a sigh of relief when he spotted him on the rank.

He checked his watch again; still no sign yet of Maxwell and four o'clock approached fast. He hoped Brownlow would manage to keep his composure and not give the game away; he had to take the risk, he just had to hope that nerves wouldn't get the better of him. He turned his thoughts to the coach that picked Maxwell up earlier, a pool coach from the Treasury — but who had authorised it? Now, that question needed answering. Names of the officials in the department were going through his mind; Dooley, the minister; Kintersbury, the department's chief secretary; also Witchet, Foogarly, Noundon and Inkley, all juniors in the department. There were others who could have access to a coach, including runners and messengers or even the caterers. Boil it all down, practically anyone could get hold of a Treasury coach. Kintersbury: now why did that name nudge the memory banks? He thought a moment longer and then remembered the handkerchief with a "K" embroidered in the corner. Could it be him? Might be an idea to see if he has some nasty scratches on his face; another task for tomorrow, he thought.

'Is this the one, sweetheart? Only I's quite happy where I's is if it ain't, youse know.'

Cornwallis heard the voice before he saw the owner and he breathed a sigh of relief, one out of two wasn't so bad. He poked his head out of the window and smiled as Rose came walking up with Fluffy cradled in her arms. She stroked him and the cat definitely grinned. He flung open the door and Coggs looked around just as Rose disappeared inside. The driver gave a low whistle of approval, but he spoilt the effect by having a mouthful of sandwich at the time.

'Just in time, Rose,' said Cornwallis. 'I was getting worried you wouldn't make it. Hello, Fluffy,' he said to the cat as he bounced against her chest as she sat down. 'Thanks for agreeing to help.'

'Youse is the boss man, ain't youse, sees youse at the window. Youse laughed at me, didn't youse?'

Cornwallis chuckled. 'Not at you, Fluffy; at Frankie. I enjoyed seeing him try to handle you.'

'Well, that's all right then. Only I don'ts like it when I gets the piss taken out o' me, people's tend to live to regret it.'

The cat settled itself on Rose's lap and began to purr contentedly while Cornwallis looked on. A definite pang of jealousy tingled his neck, but then he wondered why he should be jealous of a cat?

Rose scratched the back of Fluffy's head as he lay curled up on her lap. 'He was no trouble, only too willing to help. Apparently the box of fish worked wonders for him and can he have another?'

'When he's done what we want,' replied Cornwallis easily.

He reached forward to pat the cat but then a movement took his attention away. A carch, a cross between a cart and a coach, drew up outside Brownlow's and the driver got off to open the gate.

'Yes. I think we're in business,' said Cornwallis triumphantly.

Rose looked up and the cat took a little interest too. 'Never seen one of them before,' she said, observing the carch.

'New thing,' answered Cornwallis. 'Not many of them around. The front end is a two seater coach and the back end is a cart for carrying stuff around. That's a long wheelbase one, triple axle, should take quite a load.'

'So what's I 'ere for then?' asked the cat.

Cornwallis grinned. 'What we want you to do is sit by the gate, and when the carch comes out, hop on the back. We want to know where it goes. We will be following, but if we lose it then you would be our insurance, if you like. We would wait and you can walk back. If you get near what seems to be their destination then we will stop and wait for you to get out before going any further. Is that clear?'

'Sounds like a lot of walking to me,' replied Fluffy. 'A double box of fish at least.'

'I think we can stretch that far for a job well done. They're inside the yard now, so they've just got to load the crates and then they'll be away. We won't be far behind if all goes well.'

Reluctantly Fluffy relinquished Rose's lap and dropped down onto the floor. He stretched slow and long and then sat back down. 'Well, are one o'youse buggers gonna open the bloody door?'

Cornwallis leant across Rose and flicked the handle. Fluffy jumped down and then sauntered over to the gate. He sat down and began to lick his paw as he waited.

'You can get back up now, he's gone.' Rose tapped Cornwallis on the shoulder, who still stretched across her, looking out the door.

Cornwallis turned his head and grinned apologetically. 'Sorry.'

He sat up and looked forward, straight into a face that only a mother could love: the driver Coggs, leaning down and leering through the window.

'Oi, you need to get ready, Coggs, put your dinner away and wait for my word, okay?'

Coggs grinned. 'As you say, guvnor.' He gave a little salute and then turned back around.

'Really,' exclaimed Cornwallis. 'Give them an inch...'

Rose raised a laconic eyebrow; the exact same thought went through her mind too.

Cornwallis brought Rose up to date as they waited. He still prayed that Frankie would make it back in time but now he was losing hope; he knew the bridge could be a bugger, and it didn't take much to snarl it all up. The gate began to swing open and he watched as Fluffy stood up and walked nonchalantly through.

The carch pulled out and the gates closed behind. It then began at a steady pace down the road and Cornwallis ordered Coggs to follow. He took a last look behind and saw a cab approaching with a figure leaning out of the window, Frankie had arrived at last, but he couldn't risk stopping to wait as the carch had begun to pick up a little pace and they would have no chance of getting in contact with it again. He leant out of the window and waved, and Frankie rewarded him with a thumbs-up.

'Don't get too close now, Coggs,' yelled Cornwallis, above the noise of the cab. 'Don't want him to get suspicious.'

Coggs yelled something back that Cornwallis didn't quite catch, Rose did though and she smiled. It would be best if she didn't repeat it, as she knew for a fact that he had a father.

The traffic slowed the carch down, and as they got closer they could see Fluffy on the back by the tailgate, the cat wedged between the crates and appearing to be enjoying the ride. They had two carts between them and the carch, which appeared to be heading towards the river, but Cornwallis couldn't relax; he fidgeted and kept giving pointless instructions to Coggs, who Rose could tell was getting more and more wound up.

'Why don't you just let him drive?' she asked, with a sigh of exasperation.

'I am,' responded Cornwallis, 'I'm just helping him along a bit. There's an art to tailing someone, just don't want to give the game away.'

The traffic stopped at a busy intersection and a feeler up ahead tried his best to make things worse. His arms seemed to be waving in all directions at once, but it only created havoc. As they inched forward, Cornwallis could see Dewdrop, his face a picture of despondency, as his arms whirled around him. Cornwallis managed to find a smile, and the sight of the feeler in his agony made him at last relax. The cab stopped for a few minutes while Dewdrop tried to sort the mess out, so Frankie took the opportunity to run the few yards to jump in with Cornwallis and Rose.

'You cut it fine,' observed Cornwallis as Frankie sat down and got his breath back.

Frankie shot Cornwallis a look of distain. 'Fine? And whose sodding fault is that then, eh?'

'Now, boys,' interjected Rose. 'We're all here now, and that's the important thing.'

'You trying telling his lordship here; had me gallivanting all over the place.'

Cornwallis grinned wryly and held his hands up. 'All right, you win. Now did you get to Gerald?'

Frankie nodded. 'Yeah, it's all getting sorted. He'll get them safe, but you need to go and see him later to find out where they are. Apparently, he's heard a little about Maxwell, by all accounts a mean vicious bastard. He's come from out of town, so background's unknown. The finance place employs him as an enforcer, and he really enjoys his work. He's recruited a few of the more dense thugs that Gornstock has to offer, pays good money too. Gerald says he did for Freddie.'

Rose saw the body nailed up in her mind and gave a shudder, 'Sounds like a nice man.'

'Hey up, we're off again,' observed Cornwallis.

Dewdrop had cleared a bit of the jam which allowed the carch to go through, then stopped the vehicle in front of Cornwallis which made him seethe.

'Go around, Coggs,' he shouted. 'Ignore the feeler.'

'Right you are, guvnor,' acknowledged Coggs. 'On your own head be it.'

Frankie grinned. 'You can't do that to Lord Cecil you know.'

'Lord Cecil? What the hell are you on about?'

'Dewdrop has been calling himself Lord Cecil to attract the ladies, isn't that right, Rose?'

Coggs pulled the coach out which made a pretty little open carriage, containing what appeared to be a mother and her daughter, on the way back from a shopping expedition, swerve to avoid an accident. The assortment of bags leapt around, spilling its contents and sending clothes, cosmetics, and confectionary everywhere, into a sort of consumer's trifle. Coggs yelled an apology and carried on; he sped past the cart in front and on into the intersection, just as Dewdrop allowed a wagon from the side to move. Someone screamed abuse at Coggs who gave better back. Dewdrop stood mesmerised, unsure what to do. A cart, the driver thinking that the feeler had allowed him to move, took the chance and entered the melee at pace; another wagon didn't stop in time and ploughed into the back of a coal wagon, the bags lurching at the sudden stop and toppling over into the street. Other carts and wagons and carriages all saw an opportunity and went for it, all of them aiming straight at Dewdrop who stood forlornly in the middle. Coggs, with a devil like grin, waded through it all, standing on the plate and giving an excited "Ye, ha," as he cracked the whip.

Cornwallis, Rose and Frankie sunk down into their seats trying to hide their faces, but as they went past Dewdrop, Cornwallis looked up, gazing straight into the face of the young feeler. The feeler's face was a picture and Cornwallis decided to cast all caution to the wind and grinned back; that'll teach him to go to Mikel An' Jello, thought Cornwallis, evilly.

The screams and yells from the intersection receded as they got further away from the carnage; Coggs turned around and looked in with a wild joyous expression. 'Will that do ya, guvnor? If you want, I can turn around and we can do it all again,' he said hopefully.

'Thank you, Coggs, but I think once is enough.'

'Right you are then, guv,' he acknowledged with a serious degree of disappointment.

Rose had slunk down to the floor during the episode and was now regaining her seat. 'Nothing like being subtle and discreet is there?' she commented to Cornwallis, as she got comfortable.

'Hmmm, perhaps that didn't go quite to plan,' he replied contritely. 'Ah well, we're still in touch with the carch, if nothing else.'

'Let's hope they weren't looking behind during all that ruckus,' said Frankie, who enjoyed it all no end. 'A good bit of driving though; got to take me hat off to Coggs, the way he got through it all.'

They continued the chase as though nothing had happened, and it appeared that those on the carch had not seen the problems that Coggs had caused either. Cornwallis breathed a sigh of relief. The bridge was up ahead and they proceeded in a much more sedate fashion now, so Rose and Frankie explained about Dewdrop, much to Cornwallis' amusement.

Just before they got to the bridge, the carch turned right and went down a slope to the north shore waterfront and Cornwallis instructed Coggs to follow more slowly and carefully now. The carch pulled away and appeared to be heading towards the north docks where a few ships were moored. The carch began to slow down and Cornwallis ordered Coggs to pull up somewhere out of view; they daren't go any further without being seen and suspected.

Cornwallis got out and stood at the side looking forward, seeing lots of activity in the distance. It came to him suddenly that the carch had stopped roughly where the disused warehouse that MacGillicudy had searched was located. He scratched his chin in thought and walked forward to the edge of the river. He looked down into the murky brown depths and sniffed, smelling salt and wet vegetation, but most of all, wee and shit. A turd floated by, hit the bank and did a little pirouette before re-joining the flow once more.

'You seem to be fascinated by something, let's have a look.' Rose had come up to his shoulder and followed his gaze. 'Oooh, nice. Get another and you can have poo races.'

Cornwallis chuckled. 'The start would be interesting, arse over the rail, trousers around the ankle, three, two, one, and strain.'

Rose laughed, and it made Cornwallis think of a fresh clear

mountain stream tinkling its way down over the rocks.

'What you doing?' asked Frankie, coming to join them.

'Racing,' replied Cornwallis. 'But Rose declined to start.' He received a nudge from an elbow which actually hurt. 'Right, back to work,' he said, rubbing the spot happily.

They stared along the busy wharves towards the ships, full of activity from the loading and unloading of goods and equipment. Massive cranes were swinging out over holds and drawing up the cargo, and then teams of workers were putting it all on carts and barrows and dragging them away. Streams of workers were moving along gang-planks with the smaller boxes and crates, dodging and weaving between it all. The crane drivers were big powerful polar bears and gorillas, the strongest of the strong, as they had to power the massive mechanisms needed to lift the huge weights. It was Gornstock's hub, its lifeblood, where goods from far and wide came to the city, and exports, Gornstock's finest, for the delectation of the world, went out. Cornwallis knew that this made Gornstock tick, the thing that kept the city running, commerce on a massive scale with the whole world involved. If a country produced something commercial then it was likely to turn up here.

Because of the amount of workers flooding over the area, it made observation difficult, so now they had to be patient and wait until the cat came back. Cornwallis began to pace with the enforced hiatus in proceedings, always keeping a wary eye on the wharves and of course the seagulls, who took obvious delight in targeting anyone beneath them. A good few minutes passed and he decided, regardless of whatever was happening, that he had to know, when the cat made a sudden appearance amongst the throng, sauntering along with its tail high in the air.

'Hey, Fluffy,' cried Frankie. 'Over here, son.'

The cat swung over and Cornwallis opened the door to the

cab. The cat jumped in first followed by Rose and Frankie; he climbed in last.

'Well?' asked Cornwallis when he'd sat down. 'What happened?'

Fluffy jumped up onto Rose and padded her lap before settling down contentedly. 'They's loading them crates onto that big ship out there, but I's suspect youse thought that. The interesting thing is that the man I scratched is there, youse know, the one 'oo let yer man outta the winda.'

'Is he?' exclaimed Cornwallis. 'What's he doing?'

'Looks like 'e did the supervising. Buts when most of it were done, him and the man on the cart went into the warehouse thingy. Big and dark in there, youse knows, followed 'em a while to sees what they's up to.'

'And…?' encouraged Cornwallis.

'Don'ts know; they disappeared down an 'atch in the floor. Couldn't follow then, so I fought I'd come back to find you lot.'

'Can you show us?' asked Cornwallis, getting excited.

'Naw, don'ts feel like it.' The cat paused and licked a paw. Cornwallis, Rose and Frankie exchanged looks. Cornwallis was just about to say something when the cat sort of grinned. 'Just me's little joke, course I can.'

Another look passed between the three and an audible sigh of relief went through the cab.

'He, he, he. Youse fought I weren't gonna take youse there, didn't youse? Just fer a minute, be 'onest.'

'I think you can say the thought crossed his mind,' answered Rose for Cornwallis, just before he decided to strangle the thing. She looked over at him and cocked her head slightly.

'Very good, Fluffy, very funny,' said Cornwallis stiffly. 'Now let's get going while there's still a chance of finding out what they're up to.'

The cab door opened and they all alighted. Cornwallis told Coggs to wait until they returned, and then Fluffy led the way along the dock towards where the warehouse. They dodged past all the workers, narrowly avoiding being run over more than once and eventually came close to where the carch had stopped. The carch itself was just disappearing into the distance after unloading the coach that tried to kill Cornwallis. They looked at the ship, a big three-masted monster, weather stained and encrusted with barnacles from the open seas. The name was "Greyhawk", but where it came from, or where it was going, there was not a clue. Cornwallis filed the information away in his mind until later; it would be interesting to find out where it was destined. Fluffy rubbed up against Rose's leg and she looked down.

'This way,' hissed the cat, and led off down the side of the warehouse.

There were big double doors at the front, but they looked like they hadn't been opened in years, which indeed they hadn't; not since the Great East Company went out of business some five years ago when the chairman did a runner with all the money. He was kind enough to send back a postcard to his former associates saying "Having a lovely time, wish you were here," just to rub salt into the wound.

Fluffy took them to a little side door which had well oiled hinges, indicating that it had been used many times before. Cornwallis turned the handle and the door swung silently open. They stood inside, waiting, until their eyes adjusted to the dim light, and then they saw just a vast empty and dusty place. Dusty that is, except for large stretches of the floor which had been swept clean. MacGillicudy hadn't mentioned that, thought Cornwallis, and he was as sure as night follows day that he didn't clean up as he searched.

The cat padded softly across the floor to a sectioned off part of the warehouse where a few old bags of tea leant against a wooden post. Fluffy entered a big office which had a few old tables ridden with woodworm and a few broken chairs with their legs at odd angles, which had all been pushed up against the rear wall.

'This is where they's went,' he said, cleaning his whiskers.

Cornwallis cast his eyes around but had to admit he couldn't see a thing, there didn't appear to be a hatch anywhere. He looked closely at the floor again in case he missed something obvious; but no, he could see nothing.

'All right, Fluffy, I know you're sitting there waiting to tell us. You have that superior look on your face.'

'Ah. Us cats is always superior, didn't yer knows that? That lamp on the wall, give it a tug.'

Frankie got there first. 'You mean this one?' He pulled at it before the cat could answer and a cranking noise began, followed by the grind of machinery and then a section of the floor where Cornwallis stood began to swing away.

'What the f...!' cried Cornwallis as he found himself lowering beneath the floor at a strange angle. He jumped back up before he slid into the unknown and then looked askance at Fluffy. 'You could have warned me.'

The cat just grinned.

The floor cranked to a stop and the three craned their heads over to look. There were some steps leading down about twenty feet to the floor beneath where a passage, hewn from the rock, led in two directions. There seemed to be lanterns in a small alcove at the bottom of the steps, presumably for anyone stupid enough to go exploring. The three looked at each other until Cornwallis decided that they really had no option, they had to be stupid enough to go exploring.

Fluffy went back to wait with Coggs and Cornwallis wanted Rose to go with him, but she didn't move, adamant that she was coming along and no amount of effort would persuade her otherwise. Cornwallis, having lost the argument, led the way down and Frankie found a match to light a couple of lanterns while they decided which direction to go. Dust on the floor could come in very handy in some circumstances, and this was one of them. Rose looked down and saw footprints. A couple led off and then returned in the direction of where they left Coggs, but there seemed to be more activity in the other direction where there were several sets of prints both coming and going.

'Looks a no-brainer,' said Cornwallis, 'we'll go that way. We'll stick close together, and we'll keep our voices down. Now let's see what we can find.'

They found the switch to close the trapdoor and then began. The height of the passage allowed them to walk upright to start with, and then it seemed to lower a little as they moved further along, but just wide enough so that two could walk side-by-side; so Cornwallis and Rose went in front, with Frankie bringing up the rear. The passage seemed to change direction frequently, switching one way and then the other, and though they were listening intently, they heard no sound apart from their own shuffling footsteps. They advanced slowly, following as much as they could the footprints in the dust; there were offshoots, and they stood at these and shined their lanterns into the depths for a few brief moments before continuing. None of them voiced their fears, but all three were dreading something unknown in what appeared to be age old tunnels; there were rumours aplenty of what lay beneath the surface in old Gornstock: ancient flesh eating beasts, big fiendish ogres and devils and imps that would suck the very being out of you, leaving behind just a living breathing shell. Cornwallis shuddered as the thoughts played around his mind. He cast his eye to look at Rose walking next to him and saw her intense concentration as she looked forward into the black depths beyond the lantern light.

The footprints had gone, or more to the point, the dust had gone, so they had nothing to follow now. They decided to stay in the main passage, as there were just too many alternative tunnels, and it would take an age to check every one; Maxwell could have ventured into any one of them. They were in a labyrinthine maze with no way of telling where you were; any sense of direction had long gone and it was now just a case of not getting lost. Cornwallis voiced the opinion that they should turn back, which pleased Frankie no end, as he began to get just a tad jittery. He bunched up as close as he could get to the two in front, his nose virtually on Cornwallis' shoulder as they negotiated a sharp left turn, so close, that when the noise came eerily through the passage he slammed into their backs as they stopped. 'What's that?' he asked, his tension rising,

Cornwallis didn't answer; he just looked forward instead and tried to tune his ears to the noise.

'I said, what's that?' repeated Frankie, nearly at screaming point.

'Shush,' said Rose, bringing a finger up to her lips.

The tension grew, neither of them willing to go another step further. They heard a scraping noise again and then a sigh. Frankie gripped Cornwallis on the shoulder so hard that he had to prize the fingers off.

'It's the Multi-Headed Grip Thranglar,' ventured Cornwallis at last. 'It devours anything in its path. It favours eating its dinner from the feet up so it can enjoy the death throes of its victim; it has the added advantage of its victim not being able to run away if it feels it just needs a snack. How the hell do I know what it is?'

'Bastard,' exclaimed Frankie, 'I believed you there for a moment.'

Cornwallis shook his head. 'Look, wait here a minute and I'll go and see if anything's there.'

Frankie didn't argue, he remembered the bogey man of his childhood, and how he would always keep his hands inside the bed when he lay there in the dark, convinced the bogey man waited just under the bed to grab his arm the moment he let it dangle, a feeling that had never left him, even now.

Rose offered to go with Cornwallis but he shook his head.

'Best keep back until we know what it is. I won't be long.'

Cornwallis patted Rose on the shoulder and gave her a reassuring smile. He then began to inch his way around the corner, holding his lantern as far out in front as he could. So far so good, he thought. The passage seemed empty, so he took a few tentative steps forward, but he failed to see the passage leading off to his left, and as he came abreast of it, he felt a draft of air whistle into his ear. He stopped abruptly and swallowed hard; he could sense something there, something very close to him, and if he turned, he felt sure he would come face to face with the lurking beast. He swallowed again, then slowly turned to face his nemesis, ready to scream out loud and run.

'Sorry mate, it's the Multi-Headed Grip Thranglar's day off. But if you want, I can chew yer legs off for yer.'

Cornwallis stared ahead, straight into the blade of a very sharp axe. He then followed the handle down to the hand of the dwarf holding it.

'Afternoon,' said Cornwallis, recovering instantly and feeling a whole lot better. 'Nice day for a stroll.'

The dwarf grinned. 'Aye, that it is. But what I want to know is why you is taking a stroll in one of *our* tunnels?'

Cornwallis looked at the dwarf: yes, he might be short, but everything else about him was big. The shoulders were enormous, the arms massive, the hands big and calloused, the chest like a two hundred gallon barrel.

'Sorry, must have got lost.'

Rose and Frankie heard the exchange and came around. They stood next to Cornwallis and looked down on the dwarf, while he in turn scrutinised them.

'I've seen you,' he said to Rose eventually. 'Black Stoat, the other day. You broke up a fight. Very impressed we were too.'

'Thank you,' answered Rose, smiling down at him. 'I remember you too, Trugral, isn't it?'

The dwarf grinned back. 'It is; thank you for remembering. Most people don't, you know; a dwarf is just a dwarf to most of them, too much like hard work to remember something simple like a name.'

'I'm sorry if we're trespassing,' ventured Rose, 'only some men came down here not so long ago, and we were sort of wondering what they were up to.'

'Ah. Them.'

'You know who we're talking about?' interjected Cornwallis.

'Oh yes, you don't want to go mixing with them, they're trouble.'

'We know,' replied Cornwallis, 'that's why we followed them down. We're investigators, working with the police.'

Trugral scratched his beard with his free hand, but he wasn't letting go of his axe just yet. 'Investigators, eh? Well they certainly need investigating and that's one reason why I'm here, to prevent incursions. There are limits, you know; these tunnels are pretty much sacred to us, but they had permission to use a few of them, but not this one.'

'Permission?'

'Aye, permission from the King of the Dwarfs. They were keeping one of you lot, I mean human, down here. We kept an eye on him, so to speak.'

'Where?' asked Cornwallis, eagerly.

'Down there away's,' he pointed back the way they had come. 'You missed a passage on your right, they goes down there. The place where they held the man is an old guardroom; didn't know anything about him, but he looked harmless enough. Gave him some food and water and kept him in light.'

'I presume then that the King agreed to all that?'

'Sort of, they were just going to leave him there. We felt a bit sorry for him actually, so gave him the chance to get out, but didn't; seemed like he wanted to be a prisoner.'

'How do you mean?' asked Rose.

'We left the door unlocked. Never tried it once, did yer man. Just sat there or walked around the room.'

'Why are you telling us all this?' asked Frankie, a little confused.

Trugral shrugged his shoulders. 'Why not? They made it plain they don't like dwarfs, so I reckon, I don't need to like them.'

'Sounds fair enough,' reasoned Frankie. 'You say held, so I take it he's gone now?'

Trugral nodded. 'Took him away about ten minutes ago.'

'Ten minutes? Then why haven't we seen them?'

'Because you're in the wrong passage. If you were in the right passage; then you would have seen them. Do you want to see the guardroom?' When Cornwallis hesitated, Trugral just grinned. 'Don't worry; you'll still catch up with them.'

Trugral took them down a shortcut with Frankie moaning all the time about how they had just missed Maxwell, for some reason his fears of the dark tunnels had totally evaporated. The guardroom wasn't far, and within a couple of minutes, they were looking at the now empty room.

'Table, chair, mattress. Nothing else. He must have been bored out of his mind,' said Cornwallis. 'And you say the description Frankie gave you matches the man in here?'

Trugral nodded.

'Definitely Goup, then. I wonder why they're taking him out now?' Cornwallis tapped his lip in thought for a few moments. 'I'm going to have to speak to the King, you know, I just hope he'll be agreeable. Could they get out another way?' he asked.

Trugral shook his head. 'No, not for them. They get out the same way as you came in. I'll inform the King and I'm sure he'll be accommodating; he does enjoy all the little webs you humans weave. I tell you what, I'll take you back; that way you won't be dawdling and you can catch them up; and I can show you something you might find interesting, seeing as you're investigators.'

'And what's that then?' asked Frankie.

'Bit of patience, you'll see.'

Trugral led them confidently down the tunnels so fast that the three had to nearly run to keep up; he stopped at a couple of openings and whistled each time, waiting for a reply before carrying on. Notifying the guards, he explained, just in case they thought we were being overrun, as there hadn't been this much traffic down here for a long time. It seemed to take only about half the time to get back to the warehouse entrance, but Trugral didn't pause, he just walked on past the steps and on into the other side. He stopped a little way up and then stood aside to let them see. 'All this has suddenly appeared, but I don't know whether it's got anything to do with your friends or not.'

Cornwallis, Frankie and Rose looked into an alcove which was stacked with small parcels. Frankie leant forward and picked one up; he sniffed it at first, then slid a fingernail down the side to open it up. He grinned, and then showed it to Cornwallis and Rose.

'Drugs. There must be millions of dollars' worth here. That's what they're up to: drug trafficking.'

CHAPTER 8

Trugral brought them back to the steps and then showed them the periscope hidden in the wall that revealed the entire floor of the warehouse above. Cornwallis smiled to himself as he looked through the little glass window. He turned it from side to side as he saw three men, two of them struggling to hold on to a third as they crossed the floor.

'There they are,' he said triumphantly. 'We haven't lost them after all... and who is that?' He studied one man closely in the half-light. 'Oh, yes.' He punched his hand into the air.

'Let's have a look,' said Frankie, elbowing Cornwallis out of the way. He too then grinned when he saw the three men. 'That's Goup, the one who keeps falling over. The one on the left must be your friend, Maxwell, and the one on the right... Well, well, well.'

Rose couldn't wait any longer, and as Cornwallis and Frankie exchanged knowing grins, she too looked.

'Kintersbury, Pelegrew Kintersbury,' announced Cornwallis. The "K" on the handkerchief, the matches from the inner ring: it all started fitting together. 'They should be gone by now. How long have we been here, what, a couple of minutes? I wonder what they've been doing?' Cornwallis voiced his thoughts aloud.

'Goup looks like he can hardly walk,' said Frankie. 'If I didn't know better I'd say he was drunk.'

'Or drugged,' suggested Rose, coming away from the periscope. 'They've just gone through the door; so it's all clear now.'

Cornwallis and Frankie both looked back down the passage at the same time to the large haul of drugs that just sat there; it must have been put there by Kintersbury and Maxwell. Rose must be right; they must have drugged Goup. But why? What do they intend to do to him?

The trapdoor swung down and they thanked Trugral for all his help before climbing up to the warehouse office. The dwarf waved a farewell and then flicked the switch, just as Cornwallis turned to offer more thanks and a promise of a few drinks the next time he was at the Stoat. The floor closed with a clunk and they felt strangely exposed after the confines of the tunnels. Rose walked forward a couple of steps and saw a little packet on a table together with a bottle and a glass. She knew they weren't there when they had gone down.

'Here's your answer,' she said, examining them. 'They *have* drugged him.'

'So they have,' responded Cornwallis, coming over too. 'Not going to be easy manhandling someone smacked up to the eyeballs; so let's get after them and see what they're up to now.'

They hurried across the warehouse and tentatively opened the door a crack. Cornwallis peered out through the small gap and saw their three targets just disappearing around the front of the building. He flung the door open wide and stepped out, closely followed by Rose and Frankie.

They half ran forward to the edge of the building and then slowed as they walked out onto the docks in as casual a manner as they could. They couldn't see Maxwell and friends at first, the area was still busy, but a little gap opened up and they could see the three of them lurching along a wharf by the side of a ship, the same ship that had the carch loaded onto it earlier. A walkway led up to the deck, and Maxwell pushed Goup up and handed him over to a couple of sailors. Kintersbury then spoke to someone who looked like a ships officer, culminating in them shaking hands. The sailors then helped take Goup away, into the bowels of the ship. Cornwallis looked again at the name before ushering Frankie and Rose away.

'We can't let this ship leave,' said Cornwallis. 'I'm going to have to see the harbour master, see if we can get it stopped.'

'I think you're going to be a bit late for that,' replied Frankie. 'Look.'

The three heads looked at the sudden activity on the ship, a whistle blew and the ship filled with sailors running to their posts.

'Oh Gods,' voiced Cornwallis with feeling.

'Not to worry, Mr Cornwallis,' said a confident voice at his side.

'Sorry?' Cornwallis turned to see a small man in a round topped hat wearing a long coat and he looked down at him suspiciously. 'What are you talking about, and who are you?'

The little man smiled. 'Well, I'm me of course, but you can call me, er, Mr Sparrow.'

All contact with the shore was then broken as the last of the workmen left the ship and the gang-planks hauled up. The mooring ropes were pulled in and a tug, which Cornwallis hadn't seen, began to tow the ship out into the middle of the river.

Frankie sidled over to stand at the side of Mr Sparrow who just looked up at him and grinned some more. Rose stood behind him, just in reach.

'Your two little birds are flying away, I see; they don't like hanging around do they?' said Mr Sparrow, watching Maxwell and Kintersbury hurrying down the docks. 'They must be very busy people. I recognise Pelegrew Kintersbury, but who is the other man? And who did they escort onto the ship?' He turned his head slightly to catch Rose in his vision. 'I know you are very good, Miss Morant, but alas you are not quite good enough, not yet at any rate, and I would so hate seeing you hurt.'

If Rose had learnt one thing in life, it was that a little man with a lot of confidence could be a big problem. She sensed that there was more to Mr Sparrow than met the eye, that he could more than live up to his promise, and that she didn't really want to find out what that promise was. She took half a step back.

'Okay, Mr Sparrow, I've had enough. Have you been following us?' asked Cornwallis, getting a little angry now.

'Of course. The question you are going to ask now, is why? So I will say just this. The Bagman wants to see you.'

'The Bag...? Oh no.'

Mr Sparrow laughed. 'I'm afraid so, Mr Cornwallis. It's out of my hands and perhaps you might learn something to your advantage. He will tell you everything he wants you to know. Are you going to tell me who those gentlemen are?'

Cornwallis looked at Sparrow and just shook his head slowly.

Mr Sparrow grinned. 'So be it, Mr Cornwallis. The Bagman will inform me when you inform him.'

Rose listened in confusion. 'Who's the Bagman?' she asked, seeing the look on Cornwallis' and Frankie's faces.

'The Bagman is very bad news,' explained Cornwallis, keeping his eye on Sparrow. 'He's what you might call the last resort. If the Bagman is involved then it is likely to be something really bad. He's Gornstock's rat catcher.'

'Very apt description, Mr Cornwallis. Now, if you would like to come with me you can forget about our two friends for a while, I'm sure you will catch up with them later.'

Cornwallis sighed, he wasn't expecting this turn of events, but he knew he had no option; if the Bagman wanted to see you, then you saw him. 'All right, we'll come with you, Mr Sparrow.'

Sparrow nodded at the wisdom of this. 'However, just you, Mr Cornwallis. Mr Kandalwick and Miss Morant can take the rest of the day off.'

Cornwallis felt hamstrung as the little man spoke. He couldn't ignore a summons from the Bagman and the little man Sparrow, confident that he was going to be obeyed, stood patiently waiting with a wide grin on his face. Cornwallis began to argue, but in the end Sparrow produced the required proof of his identity and Cornwallis' arguments petered out. In the end, he reluctantly instructed Frankie and Rose to return to the office and told them he would see them later, if not there, then down at the Stoat. He told Frankie to see if Algernon had managed to ferret out any information, even if he just found out what they had already learnt; but he might have heard something else. Coggs still waited, along with the cat, so he left it to the two of them to sort out what they owed while he accompanied Sparrow to see the Bagman; a meeting that could be very short — or one that could be very long.

Sparrow kept up a steady stream of conversation as they walked along the docks, with Cornwallis doing his best to ignore. He wasn't in the mood for polite chit-chat and Sparrow's warbling's had begun to get on his nerves, though he did manage to find a grin when he noticed that the birds had splattered Sparrow's hat. The little man walked on, oblivious to the speckled state of his head attire and continued to point out various ships and their intended destinations.

Mr Sparrow had a small two-seater hidden away in an Inn up by the bridge. No money changed hands when he retrieved it so it seemed likely that they had an agreement between them. Cornwallis was just about to ask when he realised that he wouldn't get an answer; instead, he slumped down in the seat, crossed his arms and stared silently up the road.

Cornwallis had to concede that Sparrow knew how to drive, he seemed to flow through the traffic with consummate ease, and when they got to the junction where Coggs had created mayhem, he just breezed through without even stopping. Dewdrop still stood there trying to direct traffic, still confusing everything with his vague signals, but not Sparrow; Sparrow didn't even blink.

Cornwallis supposed that they were heading for the Assembly at first, but now they had missed several turns that would have taken them there in just a few minutes. He looked at the calmly relaxed Sparrow who seemingly hadn't a care in the world; he just guided the horse with a barely perceptible flick of the wrist. Cornwallis began to wonder where on twearth they were going, when Mr Sparrow u-turned in the street and then went back the way they had just come, they seemed to pick up a little speed and he then began turning into side streets as they headed back towards the river.

Sparrow briefly turned his head to look at Cornwallis. 'Can't be too careful you know; we don't want any unwelcome interest in our movements.'

'No, of course not,' replied Cornwallis, with a degree of unease. Sparrow was concerned that they might be followed, and he had taken a long detour just to check it out.

When they eventually arrived at the Assembly, Sparrow turned down by the side of the big building and then out onto the embankment at the rear. A short ramp led down into the bowels of the building and the horse didn't even hesitate as they headed into the darkness. Lamps lit the way now and the close confines amplified the noise of the coach; after a few yards, they came off the ramp and into a coach park. Sparrow eased them into a parking spot and applied the brake. An old man immediately came out and begun to unhitch the horse. The smell told Cornwallis that there was stabling nearby; either that or someone had a very severe stomach problem.

Sparrow climbed down and indicated that Cornwallis should follow. They crossed the coach park and headed to a small door on the far side. Cornwallis took the opportunity to look at some of the vehicles parked up; some were sleek and nimble, built for speed and manoeuvrability, while some others were large and appeared heavy as though armoured. Most though were nondescript, plain coaches that would blend into the background. An array of carts and wagons looked like they were falling apart, but knocking into one, Cornwallis found that looks could be deceiving; it was as solid as a rock.

The door thumped shut behind them and Sparrow stood and waited. They were in a small room devoid of furniture with just a little window at the top of the wall and another door below it. After a couple of minutes, Cornwallis heard a click and that door swung open. Sparrow beckoned him forward and they walked through into a warm bright corridor. There were noises: bangs, scrapes, squeaks and a few raised voices coming from the various doors that lined the corridor. Cornwallis wanted to look in to find out what was going on, but Sparrow led them past all these and down to the far end. He opened a door and they entered a large reception room, sumptuously furnished with sofas and small coffee tables with a variety of newspapers and journals, and of course pot plants. A desk, covered with little personal mementos and more plants, placed in front of another door, was devoid of an occupant. Cornwallis surmised that he would shortly find out where that door led. Sparrow indicated that Cornwallis should sit down.

Cornwallis picked through the titles of some of the journals; Ladies View, Classic Carts, Collider Monthly, all weeks out of date, when the door opened and a pretty little girl walked in carrying a tray with some mugs and a pot.

'Good evening, Mr Cornwallis, Mr Sparrow,' she said brightly.

Mr Sparrow jumped up from his seat and smiled back broadly. 'And a good evening to you too, Miss Wren, can I help you with that?' he enquired hopefully.

'I can manage, but thank you all the same. It's coffee you drink, isn't it, Mr Cornwallis; black, no sugar?'

Cornwallis nodded that it was.

'Mr Sparrow likes his sweet, don't you, Mr Sparrow.'

'Just like you, Miss Wren, hot and sweet.'

'Mr Sparrow, please. What will Mr Cornwallis think?' and she giggled.

Cornwallis thought that he might like to vomit. Sparrow leered at Miss Wren with undisguised lust, but when he had looked at Rose he had been completely devoid of any emotion, and you just couldn't compare the two. He looked at him properly now he had taken off his hat and coat: a wiry individual about the same age as himself with very ordinary looks. A face that could fit in anywhere in any circumstances, or it could be instantly forgotten; which *he* desperately tried to do now as Sparrow perched himself on the corner of Miss Wren's desk and spoke to her in a soft voice. Cornwallis was thankful that he couldn't hear what he said to her as she grinned and grimaced along with it, and then he whispered something into her ear which resulted in big wide eyes and a very suggestive smile.

A bell sounded and straight away Sparrow got off the desk and hurried through the door. Miss Wren became all Miss prim and proper again, told him to stay sitting down, and then tried to look busy by scribbling in a book. This surprised him, as she must have been the only girl working in the Assembly at a desk;

and not the tea girl as he thought. After a few minutes, the door clicked open and Sparrow put his head through, he winked at Miss Wren and then beckoned to Cornwallis to come through.

The room was enormous. It stretched away with chairs and couches lining both walls and a hand woven rug, all of sixty feet, ran all the way along the floor to a massive oak desk at the far end of the room. Paintings lined the wall; portraits of past Wardens of Gornstock looked sternly down, whilst on the opposite wall there were landscapes of various ages depicting Gornstock as it grew. A line of lanterns, equally spaced along the walls, cast a warm glow on the whole; which went against what Cornwallis now felt.

Mr Sparrow walked down the centre of the rug and urged Cornwallis to follow; eventually they arrived at the desk and came to a halt. As they waited, the large leather chair began to slowly spin around, revealing the occupant. A slim skeletal looking man with a hairless dome, a small pair of spectacles, giving him a sinister look, and wearing a very well cut suit. He didn't smile as he leant back in the chair.

'Good evening, Mr Cornwallis. So good of you to come.'

'Did I have an option?' replied Cornwallis through thin lips.

'Not really,' came the honest reply. 'Now, would you be so kind as to tell me who you were following, and who left Gornstock on that ship?'

Cornwallis tried to take a few moments to think, unusually, from what he heard about the Bagman, he had come straight to the point with no verbal jousting, no beating about the bush, and no lulling into a false sense of security. 'Why do you want to know?' he replied, with a confidence that teetered on the edge; the Bagman did that to most people.

The Bagman's lips widened in a smile, but the eyes told a different story; they were like two shards of ice. 'Because, Mr

Cornwallis, I have a vested interest in the assignment you are currently undertaking. Let us be frank, it will make things an awful lot easier in the long term, and probably the short term too. Now, a burglary at Roland Goup's office started it all for you, however, for me it started some time before that. It had come to my attention that Abraham Dumchuck had made a big mistake, a very big mistake, involving his tax returns.'

Cornwallis' eyes widened at this, they had thought about the name of Dumchuck back in Goup's office, so it was his file that went missing.

'Yes, our Gornstock Bank's president. Now we heard about this mistake and took steps to seize the documents ourselves. At the time we decided to do it surreptitiously, as the sums mentioned were enormous, but unfortunately, our Mr Dooley, the Chief of the Treasury, didn't make a copy; he just sent the return back. So we had to retrieve it by placing one of our operatives into Goup's office, however, something unfortunate happened to her.

Cornwallis was shocked. 'You mean Eliza Knutt?'

Mr Hawk nodded. 'Yes, her real name, I may add, as we didn't have time to establish a proper background. Quite sad really, very sad; she was one of my better agents, a tragic coincidence to have that nasty thief there at the same time. Now, would you please answer my questions: the man with Kintersbury, and who did he put on that ship?'

Cornwallis sighed to himself. It wouldn't take much for the Bagman to find out anyway, and he had already been given another snippet of information. 'They put Goup on the ship, the other man is called Maxwell, a very nasty piece of work. He has something to do with Gornstock Trust and Holdings.'

'Thank you Mr Cornwallis.' He turned to Sparrow and steepled his fingers. 'Well, you know what to do, don't you, Mr

Sparrow?'

Sparrow smiled. 'I will order it done now, sir.'

Sparrow turned, caught Cornwallis' eye, and then marched back down the centre of the room. The Bagman flicked a button on his desk and the door at the end clicked open. Mr Sparrow pulled it and went through, as the door shut there was another click. Cornwallis furrowed his brow.

'Yes, Mr Cornwallis, the door is locked. Some people try to leave in a hurry for some reason; I couldn't begin to understand why.' He scrutinised Cornwallis for a few moments and came to a decision. 'Mr Sparrow will stop the ship some way down the river, so there will be no chance of a message coming back to Gornstock.' A yelp came from the reception and then a peel of laughter. 'Ah, Mr Sparrow and Miss Wren must be getting reacquainted, the young today, eh? Never miss an opportunity, do they?'

'Obviously not,' he answered indifferently. A thought crossed his mind. 'Does everybody have bird names?'

The Bagman smirked. 'For the moment, yes, though we might change it in due course, just for securities sake.'

'So, what do they call you? Bald eagle?' asked Cornwallis, putting an edge to his voice.

A flinty glint passed across the Bagman's eyes, and then quickly vanished. 'Tsk-tsk, Mr Cornwallis, there is no need for that. Actually, I'm Mr Hawk, so you weren't far away. Now take a seat, please.'

Cornwallis looked around. The closest chair was very low and a few feet away from the desk, but there were some dining chairs a little further down the room, so Cornwallis walked down, picked one up and returned, placing it directly in front of the desk. He sat down and crossed his legs.

'Interesting, Mr Cornwallis. Most people sit down on that

one,' he pointed to the low chair nearest to him. 'But not you, you are going to try to intimidate me. The next thing you plan to do is lean forward and put your arms on my desk, but it won't make any difference, except it'll probably hurt your shoulder, but full marks for trying.'

Cornwallis raised an eyebrow, because he was planning to do exactly that; and how did he learn about his painful shoulder? Of course, he mentally slapped his head, Sparrow.

'Word travels quickly, Mr Cornwallis,' he said to the unspoken question. 'Your little coming together with the coach was most unfortunate. Now then,' he continued, dismissing the subject. 'Why have I brought you here?' Mr Hawk leant back in the chair and smiled. 'That is what you are asking yourself; and you will be pleased to know it is because you are doing far better than I thought you would.'

Cornwallis noticed that his concern over Miss Knutt had disappeared. 'And what does that mean?'

'It means I'm not going to take this investigation away from you, however, there will be some conditions.'

'Hang on,' said Cornwallis, holding up a hand. 'I'm only involved because Radstock heard a rumour and happened to be at Scooters yard at the time, he apparently said that he didn't want the police involved with the investigation.'

'Yes, he did. Mr Radstock is a very good boy, you know; he does, and believes, everything we tell him. And before you ask, he is not one of us. We intended to let you investigate the burglary, letting you flounder about, trying to find the perpetrator, which of course, you would never have done, and we would then have known what Dumchuck was up to. Also, we didn't want the police to go through Mr Goup's files, because there are a few things there that need to be kept quiet. Radstock really enjoys thinking he knows things others don't. Eliza, may the Gods bless her soul, was going to "find the burglary" and inform the police, and then Radstock was to be there to make sure you got the job. You got the job, but Eliza died and then you began to investigate a murder. It is unfortunate that the police now have the files at Scooters Yard; we thought you might put them somewhere else, so now we are going to have to retrieve them. We will have all the other evidence you have too; the handkerchief, the trousers and jacket, the rags for the attempted arson, the little matchbook, we will even take the pictures off your hands. Those are the conditions, I want all the evidence and all the information you have.'

'What if I refuse?'

'You won't, Mr Cornwallis, because if you do, you will be ruined.' The Bagman smiled without humour. 'I will make sure of that, and you know that I can. You are resourceful, Mr Cornwallis, your interest has been piqued, and you want to know how it all ends. I am giving you the chance to find out, but if you don't, then your career as an investigator will come to an end.'

Cornwallis felt deflated. 'Then I'm damned if I do and I'm damned if I don't.'

'I wouldn't put it quite like that. Just think of it as an opportunity.'

Cornwallis laughed ironically. 'Some opportunity.'

Mr Hawk swung in his chair. 'It could well be, Mr Cornwallis. Now, you can tell me what you know of this Maxwell and Kintersbury.'

Cornwallis tipped his head back and stared at the ceiling; he blew his cheeks out and then let the breath out slowly. 'Not much to tell, Maxwell has something to do with Gornstock Trust and Holdings and threatens people to get their money back. Kintersbury I don't know yet, he's only just come into the picture.'

Mr Hawk's eyes twitched momentarily and then he nodded. 'And how did you get to find out about Maxwell?'

Cornwallis noticed the twitch and for some reason felt the back of his neck tingle. 'When we were searching for the coach which took Goup away on the night of the murder, it led me to Brownlow and Son, a coach company down Woodlands. Maxwell forced Brownlow to lend him one of his coaches as he is having trouble paying back a loan; he threatened the family of the man if he didn't do as he was told. I also found the coach that tried to run me down in Brownlow's yard; that has something to do with Maxwell too.'

'That's interesting. Did you know that Kintersbury bought Gornstock Trust and Holdings some eighteen months ago?'

Cornwallis shook his head. 'No, I didn't.'

'And that he's been buying up all the personal and small business debts from the bank since then?'

'I didn't know that too. It sounds like he's being very heavy handed in getting the money back.'

Mr Hawk leant back in his chair. 'You mean like Brownlow? Yes of course, collateral damage, I'm afraid, generally sound business sense. Sometimes the company oversteps the mark, I'll agree, but as it's helped the bank, and in turn the city, that has been overlooked.'

Collateral damage? thought Cornwallis; like everyone else, the Bagman doesn't worry about the little people. 'Drugs are involved too; the dwarf tunnels have a pile of drugs and it's too much of a coincidence that Maxwell and Kintersbury have just started to use those tunnels, presumably they were brought in by that ship, so it would seem that they are dealing in them.'

'That's Kintersbury's ship. The drugs may be a sideline, or if big enough, financing.'

'Kintersbury is a rich man. The drugs are big enough, I

assure you; send one of your men down to look.'

'I might well do that, Mr Cornwallis.'

The pair regarded each other for a while as if weighing up everything they'd heard; at least Cornwallis assumed that, because he was doing a little weighing up himself. He had kept back the knowledge that the handkerchief and the matchbook tied Kintersbury to the scene, and he also decided not to say anything at the moment of his suspicions that Maxwell had killed Freddie, who had killed his Miss Knutt. He was just wondering if the Bagman knew all that when Mr Hawk cleared his throat.

'I think our little discussion has come to an end, Mr Cornwallis. Can you think of anything else that might be of some interest to me?'

'No, I think you have the lot.'

'And what a lot it is. Remember, Mr Cornwallis, your future rides on this. Find out what is going on, for your own sake.'

Like the morning sun, it dawned on Cornwallis that if it all went wrong, then the Bagman would lay the blame squarely on his shoulders. It made him feel angry just to think about it. The Bagman has all the resources there is, teams of people and equipment, but he wasn't putting any of them at his disposal. He was being threatened, oh, in a polite kind of way, but a threat nonetheless. The more he thought about it the more furious he became. The Bagman seemed to notice as his face broke out in a condescending all-knowing grin. Cornwallis felt like he wanted to explode; he stood up angrily, placed both arms on the table, and leant forward. Mr Hawk retreated just an inch, but Cornwallis noticed, he seemed to notice it all now, and he desperately wanted to say something, wanted to threaten the Bagman, wanted to make the Bagman frightened of him; but the words wouldn't come. He stared hard as he fought his temper and finally he slapped the desk and turned, then marched back down the centre of the rug and wrenched at the door. It wouldn't open.

'We will keep in touch,' said the Bagman from afar. 'We will keep in touch.'

The door clicked, and Cornwallis finally managed to drag the door open. He strode through and Mr Sparrow and Miss Wren stopped talking mid flow. Cornwallis shot them both a look and then walked across to crash the door into the next room too. Mr Sparrow hurried after Cornwallis as he strode down the corridor, he could see how angry Cornwallis was, so didn't even bother trying to open a conversation. At the end of the corridor Mr Sparrow leapt in front and opened the door, he then guided Cornwallis through the coach park and out into the evening sun.

'I will come and see you very shortly, Mr Cornwallis,' said Mr Sparrow, by way of parting.

Cornwallis turned and fixed him with a flinty look before spinning around again and marching off. Mr Sparrow let out his breath like a deflating balloon.

Mr Hawk looked up as Mr Sparrow sat down. 'Well?' he enquired.

'Very, very angry,' replied Mr Sparrow.

'Good, we need him to be angry. I think we've given him enough to get on with now; we've pointed him in the direction of Dumchuck, so that should be sufficient for him to get his teeth into it all. I just wish we could have got hold of those documents at Goup's though, it would have made things so much simpler, Mr Sparrow.'

'Yes, sir, I quite agree. Do you want me to follow Cornwallis again?'

'No, he knows you now. We'll get Mr Magpie to go

snooping around instead.'

Cornwallis' temper slowly returned to normal as he stormed through the streets of Gornstock. The steps were getting lighter and slower as his shoulders began to relax; and then he began to think. He had seen the Bagman flinch, only at the end, but there had been a definite reaction there. He smiled to himself in triumph, the Bagman may not be quite as confident as he appeared.

They weren't at the office when he called in, so that must mean they had gone down to the Stoat. Dusk descended fast, with the long shadows melding into one great lump of dark. The street lamps were being lit as he made the short journey down to the pub. He felt much more like himself now, he could put it all into perspective; the Bagman was unsure of something.

Frankie and Rose sat outside minding their drinks when he entered the square, he noticed that they had thoughtfully provided one for him and they both looked up expectantly when he came over and sat down. He didn't say anything at first, just lifted the glass and downed it in one.

'Well? asked Rose, with an enquiring twitch of her head when he'd finished.

'Well, indeed,' replied Cornwallis, now grinning, 'I think another one of these is called for.'

'Not too many,' warned Frankie. 'We have to go and see Gerald, don't forget.'

'Oh bugger.' Cornwallis had forgotten; a request by Gerald is just as important as one from the Bagman. 'I'll just have one more while I fill you in, then the three of us can go to the Brews. Anything from Algernon?'

Frankie shook his head. 'Nothing so far, but he's still keeping his ears open.'

'Bugger,' said Cornwallis and then he spent the next half hour going through his interview with the Bagman.

He was desperate for another pint, but it wouldn't do to see Gerald with anything other than a clear head. When he dropped the name of Dumchuck, Frankie gave a low whistle; the whole investigation could be the downfall of a lot of important people, but Rose couldn't understand why the Bagman had let them continue if he had known all this.

'Because,' answered Cornwallis, and he had been thinking the same thing. 'Because he's not certain. I don't think he told me everything, but he said he'd ruin me if I stopped. You have to listen to threats like that from someone like him. He wouldn't do it lightly, so that means there's something he can't get to — or someone.'

'So we have to find out who or what.'

Cornwallis nodded. 'For our own salvation, if nothing else. Right, let us go through everything again: Freddie the Weasel killed Eliza Knutt at Roland Goup's office, after she was put there to lift some papers belonging to Dumchuck. We saw Maxwell, who Gerald said killed Freddie, who also threatened Brownlow, and who, with Kintersbury, helped Roland Goup onto the ship; the same ship which is believed to be involved in drug smuggling. Now, are Kintersbury and Dumchuck working together, and where did Dumchuck get all the money in the tax return? Kintersbury owns Gornstock Trust and Holdings, who employs Maxwell. But at the moment, we only have evidence to lift Maxwell. The cat put Kintersbury at Goup's office, so we can surmise that Maxwell must have been there too; but Goup is only a witness, so Kintersbury hasn't done anything illegal.'

'He tried to torch the place,' interjected Frankie.

'Yes, but it would be the cat's word against his; and who out of the two of them is a member of the government?'

'Point taken.'

'The drugs are illegal, but we can't prove Kintersbury is involved with them, yet.'

'Gerald,' indicated Frankie, tapping the table. 'We can't keep him waiting.'

'No, you're right. Let's all think about it and we'll decide what to do in the morning.'

*

The Brews took on a different complexion during the night, the only light coming from the moon and the occasional weak candle glow seeping from a house. It was just as well really, because the squelchy stuff they were treading on didn't encourage discovery. Rose couldn't believe the poverty she saw, the children were still out and about and resembled feral creatures dressed in rags. They clung to her jacket, begging for money, for scraps, for anything at all, as she passed by. Arms like thin skeletal demons reached out of the darkness and sent shivers down her spine. The adults all stood in groups of twos and threes and watched without concern through their alcoholic mist. Occasionally they were followed, but a quick threat from Frankie generally did the trick and the followers melted away into the dark dank passageways. A scream began from somewhere behind and echoed all the way through the streets and passed them by before ending far ahead in a gentle sigh. Rose edged towards Cornwallis until she welded herself to his side.

'If you stay being an investigator you are going to have to come in here quite a lot,' said Cornwallis quietly. 'Outsiders don't last very long in here, and yes, I know you can look after yourself, but this is the Brews; it's everybody's worst nightmare. It's just as well we're seeing Gerald, he can put the word out that you're not to be touched.'

Rose didn't argue; she had never been so scared in her life.

They went down a few more alleys, past several Brew Houses and through a wide square where thin emaciated women were touting for business; the nature of the business being quite plain from the grunts emanating from the alleys that ran off to the side. Eventually they came to a large tall house that backed onto the river. Outside were several of the inhabitants drinking and playing dice. They waited until a couple of the men looked up and noticed them standing there, and then one of them grinned evilly through a rotten set of teeth. Frankie stepped towards him so he could be recognised, and with a nod of acknowledgement, the man lurched to the side to create a little gap for them to walk through. Cornwallis held on to Rose's arm as he guided her past the men. She looked at all of them in turn and saw from the returned scrutiny, that if it wasn't for Frankie and Cornwallis, she would be anything but safe. Frankie pushed at the door and it scraped open. He then stood aside as Rose and Cornwallis went past and then turned back to the men and leant forward to speak quietly into one of the men's ears. The man nodded and said something in return. Frankie's mouth opened, but then he shut it quickly before patting him on the back.

'They'll keep an eye out,' he informed Cornwallis as he pushed the door closed. 'Apparently, we're already being followed.'

Cornwallis nodded. 'That'll be Sparrow, I expect.'

'This place was bad enough during the day,' observed Rose soberly. 'But at night it takes on a whole different persona. Just how do people live here?'

'They have no choice,' replied Cornwallis easily. 'But they're used to it, it holds little fear for them as they know and understand the rules. In actual fact, to most of them it's the safest place in the world, except if you go against the rules.'

They were in a large bright vestibule with a winding staircase reaching up, it was clean and tidy and strangely aromatic. Cornwallis led the way up the stairs closely followed by Rose and Frankie. The guard at the top of the first flight nodded and indicated that they could proceed through the double doors into a comfortable lounge-type room. They waited for a few moments in the opulence, the thick expensive carpet underfoot, the luxurious sofas, the paintings on the walls; a total contrast to the area that they were in. A door opened on the far side and a dapper looking man beckoned them through.

'Here we go again,' muttered Frankie wryly.

Rose looked askance at him, her mind already a jumble of confusion made worse by Frankie's quiet mumbling. She felt Cornwallis' hand on her back as he took a step forward, and with a strange reluctance, she joined him.

The door led into semi-darkness with a thin flickering light from just a couple of candles in sconces on the wall. Another opulent room, but this one smelt a little musty. The deep red carpet had a pattern of stars amongst a geometrical design, and standing on it, a highly polished large rectangular table, with ten chairs around it. Silently they walked forward, and Rose saw at the end of the room an enormous gilded chair set on a little platform. In front of it, a half-circle of big comfortable arm chairs coming from an age long ago. Cornwallis urged her on until they came to stand in front of the big gilded chair, and then the dapper man smiled and indicated that they could sit.

'Why we have to go through all this, I don't know?' groaned Frankie. 'I were here just a while ago, it's not as we need to be dramatic every time.'

'Rose hasn't been here before,' replied Cornwallis. 'I expect this is for her benefit. Gerald likes to create an impression, don't forget.'

'Yeah, but all the same...'

A lot of muffled swearing came from behind the gilded chair, interrupting Frankie. Rose craned her neck and noticed that the wallpaper billowed, in fact, it wasn't a wall at all, but a curtain, and it looked like someone was struggling to find the gap.

'Oh, this is just great,' moaned the curtain. 'What pillock did it this time, eh?'

The dapper looking man stood there wide eyed for a couple of moments and then dived behind the chair in order to help.

'Was it you, Crinning?' said the voice, when the man drew the curtain aside. 'I specifically said to put the gap on the sodding line. If I wanted you to put the sodding thing to the side, I would 'a said put the sodding thing to the side. I wanted it there.' A stamp of a foot indicated where precisely the gap should have been. 'All right, just go and get the coffee, see if yer can get that right.'

The man disappeared behind the curtain and a few moments passed, then a grinning face suddenly emerged through the now properly positioned flap. This face belonged to someone else, a small tidy looking man with salt and pepper hair. He wore a dark suit covered in sparkly little buttons, with a white cravat tied around his neck and he carried a hat in his hand, which also sparkled. He had a cheeky face full of mischief which carried an ever present smile. 'Evening Cornwallis, Frankie, an' this must be the delectable Miss Morant, if I'm not mistaken.'

'Evening Gerald,' returned Cornwallis with a smile. 'It

seems to me that not all went according to plan.'

'Staff,' replied Gerald. 'Who'd 'ave the buggers?' He looked at Rose and winked, before going forward and taking her hand in his. 'Not one of my best entrances, my ducks, it normally works much better 'an that.'

'Really?' replied Rose, smiling.

'Oh yes, I've 'ad some nearly cack 'emselves.' He let go of Rose's hand and turned to go and sit on his chair. 'Lights,' he yelled.

Suddenly the room lit up, bright as day. Rose turned around and saw lanterns swivelling from their hidden compartments, snapping as they found their fixture. Gerald seemed to be pleased that at least something worked to plan.

'Well, Cornwallis, yer Brownlow family. Put 'em up safe we did, 'ere in the Brews, nice gaff as well. We 'ad a bit o'problem wiv the watchers though. There were two, but we did fer 'em, so's there's two less now.'

Cornwallis raised an eyebrow.

'Crinning will tell you where on yer way out. Yeah, nasty bit o'work you've picked up there.'

'Thanks, Gerald. Frankie told me what you know about Maxwell, and you're right, he isn't very nice.'

'Did you know you've been followed 'ere too?'

Cornwallis nodded. 'I expect a Mr Sparrow; works for the Bagman.'

Gerald shook his head and corrected him. 'A Mr Magpie in fact, who works for the Bagman. There is also a Mr Scrivey, who don't work for the Bagman, 'e works for your Mr Maxwell, or 'e did until a few moments ago.' He turned to Rose and mimed a hand cutting his throat. 'Keeps on at this rate an' 'e ain't going to 'ave anyone left to work fer 'im.'

Rose's eyes widened in shock.

'Um,' began Cornwallis hesitantly, equally shocked, 'er, thanks.'

'No need to thank me, Cornwallis, just keeping the place tidy. Anyway, 'e was one of 'em 'o did fer Freddie the Weasel.' Gerald smiled again, pleased at the reaction. 'Now, where the hell is that coffee? Crinning,' he yelled.

Crinning appeared with a tray and another flunkey came behind carrying a small table. The man put the table down and the tray went on top. Gerald rubbed his hands together and then began to offer each of them a mug. Cornwallis took a few moments to get himself together after the revelation — would it have been another attempt on his life?

'Now,' said Gerald, settling back into his chair. 'Miss Morant, or can I calls yer Rose?'

Rose nodded that he could.

'Good. Word on the street is you is now working fer Cornwallis 'ere.'

Rose nodded again, not quite sure yet about Gerald; there was something not quite right.

'I suspects that 'e brought you 'ere to get to know me as yer needs to know the rules.'

'Er, yes. I think so.'

'Well, the rules is simple 'ereabouts. Yer don't mess with the Brews, yer don't go a thieving or a murdering wivout my say so; but yer can investigate all yer like, an' you can arrest if yer need to as well. No one will touch yer if yer keep to the rules, it's a case of you scratch my back an' I'll scratch yours. Cornwallis and me made up the rules so's that 'e could investigate freely, as there are some 'ere 'oo like to play away. To my mind, it's their lookout if they go a thieving or somesuch outside of 'ere. But inside the Brews, it's my business.'

'Sounds simple enough,' responded Rose, with a degree of

hesitation. There was still something about Gerald that she couldn't put her finger on. She looked across to Cornwallis and Frankie, but they just sipped at their mugs. 'Er, can I ask you something, um… Gerald?'

Gerald relaxed back, nodded that she could, and beamed. 'Of course yer can my darling, harsk away.'

She wasn't sure how to ask what she wanted to know, she just wished that Cornwallis had told her more about this man than he had; in any event, she'd started, and now she had to go through with it. 'Who are you?' she asked, quietly. 'I mean, I don't mean to be rude, but I'm struggling to come to terms with the fact that you rule here. You don't seem to be like the others.'

Gerald didn't turn a hair, he just laughed. 'Yer mean a little fella like me, 'ow can 'e control it all, eh?'

Cornwallis thought he'd better intervene. 'I'm sorry, Rose, but I haven't told you very much about Gerald; things seemed to get in the way. Gerald has some special talents— '

Gerald leant forward and held his hand up. 'Yer can stop right there, Cornwallis,' he said with a frown. 'It's only right that I answer 'er. After all, you've 'ad your chance.'

Cornwallis opened his mouth to say some more, but then thought better of it. He settled back into his chair and waited for Gerald to continue; in any event, both he and Frankie had gone through something very similar in the past, and it would be interesting to see how Rose reacted.

Gerald got up and stepped down, coming to stand in front of Rose. 'Up yer get, my girl, I 'ere's your pretty 'andy in a scrap. Now we'll see just 'ow 'andy.'

Rose looked across at Cornwallis who sighed. Frankie jabbed her in the ribs with his elbow and indicated that she should do as Gerald asked.

When she reluctantly stood up, she found she could look

down on the top of Gerald's head; he was even smaller than she had first thought, wiry, yes, but she knew she could do some serious damage to him if she really wanted to.

He looked up into her face and grinned. 'Come on then my girl, try an' knock seven colours o'shite outta me.'

'I'm not sure about this,' she said nervously, already regretting asking the question in the first place. Later on, she intended to really rip into Cornwallis for not saying anything about this man before. Something was going to happen to her, but she hadn't a clue what. 'Perhaps it would be better if we just leave it there.'

'Oh no, Rosie, my luv,' Gerald sprang back and began to dance about like a prize-fighter. 'Get stuck into me girl, come on, let rip, gimme yer best shot.' He sprang forward and shot a hand out to give a playful tap on her arm. 'Yer don't react, girl, I'm going to end up 'urting yer, come on, let an old man 'ave some fun.'

Rose closed her eyes; she couldn't back out now, she had to do as Gerald asked, even though she knew she wasn't going to win, she even suspected that he might be even quicker than her: she should have seen the signs well before this. She opened her eyes again and looked at him, fixing her gaze on his eyes as she tried to gauge his strength and speed. She knew that you could read a lot in the eyes, but she was disconcerted when she found that nothing came back; he appeared to have eyes that were empty, black depths of absolutely nothing. A shiver ran down her spine; and then she went for it.

'So, my girl, now's yer understand. Yes?' asked Gerald, once they had finished.

Rose found herself nodding. She now knew how this little man could control everything about him, how he could have the power of life and death in this slum; she was only grateful that he seemed content to keep it here and not attempt to control the whole city.

She had decided to get it all over with quickly, so let him move a little closer to her as he danced around. He tapped her once again on the arm, but this time as he recovered from the movement, she pounced, spinning around and flicking out with her foot while at the same time bringing her arm scything through the air, aiming for his neck. The feeling as she connected had been unreal; like hitting candyfloss, as if the air had suddenly become sticky and the force of her blows had become bogged down. Her movement had carried on slowly for a microsecond, and then her blows found normal air again and the momentum continued. She finished spinning and then stumbled, losing balance, expecting something to happen, but not this. She sort of lurched into Gerald, and then the feeling became more intense as his head disappeared into her chest as she flung her arms out wide to stop herself falling. She then felt him move through her, straight through her, and then out the other side. She fell to the floor as his body left hers and gasped in shock. She turned and looked up at him as he stood looking down; he was smiling, full of mischief again.

'Good try, Rosie my darling, nearly got me there.'

'Wha… wha… what happened?' she spluttered, totally confused now.

'Let's sit yer down and I'll tell yer,' he said, offering his hand to help her back up.

As she sat back down her hands began to shake, and she felt a rising nausea in her throat, but slowly, little by little, it all began to subside. Cornwallis and Frankie were grinning from ear to ear while Gerald sat motionless in his chair. She couldn't comprehend what had just happened, she must be dreaming, it just couldn't happen.

'Yer didn't 'urt yerself?' he asked, now a little concerned.

Rose shook her head; this all felt very, very, wrong. Yes, after that, she could understand how he could control everything, the question now was, how did it happen?

'It's a long story really,' he said, when he saw her looking back to normal. 'I used to be a very good burglar, back in the old days, an' I made quite a tidy sum. But I got curious one day, because rumour 'ad it that a lot o' money could be made at the Collider. So being daring an' all that, I decides to take a look. There weren't much in the way of security, as they didn't expect anyone to try an' get in. I sort of got through one of the vents that took the air into the building, an' I crawled through until I found the chamber that 'oused the Collider. It took some time, I can tell yer, an' a few wrong turns as well, but eventually I found it. An' do you know what?'

Rose didn't, so shook her head.

'There were nobody there, the whole place empty. No people, no guards, no keepers, no nobody. I thinks, I'm on to a good 'un 'ere, as I looked through the grate. I lifted it up an' dropped down, an' then the Collider were there in front of me, all these little desks an' toggles an' things, all lined up in front. It looked like a great big mirror, it did, but it sort of hummed, an' I goes up to it to take a look. It were the strangest thing yer could ever imagine, there were me looking back, but it weren't me, an' behind the other me, I could see loads o' people running. What's going on 'ere? I says to myself, an' I pushes a finger towards the Collider. The other me did the same, an' our fingers sort of touched. It went even weirder then as my hand got sort of drawn in; the next thing I knew, all o' me got sucked in, an' suddenly I were on the other side, an' I wasn't in the Collider anymore. I were in a strange looking street, an' all these people were running towards me. They didn't look too friendly like, so I wanted to get back. Fortunately, I still had a foot on this side, so I tries to back into it again. Just then, these people stops, an' one of them points a sort of pipe thing at me. Next thing I know the pipe thing explodes, it goes bang, just as I manage to get back again. I felt something 'it me, an' I thought, that's me gorn; I should've been dead, but I wasn't.'

Rose looked at Gerald in disbelief; she'd never heard a tale as strange as this. 'But how…?'

Gerald chuckled. 'Ow did I do that?' He sort of mimed going through a body and Rose nodded. 'It were explained a while later. I sort of noticed that I weren't the same anymore, a bit like a ghost, but not a ghost. Sometimes I were real an' other times I weren't. Just think what it felt like, not knowing what you is. I found I could pass through things when I wanted, but could be solid too, when I wanted. Weird didn't come close to 'ow I felt. So I harsked. Found a keeper willing to talk an' I harsks him some questions. 'E said that if someone did fall into the Collider then they would probably cease to exist; not so much die as not exist anymore, as yer would just disappear into yerself on the other side, sort of fall between the universes. But I didn't, I got back, an' 'e reckoned that if someone did that, then they was here an' between at the same time. That's why I can pass through things, an' why things pass through me — because sometimes, I ain't 'ere. Over time I've learnt to control it.'

'That's incredible,' exclaimed Rose; she looked to Cornwallis who just finished draining his mug. 'It beggars belief.'

'It does, but it's true enough,' said Frankie instead. 'Now you know why Gerald has so much power, it sort of makes it difficult to hurt him.'

'But what happened to the other you?' she asked.

'Don't rightly know, but I suspect that I died when that pipe thing went off. Whatever 'it me stung a bit, I can tell yer.'

Rose looked crest fallen, 'I find that very sad,' she said. It sort of made real the knowledge that there are countless you's out there, all having different things happen to them. Her mind spun with the possibilities, some of which she didn't really want to contemplate. All of them: living, breathing, walking, talking, doing all the things that she could do, all in the other worlds. How did her life measure up against theirs? 'Very sad,' she said again; and really meaning it.

CHAPTER 9

The events of last night were still having their effect on Rose as they sat in the office. All three were trying to think of a way of taking the investigation forward and they sat staring into space until one of them could come up with an idea. Rose couldn't help but let her mind stray back to what Gerald had described the night before, she felt somewhat depressed as she had been thinking of it all night and had hardly got a wink of sleep. Cornwallis and Frankie had not comprehended the enormity of it all, despite having known about Gerald for some time. They seemed to treat it as just something that had happened, something that really didn't affect either of them; perhaps as a female, she could think on a wider level to them. There were also many Cornwallis' and Frankie's out there too, so she turned her mind and wondered what would be happening to them.

'We do need to know more about Kintersbury and Dumchuck,' opined Frankie, after some thought, 'I mean, after what the Bagman told you, we really don't have an option.'

'Yes, but only if the Bagman told me the truth. I wouldn't put it past him at all to spread a few false leads,' replied Cornwallis, tapping his teeth with a pencil. 'We also need to keep a tab on Maxwell as well; carries on like this, then we're going to need a bigger department than the police.'

'Hmmm, Maxwell, now he's a bit of a thorn in our side. It seems like he has got a tab on us, if what Gerald said was true, which means he knows we are investigating. It strikes me as a good idea to do something about him before he can do something about us, the other two can wait a while. What do you think, Rose?' asked Frankie, turning his head towards her.

'Huh?' answered Rose, coming back to the reality she knew. 'Sorry, didn't hear you.'

Frankie grinned at Cornwallis. 'I said; should we do something about Maxwell, as he's the dangerous one.'

'You're asking me? I've only been here three days.'

'Three days? Is that all it is?' responded Cornwallis with surprise. 'Seems like you've been here forever.'

'Thanks,' replied Rose. 'I'm not sure how to take that.'

'In the best possible way, Rose,' said Cornwallis with a smile.

Rose pulled a face, not quite sure whether to believe him or not. 'In that case then, for what it's worth, I don't think we can do much if we're looking over our shoulders all the time. If Maxwell has his people following us everywhere then he'll know who we're talking to, besides, we know he's involved in murder because of what Gerald said, he could be our way to Kintersbury.'

'That's my girl,' said Frankie, banging his fist on the table. 'So that's two of us, Jack. What about you?'

Cornwallis looked from one to the other. 'I agree. Maxwell would be able to implicate Kintersbury if we exert the right amount of pressure. Perhaps we could get Algernon and some of his friends to keep an eye on Kintersbury and Dumchuck for us, while we deal with Maxwell. With Maxwell out of the way, it might panic the others into doing something stupid anyway. Suggestions then, how do we get him removed from the scene?'

They discussed the best way of getting Maxwell off their backs for the next hour or so. Frankie favoured ripping his head off and stuffing it up his own arse, but Cornwallis, although agreeing with the principle that this would be a fitting result, declined the suggestion on the grounds that it might take a bit of explaining; and how would he be able to talk? He favoured a more prosaic response, and despite Frankie's protestations, they finally settled on banging him up for the threats made to Brownlow and handling stolen property, leaving the little matter of the drugs and murder to later.

They now had the problem of finding a way to corner him so they could make the arrest. The obvious answer was to go down to the finance house and pick him up there, but he would be surrounded by his own men, and that might prove a problem without enough back up. They would instead have to get in a position so that they could follow him on one of his excursions away, and to do that effectively they would have to deal with the likely tail that they already had. They didn't know the Bagman's Mr Magpie, but they thought that if they were observant enough they should be able to spot him. Maxwell's man should be equally easy to spot, and they should be able to deal with him too.

It was now mid-morning. Cornwallis left the office to take a walk down to Scooters Yard while Frankie and Rose hung back to observe from the window for a short time. They could see nothing obvious, but Grantby Street was busy with both people and traffic. Failing to spot anyone, Rose left a few minutes after Cornwallis and followed the same route. Frankie would wait a few minutes more then come after her and Cornwallis. It wasn't a perfect plan, but it was the best they could do, the hope being that one of them should be able to pick out their man.

Cornwallis took a route that led through enough quiet streets to confuse whoever might be following; they wouldn't know his destination so they would have to keep in touch or risk losing him completely. He took up a nice steady slow pace, but found it very difficult not to keep looking behind, the urge to look, almost impossible to ignore. He would just have to trust to Rose and Frankie and hope that the route they'd chosen would give them the edge they needed.

Rose saw potential candidates everywhere. She kept latching on to people only to be disappointed when they turned into a coffee shop or delivered a parcel or met with a friend and dived into a bar. She didn't know the rules to this new game and she found it extraordinarily difficult to sort out the wheat from the chaff, and there were plenty of chaffs about. Her mind kept losing concentration as she gazed about; she had never noticed just how many young people there were on the streets just aimlessly wandering around, looking lost and bored. She passed little groups just chatting on street corners, young mothers with their child glued to their hips with half a roll-up dangling from their mouths. These were the real chaffs she thought; they could be whole new underclass of society. Ahead in the distance, she could see Cornwallis as he turned down a side street; there were a few people between him and her and she prayed that one of them would do the decent thing and turn after him. A couple of youngsters hurtled by, each on a homemade contraption of a board on a set of wheels. They were standing up and yelling at people to get out of the way; maliciously, she hoped they would fall off, it would serve them right to have a scrunched up face for a few days. A tingle of excitement ran down her back as a man hesitated at the corner where Cornwallis had turned, he had his hands in his pockets and he seemed to check his step before following after. He seemed to match what she supposed would be one of Maxwell's cronies, scruffy, large, shaven headed with a hint of violence. She felt certain that this was the one.

'Don't look at me and keep walking, there are another two

behind you,' said a voice at her side. 'Your other colleague behind has spotted them. I suggest you do a bit of window shopping for a minute so that he can catch up. Good day to you, Miss Morant.'

The man passed her by without even a glance; she couldn't even see his face as he stepped right in front of her as he headed off. She gradually slowed to a stop, her heart began to pound and she felt a degree of shock. What should she do? She quickly realised that if there were more following her then they would notice that she just stood there staring straight ahead; she decided that the warning came from Mr Magpie and it might be prudent to follow his advice. She saw out of the corner of her eye that she was next to a shop, so without even looking at what it sold stepped right into the doorway and looked into the window. It took a moment to realise that she now stared at a shop window selling seedy erotica; there were censored carvings and pictures and strange looking items, all intending to give some degree of enjoyment. Her eyes widened at the miniscule items of clothing designed, she supposed, for women, and some weird looking stuff, presumably for men. Then she noticed two men pass by the window and so she cast her gaze to the door, and saw a smiling woman looking back. She beckoned Rose to come in and began to open the door. Rose felt a panic grip her throat just as Frankie pulled on her arm and whipped her away.

'You are full of surprises, Rose; I wouldn't have put you down as a fetishist.'

'Frankly, Frankie, I'm not, thank you very much. I've met Mr Magpie and he told me that you might need some help. I had to do something, so I just stopped and I happened to be here.'

'Yeah, I believe you,' he chuckled. 'But you're right, I met him too and we have a couple of handy looking men to deal with. You can see them just ahead now, one with a green coat, the other grey.'

Rose recovered quickly. 'I can see them, but there was another one in front of me.'

'Really? That makes three of them; they're hunting in packs now.'

The two they were after turned down the street that Cornwallis had not long gone down, followed shortly after by Frankie and Rose. One of them looked behind and seemed to want to stop, but the other said something then pulled him along; then they yelled and broke into a run.

'Come on, Rose; let's see how fast you are.'

Their feet hammered on the pavement as they ran for all they were worth. The men up front slewed around a corner and shot off down another side street; Frankie and Rose were only a few yards behind them and already closing. A couple walking towards them arm-in-arm hurriedly backed out of the way, the woman noticed Rose and quickly covered her partner's eyes with her hands. Rose ran past and felt the woman's stern gaze, she wondered for a moment what she had done, and then she glanced down. Oh Gods, she thought. She could see now why the woman had covered the man's eyes; her chest bounced around like two footballs in a sack. She flicked her eyes to see if Frankie had noticed and then grabbed the offending articles to keep them still.

'Forget 'em, Rose,' yelled Frankie. 'No one's going to complain.'

Shit, he has seen them. She cast caution to the wind and let go. The two men were nearly in arm reach and then one of them took a chance and looked behind. A bad move on his part, because despite his attempt to get away, the sight of Rose and her appendages put him off his stride. He stumbled, and then grabbed hold of his mate to stop himself falling, but only succeeded in bringing him down too. They both fell headlong onto the road, tumbling end over end before coming to a stop against a wall.

Frankie and Rose skidded to a halt and leapt on top of the two men, pinning them to the ground before they had a chance to recover. Frankie whipped out a pair of handcuffs and clapped them on with well-practised skill. Rose struggled with hers, until Frankie, seeing she had problems, helped out. 'Would you prefer if I went and got some padded ones from that shop back there?' he puffed, gleefully. 'Won't take me long.'

'Frankie,' gasped Rose, 'You can just sod off.'

'Yeah, Frankie, do as the lady says,' said one of the men menacingly, as he turned over. 'You've just made a big mistake; you got no chance of… umph!'

'Oh sorry,' scowled Frankie. 'My elbow must have slipped.'

Cornwallis appeared shortly after with the third man in cuffs; he explained that he'd heard a yell and had turned around to see a man pull a knife out, then another man came running up, and as he passed, he'd whacked this one on the head, and then shot off. It was just a matter then of clapping the cuffs on the semi-conscious assailant and coming back to find out what was going on. Mr Magpie, Cornwallis assumed, appeared to be keeping a very close watch on everything.

Cornwallis, Frankie and Rose had one apiece as they marched their complaining captives down the road towards Scooters Yard. It was a shame that Maxwell wasn't one of the three but at least they had a bit more breathing space for a while. The Yard wasn't far, and shortly they marched them into the reception area.

'Bed and board for three please,' said Cornwallis, relieved to see Wiggins and not Grinde leaning over from the vantage point.

'Good morning, Mr Cornwallis,' replied Wiggins. 'But it will be floor and board in this hotel. What charge please, for the record?'

'Assault with a deadly weapon, to start with, and I'm sure we can find a few more things of interest when we have a proper word with them.'

'Assault, eh? Whom, may I ask, were the victim?'

'Me, Constab… I mean Sergeant Wiggins, it was me.'

When they had safely deposited the three men in custody, Cornwallis, Frankie and Rose took a few moments respite before going to find Maxwell. They had spoken at length to the three individuals, and one of them had let slip that Maxwell had business at the warehouse. They were also curious as to MacGillicudy's fate, but no word had yet filtered down from Bough: the two were still suspended and awaiting judgement. They sat in the canteen drinking coffee and a grinning Frankie described Rose's two unfortunate occurrences, much to her discomfiture.

'Look,' she explained, 'I stopped at the shop as a result of Mr Magpie's warning that you, Frankie, might need some help, and the second is just something I can't do anything about. It's just typical that you pick up on anything remotely sexual just to have a bit of fun at my expense. What you would you feel like if I spent all day staring at your groin, eh?' She held up her hand. 'No, stop, don't answer that one.'

'I'm sorry, Rose,' said Frankie. 'But you have to admit that matey boy wouldn't have fallen if your…' He tried to find the appropriate words. 'Your, you know what's, weren't bouncing around. It was poetic really.'

'Come on, children,' interjected Cornwallis, 'let's be adults please.'

Rose turned on him. 'Adults? That's a fine thing coming from you. The other night you were virtually talking to these things before I managed to drag your eyes away. Now I'm working with you, I expected a little more respect, if you please.'

Frankie and Cornwallis were both speechless, they looked at each other for some help, but Rose had the bit between her teeth, her eyes showing her anger.

'That's it. I'm going back to my uncle's. I'm finished with you two. I thought you were different, but I couldn't have been more wrong.' She stood up and began striding through the canteen, scattering chairs and feelers in equal measure.

'Quick, Jack, get after her,' cried Frankie. 'We can't let her go like this.'

Rose had already gone through the door by the time Cornwallis got to his feet. He thought he would be able to stop her at the front desk, but she had breezed past and got out just as Wiggins let someone through. By the time he had got through too, she was outside and marching away. He ran, for the first time in his life, he ran after a girl.

'Rose,' he yelled, not caring who heard. 'Rose, stop. We need to talk.' He knew she'd heard because he saw a slight hesitancy in her step, but she ignored his plaintive cry and carried on. He ran harder and caught up with her just as she turned into a park. 'Look, Rose. I'm sorry, we're both sorry; we meant no harm. We both thought that you were okay with the banter and would give back worse than you got.' He touched her shoulder and pulled back to bring her to a halt.

She stopped, and turned, and held her head up high. There were tears in her eyes and she sniffed sorrowfully. She stood like a statue for a few moments and then let her shoulders droop; she then sort of crumpled against him. 'No, I'm the one who should be sorry,' she said eventually. 'I thought I was stronger than I am.'

'You are strong,' replied Cornwallis. 'Come on, let's sit

down.'

They moved over to a bench and sat down; he put his arm protectively around her shoulders and she leant against him, taking a few deep breaths.

'It's not the banter that got to me, Jack. I was scared. When that Mr Magpie told me there were two men behind me, I froze; I didn't know what to do. Then I felt Frankie pull me out and he showed me the two men who just went past, and I just wanted to hide. Instead, we had to run after them, and I kept thinking, is this it; are they going to turn and run us through? I didn't have a problem the other day with Snodgrass because I had control. In the Brews when we found Freddie the Weasel, I had control again. Just now? I wasn't in control, even though we were chasing. I know you told me it could be dangerous doing this, but I've only just now realised how right you were. Maybe I should go back to being a serving girl.'

'Never, you're part of the team now. We all have to go through the scary bit. I have, Frankie has. It's just something that you have to go through. You need to experience it and then come out the other side. Once you've done it once, I can assure you it gets easier.'

'What happens if it doesn't? What happens if I freeze again? I'd be letting you both down.'

'You won't. I've learnt a little about you over the last few days, and I can say without a shadow of doubt that you won't. And if you agree to carry on with us, I promise that both me and Frankie will stop the banter, we'll treat you just like another man. How's that for you?'

Rose sniffed and smiled. 'No you bloody won't. Do you think I want to be treated like a man? I've spent my life using what I've got and I'm not going to stop now. Yes, Jack, I know how I look, and I know what reaction I'm going to get. But I'm used to it, and I intend to stay being used to it.'

Cornwallis breathed a sigh of relief, they'd come through the crisis; he had thought for a moment that he had lost her, but now she was right back where she belonged. 'We had better go and find Frankie then, and then we have to find Maxwell. You can go back to the office if you want and wait there. The two of us can deal with Maxwell.'

'No chance, I'm coming too,' she replied defiantly. 'You ain't getting out of it that easily.'

They found Frankie waiting outside the Yard; he paced up and down and looked for all intents and purposes like an expectant father. He stopped when he saw them appear, and Cornwallis could see the relief in his face. Rose bit her bottom lip as they approached; she then skipped up to him and planted a kiss on his cheek.

'That's to say sorry,' she explained meekly. 'I was a naughty girl who deserves to be put across your knee.'

Frankie's face broke into the biggest smile ever. 'Ah, we've got our Rose back. Right, now where's a chair?'

She smiled and then playfully patted his arm.

'Right you two,' said Cornwallis grinning. 'We have work to do. We have a nasty little man to go and find, but first we need to see Algernon.'

When the cab dropped them off by the bridge, Cornwallis led them down the slope and onto the north shore docks. The scene was much like the day before, with all the activity associated with a busy port. The ships moored up alongside the wharves were a hive of activity with workers rushing around. The fishing fleet were in and they had docked further down on the north side, and the sight of them reminded Cornwallis that they owed two boxes to the cat; but under the present circumstances the cat could wait, Maxwell came first, and if they had time after, he would allow Frankie an opportunity to get reacquainted with his favourite fish-gutterer. Algernon had been given details of the task required and had hurried off to recruit some friends; Cornwallis had promised now to relieve him of his hairdressing enterprise, provided he proved satisfactory in this little piece of work.

'Did anyone notice if we were being followed?' asked Cornwallis, turning around and looking back up the slope. 'I suspect this Mr Magpie will be around somewhere, but try as I might, I haven't been able to spot him.'

'Can't say that I have, Jack,' replied Frankie, 'and I've been looking too.'

'Does it really matter if he is around?' asked Rose. 'He's meant to be on our side, after all.'

'Mr Magpie,' replied Cornwallis, 'is on the Bagman's side, not ours. If his objectives coincide with ours, then yes, but if they diverge at all, then no. Besides, I feel a little uncomfortable with the fact that we know someone is following us but can't spot them. Maxwell's men were easy, but this one is proving to be a bit more difficult.'

They turned back around and began to saunter off with Cornwallis deep in thought; the task now, to find Maxwell, if indeed he was here. They had the advantage, for the moment, having disposed of his men, but they needed to make full use of it. Another thought rushed into Cornwallis' mind, the King of the Dwarfs, somehow he would have to find the time to go and speak with him; but everything seemed to be gathering pace, and if he's not careful, it could all over-run him. One thing always seems to lead to another in quick succession, everything half done, nothing fully resolved. Tie it all up later, he thought to himself, one thing at a time, that's all you can do in this game.

When they got to the warehouse they decided to hang back for a while and observe; from what the Bagman had said there were now two warehouses to look at, the empty one with the drugs and Kintersbury's next door. Kintersbury's seemed to be quite busy, and even though the ship had sailed yesterday, there seemed to be a lot of activity with the coming and going of wagons. Kintersbury must be making a mint.

Maxwell didn't appear to be outside either of the warehouses, so he should be inside one of them, but which one? Cornwallis decided to search the disused one first. Yesterday they had just gone to the trapdoor and hadn't given it a proper look, today he would rectify that mistake and give it a thorough going over. One of them would have to stay outside and observe, while the other two went inside to search. Frankie wasn't happy, but agreed with the suggestion that he should be the one to keep an eye out.

'How long do I give yer?' asked Frankie. 'And what do you want me to do if Maxwell sticks his head out?'

'Half an hour should be enough in an empty warehouse, we're not going in the tunnels again,' replied Cornwallis. 'As to the second question, use your initiative, but don't do anything stupid... I'm talking to you, Frankie, aren't I? On second thoughts just come and get us.'

Frankie looked peeved. 'You certainly know how to wound a guy, don't you, Jack.'

Cornwallis grinned and slapped him on the back. 'Just don't want to lose you, Frankie.'

The pair of them hurried away and retraced their steps from yesterday. They went down the side of the warehouse to the little door and tried the handle, it opened just as easily and Cornwallis poked his head in to give it a quick scan. He couldn't see anyone, so he eased himself in, closely followed by Rose. The door closed behind them and they stood there a moment waiting for their eyes to adjust to the light.

'Seems the same,' observed Rose. 'Just a big empty shell. What do you expect to find?'

'I haven't a clue,' replied Cornwallis. 'But that far wall connects to Kintersbury's, so I think that that's a good place to start.'

They padded over to the far corner and began to walk along the wall; they could hear a lot of noise coming from the adjoining warehouse, but in here, it was eerily quiet. They walked quickly at first as there really wasn't much to see, just empty space right up to the roof, it was only when they got further along that they came across some offices to look into. There were plenty of footprints in the dust, as the floor hadn't been swept around there, but they couldn't tell who had made them and when. The likely explanation would be that MacGillicudy and the police had made them, but it wasn't wise to make assumptions just yet. The first three offices they came to were exactly the same, fading posters on the wall, a ripped calendar, a couple of old notes, and some broken old furniture; all no good to anyone. But the fourth office piqued their interest, being clean.

Cornwallis stood still and cast his eyes around. The floor had been swept, and a clear path ran all the way across the warehouse to the office with the trapdoor down to the dwarf tunnels; the same clean area that he had noticed the day before, he grinned to himself.

Rose too had noticed and was just about to point it out when Cornwallis put his finger to his lips.

'Shush,' he whispered, and then leant close to her ear. 'I think we may have found an entrance to next door.'

Rose nodded in agreement; she had been thinking the same.

She put her mouth close to his ear. 'But why are we whispering?'

'Just in case there is someone there who could hear us.'

Rose leant close again. 'Do you really think I would be daft enough to scream out loud and bang a bloody drum?'

Cornwallis jerked his head up suddenly and turned towards her; he mouthed the word "Sorry" and grinned awkwardly. Rose just raised her eyebrows and shook her head. The meaning left no room for misinterpretation.

They entered the office and began to examine the wooden wall which seemed intact and without adornment, except for a few old pins, but anything that had hung on them had long since gone. There were a couple of sconces on the side walls but nothing else. Rose stepped forward and began to look closely at the connecting wall.

Cornwallis stepped back and patiently let her look for a door. He felt relieved that she seemed back to normal now after the earlier outburst, he was worried for a time that she would change her mind and leave them, even up to a few minutes ago; and then came the indignation when he shushed her, and he felt the jolt of relief rush through him. He watched as she ran her fingers over the wall, her face full of intense concentration. She leant in closer and turned her head, feeling for a draught. He nodded to himself; she had worked all this out for herself.

Rose turned her head towards him and beckoned him over, 'Here,' she whispered. 'I can feel some air.' She pointed at the wall and indicated with her finger the line of the draught.

Cornwallis came close and checked; he could definitely feel something there. Their faces were almost touching, barely a hairs breadth between them and he could feel the warmth of her sweet breath on his face; a tingle of pleasure ran through him.

'Jack,' she said, very quietly.

'Yes?' he replied, equally quietly.

'I know we're friends and all that, but do you think you could take your hand off my arse.'

'Huh?' Cornwallis quickly whipped his hand away, not realising what he'd done. 'Oh, Gods, sorry.'

She shot him a sideways look, a half-smile playing on her lips. 'That's all right, but next time, wait for an invitation.'

They both stood back and Cornwallis coughed quietly. 'Er... perhaps we could, um... try one of the sconces, like the office with the trap door.'

Still grinning, Rose went over to the first and tried to pull it. Nothing happened. So she went across to the other and tried that, still nothing. She tried twisting it, pushing it, but still nothing. She went back over to the first again and tried everything there too, still nothing. She sighed, and Cornwallis came and tried too, still nothing.

Cornwallis looked closely at both sconces and noticed a little nodule at the base of one, so he shrugged his shoulders and flicked it. They heard a click, and his eyes opened wide. He grinned as he pulled the sconce again, and this time it gave. They heard another click, but this time it came from the wall. They both turned and saw a door shaped outline emerge.

Rose got there before Cornwallis and put her eye right up against the opening to have a look. She peered into an office and out through an open door into Kintersbury's warehouse where she could see lots of goods stacked in rows and rows. She could see men and a couple of bears busy loading various goods onto various wagons, presumably, getting ready for disbursement. Cornwallis tapped her on the shoulder, so she made way, letting him have a look too.

'I wonder if we can make use of this?' he said thoughtfully. 'If we could somehow get Maxwell to come over, then we might have a chance to grab him.'

'That's if he is in there,' responded Rose.

'Well, there's only one way to find out. Could you go and get Frankie while I have a think.'

Rose hurried off, leaving Cornwallis to activate his brain; she sneaked through the little door on the side of the warehouse and ran forward but stopped when she got to the wharf. Frankie, over on the far side, had not yet seen her, so she waited for a while until their eyes met and she beckoned him over.

'We've found a connecting door,' she informed him when he arrived. 'Come on, before he gets it into his head to do something without us.'

'Yeah, he's prone to that sort of thing,' replied Frankie. 'And I've just seen Maxwell walking around with a stack of paperwork.'

When they got back in the warehouse Rose was relieved to find Cornwallis still there, he hadn't tried anything without them and still seemed to be thinking. He looked up and nodded at Frankie.

'Maxwell is there,' said Frankie coming over. 'I saw him about a few minutes ago, disappeared back inside though.'

'Ah, good.'

'Yes, it is,' said Rose, 'and I've been thinking too. What if I went in and asked to see Maxwell and waited just here?' She indicated the office on the other side of the wall. 'When he came over you two could, well, surprise him, so to speak. I should think most of the workers are legitimate so they might not get suspicious.'

'No,' replied Cornwallis. 'I can't put you at risk. Me and Frankie will just go in and drag him off and hope for the best.'

'Oh come on, don't be so stupid. If you haven't thought up anything better than that, then my idea is the best, and you know it.'

'Maybe, but I don't want to risk you. Maxwell has probably had a description of you; he might even have seen you at the docks.'

'All the better then, it makes us even.'

Cornwallis made a bit of a mistake by hesitating, so Rose just smiled, took her jacket off and then let down her hair. She wore a loose shirt, so she tucked it tighter into her trousers then undid a couple of buttons, revealing a promise of things to come. The effect left Cornwallis and Frankie open-mouthed.

'That should do the trick.' She smiled and winked. 'Now, I'll go and ask a nice man if he can go and find Maxwell for me.'

She went through the connecting door before either Cornwallis or Frankie could say a thing, and grabbed a couple of bits of paper from the desk in front and shuffled them around; nobody had seen her yet, so she walked to the open door and stood there, looking bemused.

It didn't take long before a man wandered over; she thought he looked quite handsome in a rugged sort of way and hoped he wasn't one of Maxwell's henchmen. As he approached, she noticed that a lot of the other men had now noticed her too.

'Can I help you, Miss?' asked the man, smiling.

Rose smiled back. 'Oh, I do hope so. I'm looking for a Mr Maxwell as something seems to be wrong with my delivery.' She bent her head and shuffled the papers in her hand. 'I'm ever so sorry, but when I came in everybody seemed so busy and no one seemed to notice me.'

'Really?' The man seemed surprised. 'Well, my good fortune then. Mr Maxwell is over the other side, I'll escort you across and we can have a nice little chat as we go.'

'No, I don't want to get in the way. Could you ask him to come over for me, only I slipped and hurt my ankle, you see.'

'Oh no, that is unfortunate. Do you want me to have a look

for you? Maybe I could rub it better.' He smiled lecherously and then winked.

She bit her lip coyly, she could tell where his eyes were aimed, and it wasn't at her feet. 'Maybe after, I'd rather speak to Mr Maxwell first.' She breathed in deeply and it had its effect, this one was too easy.

The man's eyes lit up at his turn of luck. 'Don't go. I mean don't move away, I won't be long,' and with a last lingering look he rushed off to find Maxwell.

Rose found that she had become the centre of attention as all the eyes in the warehouse seemed to be turned to her, she had hoped for a reaction like this, and with the amount of people looking she felt sure that if it all went wrong then Maxwell would be limited in what he could do. Behind her, she could tell that Cornwallis and Frankie were now in the office, hiding, just behind the door.

'When you see Maxwell coming, tap your foot,' instructed Cornwallis behind her. 'Then walk in here. We'll grab him as soon as he comes in.'

Rose thought it best not to reply, so she put a hand behind her back and twitched her thumb in acknowledgement that she'd heard.

Cornwallis legs felt uncomfortable crouched down, and he supposed that Frankie probably felt the same. They had been waiting for a while now, and the pain behind the knees began to indicate its presence; it had got to that exquisite stage, where it took a great deal of conscious effort not to move. Frankie began to shuffle a little, and Cornwallis opposite, gave him a warning glance.

Rose watched and waited with an ever increasing anxiety; she could feel her heart beating faster, and then it nearly missed a beat as she saw Maxwell emerge from between the rows

231

together with the man who went off to look for him. She tapped her foot as she watched them approach. He looked even more brutish close up than when she had seen him through the periscope, and she thought that perhaps they had bitten off a little more than they could chew. She took a few steps backwards, still keeping Maxwell in her view, until she felt the rim of the desk on the back of her legs. As he came closer she saw the look of recognition dawn on his face, and a smile played on his lips; but the smile was not a pleasant smile at all. He stopped briefly and then sent the man with him away; who cast a last look of longing and disappointment as he trudged back to work. She swallowed, desperate to look down at Cornwallis for reassurance, but sense got hold of her and she kept her eyes firmly fixed ahead. Maxwell continued forward and came to a stop just beyond the door and stood there, regarding her with his gimlet eyes, staring at her, undressing her, and she stifled the shiver that shot down her spine. Maybe playing the vamp was not such a good idea after all.

'You're Cornwallis' tart, aren't you?' The voice matched his persona, harsh, grating, with a hint of menace. 'What's he sent you here for then, eh? Has he lost his bottle?'

Rose felt the shiver return. 'I don't know what you mean, who's Cornwallis?'

Maxwell's smile widened. 'Don't take me for a fool, girl. I've heard all about you. You're here, which means he's been looking for me; his enquiries have made a return at long last. I reckon he's behind the hidden door there that you left slightly open, should think he's waiting until I come in and then he'll spring out, am I right?'

'No,' she replied in all honesty.

Maxwell laughed mirthlessly. 'Well, even if he isn't, I won't take the chance. Turn around girl and push it closed, and then push the desk right up against it.'

Rose hesitated for a moment and then did as he asked. Somehow, she succeeded in not looking at Cornwallis and Frankie, despite the overwhelming urge. When she'd closed the door, she turned back around and stood waiting.

'That's better,' said Maxwell. 'Now you and I can have a little fun, no prying eyes, you see. You can tell me what you want, and then I will tell you what I want, and seeing as you've already got everything hanging out, I think that what I want is pretty obvious.' He stepped forward and pulled the door to as he went through.

Frankie moved first. As the door closed he launched himself upright with his fist bunched and aimed at Maxwell's jaw, Cornwallis moved a split second later and went to wrap his arm around the throat. Frankie's blow made a sick crunching sound as the slack lower jaw met the solid upper and sent the head whipping back, Cornwallis' arm snaked around the neck and then he threw a punch into the kidneys, just as Frankie let fly with his second blow to the side of the head. Maxwell grunted, and then collapsed in a heap on the floor.

'Oooh, that was easier than I thought,' remarked Frankie, looking down. 'I'd a thought he would've put up a bit more of a fight than that.'

'Well, I'm not complaining,' replied Cornwallis. 'The easier the better as far as I'm concerned. You all right, Rose?'

'Yes, thank you. What a horrible piece of shit he is, I've half a mind to cut his bollocks off for what he just said to me.'

'You can as far as I'm concerned, but we need to get him to the Yard; and if you've whipped his bollocks off it might make walking him a bit difficult.'

'Do it later,' suggested Frankie. 'You'll enjoy it more if he's conscious when you do it.'

Cornwallis pulled out a pair of cuffs and clapped them on, they weren't his normal ones as they were still at the Yard; these were an old pair that he had picked up when he left the cells, and he looked at them with a degree of distrust. 'I'm not sure about these you know, they look a bit rusty.'

'They should still do the trick though,' said Frankie. 'We'll just have to keep a good hold of him as well.'

Maxwell groaned, then someone knocked on the door and Cornwallis and Frankie froze.

'Are you okay, Mr Maxwell? asked the knockee, 'only I thought I heard voices.'

Maxwell groaned again and Cornwallis thought quickly, he beckoned Rose over and said quietly. 'Pant, and very loudly.'

Rose's eyes widened at the request, but Cornwallis urged her on. Frankie just grinned and then sat heavily onto Maxwell's back, which elicited an even louder groan. It suddenly dawned on Rose what they wanted her to do, so she began to pant rhythmically, and in time to Frankie's bouncing. It very nearly became too much for them all, as they could hear the person outside push up against the door in order to hear better. Maxwell groaned, Rose panted, and Cornwallis and Frankie dissolved into hysterics. With tears streaming down her face, Rose carried on for a couple of minutes longer, getting slowly louder and more desperate sounding. Frankie had got well into the rhythm now, and then Cornwallis decided to make things worse by playing the conductor. The crescendo approached at a pace, until Cornwallis indicated a last long note and both Frankie and Rose obliged.

In the silence that followed, they could only hear footsteps walking forlornly away from the outside of the door.

Rose, Cornwallis, and Frankie looked at each other, all three biting their lips as their shoulders shook. Frankie desperately waved his hand trying to get the other two to stop laughing, which largely proved unsuccessful. Quite a few minutes passed before some form of decorum returned and they could all speak properly.

'Oh, Gods,' remarked Cornwallis, wiping his eyes. 'That wasn't fair.'

'No, it wasn't,' replied Rose, grinning. 'Just think what his reputation will be now; you made it go on far too long.'

Frankie creased up again, but only for a few seconds. 'Oh Gods, I love this job,' he said at last.

As Maxwell began to regain consciousness, Frankie felt him begin to move beneath his knees; he clamped a hand quickly over the mouth to stifle any shouts that might come and then looked at Cornwallis. 'Search him, Jack, I bet he'll have a stack of weapons.'

Cornwallis found a knife, a cut-throat razor and a garrotte, which he thrust into his pockets. 'The door, we need to find the trigger mechanism,' he said, suddenly jumping up. 'It's going to be the sconces again. Come on, Rose, you that one, me this. Don't let go of the bastard, Frankie.'

It was one of the sconces, and Rose found the catch and the secret door clicked. Cornwallis pushed the desk out of the way and flung the door open wide, and then went to help Frankie drag Maxwell through. Once back in the deserted warehouse they shut the door and began to breathe a little more easily.

Maxwell lay on the floor and jerked around as he came fully to. 'Bastards,' he snarled. 'You're going to regret this; you've made some really powerful enemies now.'

'Yeah, right,' replied Frankie, wanting desperately to kick the shit out of him. 'As if we care what you say, a few nights banged up might let you find out who your friends really are.'

'Come on,' said Cornwallis. 'Let's get him away, you can carry on your friendly conversation later; down at the Yard.'

As they had cuffed Maxwell with his hands behind his back, Frankie and Cornwallis had trouble dragging him upright. He didn't help them much, using his weight to cause as much as a problem as he could, but finally, they got him to his feet and marched him across the warehouse to the little side door. Cornwallis looked around to Rose, motioning that perhaps it might be a good idea to sort out her shirt. She looked down and gave a little squeak of horror at what she showed; with everything that had been happening she hadn't noticed that another few buttons had come undone. Quickly she covered up, making herself respectable once more, with Maxwell watching with undisguised lust.

Rose led them out and down the side of the warehouse into all the activity on the wharf.

'It ain't going to make a blind bit of difference if you yell and shout,' warned Cornwallis to Maxwell, as they stopped. 'You've been arrested, and even your friends next door won't be able to lift a finger to help. Do what you want, but all you'll do is show yourself up as the coward you really are.'

Maxwell turned his head and sneered at Cornwallis. 'You're going to be very dead, very soon, so make the most of your time left, because it ain't gonna last much longer.'

Cornwallis laughed at him. 'We'll see, Maxwell. You're just shouting hollow threats.'

They marched out onto the wharf and away from the warehouse and a few of the workers turned to look as the little group went by. Rose took the lead with the others coming on behind; keeping an eye out for a likely mode of transport that they could commandeer to get them to the Yard. Maxwell wasn't making it easy for them; he kept struggling and fighting, trying to get free. The workers blessed him with catcalls and jeers as they watched his vain attempts to resist arrest, then suddenly that changed into a collective sharp intake of breath. Cornwallis sensed that something had gone wrong just a split second before he felt a knee thump into his thigh. Frankie had sensed the change too, and found out why when a fist smacked into his face. Maxwell had broken free and bolted forward to the gasp of the onlookers.

Rose only realised that something was wrong when she felt an arm wrap tightly around her waist and heard the gasps of the crowd.

'Gotcha now, you little tart,' hissed Maxwell into her ear as he spun her around to face Cornwallis and Frankie.

Maxwell had hold of Rose: the cuffs had given way.

Cornwallis had been right to be worried about them but now it was too late. He limped a few steps forward cursing the dead leg he received.

'That's as far as you go, Cornwallis,' warned Maxwell, reaching down to his leg and whipping out a small four inch knife which Cornwallis had missed in the search. He held it to Rose's neck and pressed the point into the flesh. 'Time to negotiate, I reckon.'

A wide gap developed in the throng on the wharf, with just the four of them in the middle. A standoff now occurred and the audience waited with baited breath to see the outcome.

'No chance of negotiations, Maxwell, let her go,' ordered Cornwallis.

'Let her go? No way,' said Maxwell. 'She's coming with me as we have some unfinished business, ain't that right, my lovely?' He moved his hand upwards to give one a squeeze.

'Don't even think it, Maxwell,' warned Cornwallis. 'Because I promise you, I'll rip your head clean off your shoulders.'

Maxwell laughed. 'Too late for that, I'm already thinking it.'

'Then you're a dead man walking,' said Frankie menacingly.

Rose felt Maxwell's hand squeeze and tried to ignore the nausea sweeping over her; she had to keep her mind clear, be able to think quickly when the time came. She determined not to let Maxwell do what he wanted. His grip on her changed again and she felt a lessening of the pressure of the knife at her throat. Ahead she could see the anxiety on the faces of her two friends as they watched, powerless at the moment to do anything. She came to the conclusion that Cornwallis would try and negotiate after all, whatever he had said to Maxwell, and after all this, she wasn't going to allow that to happen. Maxwell won't be getting away with it.

The next few moments were going to live with Rose for the rest of her life. She closed her eyes and swallowed hard, waiting for her muscles to relax. Then without warning, she picked up her leg and stamped as hard as she could down Maxwell's shin, whilst at the same time striking upwards at the hand holding the knife. Maxwell yelled in pain as his leg burned in agony, but he hardly had time to register that his hand had been pushed away when Rose whipped her elbow back into his ribs. He grunted and then let go as the blow knocked the wind right out of him. Rose spun around, and with Maxwell gasping for breath, she let fly at her preferred target with the toe of her boot. As her boot connected with Maxwell's bollocks, he cried out in pain and bent double, just as a cry of warning came from the audience. She turned to look and a crate came swinging towards her. She ducked, and felt the draught of air as it passed closely over her head, but Maxwell wasn't quite so lucky, as just as the crate came swinging by he began to straighten up. There came a thwack, and suddenly Maxwell disappeared backwards in a graceful somersault over the edge of the wharf towards the mast of a small boat. Maxwell flew upside down towards it, hitting the mast and making the boat lurch sideways. As his stomach smacked against the mast his legs curled around it; and then everybody on the wharf watched as he slid down the mast and out of sight.

They heard a crash and a splintering of wood, and Rose, Cornwallis and Frankie rushed to the side to look down. There, below they could see most of Maxwell, his head having smashed through what appeared to be the rotten bottom of the boat. Water poured in through the damage around Maxwell's neck and his feet jerked as they watched him pushing with his arms, trying to force his head out from the splintered wood.

'Hey, Chalkie, you gonna do something?' shouted a man.

Cornwallis turned to see a big polar bear loping towards them, he had his arms shaved and had tattoos in place of hair. He was the driver of the crane whose crate had just smacked Maxwell.

'Sorry about that,' he growled. 'Took me eye off it for a moment.' He leant over the side and gave a low whistle. 'Ooh, will you look at that.'

Chalkie jumped off the side and landed expertly on the boat. The jerking's of Maxwell had now slowed to an almost complete stop, and the boat had let in a great deal of water. Chalkie wrapped his arms around Maxwell's legs and tried to heave, but nothing happened, so he changed his grip to get a firmer hold just as the last twitch left Maxwell's body.

'Reckon you're too late now, the bastard's dead,' shouted another man, just along the wharf.

Chalkie looked up and sniffed defiance. He grabbed hold of Maxwell again and gave an almighty heave; and this time he felt something give a little. Chalkie licked his lips and heaved again and the water around Maxwell's neck began to bubble. Chalkie, feeling that once more should do it, used all the power he could muster. He heaved, and something gave way.

The crowd looking over the edge of the wharf heaved too. A few vomited as Chalkie held the result of his rescue up towards them; Maxwell dangled by a leg in the strong paw of the bear.

Then a wag shouted down. 'You left something behind, Chalkie,' and a peel of laughter rang out.

Chalkie looked down and his grin of success turned to a grimace of disgust. 'Oh, bloody hell!' he whined, as the river turned red.

'That's sodding torn it,' observed Frankie wryly. Maxwell dangled, well most of him dangled, that is. His head had parted company with his body and now it settled in the slime at the bottom of the river. 'You still want to talk to him, Jack?'

CHAPTER 10

The feelers arrived to sort out the mess, in the guise of a sergeant and two constables. Cornwallis' face broke into a grin when he saw that one of them was Dewdrop. They arrived with a cart to transport the body of Maxwell and a reluctant Dewdrop looked down onto the headless corpse lying at the edge of the wharf.

'Where's the top end?' he asked with a grimace of distaste. He looked up and then saw Cornwallis, Frankie, and Rose standing in the row of onlookers. 'Oh,' he exclaimed in embarrassment.

'Well, if it isn't the Lord Cecil Toopins,' said Frankie grinning. He then turned to Cornwallis and asked. 'Have you by chance met his Lordship?'

Rose rolled her eyes; for some reason she knew what was coming, but even so, she found it hard to suppress the smile.

'I must admit that I haven't,' replied Cornwallis conversationally. 'I have met a Constable called Toopins though, are they one and the same?'

'They are indeed; I would have thought you would have known all about him as you nobby types tend to stick together.'

'But I'm only an Honourable, you see, a Lord outranks me.'

The sergeant and the other constable looked askance at Dewdrop as they listened to the exchange, the implication being that the whole station would be hearing about this.

The crowd of onlookers took its collective attention away

from the corpse and concentrated on the banter going back and forth between Frankie and Cornwallis as they mercilessly took the piss out of the hapless feeler.

'Does that mean that a Lord lives in a bigger house than you?'

'Well, he should have a family pile, or possibly even several.'

'Interesting. Excuse me, Lord Cecil, how are your piles?'

Dewdrop's face went crimson as the crowd laughed; there were about thirty of them in all, with three polar bears, a gorilla and an orangutan, all tough dock workers and all of them looking straight at him.

Rose found some sympathy in the end and stepped forward, trying to divert the attention away from Dewdrop and back to the corpse. 'Can you swim?' she asked, when she had unclamped her teeth from her bottom lip.

Dewdrop nodded.

'In that case,' she leant closer so that only he could hear. 'If I were you I would volunteer to dive in and retrieve the bit that's missing; and Cecil, when you lie in future, make sure that it's a lie that can never be found out.'

Dewdrop nodded again and stepped forward to the edge of the wharf to look down into the murky depths of the river, mulling over what he had just agreed to do. He swallowed hard, but it would better than listening to all that piss-taking.

'Constable Toopins has volunteered to go into the river to retrieve the head,' announced Rose, turning to face everybody. 'Now, let's see what help we can give him. First though, we need to get that boat out of the way.'

The sergeant and the other constable raised their eyes in surprise; this was turning into a really interesting day.

Rose's request turned into a kind of reflex action from the dockers as they gathered up the equipment they might need. A few ropes appeared and then a small row-boat splashed down on the river below. The arm of a crane swung gently over and a chain clanked down to dangle just above the sunken boat.

'Right now, Constable,' intoned the sergeant. 'I assure you that the Captain will hear about this; now get stripped off and could someone hand me that rope, we don't want another corpse on our hands, now do we?'

Dewdrop looked worriedly at the sergeant.

'Come on lad, hurry up, don't be shy. We're all lads together here.'

Dewdrop pointed at Rose. 'But she's not a lad, Sarge.'

The sergeant regarded Rose and sighed. He could imagine what might happen if he had to strip off in front of her, but as Dewdrop would be doing the stripping, then it didn't matter. 'No, but she don't count as a girl as she is an investigator. Take no notice of her, as I'm sure she'll take no notice of you.'

'Aw, Sarge.'

'Come on, lad, can't get police property wet, now can we?' the sergeant leant forward and whipped off Dewdrop's hat. 'Let's get going; we ain't got all day.'

Reluctantly, Dewdrop took off his jacket and then sort of hopped around as he tried to take off his boots. He eventually sat down on the mooring post and achieved his goal, two big toes stuck out of his threadbare socks and he then stood up as if ready.

'The rest of it, lad, shirt and kecks please.'

'Sarge,' wailed Dewdrop as if pleading for his life.

He couldn't get away with it; the sergeant wasn't going to let him. Chalkie, feeling a little guilty, but not guilty enough to dive in, came to stand behind Dewdrop to collect the clothes as he discarded them. The shirt came off next and a ripple of amusement ran through the crowd as the less than manly chest came into view.

'Could someone give the poor bastard a meal, the last time I saw ribs like that they were on my plate with a dose of sauce on them,' shouted one of the crowd.

Dewdrop turned his back while trying to cover himself with his arms. He cast a forlorn look to the sergeant who replied with a stern look of disapproval. Dewdrop sighed, and then began to remove his trousers. Two skinny stick-like legs appeared below a pair of very grey underpants. The crowd whooped in delight at the lad's suffering and someone shouted out, as someone had to with Chalkie standing there. 'Watch out lad, you have a bear behind!' The crowd laughed in response as the pale thin Dewdrop stood there trying to cover his lunch box.

Rose took hold of the rope and stepped forward to loop it around his middle.

'Nooo,' yelled Dewdrop, grabbing his bits even harder. 'You do it, Sarge — please.'

A smiling Rose handed the rope over and retreated a few steps; tempted, out of curiosity's sake, to try and have a peek at what he covered up, but she kindly ignored the devil on her shoulder.

Dewdrop dropped over the side of the wharf and clambered down the iron steps fixed to the wall to where the little row-boat bobbed up and down; he stepped in, and the boat moved away, over to the spot where the dinghy and Maxwell's head lay. He found just enough courage to climb over the side and then slide into the water. He looked up and saw a whole load of faces staring down. From somewhere he found a little more backbone and waved, before taking a big gulp of air and disappearing below the surface with the ends of the crane's chain in hand. The crowd hushed and waited expectantly as the ripples died away. About thirty seconds later, his head broke the surface and he trod water while he caught his breath, he gave the thumbs-up and held onto the boat as it moved over to the side. The crane took the strain and then began to lift. He had attached the hooks to the rails and as it broke the surface, the rails began to bend. With yells of encouragement, the crane's driver swung the thing over onto the wharf, and it was only just in time as the rails gave way and the dinghy crashed to the ground. The crowd cheered, and then everyone started pointing into the water. The row-boat came back, and to shouts of encouragement, Dewdrop slipped again into the water. He dived down three times, each time a failure and he surfaced panting from the effort. But he persevered and tried again as the crowd waited patiently. It seemed as if he was down an age this fourth time, and the crowd actually began to get anxious. But then something broke the surface: like an ethereal arm from one of the river Gods, a hand gripped Maxwell's head by the hair. Dewdrop knew how to play to the crowd despite his shortcomings. The young feeler's head came up shortly after, beaming with satisfaction. The crowd cheered, the sergeant threw a sack down and Maxwell's head disappeared inside the canvas.

The sergeant pulled on the rope to help Dewdrop as he swam to the steps and climbed up to a round of applause. The dripping Dewdrop stepped onto the wharf and found Rose standing in front of him, holding a bit of cloth for use as a towel, he reached forward for it but found he stared straight down the front of Rose's open necked shirt. He blinked, but his eyes wouldn't move. Then he realised that water did something to cloth, especially very thin underpants cloth, and he felt something begin to happen. Worriedly he looked down. In a way it was a mistake, because Rose couldn't help it either — she looked down too.

Cornwallis had a task to do in town, so he left Rose and Frankie at the wharf, agreeing to meet up later at the Stoat for a couple of pints, while he nipped back to the office to pick up a package before heading off.

The brown paper bag tucked beneath his arm contained the suit worn by Freddie the Weasel.

He still chuckled to himself at Dewdrops indiscretion as he pushed open the door and stepped through into the interior of Biggins and Shute, Cavel Row; considered the epitome of luxury tailoring with good quality coming at a price, and Biggins and Shute certainly charged a price.

Refined with quiet respectability, the tailor's had a plush carpet on the floor with scattered upholstered chairs around a few low tables for customers to relax while they waited. There was no counter, just a curtained door, which twitched aside, as an immaculately dressed assistant came out to greet him.

'Good afternoon, sir,' he intoned gravely. 'May I be of assistance?'

Cornwallis smiled, he hated the place and all it stood for, but his father used it and insisted that he did too; but he had to admit that when they made a suit, it stayed made. 'I do hope so. Mr Gillimot usually deals with me; I'm Jocelyn Cornwallis. You must be a new member of staff as I don't believe I have had the pleasure?'

'Indeed no, sir, I've been here this last six months, sir, and I believe you are right. I am Mr Ollivant. Mr Gillimot is indisposed at the present, sir, but if you will allow me, I will do what I can to help.' He smiled and tilted his head to the side.

Priggish jumped up little shite, thought Cornwallis, but returned the smile and said instead. 'Perhaps it might be better for me to wait for Mr Gillimot, nothing personal you understand, but continuity and all that?'

'And rightly so, sir. If you will excuse me I will just go and see how long he'll be.'

He dived back through the curtain with a graceful bow of the head and Cornwallis sighed; he wondered where they found these people, whether a tree grew somewhere that produced total stuck up knobheads like Ollivant. He could understand the wealthy and the titled having airs and graces, but Ollivant wasn't one of them; he imagined that he must have been bullied at school. Another thought crossed his mind though, and at this, he smiled to himself. What did Ollivant think of him? It was very probable that they had a common thought.

Frankie and Rose had gone off with two crates of fish for the cat while he decided that he'd better find out whose suit Freddie had been wearing before the Bagman came to collect. So after they had sorted out the headless corpse, they bought the fish and had parted company until later.

As he waited, Cornwallis mulled over the unfortunate event of their afternoon's endeavours; he really could have done with speaking to Maxwell at length. Though he doubted that Maxwell would have been forthcoming, he might have let something slip. The sight of his headless corpse dangling from the bear's paw, which looked a bit like a trophy hunters painting in reverse, was going to be the talk of the docks for months to come.

Maxwell's demise must throw a spanner into the works for Kintersbury. Would he continue now that his henchman had been eradicated? He certainly must be running short of them, as three were incarcerated at the Yard, one had his contract terminated by Gerald in the Brews, another two at Brownlow's, and now Maxwell, which makes seven. How many did he have left? However many there were, they must be thinking that perhaps their long term employment prospects with the treasury secretary would not be good.

'Good day, Mr Cornwallis, I'm so sorry to keep you.' Mr Gillimot flounced through the curtain with a flourish, and then stopped short. 'Oh. That will not do, Mr Cornwallis, if you don't mind me saying,' he said, scrutinising Cornwallis' suit which had been through the mill in more ways than one over the last few days. 'A good clean and a press I think.'

Cornwallis grimaced and then brushed himself down a little, he felt like he'd had his wrist slapped. 'Maybe later, Mr Gillimot, but first I have a request to make.'

'Request away, Mr Cornwallis, request away.'

'Good, I appreciate it. I have here something that has turned up during one of my investigations, and I wondered if you would be so kind as to take a look and give me what information you can.' He pulled the brown paper bag out from under his arm and handed it over.

Mr Gillimot screwed up his face in disgust as he tentatively opened the package. 'Oh, the smell. Where has it been?'

Cornwallis put on his sombre face. 'I'd rather not say if you don't mind, but I don't think you'd like to know anyway.'

'Really? Oh well, you young men and your adventures. You had better come through so we can have a proper look.'

Mr Gillimot led Cornwallis through the curtain and into the fitting room where a big long table, ordinarily used for cutting, took up half the space. He placed the package on the table and drew the manky suit out. He sniffed with disgust again at the smell and then separated the jacket from the trousers. 'Definitely one of ours, though I have never seen one in quite such a bad way before.' He fussed over it, like the prodigal son returned from adversity.

'I wonder if you can tell me who it belonged to?'

Gillimot scratched his chin in thought and then, realising what he had just been handling, stopped abruptly. 'We do have a thing called client confidentiality, I'm afraid, Mr Cornwallis. I'm sure you understand,' and then he smiled at Cornwallis, holding eye contact.

Cornwallis returned the scrutiny. There were a few moments of silence between them, and then finally Cornwallis pulled out his wallet. He counted out ten dollars and placed it on the table, with Mr Gillimot watching the fall of each note. Mr Gillimot kept smiling, but said nothing, so Cornwallis counted out another ten and placed that on the table too.

'That'll do very nicely, sir; now let's see what we've got.' The money disappeared in a flash into one of his pockets and then he got down to business. 'Classic cut, Mr Cornwallis, see the lapels? They are slightly wider than yours, and slightly longer in the length; the back is slightly longer too which would indicate one of our more old fashioned clients.' He reached into the inside pocket of the jacket and pulled out a little label. He moved closer and squinted, and then wrote in his little pad. 'I'll just go and get the ledger and see what we've found.'

Mr Gillimot went through into a back office and returned a few minutes later carrying a large leather book. He placed it on the table next to the suit and began to turn the pages. 'Here we are.' He ran his finger down the entries and then stopped hesitantly with his finger poised. 'Oh my!' He checked his pad again, then checked the little label again, and then checked the book again. 'Well, this is a surprise.'

Cornwallis leant over and saw the name beneath the finger: Pelegrew Kintersbury.

*

'Maxwell is dead.' Kintersbury paced the office with his hands thrust deep into his pockets.

'How?' asked Dumchuck, shocked. He sat back in his chair and just stared in astonishment. 'Who?'

'Cornwallis; who else?' replied Kintersbury. 'I've just heard and came rushing here. Maxwell was at the warehouse when they came to take him, apparently when he tried to escape they just ripped his head clean off his shoulders.'

'Oh, that's gross.'

Kintersbury nodded. 'It means that we will have to bring it all forward now. Don't worry, it's all been agreed by the other party. Steps have been taken to ensure that we're safe.' He scratched at the cuts on his face which were now starting to itch. 'We won't contact each other again until it's all in place. The day after tomorrow should give me enough time to sort it all.'

'Oh, I do hope so, Pelegrew. I do hope so.'

*

They sat around the table in the piazza outside the Stoat, each of them nursing a pint pot as Cornwallis told them what had happened at Biggins and Shute and that now they could at least connect Kintersbury to Freddie the Weasel.

'It doesn't prove anything though,' said Rose. 'Only that Freddie wore one of his old suits.'

'No,' agreed Cornwallis. 'But it is circumstantial, and when we add everything else to it, a judge would sit up and listen.'

Frankie smiled to himself.

'What's tickling you?' asked Cornwallis, after taking a long gulp.

'His Lordship actually, what wouldn't he give for a quarter of what Freddie had, eh?'

'Oh Frankie,' admonished Rose. 'That's not exactly fair. He'd just come out of the river and stood in a draught, he was wet through and shivering. Even I know that everything disappears when it's cold. Poor little Cecil looked mortified.'

'Little is the right word there,' laughed Frankie. 'Ye Gods, he stood at the back of the queue when that got handed out.'

'When what got handed out?' asked MacGillicudy, making an appearance. He pulled over another chair and sat down. 'Might as well come and annoy you lot, it's either that or sit at home waving goodbye to my career.'

Rose smiled at him and patted his arm. 'I'm sure things will work out.'

'Hmmm, we'll see. Who handed out what then?'

'Dewdrop,' explained Frankie. 'You missed a good day today. Dewdrop came out of the river sopping wet in just his underpants; Rose here stood just in front of him. You can imagine what happened next, can't you?'

MacGillicudy opened his eyes wide. 'Oh, he didn't, did he?'

Frankie nodded and then raised his little finger in demonstration.

MacGillicudy laughed. 'Oh, how I wish I could have seen that. Why did he go in the river anyway?'

'Fishing out Maxwell's head,' explained Cornwallis.

MacGillicudy looked confused.

'Oh, I forgot, you've been out of the loop. Maxwell killed Freddie, who we can connect to Pelegrew Kintersbury and the Gornstock Trust and Holdings. We found him down the docks, and when we tried to pick him up, he broke away and fell into a boat. One of the workers down there tried to pull him out of the boat by his legs, but unfortunately his head had gone through the timbers, and when he pulled, the head and the body parted company, end of Maxwell.'

MacGillicudy still looked confused; he looked at each of them in turn with his face a blank. There were a few seconds of telling silence, and then Cornwallis said. 'I tell you what, let's get you a pint and we'll tell you all about it.'

It took two pints to get MacGillicudy up to speed on the investigation, and another two to dissect it. All that excitement and he'd missed it, just for a moment's aberration when he landed that punch on Grinde. A couple of clues, one or two questions in the right ears, a bit of observation and leg work, a murderer discovered, albeit now a dead murderer, and he had missed it all.

'What next then?' asked MacGillicudy, feeling deflated.

'We have to tie Kintersbury in with Dumchuck. Algernon is keeping an eye on them for the moment, so we'll just have to see if he comes up with anything,' explained Cornwallis. 'Those are two men who we will have to be very careful with.'

Frankie drained his pint, stretched his arms and grinned. 'Well, if you ain't gonna need me anymore, I'm off to bed.'

'This early?' queried Cornwallis.

'I didn't say mine, did I?'

Rose tutted and wagged a finger. 'If I had said something like that you would have accused me of being a loose woman.'

'That's because all the virtue goes to the giver, and not the receiver, my darling,' replied Frankie, just ducking in time.

MacGillicudy laughed. 'At least you have all cheered me up; I'll walk a little way with you, Frankie, if I stay here any longer I won't want to move.'

Frankie and MacGillicudy left the table and together walked towards the alley at the far end, they were talking and laughing animatedly as they disappeared from view, and Frankie's raucous laugh could still be heard long after they'd gone.

Cornwallis and Rose sat quietly for a few seconds

luxuriating in the peace. He leant forward and toyed with his glass for a few moments as if in contemplation, then sat back again as if he'd made up his mind. He turned to look at Rose and smiled, and then she smiled in return. The light from the oil lamps cast a gentle romantic glow around the piazza on the warm balmy evening and a low hum of conversation from the tables around accentuated the intimate atmosphere. They both took a sip of their drinks and gently placed the glasses back down.

'There's something I'd like to talk to you about, Rose,' began Cornwallis quietly, thankful that at long last he'd found the courage to say what he wanted to. He felt awkward, and a little bit scared of what she might say; she might turn him down.

She waited another few seconds and then gave a half-nod. 'I know, Jack. I thought you wanted to, and you're right, we should discuss things,' she replied seriously. 'It's not something we can hide from, I know that, but I'm just worried that you might think it would affect our work.'

He reached out and held her hand. 'It won't affect our work, I promise you that.' He looked directly into her sultry eyes.

She squeezed his fingers in hers. 'Thank you, Jack, that means a lot to me.'

He smiled again, and for the first time didn't struggle to keep eye contact. He could sense her chest heave as she took a deep breath, but he manfully managed to hold her gaze; after all, things were going far better than he expected and there would be plenty of opportunity later. 'I think just one step at a time; I won't push you into anything before you're ready, but sometimes it happens, just the same; we have to go with the feeling. Neither of us are children, so if it happens, then it happens for the best.'

Rose nodded her agreement and smiled, her lips moist and slightly parted. 'I think you understand these things much more than me, you've had so much experience.' She reached over with her other hand and clamped his hand in hers, squeezing tightly. She then leant her head back and sighed as if a great weight had been taken off her mind. 'I've been thinking about it most of the day, even when…' and she chuckled '… your hand kept stroking my bum.'

Cornwallis looked at her longingly, feeling that everything was going to be all right; but from behind, he heard a very soft exclamation.

'Lucky bastard,' it said.

He whipped his head around, but all he could see were the backs of the drinkers as they picked up their glasses.

'Yes,' continued Rose. 'It's been a strange day, and it also crossed my mind when you made me have that orgasm in the warehouse.'

'Oh no, this ain't fair!' The voice came again, and this time with a hint of desperation.

Cornwallis thought he was quicker this time, but he still couldn't discern where the voice came from. His eyes bore into the backs of all within sight, willing one of them to turn. When nobody did, he eventually returned his gaze to Rose.

'So I'm glad we can talk about it,' she said, with not a hint that she had heard the errant voice. 'I promise that I won't do it again, Jack. Think of it as a one off, and it only happened because it scared me.'

Cornwallis continued to look at her with a smile on his face, and then as she spoke his brow became furrowed in confusion. 'Er…?'

Rose returned the look and smiled, her tongue licking her lips. 'You know, at Scooters Yard, when I had a little panic.' She patted the hand she still held. 'I'm glad you understand.'

'Oh, er… yes, of course I do.' He groaned inwardly, there wasn't a hole big enough for him to fall into at that moment. 'Yes, er… right. I'm sure it won't, Rose.'

She sighed again, her chest heaving. This time Cornwallis looked, and mentally waved them goodbye.

'Do you know, Jack, I've just replayed that conversation in my mind, and it sounded very much like you and I were talking about, you know, having a relationship.'

Cornwallis recovered well. 'Did it really?'

'Yes,' she said. 'I'm so glad we weren't talking cross purposes; that would have been so embarrassing.'

'Yes, it would,' he agreed, quietly.

They lapsed into silence again while Rose sipped at her drink. 'You know, it's so warm tonight; we could do with Big George and his fan.' She held the front of her shirt open and gave it a shake to move some air.' I won't be able to wear a thing in bed tonight; I'll just have to gently perspire, as that's what good girls do instead of sweat. I'll be all slippery; I just hope I can sleep.'

A groan came from behind Cornwallis.

'Right. That's it. Which one of you is it?' he demanded, spinning around and standing up. 'Which one of you has been listening to our conversation?'

Nobody moved, and nobody said a word.

'The next time I hear any of you say anything, I'll arrest the sodding lot of you, understand?'

'Jack? What's going on?'

He stood there for a few more moments looking daggers, and then relented again. 'You didn't hear anything?' he asked.

Rose shook her head. 'No. Anyway it's not important.' She finished her drink and put the glass down. She had in fact heard, and out of the corner of her eye, she had seen the men at the table lean closer to hear better; but she'd decided that she didn't want an audience when talking about how they felt about each other, and perhaps they should wait until this job had finished anyway. 'Ah well, it's been a busy day. I'm off to bed now, just me and my slippery sweat.' She flicked an eye to the men. 'If I can't sleep, I'll think about that orgasm all night long.' She winked and placed a kiss on his cheek. 'Goodnight, Jack.'

'Goodnight, Rose,' he said, as hope left him.

As she made her way to the door, a quiet voice came to Cornwallis' ears again. 'I know I won't sleep, slippery and orgasm, oh ye Gods!'

*

The next morning saw them all in early at the office, with Rose coming in slightly nervously. Cornwallis still wondered if she really knew what he wanted to say last night, but thought it best now to forget it; the opportunity came and then it went. He decided that she had diverted the conversation just in case he became embarrassed when she turned him down. She had turned the conversation like an expert and it left him floundering. Maybe he'd misread the signs and perhaps friends were all they were destined to be. He watched her sit down and then his eyes focused on the copy of yesterday's Gornstock Chronicle that she had tucked under her arm. As they scrutinised it, Cornwallis and Frankie were momentarily lost for words. They were looking at an advert, in the recruitment pages.

Secretary/Office worker required

Apply

Cornwallis Investigations

'Why didn't you tell us?' asked Cornwallis eventually. 'We don't need a secretary.'

Rose became defensive. 'You didn't say that, so I assumed that you agreed to it.'

'But I had a hangover.'

'Yes, but that was hardly my fault,' she said indignantly, pointing a finger at her chest.

'All right. All right.' He held up his hands in surrender. 'We'll give it a go, see what turns up. But we'll only take someone on if they're perfect for the job. They can have a week's trial, and if they're no good, they go. Does that satisfy you?'

Rose huffed and nodded, and then sat there with her arms crossed, hiding the feeling of triumph as advised. Cornwallis' father had made the suggestion the other night at dinner, he had told her that his son would never get around to getting a secretary if left to his own devices, and he agreed that they desperately needed one. So when they had finished eating, he had helped write out the advert, and together they dropped it off at the offices of the Gornstock Chronicle. He also told her not to tell him until the applicants were imminent, as he would probably do all he could to get out of it. It was now eight o'clock and they should all be queuing up very soon.

Frankie warmed to the idea very quickly. He had a vision of what type of secretary they should have, his primary requirement being that she would be young, attractive, and eager to please; just being eager would be enough. He rubbed his hands together and then slurped his coffee. 'You know, Jack; it ain't such a bad

257

idea after all. Just think of the saving in time; we could devote all our energies to the job in hand.'

'Frankie,' began Cornwallis. 'We spend most of the time doing nothing as it is, we are reliant on people walking through that door wanting our services, and if no one comes through, then we don't work.'

'Yeah, but if there's always someone here, then anyone who does come in, ain't gonna go away, are they?'

Cornwallis had to agree with Frankie's logic there, but would it really work? Some of the cases they deal with are very sensitive, and to have someone they didn't know handling the files could be asking for trouble. When he voiced those concerns, Rose shot them down.

'You didn't know me until the other night,' she reasoned, 'and now look. Are you telling me you don't trust me?'

'No, no, of course I trust you. But you're Rose, you're different.'

'Jack, I could have been a homicidal maniac and you wouldn't have known. If you cast your mind back you spent more time talking to my chest than you did to my face. It's only in the last couple of days that I've been confident that when I do speak to you, you are going to look back at me properly.'

Cornwallis felt his cheeks flush because she had a point. He and Frankie had spent a long time that night talking about her various points of interest, and he agreed to try her out because of the effect she had on the men at the Stoat, and the fact that she could scrap,. The main reason though, and he had to admit it, had to do with the effect she had on *his* trouser department. But things had changed since the other night. He could still see the same strikingly beautiful girl with all the skin and breasts and hair and legs but he could now see more than that. He'd scratched the surface, and underneath it, he found a clever spirited girl, as vulnerable as everyone else. He had already come to the conclusion that she would stay; she had become an integral part of the team. He knew now too, that the likelihood of the relationship developing into something more, would be remote, to say the least, but somehow that didn't matter; it was more important to be friends, which is as it really should be.

'Er, yes,' he stretched the word out as if contemplating his reply. 'But I know you now.'

Rose changed the pout to a smile. 'My point exactly, you should give people a chance.'

A knock came at the door, swinging open without invitation and Sparrow walked in. Behind him, followed three men in overalls, and Sparrow pointed out the pictures that they were to take before even saying good morning to Cornwallis. The three looked on speechless as the men got to work.

'You caused quite a stir yesterday,' said Sparrow by way of a greeting. 'Very messy.'

'Well, Sparrow,' replied Cornwallis, leaning back in his chair and fixing him with a firm gaze. 'Maxwell wasn't trying to kill you, so I think that you can just bugger off. I don't give a toss what you think. You and the Bagman had your chance, and you declined to take it.'

'We were biding our time, Mr Cornwallis, letting things fall into place.'

'Yes, and in the meantime one less investigator wouldn't have mattered.'

'I wouldn't go quite so far as to say that, we do have your best interests at heart. Take your near miss yesterday, if it wasn't for us you would be looking up at six feet of dirt.'

'I could have dealt with him easily enough.'

'Perhaps, but now we will never know. You know Maxwell could have unlocked a few closed doors for us.'

'I know, Sparrow, that's why I wanted to talk to him.'

Sparrow smiled benevolently. 'Bit too late for that now though, don't you think? Perhaps next time you might listen to us a little more. Incidentally, we have already been down the Yard and removed all the files and the rags that were there. Oh, and the three men you took yesterday as well. If anything arises from our discussions with them we will of course inform you.'

Cornwallis tried hard to keep his temper in check; he intended to go and speak to them some more later that day. 'Take what you want, Sparrow, and then go. I'm getting a bit bored with your company.'

Sparrow smiled some more. 'Just hand over the handkerchief, and, oh yes, the pictures that MacGillicudy had done of Mr Weasel, plus the suit; I think then that we will be done. Incidentally, there is quite a crowd of women waiting downstairs, are they all for you?'

Cornwallis swore to himself, the pictures of Freddie the Weasel had only arrived last night and he hadn't had time to look at them properly. He got up, went over to the cupboard and pulled them out; there were only a few, and they were small, as they should be. He quickly flicked through them and decided that nothing there would give them a further clue. 'Here, now go,' he said, handing them over.

Sparrow waited, and then Cornwallis handed over the rest of the stuff.

'Thank you, Mr Cornwallis. We will meet again. Goodbye Miss Morant, Mr Kandalwick.' He doffed his hat and walked out behind his men.

'Bastard,' muttered Frankie to his back.

Rose thought hard. 'Do you know, Jack, I think that they are going to let us do all the work, and then when we finally sort it out, they are going to jump in and take all the credit.'

Cornwallis nodded. 'Yep, that's exactly what they intend to do. So it will be up to us to make sure that it doesn't happen. Agreed?'

Frankie and Rose nodded. The Bagman was going to find out that they were more than a match for him.

'Let's get this other business sorted out now,' said Cornwallis, shaking off the effects of the visit. 'Sparrow said that there were loads of women down there, so we had better start thinning them out.'

They arranged the desk so that it was directly in front of the door, with three chairs placed behind it so that they could sit and watch each applicant as they came in. Rose placed a single upright chair in front for the victim. Cornwallis sat in the middle, flanked either side by his friends. He had given Frankie and Rose a wad of paper and a pencil each, and the three looked quite professional sitting there.

'Right,' said Cornwallis, satisfied at the layout. 'Let's get this show on the road. Who's going to drag the first one in?'

Frankie and Rose sat there and looked at each other. Neither of them moved, each reluctant to initiate the process while Cornwallis tapped his pencil impatiently on the desk. Finally, Rose sighed and got up; she sauntered over to the door and flung it open, calling down the stairs for the first person to come up before hurrying back to her seat to get ready for when they came through the door.

'Good morning,' said Cornwallis, as the girl came in, 'and what is your name?'

The girl shut the door and then walked forward slowly. 'Gladys, sir, but I'm known as Peaches.'

Cornwallis smiled as she came over. 'Please sit down, Gladys, or Peaches, I should say.'

She smiled, bit her lip, and pouted all at the same time.

'Thank you, sir.' Peaches sat down and arranged herself demurely with her hands on her lap.

'And why, may I ask, have you applied for our vacancy?'

'Well, sir.' She held Cornwallis' gaze and refused to let go. 'Because I want to have a worthwhile career, sir.'

Rose sniffed. 'What experience do you have, Gladys?' she asked pointedly.

Peaches didn't even turn to look at Rose; instead, she kept her eyes firmly on Cornwallis. 'Oh I have plenty of experience, sir.' She smiled, and then she squeezed her arms together; two little domes of flesh popped up, her nickname's origins becoming quite obvious. 'But in the service industry mainly, I'm a girl that does, sir, very willing I am, sir.'

Frankie leant forward to get a better look and kicked Cornwallis hard under the table; he for one had got the message.

Cornwallis shot Frankie a look and then returned his gaze to Peaches. 'We work strange hours here, would that prove difficult for you?' he asked, ignoring her obvious body language.

'Oh no, sir, I'd be here at your beck and call, at any time you require, sir. I'd always be ready for anything you need, anything, sir.' She flicked her eyes to Rose as if weighing up the opposition and then looked at Frankie, her eyes smouldering with the promise of things to come.

Frankie clamped his jaw shut as it had been hanging open and he smiled back. 'Does that include the occasional night shift?' he enquired, in hope.

Peaches licked her lips as if thinking. 'Well, of course, sir. I would always do my best to be accommodating.'

Cornwallis coughed politely. 'Thank you for coming, er, Peaches; we will let you know.'

'Thank you, sir, always ready to be of any assistance, sir, you understand, sir?' She almost winked, but held it back, inclining her head slightly instead and handing over a piece of paper. 'This is where I live, sir, if you wishes to discuss things further.'

'Well.' Rose exclaimed when she had gone. 'The nerve of the girl.'

Frankie grinned. 'I don't know what you mean, Rose, I thought she was a good candidate.'

'Yes, you would, Frankie. But not with regards to her office skills.'

'Let's get the next one in,' said Cornwallis laughing. 'I don't think we need a Peaches here, we'd never get Frankie to do any work.'

Frankie put on his indignant look. 'Bloody cheek, I noticed you had a good look too.'

'I may have cast my eyes in that general direction, Frankie,' agreed Cornwallis. 'But then I didn't really have a choice, they sort of waved, if you know what I mean. Let's see what the next one's like.'

Rose called down for the next one and this time two came through the door.

'This is Mildred,' said the older of the two as she sat down. 'She's come fer the job, she's me daughter.' Mildred chewed on gum and looked around the office like the stroppy skinny teenager she was. Her mother regarded Cornwallis keenly. 'Good girl she is, too, yer know.'

'I'm sure she is,' replied Cornwallis, looking from one to the other. 'Er… Mildred, what sort of work do you normally do?'

'She works as a kitchen maid,' replied the mother. 'Scrubbing the pans and the like.' Mildred just stared and chewed, her boredom obvious.

'Really?' responded Cornwallis. 'Well I never.'

'Yeah, but I tells her to get her finger out an' get a proper job. No future in being a scrubber, yer know.'

Cornwallis smiled indulgently. 'You're so right. So Mildred…' he began.

'Oi, Mildred, listen to the man. He's talking to you,' interrupted the mother.

Cornwallis tried to smile again, but it was becoming increasingly difficult. 'Yes, well. Perhaps Mildred would like to tell us what she expects from this position.'

'She expects to work is what she expects, don't you, Mildred?'

Mildred obviously didn't care what anyone expected. She huffed, dug her hands deep into her pockets, and then tried to blow a bubble.

'I expect Mildred might be more suited to another line of work,' ventured Rose after a few moments silence.

'Yeah, p'raps yer right,' replied Mildred's mother. 'Come on, girl, yer no good fer nuffing.' She clipped her daughter around the ear and then hurried her out of the office.

'I felt a little sorry for that one,' said Rose, when they'd gone. 'What chance has the poor girl got with a harridan like that for a mother?'

'None, I should think,' replied Cornwallis with a sigh. 'Gods, I've had enough of this already.'

The next few applicants were just as unsuitable as the first two. Two couldn't read, which could be thought an advantage, considering what some of their clients had got up to, but left them all at a loss as to how they had known there was a job on offer in the first place. Another one had a serious body odour problem, and yet another didn't stop talking from the moment she entered the office until the moment she left, leaving all three quite breathless from the experience.

Cornwallis wanted to stop the whole thing there and then, but Rose would have none of it, determined to find someone suitable. She reasoned that there must be at least one person waiting who could do the job, and it only required a little bit of patience to find them. Frankie tried again to get the first one back in the frame, quite rightly saying that she was the best of all that they had so far seen, but Cornwallis just shook his head slowly, adamant that they wouldn't have a Peaches working there.

Rose left her chair again and called down the stairs. Shortly a woman of indeterminate age walked in, dressed rather plainly but she had clear, smooth skin with dark hair twisted into a tight bun. She smiled at the three of them as she sat down, waiting for the questions to come.

'And you are?' began Rose with a smile.

'Mrs Gridlington,' said Mrs Gridlington.

Cornwallis shuffled the pieces of paper in front of him. 'Well, Mrs Gridlington. Could you tell us what experience you can bring to this office?'

'Why certainly, Mr Cornwallis. At present, I am a housekeeper, but prior to that, I worked for Mr Flammery, the lawyer, until he passed away, may the Gods bless his soul. Before that, I worked with Mr Plugnill, the accountant, until he too passed away, may the Gods bless his soul also. I used to deal with all their correspondence and appointments; kept everything nice and tidy.'

'Oh, really? I remember Mr Flammery, wasn't there something a little strange about his passing?'

'Er, yes, but I'm not one to gossip, Mr Cornwallis. Suffice to say that it was most unfortunate.'

'You are so right; we need someone who understands confidentiality. Oh, yes, I remember now. Didn't he expire as a result of, er…'

'Confidentiality, Mr Cornwallis. I believe the lady involved wishes to remain anonymous.'

Rose wrote on the bit of paper in front of her and passed it to Cornwallis. 'You say you are at present a housekeeper,' said Rose, regarding her again. 'Why the change?'

'I have always liked working in an office,' replied Mrs Gridlington, 'and I only went as a housekeeper on a temporary basis. My intention is to return to the profession as soon as something worthwhile comes up. The lady I work for now is well aware of that and encouraged me to apply this morning. I have a reference here from her if you would like to have a look.' She then handed over a neatly folded piece of paper.

Cornwallis read it and then passed it along to Rose. Frankie sighed as he could see where all this was going.

Rose read the reply to her note too, saying Mr Flammery died happy wearing a nappy at a special club. She looked at Cornwallis and he winked at her.

'Most impressive reference, Mrs Gridlington,' observed Cornwallis, getting back to the job in hand. 'There would be a lot of comings and goings here; and at odd times too. You would be pretty much left to deal with things as they happen on your own. Would that be a problem?'

'Oh no, Mr Cornwallis, I'm sure I will quickly pick up how you like things done.'

Cornwallis cast his eyes to Rose and Frankie and then wrote something down on the piece of paper in front. Rose leant across and put a tick next to it, Frankie reluctantly followed suit.

'Well, Mrs Gridlington, if you still want the position, then I am pleased to be able to offer it to you.'

Mrs Gridlington clapped her hands together and beamed. 'Oh, thank you, Mr Cornwallis, I will be delighted to join you all.'

'Well, that's all done then. When are you able to start?'

'Would tomorrow morning be all right for you?'

'That would be splendid,' replied Cornwallis. 'We will all look forward to seeing you.'

Mrs Gridlington stood up and nodded her thanks. 'I'll be here bright and early, Mr Cornwallis, and I'm so looking forward to it all.'

She closed the door as she left and Cornwallis slumped down in his chair. 'Thank the Gods for that. I thought we would never find someone. I dreaded any more dross coming through the door. Frankie, would you be so kind as to tell everyone else that the position has been filled and then thank them all for coming.'

Frankie shot Cornwallis a forlorn look and then got up slowly. 'I still reckon that we should have taken on Peaches, can't we find a place for her too?'

'No, Frankie, we can't.'

'Oh well, you have her address there, perhaps I might pop 'round there to tell her she's been unlucky.'

Cornwallis sighed heavily, Frankie's priority emanated from just below waist height, and he supposed he wasn't going to change now. 'Before you do any popping, we have to go to work; we've spent far too long here this morning as it is. You and Rose can go and check with Algernon, see what our friends have been up to, while I'll go and see the King of the Dwarfs. When you've done that, you can go and see Gerald, he will probably want to know that Maxwell is dead.'

'Aw, Jack; seeing Algie ain't gonna be the same.'

'Clear the women out of the place, Frankie,' ordered Cornwallis with exasperation.

CHAPTER 11

Cornwallis felt that it was only polite to speak to the King of the Dwarfs, but he doubted whether he would be able to tell him anything he didn't already know; but seeing as he had told Trugral that he would pay a visit, it seemed churlish not to do so now. Good relations were something to be cultivated; he never knew when it would come in handy. A contact was a contact, even if the contact lived deep underground.

The nearest underground entrance was near the Guilds Hall, thankfully not far away. He knew the mines were extensive, so where in all those tunnels he would end up he just didn't know. He had arranged to meet up with Rose and Frankie in a coffee shop later in the afternoon; he'd give the pub a miss for once in the hope of getting a good night's sleep. He just hoped he'd got his timings right. He left the office and began the trek down the road whistling to himself for no other reason than it made him feel better. He had not been in a particularly good mood because of both his lack of success with Rose, and having to interview all those women; but with reflection, perhaps it might not be such a bad idea to take on some help. He smiled to himself at Frankie's infatuation with Peaches, he could see the attraction, but he dreaded to think what would have happened if he had taken her on.

He crossed the street and then slipped down a side road, a little further on he dipped down another, leaving all the people behind him. He then thought he heard a little click, and then a sort of soft whoosh, and then a thump. He turned around to look, but couldn't see anyone there. He stood still for a few moments and then shrugged his shoulders and carried on.

*

The small crossbow he carried had especially strengthened limbs, accurate, but to only about sixty feet. He pulled it out ready primed from the special reinforced pocket of his jacket, and then slid the bolt onto the string. It packed one hell of a punch at short range, but was a bugger to reload; he had to make this shot count. He peeked around the corner and levelled the bow to take aim; he licked his lips and took a deep breath just as his finger increased the pressure on the trigger. He centred his aim on Cornwallis' back, a good target, and with the power of the crossbow, would turn his insides to mush.

He concentrated hard, which though a good thing, could also be a bad thing because while he focused his aim at Cornwallis, he couldn't see what was happening behind. Had he been able to see, he would have seen a seven inch long tempered-steel throwing-knife travelling towards him at about a hundred miles an hour, and about to come into serious contact with the back of his neck; but he didn't know that, although shortly it was going to become very apparent.

The knife hit home, the arm twitched, and the finger finished the pull. The crossbow fired. He had a brief instance of comprehension as the knife sliced through his flesh and bone and came to rest with the pointy bit just below his chin; life waved goodbye and oblivion said hello.

Mr Magpie drew the blade from out of the body and peeked around the corner. He saw Cornwallis just as he turned back from looking and watched with a knowing grin as he continued on his way. The crossbow bolt had missed Cornwallis by a good few feet thanks to his intervention, now reverberating in a door post on the other side of the street. The assailant's reverberations though, were well and truly over.

*

Cornwallis walked up to the underground entrance in Beltide Park and descended the few steps cut into the pavement behind the park railings, where a protective barrier around the entrance stopped anyone falling down. Large iron gates blocked the way a few steps down and Cornwallis stood and rang a bell which indicated that he might quite like to come in. He stood there for a good few minutes tapping his feet and checking his watch, it was getting to the point where he felt he might have to go down to the warehouse entrance when he heard the slow steady pace of footsteps coming towards him.

'What you want?' asked a deep gruff voice from the black depths behind the gate.

Cornwallis looked through the gate and tried, and failed, to see the dwarf. 'To see your King,' he replied with confidence.

'Do you now. Well, what if I said that the King don't want to see you.'

'I would say that perhaps you'd better ask him first.'

The dwarf sniffed contemptuously. 'If the King wanted to see you then he would have told me he wanted to see you.'

'You don't even know who I am, so how would you know?' reasoned Cornwallis.

'Don't need to know who you are, you got a word?'

'A word? What do you mean?'

'Exactly. If you ain't got a word then the King don't want to see you, so sod off long-legs.'

Cornwallis heard footsteps now going away from the entrance back into the deep tunnels beyond. 'Go and ask him, my name's Cornwallis,' he shouted into the blackness.

He just heard silence as a reply and Cornwallis sighed; he would just have to go to the warehouse on the wharf instead, which would eat up another chunk of his day. He hadn't thought that getting in would be such a problem. He checked his watch again and calculated the time it would take, as he had to meet up with Frankie and Rose later.

'You said you didn't have the word.'

Cornwallis had just taken the first step back up when the voice seemed to explode into his ears. He spun quickly back around and saw the dwarf unlocking the gate. How he had appeared there so quickly and quietly Cornwallis would never know.

'Uh? Er, thanks, I mean. Out of curiosity, the word is Cornwallis?'

The dwarf nodded and swung the gate wide open to let him in. 'You're to follow me.'

Cornwallis stepped in and the gate clanged shut behind him. It felt a bit like a prison cell for a moment or two, but then the dwarf hurried away. Cornwallis hesitated and then rushed after, he had no desire to get lost anywhere in these tunnels; it would take forever to find his way out again.

His guide carried an axe looped in his belt as well as a hammer, and looked as if he knew how to use both in more ways than one. He held a small lantern in his hand, presumably for Cornwallis' benefit only. Unlike most of the dwarfs he had met, this one appeared gruff and uncommunicative and Cornwallis quickly gave up trying to engage him in conversation; he just followed meekly, down tunnel after tunnel, always sloping down, and obviously going far underground. In many

271

areas, he had to keep his head bent down to avoid smacking his skull on the roof, but generally, he found that he had far and away enough head room to walk upright. This surprised him, as he had supposed that he would be spending a lot of the time bent double. There were a few flights of hand-hewn steps when descending to an obviously new level, and then the trip through the tunnels continued.

Time in the dark seemed not to exist, and he quickly lost track of it. The only noises were the whistles and grunts from his companion as he indicated their presence to a guard. Eventually they came to a busier section and he could see dwarfs moving around and could hear the low buzz of them talking, and in the distance, the obvious clacks and smacks of picks at work. A few dwarfs eyed him warily, but most seemed to take no notice as he dutifully followed his guide.

They entered an enormous cavern, cathedral like in its sheer splendour with the walls shining with precious stones. Here, a great gathering of dwarfs sat on rough stone benches facing one way towards a raised area hacked into the wall. Cornwallis thought it looked a formal occasion and did wonder whether he'd been taken to a court of some description. On the raised section there were a few dwarfs sitting at tables, one of them writing furiously as another spoke in a deep guttural language.

Cornwallis looked around, trying to make sense of it all, when his guide grabbed hold of his arm and dragged him from the cavern, taking him down a small brightly lit passage to a small neatly laid out room. The guide indicated a chair, and Cornwallis obliged him by sitting down. With a grunt of approval the guide left, he slammed the door and then the unmistakable sound of a key turning in its lock. Cornwallis had reached his destination.

He regarded the bare bones of the room for only a few

minutes before the key clicked in the lock again and the door swung open. A dwarf stood there wearing a dull green cloak and polished leather trousers, a tan coloured shirt, with a medallion hanging from his neck. His beard was plaited and hung down to below his waist, as did his long grey hair.

'Hmmm.' The dwarf scratched his chin thoughtfully. 'So you're Cornwallis then?'

Cornwallis stood up and took a pace forward and held out his hand to shake. 'I am, and are you the King of the Dwarfs?'

'King? Me?' he chuckled, accepting the proffered hand. 'I'm more of what you might call the welcoming committee. Can't have anyone coming down here wanting to speak to the King, the place would be overrun with the likes of you lot. I'm Goodhalgan.'

'Oh, I suppose so,' conceded Cornwallis. 'So, when do I see the King, er, Goodhalgan?'

Goodhalgan smiled. 'Soon, Mr Cornwallis, very soon.'

'So I have to pass something then? Satisfy you that I'm not a danger to his health or whatever?'

'No. You're never going to be a danger to a dwarf, Mr Cornwallis,' and he chuckled again. 'Dear me, no, the very thought of it.'

'Then what?' asked Cornwallis, getting a little exasperated now.

'You haven't got a toothbrush on you by any chance, have you?' the dwarf asked, somewhat hesitantly.

There was a moment's pause. 'A toothbrush?' responded Cornwallis, confused at the question. 'Why do you want...? Ah!' Cornwallis suddenly remembered, Bough had told him about Psycho Pete. He grinned and shook his head. 'I'm not going to start polishing the quartz, if that's what you mean.'

Goodhalgan looked a little embarrassed. 'Oh, so you heard

then.'

'I did, but I don't think it made the front page of the papers. Your reputation should be safe.'

'The papers?' Goodhalgan's face crumpled. 'You don't think it will be in the papers do you?'

Cornwallis shook his head. 'Someone with an addled mind being thrown out the mines? I don't think that will sell papers. However, how many dwarfs were hurt?'

'Three,' conceded Goodhalgan. 'But only slightly, we're still trying to figure out how he got in.'

Cornwallis debated whether to prolong the agony for the dwarf, but then decided it might not be to his best advantage, considering he still had to see the King. 'I haven't heard anything, or read anything in the papers. Captain Bough is as discreet as they come, and I only know about it because I happened to be there when they released his cell-mate.'

Goodhalgan seemed to relax a little; he nodded and then smiled again and indicated the chair. Cornwallis sat back down and waited for the dwarf to continue.

'I'd better backtrack a bit in that case, Mr Cornwallis,' said Goodhalgan, apologetically. 'I am indeed the current King of the Dwarfs, and I bid you welcome to Under Gornstock.'

Cornwallis inclined his head and grinned, 'I thought so; Goodhalgan, please tell me, what's happening in the cavern down there?' and he pointed to the way he came in.

'You guessed I am the king? I thought I did rather well. Oh well, never mind. The cavern? Hmmm, that's school for the under forties, dwarf lore and all that; got to keep the youngsters interested in their history, don't you know. Dwarfs are proud of their heritage, Mr Cornwallis, miss one generation and it's all gone, never to be got back.'

'Under forties?' gasped Cornwallis. 'You do mean under

forty years old?'

'Of course, forty is very young but we believe in getting at them early. Now what can I do for you? Trugral told me you wanted to see me.'

Cornwallis' mind performed somersaults in trying to get around the idea that forty year old dwarfs were learning at school, and for a brief few moments, he struggled to get his mind back to where it should be. 'Er, yes, well. I mean… *forty*?'

Goodhalgan sat down and looked at Cornwallis sympathetically. 'Yes. Dwarfs live to a very old age in comparison to humans, Mr Cornwallis, unless of course they meet with an unexpected incident; like a war or a skirmish or a tunnel collapsing, which would really be their own fault as they should have built it properly to start with, or something like that. I am only a hundred and thirty two, in the prime of life, hale and hearty and ready for a good few years yet. Now, let's get to the purpose of your visit, shall we?'

Cornwallis sat still for another few moments as his face did contortions whilst his mind digested the information. 'Er, right then. Why did I want to see you? Oh yes, I definitely wanted to see you.'

Goodhalgan waited patiently.

'Yes, all right then.' Cornwallis closed his eyes and took a deep breath. He turned back to Goodhalgan and smiled. His mind sort of stopped bouncing and got onto a level field again and he felt now a little more in control. 'I'm here because you allowed a man to be kept in your old guardroom, can you remember?'

Goodhalgan returned the smile. 'I do, Mr Cornwallis. A bit of a mistake that, but we live and learn. What exactly is your interest in him?'

'I'm investigating the murder of the gentleman's cleaner.

Unfortunately, I haven't been able to interview him, owing to the fact that you allowed a couple of men to incarcerate him in your guardroom,' responded Cornwallis. 'What I need from you is, well, really anything you can tell me.'

'I don't know if I should really, confidentiality and all that,' answered Goodhalgan. 'Trugral told you they weren't nice people, I believe, but we can't go around gossiping to anybody who asks, now can we?'

Cornwallis nodded solemnly. 'Normally I would agree with you, but in this case the men concerned are, I believe, involved in murder and other crimes. One of them has just recently ended his days by having his head ripped off by a polar bear. So you see it would benefit the city if you would stretch the point a little.'

'Polar bear, eh? Ooh, nasty.'

'You should have been there,' replied Cornwallis with a shudder, the memory still fresh in his mind.

'In that case I suppose it would be all right, which one died?'

'Maxwell, the thug. The other one is still on the loose.'

'Kintersbury you mean?'

Cornwallis nodded.

'Yes, we did notice his presence, but Mr Maxwell arranged everything with me a few days ago,' answered Goodhalgan. 'He came down and said that he had to hide a man for his own protection and did I know anywhere suitable. He paid well, so I didn't argue. The man they put in there seemed a sad type, we felt sorry for him, but he wouldn't leave on his own; though we did leave the door open.'

'He didn't say anything to anyone?'

Goodhalgan shook his head. 'No, just walked about the guardroom, didn't even try the door. You humans can be so strange.'

'I would agree with you there,' said Cornwallis, having had a lot of experience with strange people. 'What about those drugs in your tunnel?' he then asked, changing the subject.

Goodhalgan rocked his head as if weighing up his answer. 'The truth of the matter is that I don't know. We hardly used that tunnel and we only noticed them when they hid this man in our guardroom. Couldn't tell you how long they've been there,' he added a little embarrassedly. 'I take it you are going to remove the drugs from our tunnels? We don't want a reputation for dealing in your little habits, you know.'

'In due course, Goodhalgan. I would rather like to leave it all there for a while, you know, just to keep an eye on who comes and goes. Would it be possible for one of you to, er, take notice, should anyone take an interest?'

'As long as it's agreed that it won't be for long.'

'Good, I think we have an agreement then. You know Gerald from the Brews?'

Goodhalgan nodded.

'I'm going to ask him to help too, if you do below the ground, he'll do above.'

They heard a cheer coming from the cavern next door and then the sound of a tidal wave rushing through the tunnels. Cornwallis looked startled while Goodhalgan just sat there and grinned.

'Dinner time,' explained the King. 'Our youngsters do get a little exuberant when it's time for their lunch.'

*

They'd found Algernon up near the Assembly, still keeping an eye on Kintersbury. Nothing had happened last night after he got in place, and so far, nothing had happened today. Frankie made the decision to leave him to it and hope that at least something would happen soon. Algernon had told him that Dumchuck had stuck to his house last night, while his wife only went out to do the soup run, and today he'd only ventured as far as the bank. Kintersbury had been up to much the same, with the only movement last night coming from his servant, who popped out for a short time to deliver a letter. Today he just went to the House of Assembly, presumably to do whatever a Chief Secretary to the Treasury did; which, in Frankie's opinion, was not a lot.

Rose fell into step with Frankie as they made their way down the road towards Sal's to grab some lunch. She gave them a big welcome, and an even bigger lunch: for him, a special, and for her, a smaller version. They would try to cadge a lift to the Brews to see Gerald after they'd eaten, as they would probably be too full to move.

'Still feel a bit guilty about forcing a full special on yer the other day, my girl,' said Sal, as she made them comfortable. 'But sometimes you can't resists the temptation. I was impressed though, you managed to eat it all.'

'And very nice it was too, Sal, but I don't think I'll try another just yet.'

'No, you wouldn't keep that figure fer long if you did.'

Already the crowd around Sal's Sizzler began to increase with the presence of Rose sitting behind the counter. Rose hadn't noticed, but Sal had; and she grinned in gratitude for the extra custom, now prepared after the chaos she caused the other day.

'You come here as much as you like my girl,' she said, counting the money, 'even if Frankie ain't with you.'

'Thanks, Sal,' replied Rose between mouthfuls.

'Yeah, you and I can have a good old chinwag at some time. I reckon that once we start we won't be able to stop. Take your employer, I can tell you a good few things about him, I can tell you. When I used to work with his—'

'Mum,' interrupted Frankie. 'We ain't got time for all that. We're working.'

'Oh well, you go and spoil a couple of girls' fun, why don't you my lad. Us girls always have time for a chat, ain't that right Rose?'

'It is, Sal, but I'm afraid Frankie's right, we have work to do. If we got started where would we end?'

'Probably at the point where I tell you about when I smacked your Jack's backside for being a naughty boy.'

'My Jack?' Rose stopped chewing and looked up in surprise.

Sal hesitated for a second as Rose's question fed into her brain. God's, you wait 'til I gets holds o'him, she said to herself. 'I just mean yer boss,' she answered in the end. 'Just my way of talking.' She cast her eyes to the far end of the stall. 'Oi, Manuel. Get yer finger out o'that pie.'

Rose pondered a thought as they bounced along the road. They were sitting in the back of a draper's cart that headed across the river, the jolts being thankfully absorbed, as the wheels hit the potholes, by the cloth bundles on which they were presently reposed. Frankie had forced the lift, and was once again thankful that the folk in the city were largely an obliging lot.

'Frankie?' she asked hesitantly. 'How discreet can you be?'

'Uh?'

'I mean, if I told you something, would you be able to keep it to yourself and not blab it around?'

'Discretion is my middle name, my darling,' he replied, his interest now piqued.

'Hmmm.' She pondered the thought again, and looked at him as she chewed her lip.

He raised his eyebrows in question, and then made an encouraging hand gesture.

'I'm not really sure I should say anything really, it's a bit personal,' she added in the end.

'Rose, how long have we known each other?'

'Barely a week.'

'Ah, but a week for us is like a decade for someone else. Look what we've been through?'

'Perhaps you're right, but I warn you, if you breathe a word of this to anyone, I will cut your knadgers off and feed them to the fish.'

Frankie automatically dropped a hand down to his lap for protection. 'Ooo, that's mean. Sadie wouldn't like that.'

'No, she wouldn't, and I wouldn't like doing it, but you know I would.'

Frankie held up his hands. 'Okay, you've convinced me. I don't want to know.'

'You don't?'

'No. You're being serious, and I like my knadgers where they are, thank you very much. If you want to unload, then unload onto Jack. He likes that sort of thing, and the nobs have a code of silence when they want to use it. Tell him and I promise you he won't say a word.'

'I can't, because it's about him.'

'Rose. That's not fair. I like my knadgers, Sadie likes my knadgers, especially when they—'

'Frankie. Stop. Too much information, thank you.' She clapped her hands over her ears and pleaded with him to shut up.

Frankie stopped mid-flow and regarded Rose, her hands dropped and they both pursed their lips, until Rose poked her tongue out at him. The cart bounced again and Rose grabbed Frankie's leg to stop herself from falling.

'Easy, girl,' said Frankie, 'I didn't tell anyone, honest.'

Rose sniffed in return.

After a few minutes of quiet, as they watched the city retreating over the bridge, Frankie slowly stirred again. 'All right, I've got to know, haven't I?'

'Only if you want to,' replied Rose with a sigh.

'I don't *want* to, but you've said too much anyway, so you might as well carry on.'

'Only if you're sure.'

'I'm sure.'

Rose pondered again, and Frankie waited patiently. 'It's not a big thing you know; if I tell you, you will probably wonder why I bothered at all. It's just that—'

'Fer God's sake, Rose, get on with it, we're nearly there.'

'Frankie, I'm unburdening myself, so let me take my time.'

'Sorry.'

'Yes, well.' She waited a few seconds longer before beginning. 'It's just that last night, after you and Jethro left, Jack became a bit, er, romantic, if you like.'

'Oooo! He didn't say anything this morning.'

'He wouldn't, because nothing happened. He started to tell me something, but then I noticed some people listening, so I turned the conversation around and made it into something else. I was grateful really, because I wouldn't have turned him down. I made light of it all, and I think he was disappointed; but I'm sure he thinks I turned him down.'

'So what's the problem? Take him aside and finish talking

then.'

'I can't. If I did, and we sort of started seeing each other, then he might become a little over-protective.'

'Well, probably.'

'But I don't want that, not at the moment; I want to be in the thick of it, especially while this job is going on; but I still want to say yes to him.'

'So why are you telling me this, if you don't want me to tell him?'

'He's a man. So when a man thinks he's got turned down by one girl, he will probably look for another who won't turn him down, won't he?'

'Ah,' the penny dropped. 'You want me to stop him.'

Rose reluctantly nodded. She shrugged her shoulders apologetically and settled back into the cargo. 'Only until this job is finished, then I'll say yes.'

'If I can't tell him, then I can't promise anything, you know that, don't you?'

'Yes, but he listens to you, and I know you would do your best.'

He grinned. 'On one condition.'

'What's that?'

'You give your old Frankie a hug.'

Rose now ventured into the brews for the third time, and it didn't improve with familiarity. Night-time had been by far the worst, because of the difficulty in seeing who was coming up behind to tap you on the head, and there were the screams of course, which tingled the spine, because the reason and the whereabouts of the screamee were unknown. Now, with the daylight, it became a busy trading area, with shops and stores selling all manner of things. Unlike the first time, there seemed to be many more people out and about and the noise increased as they passed through, everybody being out to make a quick dollar. As they passed the Colliderscope again, Rose stopped to have another look, because she just thought how sad people were to trust in something like that. It looked busier than last time, with at least seven customers all staring at their little screens, or, as she thought, mirrors. As she watched, one of them came to the end of his time, so the proprietor walked over and covered the screen. The customer pleaded with him for just another few minutes, but the man shook his head and held out his hand indicating that it would cost another ten dollars. The customer's head sunk and he slowly got up, heading reluctantly for the door.

Frankie nodded at the man as they made eye contact. 'Any luck?'

'Yep, and all of it bad. Every bloody time he covers the screen, I sees something, just as the cloth comes down. Every bloody time. He won't give me even a second more, and that could be just the thing I'm looking for. I tells him he can have half, but he just don't want to know.'

Rose and Frankie watched him as he walked bow-legged down the street, muttering and swearing and bemoaning his lot to everyone he passed.

'If he sees something, then it's a trick of the mind, isn't it?' asked Rose.

Frankie nodded. 'Yeah, how many times have you looked in a mirror, and just as you move away, think you saw another movement behind you?'

'Especially when you're looking in earnest, yes, I can see that, but how can the man who owns this place have the nerve?'

'Makes money. Everyone wants to make money. This guy used to be a middle man for the smiths hereabouts, until he copped on to this little scam. Better than selling spoons and knives to those north of the river. It's the middle men, like him, who are the scum around here, well everywhere really. They do none of the work and take all of the money, from both ends. I tell you, get rid of all of them and this place would be a whole lot better for it. They've got no conscience, they don't care, they just see the dollar signs; they're nearly as bad as lawyers and bankers, but I must say, nowhere near as bad as politicians.'

'Jack's father's a politician.'

Frankie nodded again. 'Yeah, but he's the exception which unfortunately proves the rule. That's why he never gets a major post in government, but they have to keep him close so that they can keep an eye on him.'

'Lawyers and bankers aren't bad though.'

Frankie laughed. 'The Lawyers sit between the victim and the accused, charging the twearth, and making any trial or litigation last for as long as possible; for the simple reason to screw as much money out of everyone that they can. Bankers, well I call them the merchant wankers, because that's what they are. You put some money in a bank and they're meant to keep it safe, but what do they do? I'll tell you, they use our money to fund their gambling habits, they gamble our money and take as much as they can from us, and then plead that the markets are bad, so it's our fault that they lost it all. Middle men, all of them.'

Rose moved her head from side to side, weighing it all up, and then nodded, as she could see that Frankie had hit the nail on the head. The reality of the fact is that those who are meant to help only help themselves, and it made her feel hollow inside. She then thought of the hopes of all the people around here. 'Ten dollars is a lot of money for these people, I suppose?' she said, looking through the window.

'Oh yes. If they do work, ten dollars is a week's pay for

them. Most of them work on the docks, or for the tanners, collecting piss and shit. I told you the other day, hope isn't cheap.'

They left the Colliderscope behind them just as another victim walked into the shop. Rose shook her head at the sadness of it all, but inside knew that you would never be able to stop people dreaming; and there would always be someone around to make money from them.

News of their excursion into the Brews had gone ahead of them as always and Gerald waited for them with mugs of tea for a change, the beverage brewing in the pot as they arrived. Crinning hovered around his master's elbow until Gerald waved him away with an impatient twitch of his hand. His jacket and hat of hundreds of buttons had gone, replaced by just a plain and simple waistcoat. He grinned as he held out a comfy chair for Rose to sit down on.

'Come on my lovely, park yer harse down 'ere.'

Frankie waited, but an invitation for him didn't come, so he shrugged and sat down anyway.

Gerald sat opposite. The three gathered in a little circle, rather like a mothers meeting, until Gerald poured the tea and they sat back, cradling their mugs. 'So,' began Gerald, 'to what do I owe this little pleasure then?'

Frankie leant back and took a sip. 'Drugs, Gerald. And a whole heap of them too. You've probably heard about Maxwell by now, how he and his head parted company.'

'Oh yes, lots o' talk doing the rounds about that.'

'Well, he's been one of the men bringing the drugs in, and obviously we wanted to have a little word with him about that. Unfortunately, it didn't happen, but the drugs are still sitting there; and now we want to know who is going to take up where Maxwell left off. This is where you come in.'

'Don't like drugs, never 'ave,' said Gerald, dunking a biscuit. 'Anyone 'round 'ere 'o gets involved in that sort o' thing gets turfed out pretty damn quick. Snodgrass was one, but you now got him banged up. Why me?'

'For the simple reason you don't like them. We could ask the feelers, but they're so bloody clumsy they'd get spotted straight away. You though, have different resources, shall we say.'

Gerald nodded, acknowledging the sense of that as he listened; his mind drifted a little, and while he contemplated, the soggy part of the biscuit teetered on the brink. Rose watched mesmerised as it wobbled precariously, until he finally rammed it into his mouth at the very last second. 'Got loads o' resources I 'ave,' agreed Gerald. 'So what exactly would yer want me to do?'

'Well, Cornwallis should at this moment be speaking to the King of the Dwarfs. The drugs are stored in the dwarf tunnels down by the docks, under a warehouse. He's going to ask the King to keep an eye on the pile. What we want you to do is to keep an eye above ground to see where it goes and who's doing the fetching. I tell you Gerald, the pile of drugs is huge. We reckon it's the main supply, not only for Gornstock, but for everywhere else besides; that's why we want to see what happens, find out who controls it all.'

'Huge you say? Don't like drugs at all, eats away at society, it does, all that shooting, snorting, sniffing, smoking. Stops people doing what they should be doing, gives 'em a false outlook on life. Life is fer living, get into drugs an' life is fer dying, if you harsks me.'

Rose found Gerald's opinion hard to reconcile, even though she agreed with it. 'But you rule in the Brews, which is a crime ridden society.'

'Crime, yes, my girl, but folks 'ere are poor, an' they's gets into crime in order to make better lives fer themselves. Put drugs into the equation an' the whole thing changes, crime is a way to get the next fix. Drugs makes 'em lazy, they won't work to get out, but just to get smacked up to forget. Then they forgets 'ow to do anything else; they lose all pride in themselves, so they become parasites. I ain't naive, my girl, we got a drug problem in the Brews, but I do all I can to get rid of it; an' that is why I'm going to help you wiv this little problem o'yours.'

CHAPTER 12

'Now, Mrs Gridlington, all the files are there on the shelves, they're a little dusty, but they have been there for a while.' Cornwallis conducted the new secretary around the office, which didn't take long as there wasn't much to see. 'You can use my desk until the new one for you arrives, which should be later on this morning. Any questions?'

'No, Mr Cornwallis, it all seems very fine. But the files, do you not keep them locked away?'

'That's a question, Mrs Gridlington; you said you didn't have any.' Cornwallis groaned inwardly as he said this, he wanted to be jocular, try to put the woman at her ease, but it came out more as an accusation than a joke. He gave a lopsided smile and watched as she crossed her arms and tilted her head to the side. All she has to do now was to impatiently tap her foot. 'My little joke, Mrs Gridlington,' he added, lamely.

'So it was, Mr Cornwallis, a very little one.' She raised one eyebrow, very much like a schoolmistress when she sees a child being naughty. 'However, the files I believe are confidential, and as such should not be on public display.'

'They're not, they're in the office.'

'To which the public has access, and so they are in full view of the public; therefore they are on display.'

Cornwallis had to concede the point in the end, so he had to also concede that there needed to be somewhere to store the files, which meant using the room next to the office. At the moment, they had a wall in the way, so he agreed to get someone in to make a door and to brick up the entrance in the hall. This was all getting very expensive. He'd taken on two new people in the last few days, and now he had to redesign the whole office just to accommodate a secretary that he didn't really want in the first place. He decided to make a point and send the bill to his father, considering he and Rose came up with the idea.

He'd sent Rose and Frankie off first thing this morning to see what they were doing at the finance house. Algernon was still keeping an eye on Dumchuck and Kintersbury, so he would have to see him later to find out what they had been up to overnight. Frankie and Rose had met up with Algernon last night, and they said that they had been keeping a low profile since Maxwell's demise and hadn't ventured outside their houses. Perhaps the dark might have encouraged them to be a bit more adventurous.

Mrs Gridlington began to pull a few of the old files and parchments off the shelf; Cornwallis offered to help as she had to reach up, but she turned him down flat. 'No Mr Cornwallis, I need to get all this in some sort of order, so I would prefer it if you would just leave me be.'

Cornwallis had already begun to help and he pulled at a very thick file just above her head, unbalancing everything below, encouraging it all to slide off. Mrs Gridlington looked up just as everything began to fall. She leapt backwards out of the way but went straight into Cornwallis' arms. He stumbled back and lost his balance, and the two of them crashed to the floor. Cornwallis' arms flailed around, and he found he grabbed Mrs Gridlington in all the wrong places; in fact, he suspected he grabbed some bits that even Mr Gridlington had never touched. The experience left him bemused to say the least, because Mrs Gridlington dressed in a tidy but very matronly way, but what he had touched did not equate with what he had seen. Mrs Gridlington had a very well-toned, slim and lithe body. She didn't squidge, nor did she squash, except when he felt her chest scrunch up against him; and there too he found an anomaly, because they were firm, round and quite large.

'Mr Cornwallis,' she breathed, just inches from his face. 'If this is what you call "a getting to know your employee" session, then I think it might have gone a bit too far.'

Cornwallis rolled her off and clambered to his feet with his face burning bright red, he held out a hand to help her up and offered a grovelling apology. 'I am ever so sorry, Mrs Gridlington, I do beg your pardon; a complete accident, I would never… I'm sorry, but I would never…!'

'It's all right, Mr Cornwallis, my fault entirely.' She stood up and brushed the dust off her dress. 'Those files were to blame, coming down like that; I hope I didn't hurt you.'

'Not at all, Mrs Gridlington, I apologise again, I shouldn't have reached up.'

Her eyes sparkled just for an instant, and a hint of a smile played at the corner of her lips; and then she shut it all away again. 'Mr Cornwallis, consider it purely an unfortunate accident. Let's put it behind us both and think no more of it. Now, you go about your business and leave me to sort everything out here,' and she began to shoo him out the door. 'Just one thing, Mr Cornwallis; where do you plan to be today, just in case anything comes up? A secretary must know how to contact her employer in the event of an important development.'

'Oh, right,' mumbled Cornwallis. 'Er… I… er, I should be meeting my two colleagues at the Gornstock Trust and Holdings, Mrs Gridlington; it's a finance house, but it's all hush-hush. We won't be in the building, you understand. Then later I will be seeing someone, but I couldn't tell you where.'

'Of course, Mr Cornwallis, I understand totally,' she said, tapping her nose. 'Discretion is my middle name.'

Cornwallis bounded down the steps as if in a hurry to put distance between himself and Mrs Gridlington, he stopped briefly before venturing outside and took a deep breath. He thought all that business upstairs very disconcerting, she hadn't got ruffled or shocked by what happened, whereas he felt mortified. Perhaps Mrs Gridlington had hidden depths, and if so, Mr Gridlington might be a lucky man. The door to the left of him swung open and his newest tenant poked her nose out.

'Good morning, Mr Cornwallis.'

'Oh, good morning, Miss Thrape. How's business?'

'Steady, thank you,' Miss Thrape replied sweetly. 'Could I have a quick word with you before you go?'

Cornwallis smiled. 'Of course, though it will have to be quick.'

Miss Thrape returned the smile and turned to lead him through into her inner sanctum. Cornwallis hadn't been in here since she had taken over the rooms and the plush furnishings and deep rich colours impressed him; an amalgam of tastes, from the antique to an eastern harem, old furniture and velvet wall hangings with cushions everywhere. His nose noticed a sweet smell of incense from joss-sticks smoking lazily from a vase standing on the table. It might not be to everyone's taste, but he quite liked it.

'I have been contacted from someone from the other side who wishes to give you a message, Mr Cornwallis.' She sat down in a tapestry covered armchair and indicated that he should sit opposite. Sitting demurely with her hands placed on her lap, she began to bite her lower lip. 'You have to understand that I wouldn't normally do this sort of thing, however the departed insisted and wouldn't let me rest until I promised to speak with you.' She looked at him with soft apologetic eyes. 'I hardly had a wink of sleep last night as he kept going on and on and on.'

'I'm sorry, Miss Thrape,' replied Cornwallis, somewhat surprised. He avoided this sort of thing as a rule as he had no wish to know what anyone from the other side wanted or thought. Mostly, or so he'd heard, the messages were always obscure and bore little relation to reality. He'd come to the conclusion that most mediums were charlatans who were only in it for the money they could screw from potential clients. He knew that a few were real, but they were very few and far between. He hoped Miss Thrape was one of these as he found her attractive with her long dark hair and slim figure. She had a heart shaped face with deep brown eyes, which, he couldn't help but notice, now began to smoulder as she looked back at him. She wore a long tight fitting black skirt with a tight red blouse, low cut to show a cleavage that held a lot of promise. So as far as he was concerned, as long as she didn't hurt anyone, she could do as she pleased. 'Perhaps you could tell me what the message is?' He continued, as he crossed his legs.

'I will, but you must understand, it's not me speaking, but the departed. He insisted that I tell you word for word and leave nothing out.' She fidgeted a little in her chair as though uncomfortable. 'Word for word, you understand.'

'I do, Miss Thrape. Who sent it?' Cornwallis felt equally uncomfortable now, but for a different reason.

'I don't know the name as he wouldn't say, and quite frankly, I'm pleased about that. A most obnoxious man and I would be grateful if you promise not to try and contact him through me again.'

'Really?' This piqued Cornwallis' interest.

'Really,' she answered. 'The departed said; and I would prefer not to say this, but I have to. He said. "Tell him he's a dead man walking and it won't be long before he gets here, and when he does, then I'm going to rip *his* bloody head clean off, and then we'll see how *he* likes it." He didn't seem to be a very nice man at all.'

Cornwallis grinned. Miss Thrape was the real thing after all. Maxwell, it could only be Maxwell. 'Thank you for that, most illuminating. Did he say anything else?'

She shook her head. 'Not to you, but he did give an indication that my virtue would not be intact if he was still around. Most unsavoury, as if I would.'

Her eyes held his for a few moments and unmistakably they were saying that she most definitely would. 'I apologise again, Miss Thrape,' answered Cornwallis with a little awkward cough, he uncrossed and then re-crossed his legs and tried to get the thought from out of his mind; she was a tenant of his, and that ruled out any thought of playing hide the sausage. 'He only went yesterday, a very nasty character too.'

'Well, from my understanding of the other side he won't be a problem for you when you go. He'll be sent on an anger management course, and then will probably go for reincarnation, something apt no doubt.'

Cornwallis stood up and quickly placed his hands in front of his trousers. 'I do hope so, Miss Thrape, I'm only sorry that you were subjected to his obscenities.'

'All in a day's work, Mr Cornwallis.' She smiled a little shyly and as she stood up, she quickly glanced at his nether regions. 'Er, before you go, would you consider putting a clause in my lease saying that should you pop off to the other side, then I would still be safe from eviction? You know, I don't expect for a moment that your demise is imminent, but it does pay to be careful.'

Cornwallis laughed.' Of course, Miss Thrape, remind me

when I'm a little less busy.'

Miss Thrape's smile broadened. She stepped forward and rested her hand on his wrist, perilously close to resting on something else. 'Thank you, Mr Cornwallis,' she said softly.

With their close proximity, he could smell her breath and feel his arm cradled between her chest ornaments; she stayed there for a brief second before stepping back.

'Now, please take my card. If there is anything I can do for you, you just have to ask. Contacts, ghosts, anything at all; in actual fact, I will be trying to persuade a ghost to pass over properly tonight.' She bit her lip again and then continued with a little hope in her voice. 'Perhaps you might like to come with me and see how it's all done?'

He couldn't help himself; he had a brief vision and before he knew it, he had asked the question. 'Where would that be then?'

'Do you know the Jerkey Turkey, down Poulterer's Way? They are having problems in one of the bedrooms. As you know, ghosts are those unfortunates who won't except that they have passed over, so we will have to wait in the room for this one to appear. I'm afraid that there is only a bed there, and it must be dark, so we will just have to make ourselves as comfortable as we can while we wait. Sometimes it can take all night,' she added, with a glint in her eye.

Cornwallis opened his mouth, but struggled to find a reply. All night, in a bedroom, with Miss Thrape! 'If I have the time then I might just take you up on your kind offer,' he managed in the end. Bollocks to her being a tenant he thought, gift horse and mouth sprang to mind. Besides, it was clear that nothing would happen between him and Rose, and even if there had been an opportunity, it had now gone, so he didn't need to feel guilty. 'Until later then, Miss Thrape.'

Miss Thrape smiled warmly. 'Isabella, please. Er, Jocelyn?'

'Jack,' amended Cornwallis.

Once back outside Cornwallis breathed deeply and leant against the door frame. First Mrs Gridlington with her hidden charms and now Isabella with her not so hidden ones, all in the space of about ten minutes. His luck was turning.

*

Rose waited in the shadows while Frankie nipped around the side. There had been a lot of activity around the entrance to the finance house and Frankie decided to find out why. Bored with the waiting, she took the opportunity to clean her nails while Frankie did his little bit of investigating. She supposed he wouldn't be too long, but in-between scraping her cuticles and filing her talons she cast glances in the direction of the street and the front entrance. It was a busy thoroughfare and people hurried by just a few feet from where she stood, in an old disused shop-front which used to sell potions and lucky charms, according to the dusty signs lying on the floor; not so lucky, she mused, as she polished a nail on her shirt.

'Er, excuse me, darling, but do you do special rates for senior citizens, like?'

'Uh, sorry?' Rose, startled out of her reverie, turned to see a small old man in a cloth cap with a woollen cardigan, leather patches were on the elbows and his head only came up to her chest.

'You know, like they do in the Brews; half-price or a two-for-one in the mornings, when business is slow. Only I 'ad a bit a luck wiv the dominos last night, and if I went 'ome now the missus'l clean me right out. Fought I might have a bit a fun first, like.'

'Ah.' Clarity eased into Rose's mind. 'No, sorry. Even at half-price you couldn't afford me, best get yourself home.'

The old man smiled. 'I reckon I could afford you, I 'ad a *very* good night,' he said, tapping his nose knowingly.

'No, you couldn't,' replied Rose, firmly. 'If you're that desperate then go to the Brews and have your two-for-one.' She thought she would have a bit of fun to start with, string him along just to see how much he'd pay; but she should be working and her conscience wouldn't let her take it very far, and besides, the joke had already worn thin.

'Tried that the other week. Two lovely young things they were and they both took great care and helped me out o' me clothes. They's then gets stripped off and, well, they starts wivout me. Next thing I knows is that I've sort of finished before I gets started, so to speak. They tries to get a bit o' life out o' me, but at my age it's a once and it's gone; the buggers still bloody charged me though. Only want the half-price now. Won't take long you know, we could go down the alley 'round the corner, do a stand up; I'm sure I could find a crate to give me a bit o' height.'

Rose fixed him with a stony stare. 'I said, no. Anyway, you've made a mistake; I'm not that sort of girl.'

The old fellow stood up as tall as he could and sniffed contemptuously. 'Oh, I see, your being ageist now, then. That's the trouble wiv the likes o' you, we old un's just ain't got the stamina, eh? Not good enough, eh? A quickie 'round the corner too demeaning, eh? I tells you there's many a girl who's been glad of my attention and my folding stuff; you wait until no one wants you, and then you'll come running to the likes o' me. Be glad then, won't you?'

Rose's head span. She couldn't believe the diatribe aimed at her, and besides, all she'd been doing was standing there. 'Look, you odious little man, for the last time, I am not for sale. I'm not a street girl. I do not let a man take me in the back alley.' She thought for a second. 'I mean take me down the alley, in the alley, or anything to do with an alley, stand up or otherwise. I do not sleep with men for money. I am not a prostitute!' Her voice rose with every word she spoke, and she punctuated every word with a finger dabbing into his chest, until at the end she practically shouted.

'Oh,' exclaimed the old man. 'I'm sorry, I fought you were.'

'No, I'm not. Now, will you please leave me alone.'

'Right you are then, I'll go.' He turned away and slunk out of the doorway, his hands dejectedly thrust into his trouser's pockets. He stopped after a few steps and turned back. 'Er, you don't fancy starting now, do you?'

Rose stood with her hands on her hips and thrust out her chest with her feet planted, shoulder width apart. She shook her hair with a flick of her head and yelled down the street. 'No, now sod off!'

The people in the street heard and they hesitated and turned, looking at Rose for a brief half-second, but long enough to make her cheeks turn red. She felt the blush rise and couldn't believe it. She just didn't blush.

'Nothing like keeping a discreet watch,' observed Cornwallis as he came up behind her with Frankie in tow. 'Poor old fellow, and what may I ask forced you to use such unladylike language like that?'

Rose looked at Cornwallis and chewed a wasp for a second or so while she thought. 'If you must know, he propositioned me. Really, no girl is safe in this city.'

Cornwallis burst out laughing. 'Well, well, well, the nerve of the man. Just out of curiosities sake, though,' he began with a glint in his eye. 'What did he propose?'

Rose's lips took the shape of a smile, but the eyes said something else. 'He wanted to take me down an alley and have a stand up, if you must know.' She looked hard at him, daring him to respond.

He dared. 'Really? Now there's a thought. How much did you want?'

The wasp returned, doing the rounds. 'We didn't get around to discussing the financial implications of the transaction. Only got so far as me telling him that it would be prohibitively expensive should I respond positively to his suggestion to take me up the back alley.'

Frankie's initial giggling erupted into a snot filled guffaw. He bent double with laughter and had trouble catching his breath.

'Really,' exclaimed Rose. 'You men are all little schoolboys at heart, aren't you?'

Cornwallis nodded his agreement whilst stifling his laughter. 'Back alley, front alley. Whatever takes your fancy, I suppose?'

Frankie erupted again.

She looked at Frankie and then back at him, thought of a response, and then changed her mind; remembering that they had all creased themselves with laughter in the warehouse while she pretended to have a multiple-orgasm. 'All right,' she said, smiling at last. 'But if you think that you can make me an offer to take me up the alley, then you've got another thing coming.'

Cornwallis let his laughter flow for a minute or so longer and then managed to compose himself. 'Oh Rose, you can be such a staid old lady sometimes. Besides, I don't need to make you an offer; I've already got one. Miss Thrape from downstairs has invited me to see her working tonight, and the indication is that there won't be a lot of work being done.'

Rose's mouth hung open in surprise while Frankie

immediately regained his composure.

'What's that again?' he asked Cornwallis, somewhat shocked. 'Did you say Miss Thrape?'

'I did indeed, young Frankie. She has invited me to the Jerkey Turkey to wait for a ghost in one of the bedrooms. Just she and me and all night to do it in; what do you think of that, eh?'

Frankie glanced at Rose to see her reaction, and he saw her stiffen just a fraction. He returned his stare to Cornwallis and hoped that he could see that Miss Thrape should not come into the equation, and definitely not now. 'Are you sure, Jack? I mean she's a nice girl and all, but is she your type exactly? Besides, she's a tenant.'

'And what's the problem with that, then?' asked Cornwallis.

'Well, it's obvious, innit?'

'No, Frankie, it's not; anyway, it's not your concern.'

'Well, it might be.'

'Why?'

'Because... because...' Frankie struggled to find a reason with Rose standing there. If she hadn't been, he might well have said that he was throwing away the chance of his life, but instead he flummoxed around searching for something he could say.

'I'm sure she's a nice girl, Jack,' interjected Rose. 'After all, it's not as if you have someone else around at the moment, is it?'

'It seems not,' replied Cornwallis, in a flat monotone. 'So,' he clapped his hands together signalling the end of the conversation. 'Back to work, then. Frankie has been telling me that the finance house has closed down,' he explained to Rose. 'They have apparently lost all their money and are now clearing out.'

'Yes,' agreed Frankie. He shot Rose a look, but she replied with a barely noticeable shake of her head. 'I just spoke to one of the removal guys; he said everything's going into storage.'

'So, the question now, is why? I don't know about you, but it seems to me a bit sudden; and after all we've learnt about this place, I suggest that the reason is not altogether legal. I'm going to leave you two to catch up with Algernon, to see what's been happening overnight to our two little friends. In the meantime, I will go and see my father, to see if he has heard anything of interest in the Assembly. I don't think we'll gain anything by looking at this place anymore.'

The other two agreed, and they stepped out of the doorway casting a last look at Gornstock Trust and Holdings. They stood together just a little longer, and then Rose noticed a little flutter of dust coming from above. She looked up out of curiosity and saw a further cascade coming from the chimney, a frown creased her brow, and then she saw a hand on the side of the brickwork. 'Look out!' she yelled, just as the chimney began to tip.

Frankie and Cornwallis dived back into the doorway for cover, pulling Rose with them, just as a WHUMPH noise came with an almighty crash, sucking the air away with brick dust rising up like a fountain. The chimney had crashed to the pavement in the exact place they had been standing. Pedestrians had heard the shout from Rose and also took cover, and thankfully, no one appeared injured, but a few were standing around in a degree of shock at their close encounter as the bricks rattled to a stop. Cornwallis, covered in dust like a red shrouded ghost, tentatively edged out onto the pavement and looked up; there, three floors up, he could see a curly mop of brown hair looking down.

'Bastard,' he yelled. 'He meant that for us. Rose, Frankie, if we're quick we might just catch the shit.'

'Wha... what?' cried Frankie. 'How the hell are we going to get up there?'

'The short cut, that's how.'

Cornwallis grabbed a brick and threw it through the window of the disused shop, glass shattered, and he began to kick a hole big enough for them to get through.

'Somebody ain't going to like this,' observed Frankie.

'Maybe not,' replied Rose. 'But I find that I don't care.'

'Come to think of it, neither do I.' Frankie grinned, then joined Cornwallis in kicking out the shards.

As soon as they could, Cornwallis and Rose dived into the shop and hurried through to the back, leaving Frankie to keep an eye on the roof. There were always stairs somewhere, and they found them straight away. They rushed up them, taking the steps two at a time; dust billowed out behind them and lay on the stairs like a carpet. Both of them pelted around the turn in the stairs and headed upwards, right to the top of the building where Cornwallis knew there would be a trapdoor leading to the roof. All the buildings around here had easily accessible roofs. They ground to a stop at the top and looked up, nothing there, so Cornwallis kicked a door and dived in. They found the desired trap, but with no means to get up. Cornwallis took the opportunity of the pause to catch his breath, as he didn't want his chest heaving with exertion, God's he felt unfit. He had a momentary thought of Miss Thrape, and hoped that she didn't expect a marathon; just a bit of light jogging would do. Rose though looked like she'd just had a stroll in the park; it was so unfair. Time ticked by with every second, giving the assailant more of an opportunity to escape. Rose saw a table in the next room along and hurriedly dragged it through. She placed it under the trap and Cornwallis jumped up, wheezing as though he was a fifty-a-day man. Reaching up, he drew the bolt and pushed hard until the door gave way in a shower of dirt and leaves. He jumped up and pulled himself through, and then hurried to the edge to look down, searching for Frankie. Rose scrambled her way up, and just as she joined him on the edge, Cornwallis spotted Frankie gesticulating wildly.

'There's Frankie, he's pointing that way,' puffed Cornwallis.

The pair of them set off running. They skipped over the debris littering the roof whilst keeping half an eye on Frankie down below. They skirted a rusty pram and then an old bedstead; Cornwallis wondered how the hell did they get up here? They came to a small gap as the building ended where an alley ran below, only a few feet wide, and Cornwallis leapt over with barely a pause. Rose hesitated, judging the gap, but took a deep breath, closed her eyes, which probably wasn't a good thing to do as it would have been better to see the ridge on the other building, as opposed to opening the eyes to see a pavement rushing up towards you, and leapt. Luckily, for her, Cornwallis waited, as she only just managed to get one foot on the ridge, the other missing, and as she opened her eyes she both saw, and felt, Cornwallis grabbing onto her arm and pulling her to safety; just as gravity woke up and decided that today was going to be a good day.

'Stop playing about, Rose, come on,' yelled Cornwallis.

Rose opened her mouth to reply that she wasn't, when Cornwallis turned and hared off again. They jumped over a roll of carpet and swerved around a ventilation stack, a skylight offered a particularly interesting view of a couple in the room below, but Cornwallis didn't feel he had the time to offer an opinion on their technique. Another gap, and neither of them stopped this time as they jumped over it together, and this time Rose kept her eyes open. Up ahead a mop of brown hair dodged between the stacks; they had spotted their prey, and Cornwallis grinned triumphantly.

'There's the little bastard,' he cried, pointing.

They set off with renewed enthusiasm, just as the assailant turned, and in turn, spotted them. He gave a little start and then increased his pace accordingly, climbing up a low wall and running on. Cornwallis and Rose were gaining fast, at some point the man would have to find a way down; perhaps that would be the opportunity they were looking for. They were only about thirty paces behind him now and the man cast a quick look over his shoulder; for some reason he grinned, and Cornwallis felt that perhaps he knew something that they didn't. He darted around to his right behind a big chimney stack, and by the time they'd followed, he had disappeared. Cornwallis and Rose ground to a halt and looked around perplexed. The man had just vanished.

A peel of laughter then drew their attention and they moved forward to the edge. Below them, and just a few feet away, their assailant looked at them and smirked as he dragged the plank that had bridged the gap, the gap being far too wide to jump. He stood up as the plank banged down and gave a time honoured gesticulation from the waist down. Cornwallis and Rose looked on with fury.

High above flew a Janker on its migratory path to the southern mountains from the northern territories. It had got a little lost as normally the bird would not come anywhere near the city, but it knew that if it kept going, at some point it would get to where it wanted to go. An enormous bird, the Janker had a prodigious appetite, and it wasn't unknown for one to take a fully grown bovine for a snack. The only way it could get airborne was to stand on the side of a mountain and leap off, and hope that by the time it got to the bottom the wings would work. People mistook them for Dragons, but Dragons were way out east and never came this way. The Janker had eaten well before it started on its long journey, and now it felt the growling in its stomach. Its tail feathers twitched, and then the biggest anus in the natural world came open.

Cornwallis called across the gap. 'Don't think you've got away my friend, you're going to be a hunted man from now on.'

'Yeah, right,' replied the man indifferently. 'I'm going to do for you the next time, though.'

A speck in the sky was getting larger by the second as it hurtled to twearth. The assailant looked above Cornwallis' head and saw it coming; grinning as he noticed the perfect trajectory. Cornwallis turned to see what had taken the man's eye, and seeing what amounted to the biggest dollop of shit ever imagined coming straight down towards him, grabbed Rose and dived for cover. Unfortunately, the man hadn't done well in geometry at school and his judgment of angles could have been better, his assumption that Cornwallis would cop the lot was out by about twenty feet.

The stinking steaming mass plummeted to just above where Cornwallis' head would have been had he been upright, but fortunately, sailed harmlessly by. The man opened his mouth and began the fateful words. 'Oh. Sh…!' Which though remarkable accurate, was in fact, a trifle understated, when it struck him perfectly in a soft thudding kind of way. The shit may well have been soft and squidgy, but it travelled at an enormous velocity, and a ton of shit is just that, a ton. Open-mouthed with dismay, the man realised just a split second before it hit, what was going to happen, and perhaps if he hadn't opened his mouth, his demise might well have been very different.

'Well now, will you look at that,' exclaimed Frankie, as he finished shovelling the shit away.

Cornwallis gave a low whistle while Rose fought down the impulse to vomit. The would-be assailant had a massively engorged stomach, bloated with the forced entry of about fifty pounds of Janker shit. The startled look on his face really said it all.

Sergeant Jethro MacGillicudy eased himself through the trapdoor and sauntered over towards Cornwallis. 'I knew it was you,' he said with a grin. 'Man downed by Janker droppings, on a roof, in Gornstock, and I knew you had to be involved somewhere.'

Frankie turned and grinned back. 'Jethro. What are you doing here?'

'Doing, Frankie? I'll have you know I'm doing my job.'

'You mean you're back? What happened?'

'All in good time, all in good time,' he replied with a wink. 'Oi, Dewdrop. Hurry up man, got just the job for you.'

Dewdrop appeared on the roof and immediately gave a look of dismay as he saw Rose standing there. 'Oh Gods,' he muttered. 'Not her again.'

'Right, Dewdrop,' began MacGillicudy. 'I am going to take our friends here downstairs and take some statements, while you are going to clear all this mess up. Frankie, give him your shovel please, and Dewdrop, you will arrange to get that body removed and then bag up all this shit for removal to the station allotments. You got that, boy?'

Dewdrop nodded dumbly and took the shovel from Frankie's hand. 'Yes, Sergeant.'

'Good. I'll send your colleagues up to help, now get to it.'

MacGillicudy took the statements and sat back with a triumphant look on his face, he grinned from ear to ear as he looked from one to the other. 'Go on, ask me then.'

Cornwallis obliged.

'Well, you just wouldn't believe it. Yesterday Bough called both me and Grinde back into the office and told us that having thought the situation through he had only one option, and that we were to be both reduced in rank for a period of six months. Well, Grinde just couldn't believe it. He went puce and could hardly speak, and when he did, he just looked straight at Bough and told him that if he down-graded him then he would resign from the force. Bough's face lit up like a beacon it did. Grinde hardly had the words out of his mouth when Bough stood up and offered his hand, excepting the resignation on the spot. Grinde couldn't believe it. He thought that Bough would back down, he doesn't know Harold Bough like I know him.'

Frankie burst out laughing. 'You mean the old bastard's actually gone?'

MacGillicudy nodded. 'That just left me. Bough took my stripes, leaving me just a constable again, and said he would speak to me again when I'd learnt my lesson. So I just marched straight out and went on a patrol; it were just like the good old days, me, the pavement, and no responsibility. I strolled around cadging tea and chatting to the locals, I even for old times' sake dived into some of my old haunts for a crafty puff on the old roll-up. I can't tell you how good it felt. Then this morning, when I turned up, I got the message to go back and see Bough again. I stood in front of that desk while he gave me the biggest bollocking of my career. He then said that I'd spent enough time as a constable and he'd decided to re-instate me as a sergeant, and what's more, now that the Yard had lost a senior sergeant, I was to be immediately promoted.' He held his hands out in supplication. 'What do you think of that?'

'Congratulations,' smiled Rose.

'Ditto that,' said Frankie. 'The old bastard has actually gone then?' he repeated. 'Well, well, well.'

MacGillicudy grinned. 'He has indeed. So now it's been left to me to organise the place properly, and Gods are there going to be some changes. Bough has given me a free rein to do what I want.'

'Sounds good,' added Cornwallis. 'Perhaps you might find one or two more to help us then?'

MacGillicudy chortled. 'Yes, I've been thinking about getting you a bit more help. The decapitation of Maxwell is the talk of the station. Poor old Chalkie though, he's still upset.'

'Not half as much as me,' said Cornwallis dejectedly. 'I really wanted to talk to him.'

Cornwallis headed off to the Assembly, leaving Frankie and Rose to chat to MacGillicudy for a while. Then they were to go and see Algernon, who hopefully this time, might have something to tell them; Kintersbury and Dumchuck must have got up to something last night. He grabbed a double minced-beef patty bun with bacon, cheese and ketchup from Sal's before going across the road. As always, she bent his ear, and again it had to do with Rose. What was he waiting for? Why hadn't he done it yet? Girls like that don't grow on trees you know. He tried to explain between mouthfuls, but as always, Sal never listened to anything she didn't want to hear. Sometimes she was more like his mother than his mother, which left his brain whirling. Eventually he managed to escape the tirade and kissed her lightly on the cheek before heading across the road.

Entering the Assembly was always an experience; thankfully, it had gone midday, so he didn't have to suffer the excruciating display of the opening dance. The guards were standing at ease, one each side of the door, and they came to attention with a little ting-a-ling as the bells on their ankles jangled; then watched him warily out of the corner of their eyes as he walked past and into the building. Perkins was in his customary position behind the porters' desk, and he greeted Cornwallis with all the courtesy he could muster.

'Good afternoon, Mr Cornwallis, sir. My my, twice in a week, sir, are you thinking of taking up your seat on a permanent basis, sir?'

Cornwallis smiled ruefully. 'No, Perkins, there's no fear of that. Just need to keep in touch with my father. I assume he's in today?'

'Yes, sir. I believe he's in his office,' he leaned a little closer and softened his voice conspiratorially. 'If you don't mind me saying, sir, there's a little bit of a kerfuffle in the house today. I would keep clear of the Inner Ring if you can.' He tapped his nose and winked.

Cornwallis felt the hairs on the back of his neck stiffen. 'Any idea why?' he asked, equally quietly.

'Not for me to say really, sir, but it seems that some of the members are having a little money problems.'

Cornwallis bit back the twitch of a smile that formed on his lips. 'Really? Well I never.'

Perkins looked about him in case anyone overheard. 'I'm not one for gossip as you know, sir, but it is said one or two of them might even be bankrupt.'

'Oh dear, that's not good news. I'll take your advice and steer well clear of the Inner Ring then.' Cornwallis reached into his pocket and deposited a couple of dollars into Perkins' hand. 'If you happen to hear anything else of interest, then perhaps you might let me or my father know?'

'Of course, sir,' answered Perkins, pocketing the money deftly. 'Have always looked after each other, we have, sir. I mean the Cornwallis' and the Perkins'; we go back generations, do we not?'

'We have indeed, Perkins,' replied Cornwallis, stepping away and heading for the door to the lobby. 'We have indeed.'

Cornwallis senior was, as Perkins said, in his office, but far from being alone. A melee of members congregated, either inside or outside his office, all waving bits of paper and clamouring to have a word with the earl. Cornwallis shook his head and leant against the wall a little further down the corridor as he watched the entertainment.

'Enough!' The great bellow shot out of the office and then bounced along the corridor. The crowd quietened for a few seconds and then quickly started up again. 'I said enough!' screamed the voice, obviously at the end of his tether. 'Gentlemen, I will see each of you in good time, but only one at a time, and I will send for you when I need you.'

The crowd reluctantly began to back out of the office and the shouts subsided. Cornwallis fleetingly caught a glimpse of his father's arm as he pushed the last of them out and slammed the door closed. Suddenly, the corridor seemed awfully full with people filing by; but fortunately, nobody seemed to recognise him, which gave him a bit of leeway, as he knew damn well that if they did recognise him, then they would turn on him like a pack of hungry wolves.

'Go away,' yelled his father as Cornwallis knocked on the door. The corridor had now emptied, though the floorboards still seemed to vibrate from all the stomping that had just gone on.

Cornwallis turned the handle and let the door swing open a tad before poking his head through. 'Even your own flesh and blood, the fruit of your loins?'

'Oh Gods, boy,' groaned the earl. 'Come in and be quick. Have they all gone?'

'Like a morgue out there, what's going on?'

'A morgue? You ain't far from the truth with this place,

except where their money is involved.'

Cornwallis raised an eyebrow in question.

'Expenses. I have been given the dubious honour of looking into the members' expenses. The thought being, that as I don't claim them, then I should be impartial. Word got out this morning and everyone is worried about what I am going to do. I have a mandate to bring any false claims to the attention of the law. No Assembly privilege, anyone found being underhand will find a ton of bricks landing on their head.'

'I would have thought that that would be ninety per cent of the Assembly.'

'And the rest. The other day, we had a debate in the house and the vote went through not to change, then the Warden decided that it should be investigated anyway. He said he didn't intend changing anything, so if fact, he's not gone against the house. As you can imagine there are a lot of arses squeaking at the moment; hence that lot,' and he indicated the door.

Cornwallis grinned. 'And what have you found so far?'

'You wouldn't believe it. So far I have looked at a member who has four houses; over the last four years he's had an office extension on one house, a summer house built on another, his garden landscaped on the third, and a drive gravelled on the fourth.'

'Well, a drive gravelled ain't too bad, I suppose.'

'The drive is a mile and a half long.'

'Oh.'

'Yes, and another member has put down for entertainment costs; I've checked the address and it turns out it's a brothel and he's the owner. The gentleman has let the Government fund his little business.'

Cornwallis' grin widened. 'Then, you'll be going to shaft him now.'

'Too bloody right I will. I could go on and on and on. This member, and I know it's not a lot of money, has even claimed for... No, hang on, I've misread this one. It *is* for a lot of money. The cheek of the man.'

Cornwallis stepped around to the other side of the desk and looked over his father's shoulder. '$26 per item,' he read, and then his father turned the page and his finger pointed to the bottom line. '283@$26 ea. Total $7358.00. Bouquets delivered to a Miss A A Arbuthnot, for continuing services.'

Cornwallis senior flicked the document with the back of his hand and leant back in the chair. 'Seems like we're paying for a daily bunch of flowers for his bit on the side, I dread to think what I'll find when I start to dig down into all this, and I've not even scratched the surface yet.'

'You sound as if you're surprised. If you show a dog a bone, it's going to chew it.' Cornwallis returned to the other side of the desk and sat down.

'I know. A little bit here and there we can ignore, but this amount is far more than even a cynical old man like me would've thought. Anyway, my boy, what brings you here today? I'm sure it's not to listen to the moans and groans of your father.'

'No. Actually, there are a couple of things. Firstly you connived with Rose to get me an office manager, didn't you?'

The earl smiled. 'Now, there's a girl. Rose, what I wouldn't give for... Well, never mind that, she's yours, and I suppose I shouldn't be jealous, but you should have seen them fawning around her when I took her to dinner. Word has got about and I've had three people asking how much she costs. Take your father's advice and don't let her get away, my boy.'

'She's hardly mine, actually I don't think she's that interested.'

'Not interested? She didn't stop talking about you; damn

near put me off my pudding. I suggest you pull your finger out and get in there quick, my boy. Incidentally, did you take someone on?'

Cornwallis nodded. 'Started this morning, a Mrs Gridlington. I'll give her a few days to see how it goes. You say she didn't stop talking about me?'

Cornwallis senior shook his head. 'Jocelyn, you sound like a schoolboy. There are times when I really wonder about you.'

'There are times when I wonder about myself too. I'm due to see someone else tonight.'

'Someone who is not Rose?' replied his father aghast. 'Get some sense, Jocelyn; how can you do that when that delectable creature is just waiting for you? For God's sake don't say anything to Rose and get yourself out of it.'

'Too late for that,' sighed Cornwallis. 'I've already told her.'

'You Idiot. Then tell her you've changed your mind. You go ploughing a furrow now you might end up with a crop.'

Cornwallis tapped his lip in thought. 'I'll think about it, but you're one to talk,' he said, accusingly. 'You've been ploughing different furrows all your life.'

'Yes, but I'm an Earl and a member of the government, so it's expected. Gentry *do* that sort of thing.'

'I'm gentry.'

'At the moment, yes, but I might disown you for being a bloody fool.'

'Okay, Okay,' he held up his hands to stop the tirade. 'I said I'll think about it. Now the other thing I wanted to talk to you about, if you can just drag your mind away from Rose, is Gornstock Trust and Holdings. Did you know that it's closed its doors, gone bankrupt?'

'Has it by Gods? No, I didn't. When?'

'This morning, as far as I can tell. I think you said that

Pelegrew Kintersbury tried to get you to invest?'

'Yes, he did, but if you remember, I declined. This morning, you say? Well, well, well. I've been so busy with this expenses lark that I haven't had time for anything else.'

Cornwallis nodded. 'Just as well you didn't invest then, as it turns out. Abraham Dumchuck is involved somewhere too. Look father, I went to see the Bagman the other day, and I suppose I shouldn't be telling you this, but he tried to get hold of Dumchuck's tax return, which was mistakenly put in. The two names, Kintersbury and Dumchuck, are interwoven into this whole thing.

'The Bagman? Oh Gods, then it must be bad.' He shook his head as though to clear out his ears. 'I believe a lot of members have invested in the Gornstock Trust and Holdings, if that has gone bankrupt...!'

'Look, keep your ears open for me, will you, but don't mention Kintersbury and Dumchuck. Incidentally, you spoke to Radstock for me as you said you had a little leverage with him, I'd be interested to know now what that is. Only he's the Bagman's poodle, and he's feeding him information.'

'I... I don't know if I can do that, it's rather personal, you know.'

'Look, father,' Cornwallis' temper began to rise. 'So far I've had three, possibly four, attempts on my life; thankfully each one has failed, but there could be another. I need to know all I can about everyone involved, and Radstock *is* involved somewhere.'

The earl wrestled with his conscience for a time, but at the end of the day Radstock was only an Assembly member, and if his son's life was truly at stake? 'Only if you promise to keep it to yourself.'

Cornwallis nodded and breathed a sigh of relief.

'Well, Radstock,' began the earl, 'has a little problem with the ladies. He can only get off, if you pardon the expression, when he is being humiliated. He goes to a dominatrix not far from here, for... er, relief. He is particularly sensitive about it, which I find strange, as half of the Assembly are into something along those lines, but he tries to keep it quiet.'

Cornwallis' face took on a grin, his temper deflating rapidly. 'Oh, that is interesting. And how do *you* know about it?'

The earl grinned too. 'Not what you might think. He drunk a little too much one night after a busy day in the house, he and I were up in the bar when a cleaner began working; he got quite excited. I suppose he thought I hadn't noticed to start with, but it became a little too obvious, to his shame, so over a few drinks it all came out — not that, thankfully,' he added, as his son's grin widened.

'Takes all sorts, I suppose,' replied Cornwallis, 'I expect that the Bagman knows all about this. Do you know the address of the lady he sees?'

'Oh, now you're asking. Let's have a think for a moment.' He drummed his fingers on the desk while he wracked his brain. Radstock had told him, now where did he say...? 'Got it,' triumphed Cornwallis senior. 'Havelock Crescent, very upmarket; which is why I remembered.'

'Expensive area,' agreed Cornwallis. 'Thanks for that.'

'Just keep it to yourself, if you would. What are you going to do now?'

'I'm going down to see the Bagman, see what more he'll tell me. Oh, by the way, I believe Roland Goup is in his clutches, if everything went according to plan. I'll find out while I'm down there.' Cornwallis got up and headed for the door. 'I'll catch up with you later if I can, do you know the quick to the Bagman?'

The earl shook his head and then looked at his son

earnestly. 'No. Nobody wants to know that little bit of information, in case he gets to hear that you've been speaking about him. There are a lot in here who don't believe he even exists. Jocelyn, take care.'

'Don't worry, I will,' replied Cornwallis, turning at the door.

'And Jocelyn,' called his father as he pulled the handle. 'Don't forget about Rose!'

CHAPTER 13

The problem in trying to find a secret department in a building as big as the House of Assembly is where to start. Cornwallis knew that if he went outside and around to the back he could probably get in through the underground coach-park, however, Mr Magpie would probably still be following him, and at the moment he felt like he wanted to catch the Bagman unawares. He suspected that Mr Magpie waited outside, ready for him to come out, so he would only do that if he found no other way. Perkins was the obvious choice; he'd been in the House so long he must know everything about the place.

The elevator pinged to announce that it had reached the floor and the door opened slowly. Cornwallis stood in front and waited while the flunkey inside helped an old member out. The flunkey looked at Cornwallis and beckoned him in, but Cornwallis shook his head and wondered how the man could bear to stay all day in that infernal contraption. The stairs would be a bloody sight safer.

Perkins polished the big wooden desk with an oily rag, moving it in neat little circles and bringing about a shine that would shame a diamond. He paused for a moment and then vigorously increased his effort until the offending blemish departed.

'Ah, Perkins,' said Cornwallis coming to stand at the desk. He leant forward and rested his elbows just on the spot which had received the extra oomph. 'I need to ask you a question.' He noticed that it wasn't exactly a rag he polished with, but a gerbil.

Perkins stopped polishing and looked up. The gerbil squeaked, shook itself, and then scampered to the edge of the desk and jumped down. Perkins looked down at Cornwallis' elbows and then looked up again. 'Of course, sir, how can I help?' he replied, without a hint of rancour.

Cornwallis smiled back. He felt a little guilty about leaving a mark on the desk, but the Assembly worked like this and he had to act in the appropriate manner. A porter was a servant and the members the masters, when he'd gone, he would just polish the desk again, but if anyone else did the same, then Perkins would read them the riot act. 'I think it might be an idea to speak a little quietly, if we may, I need to see the Bagman.'

Perkins hardly even blinked. 'The Bagman, sir? I'm not sure I know whom you mean. There's not a member here of that name, that I can recall.'

'I think you do know who I mean,' he replied, leaning in closer. 'In fact, I have already seen him, but now I need to see him again, and I don't really want to have to go outside, if at all possible.'

Perkins opened his mouth to deny the existence of the Bagman again, but then thought better of it as he looked into Cornwallis' eyes. He coughed politely and then flashed a wry grin. 'The Bagman you say, sir?'

Cornwallis nodded.

'Perhaps I may have heard of a gentleman who holds that title,' conceded Perkins, after a pause. 'Now, let me think.' He tapped his lips with his finger as he regarded Cornwallis thoughtfully. 'Perhaps it might be better for me to send a note to someone who could be of assistance to you,' he said in the end.

Cornwallis looked back at Perkins and felt the jarring in his ear; Perkins had not uttered the word "sir" once in that last sentence. 'I think the best idea would be for you to show me the way, while your assistant takes over for a while. After all, as you said earlier, your family and mine have always looked after each other.'

'Er…Well, that's right, sir.'

The "sir's" back now is it, thought Cornwallis. Then it dawned on him. 'Perkins, I would like to ask you a question, if I may?'

'Go ahead, sir.'

'Thank you. Now, how do you think the members here would take it should someone start spreading the rumour that the head porter is in fact working for a Mr Hawk, otherwise known as the Bagman, eh? That nondescript entity that hides away and is always digging around and looking for information to use in, perhaps, not a nice way. That secret department which deals with all the nasty, grubby, damning and grotesque activities that could be used to exert a little pressure here and there. Would you say that it wouldn't exactly help your career prospects?'

Perkins stared at Cornwallis for a few seconds as if weighing up his answer. The threat implied was all too clear. 'I would say, sir,' he said in the end, 'that a situation like you describe would not exactly be desirous. Although I refute the implication that I am in the employ of the man you describe, I think that it might be wise for me to follow your suggestion and take you to see the man that I believe you would like to see.'

Cornwallis grinned. 'A good decision, Perkins, I knew you wouldn't let me down.'

It was obvious really. Perkins was in a position to hear all the tittle-tattle, all the gossip, see who met who and for what reason and where. Totally anonymous, as all servants are, to the ruling classes who could speak in his presence of things that they would never dream of saying to someone who actually mattered. Perkins must hear all the snippets of information, just the sort of thing that the Bagman would want to hear. Cornwallis watched as the Porter instructed his assistant and then spoke to the guards behind, clearly Perkins wasn't exactly comfortable in letting his assistant loose on the desk without a martial presence — who knew what mischief the youngster could cause in his absence?

Cornwallis followed as Perkins led the way into the lobby and over to the elevator, they then waited for a few moments until the elevator pinged its arrival. The door opened and the flunkey, who Cornwallis saw earlier, gave a deferential nod of the head; Cornwallis suspected that the nod wasn't for him, but for Perkins.

'Where to, Mr Perkins?' the flunkey asked jauntily.

'Below please, Kelvin, the basement if you please.'

'Right you are, sir,' he replied, as he closed the door. 'Hang on to the rails please.'

Cornwallis had never been in the contraption before, and as the door closed, he wished he had kept up with that tradition. Kelvin pressed a button and he heard a grinding noise as the machinery came to life. As the bears began to pedal, the elevator lurched up a few feet as the ropes twanged, and then they began to descend. Cornwallis gripped the rail even harder, and his face paled as he waited for the inevitable plunge to his death. The sound of a flute began to fill the compartment as it slowly rode down; Cornwallis looked around in confusion until Kelvin pointed to the roof and smiled.

'We decided to try to entertain our customers,' he explained. 'Makes the trip go all the quicker and takes the mind off the claustrophobia. We've tried a few different instruments,' and he shook his head as he went through the list. 'The bagpipes were okay for a time, but the squeal as they started up began to fray some o' the members nerves. We tried a string quartet once too, but then the viola player fell off and unfortunately, the union said we couldn't use any more than one musician after that. I said we'd make do with a trio, but they wouldn't have it; a bloody viola player, what use is one o'them anyway?'

Cornwallis nodded as Kelvin droned on; he really wasn't interested and just wanted the whole bloody thing to come to a stop, properly of course, and not a bone crunching, wood splintering crash that heralded an elevator incident.

'Here we are, Mr Perkins, basement level.' The elevator pinged its arrival and the flute abruptly cut off as if someone had grabbed the thing in frustration and had bent it over their knee. 'Thank you for riding with us today and we hope to see you again for your return trip,' intoned Kelvin, keeping to the script as he opened the door to allow them out.

Perkins went to walk forward but then turned around and stepped back in; he prised Cornwallis' fingers off the rails then helped him out. 'Takes some getting used to, these things, but once you've done it once, it's a lot easier the next time.'

'There's not going to be a next time,' growled Cornwallis. 'I assure you, Perkins, it's the stairs for me, and I don't bloody care how bloody far it is.'

'And I thought you young men were all for new technology.'

'Not this young man, Perkins,' replied Cornwallis, leaning against the wall. 'That thing is a step too far as far as I'm concerned.'

Perkins hid the smile and then coughed as he grabbed hold of a lantern and lit it from the one next to the elevator. 'If you would like to follow me, sir. I will guide you through. Very few members have ever been down here, so you might find it's not up to the standard you're used to, a bit dusty and dirty you see.'

'Dust and dirt are fine by me, Perkins. Lead on.'

The basement level is what Perkins had called it, but it seemed more like the bowels of the House. Deep beneath the Assembly, there were a series of tunnels all disappearing off into the dark dank reaches to only the Gods' know where. It occurred to Cornwallis that if this were the bowels, then perhaps the Bagman presently sat in the arse-hole. He grinned to himself; and the thought cheered him up no end.

'Where do all these tunnels go?' asked Cornwallis. 'And what are all these pipes?'

'The tunnels have been here for years and years. They were here before the Assembly in the days of the Morris Council,' explained Perkins. 'Some of them go on for miles. The Morris was a different thing in those days, they ruled by fear and violence and they would move around the city unseen and without going above ground. Most entrances have now been blocked up, sir, but you'd be surprised where some of them came up. Don't you read your history, sir?'

Cornwallis shook his head. 'What about these pipes?'

Perkins sniffed. 'Sir, these are the sewer pipes. There must be over a thousand people in the Assembly and, if you pardon my expression, sir, all that shit has to go somewhere. Beneath us are the main sewers which take the waste out to the river; if someone upsets the maintenance manager then he gives them a shovel and sends them down. Doesn't do to upset the maintenance manager, sir.'

Cornwallis grimaced. 'No, I'll bear that in mind.'

They carried on passing storeroom after storeroom, with Cornwallis looking in when he noticed an open door. He saw that some were stacked with books and parchments, others with sacks of grain, and there were barrels and barrels of wine and beer. There were all sorts of things, everything, he supposed, to keep a well-oiled machine like the Assembly going, and all down here. It really opened the mind; he had never giving this sort of thing a moments consideration before, but now it quite impressed him. Perkins got a bit of speed on and he hurried to catch up. Lanterns down here were few and far between and Perkins had stopped giving a commentary and just ploughed on silently, expecting him to keep up as he darted into different entrances. Cornwallis generally had a good sense of direction, but now he was totally lost. A few furtive looking men passed by occasionally, doffing an imaginary cap at Perkins and scurrying about between the various rooms that were down there. Eventually they came to a thick oak door bound in iron and looking as formidable as a castle, with an eye-slit that could be dragged open from the other side. Perkins stopped and turned.

'Here we are, sir. I think this is the place you're after.' He tugged at the lever that jutted out from the wall and waited.

Perkins stood patiently waiting with his arms crossed. The minutes passed by slowly with the only communication between the two being a few brief half-smiles. Cornwallis began to think that maybe they should pull the lever again, or even better, start hammering at the door, because at least then he would be doing something to get some sort of attention from whomever happened to be on the other side. Suddenly, he heard a click and a thunk, and a pair of eyes stared back at them through the slit in the door, the eyes regarded them for a second or so and then the slit shut. A moment later a blaze of light came from mirror backed lanterns that were hidden in the walls; the whole tunnel lit up in a sunburst, and then the slit thunked open again. The eyes regarded them for a second time.

'What you want?' the eyes asked curtly.

'This is Mr Jocelyn Cornwallis and he wishes to see a Mr

Hawk,' replied Perkins evenly.

'Appointment?'

'Er, not that I am aware of.'

The slit slammed shut again and then the lights went out.

'What happens now?' asked Cornwallis, already wishing he had gone around via the coach park.

'We wait, sir,' replied Perkins. 'It could be a while though.'

But strangely, it wasn't a while, as after only a few minutes the lights came on again, the slit opened, the eyes looked, and then there came a creak and a clicking noise as keys rattled in the door. Silently the door swung inwards and the eyes beckoned Cornwallis in.

Cornwallis turned to thank Perkins but the door had already closed, the words petering out in his throat as the door clunked shut, the clinking of the keys following immediately.

The owner of the eyes turned and looked at him, with the distinct impression of not being impressed. The man had a shaven head, solidly built with muscles along his arms where there shouldn't be muscles; like a brick outhouse with the sinews being the pipes.

'Just need to see Mr Hawk for a short time,' said Cornwallis, his confidence ebbing a little under the intense scrutiny of the eyes. 'Will you show me the way?'

'I'm afraid he can't, Mr Cornwallis,' said Mr Sparrow, walking into the room and nodding at the eyes. 'What would we do if we had another visitor, eh? However, I can.'

Cornwallis let out a groan of disappointment, he so wanted to catch the Bagman unprepared, but now there was no chance of that; might as well have gone the long way around after all.

Sparrow smiled. 'Now, now, Mr Cornwallis, aren't you pleased to see me?' He turned his attention back to the eyes. 'Checked?' he asked.

A shake of the head followed and then the eyes took a pace forward and grabbed Cornwallis roughly and spun him around so that he faced the wall. A shove in the back pushed him forwards and his legs pulled back so that they splayed out. He then had the most disconcerting experience he had ever had as the eyes frisked him from top to toe in the quickest and most thorough way possible; he half expected the rubber gloves to come out.

'Oi, mind the jewellery department,' Cornwallis exclaimed indignantly, as he felt his groin being examined.

Sparrow laughed. 'Very witty, Mr Cornwallis, but you can never be too careful.'

The eyes finished and stood back with a brief nod of the head.

'Looks like you've passed, Mr Cornwallis,' acknowledged Sparrow. 'Now you may come with me.'

Cornwallis regained his posture and adjusted his clothes, casting a contemptuous glance at his frisker, who returned an even more contemptuous glance; this with the added promise that next time he *would* get the gloves out.

'Come on, Mr Cornwallis, we can't keep Mr Hawk waiting, now can we?' Sparrow held open the door and Cornwallis stepped through, still adjusting his trousers, into the corridor beyond. 'This way,' instructed Sparrow, stepping in front and heading away.

Cornwallis followed more slowly while suppressing the urge to grab Sparrow around the throat and wring his supercilious neck. Perhaps another time, he conceded in the end, and shook his shoulders to get rid of the feeling before it came back stronger; he would be better off taking note of where he was and what he saw for possible future reference.

It wasn't so much what he saw, that sent a shiver through

him, but what he heard. They walked down a dimly lit corridor, but the noises behind some of the doors left little to the imagination. He heard thwacks and whimpering sounds and jangling noises, and then occasionally, a high pitched scream would rent the air. He began to feel his hackles rise as he went further into the place, while Sparrow up ahead, ignored everything. Eventually he had had enough and lurched for one of the doors and flung it wide open; staring at what he saw in disbelief.

In a corner of the room, he saw a man strapped to a chair. In front of him were five other men, all standing with batons in their hands, panting from exertion. The man in the chair was crying, with a look of sheer terror on his face.

'And again,' instructed one of the men. The group of five then began to dance, and Cornwallis recognised it as the "Fair Maiden's Dream".

Sparrow appeared at his side. 'Been going on now for three days, this one; you have to admire the man. Can you imagine having to watch and listen to that for three solid days? No respite, no nothing, just full on Morris dancing for three days! He will break eventually, they all do in the end, just turns the brain to mush, you see.'

Cornwallis shook his head in sympathy, he could stand five minutes of it, but any more and he would be climbing up the wall. Three days? It didn't bear thinking of. 'What's he done?' he asked, not sure whether he wanted to know the answer or not.

'He's a sleeper, we believe, an agent of one of the Eastern states. Not sure which as he hasn't told us yet, but he will. Found him handing out leaflets supporting an autonomous state with free speech and equal rights for all, I mean free speech and equal rights — in a democracy? Absurd!'

'Isn't it,' replied Cornwallis sadly. He hoped the man would hold out, but he doubted it somehow. The state always won in the end.

Sparrow shut the door and dragged Cornwallis away; they went up several flights of stairs and along a couple of corridors until they reached the Bagman's outer office where Miss Wren received them with a cup of coffee and a biscuit already waiting. She smiled demurely at Cornwallis and more provocatively at Sparrow as she handed the coffee out.

'Mr Hawk said he won't keep you long, Mr Cornwallis, just take a seat for a moment.'

He heard a coffee cup rattle in its saucer as Miss Wren brushed past Sparrow to get to her desk, leading him to think that perhaps now Sparrow received a frisking, but his was of an altogether different experience. Cornwallis felt a pang of jealousy for a split second, but then remembered that he had Miss Thrape to look forward to later on in the evening. He had a brief vision of what they might get up to tonight, but then disconcertingly, the form of Miss Thrape faded away to be replaced with the form of Rose. Cornwallis sighed, and then crossed his legs.

The bell behind Miss Wren's desk sounded and then a click as the door unlocked. Without being prompted, Cornwallis stood up and headed for the door, leaving his half-drunk coffee on the table.

Cornwallis marched down the centre of the office with a sense of determination, disregarding all the paintings and ornaments that lined the wall he came to stand in front of the Bagman's desk and drew a chair forward. He plonked the chair down in front of the desk and sat down. Mr Hawk watched his progress without a word, he just leant back in his chair and steepled his fingers while thoughtfully tapping his lips. The two regarded each other for a few moments in a heavy silence.

Eventually, the Bagman broke the tension. 'Mr Cornwallis. How delightful to see you, and so unexpected too.'

'I doubt that,' growled Cornwallis. 'On both counts.'

Mr Hawk smiled, 'Maybe you're right and then again, maybe you're wrong. I did say we would keep in touch though, so tell me, how is the investigation going?'

Cornwallis had a moment of confusion, he didn't come here at Mr Hawk's invitation; he came here because he had had enough and wanted to know the truth of what had been going on. If at all possible, he would have kept as far away from the Bagman as he could, it was only after that mornings attempt on their lives that he had decided that he'd had enough and it had become far too tedious to keep looking over his shoulder all of the time. He and Frankie were used to taking risks, but Rose very nearly became a victim too, and that made him think a little differently. He decided to ignore the Bagman's question.

'What have you learnt from Maxwell's associates? You took them into your custody, so you must have learnt something; and what about Roland Goup, I assume you managed to stop the ship and drag him off?'

'Well, it was a shame about Maxwell, I would so like to have talked to him, but you certainly put a stop to that. You also neglected to mention that he was involved in the killing of my Miss Knutt. As to his associates? Well, in truth, they were just thugs, paid to do a job, but fortunately for you, didn't manage to do it. They're still down below, helping us with a few other things, they have been busy boys you know. Quite a few crimes are being cleared up.'

'What about the drugs, did you send someone down?'

'Oh yes, and you were right, too right in fact. There wasn't millions of dollars' worth there, but hundreds of millions of dollars' worth, and that in trade prices; street value would be far

far higher. Snodgrass is with my people now. You are a naughty boy, you didn't tell me about him either, did you?'

'You didn't ask.' In actual fact, Cornwallis assumed that he probably already knew. 'And Roland Goup?' he asked, to change the subject.

'Ah, Mr Goup.'

Cornwallis noticed the question had not gone down well; he hesitated a little, a degree of tension, a flicker of frustration. 'Well?' he encouraged.

Mr Hawk coughed. 'In truth, Mr Cornwallis, we don't know.'

Cornwallis screwed up his brows in confusion.

'It, er . . . it seems that Mr Goup has disappeared. We found the ship, but unfortunately, he wasn't on board. According to the Captain, Kintersbury and Maxwell did take someone on, but he left soon after, at least before the ship sailed. We have the ship somewhere and we're taking it apart, and the crew are being, er, spoken to. Someone must know something.'

'But I saw Goup go on and then your trained puppy interrupted me. If anyone's to blame then it's you and Sparrow. Job half-done, I think. Call yourselves professionals?'

Mr Hawk squirmed in his chair. 'There's no need for that, Mr Cornwallis. I admit now that we could, and should, have left it a little longer, but Mr Sparrow saw the man, he now knows as Goup, board the ship, so he deduced that he sailed in her.'

'Wrong call.'

'With hindsight, yes. But I trust my agents, Mr Cornwallis, and if I didn't then you would by now be very dead. How many attempts is it now?'

Cornwallis sniffed. 'On my life you mean? Then it's three or four if you count intent, all of them have failed.'

Mr Hawk grinned. 'Actually, it's five. Crossbow bolt in the

back. You missed that one, and thankfully for you, so did he; but Mr Magpie didn't miss. So you see Mr Cornwallis, neither of us are perfect. I suggest you put your antagonism towards me away for now, I'm sure you can make up for it another time.'

'What? When?' stammered Cornwallis.

The Bagman smiled. 'When you were on your way to the dwarf tunnels,' he held up his hand and indicated with his thumb and finger. 'You were that close away.'

Cornwallis cast his mind back and immediately remembered the click, the whoosh, and the thump. His spine tingled and he felt the goosebumps pop out all over. 'Oh,' he said lamely.

Mr Hawk sat back in his chair with a look of triumph on his face, he'd returned the ping-pong ball of antipathy quite well, he thought; he would now try a back spin curve shot. 'Don't worry, Mr Cornwallis; I'm sure there will be more.'

Cornwallis sighed and then slumped back and stared at the ceiling. 'Tell me again why I'm doing your dirty work.'

Mr Hawk picked up a pencil and twiddled it around his fingers. 'Because, Mr Cornwallis, this department is part of the government, and the police are part of the government. You, although a member of this government, are not answerable to it. If a government department investigated the events that you are currently investigating, then it could be said that the government had a vested interest in the outcome, seeing as a member of the government is central to it all. If all the rumours, which are currently circulating around the Assembly as of today, are to be believed, then that would not be a situation that the government would appreciate. Let us consider what you already know. Kintersbury, allegedly, is using his ship to bring in vast amounts of drugs, far far more than this city needs. So it is likely that it is also destined for other parts of the country; however, at the moment, we can't prove that. He also heads up Gornstock Trust and Holdings, which this morning, as you know, has declared itself bankrupt. Dumchuck is head of the Gornstock bank, which has just received a large sum of money from the government; and all this started when his tax return was, er, returned. Now, the lately deceased Maxwell, who worked for Kintersbury, got it back from Goup, via the little sneak-thief, who, in the process, murdered my Miss Knutt. As Dumchuck and Kintersbury are obviously working together, what do you suppose is going to happen?'

Cornwallis thought for a moment and then slapped his head. 'Dumchuck will bail Kintersbury's business out.'

'Exactly. The big problem now is that because Gornstock Trust and Holdings has declared itself bankrupt, the stock exchange has gone, er, mental. Prices have dropped, no, that would be an understatement, they have not only dropped but have gone through the floor and are presently burrowing to the other side of the twearth. The Warden has summoned Dumchuck to a crisis meeting, which I believe is going to be held tonight in order to sort out the situation, Dooley and Kintersbury have been told to attend as well. From what I hear they will be there all night long.'

'So the bank is going to have to prop up the stock market as well as Kintersbury?'

'Only Kintersbury. If Gornstock Trust and Holdings is re-floated then that should stave off the crisis. The word is that there is an enormous sum of money tied up in Kintersbury's company, which is why the Warden has summoned Kintersbury as well.'

'So where has all the money gone?' he asked, now knowing the answer.

The Bagman smiled. 'That, Mr Cornwallis, is the question.'

Cornwallis took a few moments for thought. 'If I pull

Kintersbury in now for questioning then I assume that there will be no chance of saving the company, and in consequence, preventing the stock market collapse, which I presume will then plunge the city into a financial crisis. So I'm hamstrung until this is sorted.'

'In effect yes, you need to hold back at least until this meeting has been held tonight.'

'Hmmm,' mused Cornwallis. He moved his thoughts to more concrete evidence. 'I'm keeping an eye on the drugs to see what will happen now that Maxwell is dead. I know Maxwell went regularly to pick the drugs up, but I only saw Kintersbury in the vicinity, he wasn't actually standing in front of it all. I presume you have found traces of it on his ship?'

'There hasn't been as yet, and the Captain is pleading ignorance.'

'So there is no proof of anything yet, other than supposition and the fact that I saw Kintersbury in the vicinity of the drugs?'

'No.'

And the fact that you knew it all but decided not to tell me, thought Cornwallis scornfully.

*

Frankie and Rose were discussing things as they searched for Algernon. They eventually came up with a strategy that might have the desired effect of putting a rather large boot in the way of Cornwallis' encounter with Miss Thrape. Frankie felt sure that in the fullness of time, Cornwallis would actually thank him for it, but in the short term, the reaction might well be quite different.

They finally found Algernon propping up a doorpost close to the Gornstock Bank. In fact, Algernon found them as they walked around, as he had disguised himself in the rags of a down-and-out and scuttled about handing out pamphlets of advertisements. Frankie had waved him away to start with, but recognition finally dawned as the persistent beggar latched on to his coat-tail and wouldn't leave him alone.

The Gornstock Bank dwarfed all other buildings around it. It screamed money, with rich decorations and marble pillars, loads of them, all standing guard around the front of the sandstone building, propping up a large overhanging portico. The square it sat in had been designed around the bank and a series of steps led right up to the front door, lending the building gravitas. Around the square, the populace walked and sat and talked in the comforting knowledge that the bank, the financial backbone of the city, would be, and always had been, there. Its presence indicated that all was well with the world. People trusted the bank; after all, it printed all the money.

'Took yer bloody time,' said Algernon by way of a greeting. 'Been here all sodding morning, waiting for one of you to come along.'

'We're here now, Algie, is there a problem?' asked Frankie, grinning at his apparel.

'Not so much a problem. I sent one of the boys around to your place earlier, but a woman just said that you were all out.'

'That would be Mrs Gridlington,' answered Rose, nodding. 'The new office worker. What did she say?'

'Just that you were out and that she didn't know when you would be back. Suggested he left a message and that you would contact him when you were available. Apparently the way she spoke didn't leave room for a response, very formal.'

'Progress. Jack is moving the business along. Anyway, why did you send the lad around?' asked Frankie.

Algernon grinned triumphantly. 'Because of your Mr

Dumchuck. He took a trip out last night, he did, and so did your Mr Kintersbury.'

'Did they now, and where did they go?' Frankie felt his interest stir.

'All in good time. You are going to feel sorry for an old homeless person now and will buy him lunch. I think a good three courses in that pub just over there; and a couple of pints.'

'It'd better be worth it.'

'Oh, I think you'll find it will be.' He indicated to another man that he was taking a break and then strolled over to the Sack of Plenty, named after the bags of coins that were historically delivered to the bank in its early days, but because of the way the sign had been painted, was known locally as the Dog's Bollocks. He sat down at one of the little outside tables.

Algernon perused the menu for a few moments and then beckoned a waiter over. 'My friends are paying,' he said straight away to the worried looking man. 'I'll have a prawn surprise to start with, followed by pork cutlets braised in cream with season vegetables and a treacle sponge for pudding; oh, yes and I'll have two pints of best. You two having anything?'

Frankie began to shake his head, when it occurred to him that his throat felt a tad dry, and his stomach just gave a little rumble, plus he'd noticed that the waiter had *noticed* Rose. 'I'll have a pint too, as well as a meatball and cheese footlong, with chilli relish, please.'

'And you, Miss?' asked the waiter, pencil poised as he looked lecherously down Rose's cleavage.

'She'll have the same,' answered Frankie, before she had a chance to open her mouth. 'She's never satisfied with anything less than twelve inches, ain't that right, Rose?'

It took a micro-second before the comment hit the waiter's brain and then he sort of said "Gneughh" as he coughed and spluttered. He then pressed too hard with his pencil and the end snapped off.

'Oh dear,' said Frankie. 'Looks like you've shot yer end off; such a nice *little* pencil too.'

He hurried away quicker than a rat up a drainpipe.

'Frankie,' admonished Rose. 'There wasn't any call for that.'

Frankie grinned. 'You didn't see what I saw; you were the subject of extreme scrutinisation.'

'Sometimes, Frankie, a girl likes to be scrutinised.' She actually enjoyed the attention, the waiter being young and quite good looking. 'Anyway, since when have you been my guardian angel?'

'Since the day you joined us, Rose.'

Algernon looked at each in turn. 'Gods, are you pair like this all the time?'

Rose rolled her eyes. 'I'm not, he is,' she said pointedly.

'Just looking after you, Rose,' responded Frankie. 'That's what colleagues do.'

'Well, if you hadn't noticed, this colleague can look after herself.'

Algernon thought of saying that he would be quite happy to look after her too, but thought better of it as Cornwallis was bound to hear with Frankie sitting next to him, and he didn't want to put his release from the hairdressers at risk. 'Don't you want to hear what your friends have been up to?' he asked instead.

'Oooh, yes please,' replied Frankie, rubbing his hands together.

Algernon leant forward with his elbows on the table. 'Well, as you know, the night before last they just went home and bolted the door, neither of them got up to anything. Mrs Dumchuck went out for a while to help out with the soup run, but she came back a couple of hours later. One of Kintersbury's servants went out too, but he didn't take long neither, however, where he went might be of interest now, after last night.'

'Really, how?'

'In a moment. Yesterday Dumchuck went to the bank as usual and stayed there all day, and Kintersbury went to the Assembly. However, last night things started to change. Both Dumchuck and Kintersbury went out.'

The beer arrived, and Frankie and Rose waited patiently until Algernon had his prawns served, but this time from a different waiter who steadfastly refused to look at Rose. A couple of minutes later the prawns had disappeared and the waiter arrived again with a couple of footlongs and the cutlets. Algernon began digging in and at last remembered he should be saying something.

'Well, Dumchuck went out first and went on a visit to an address not far from here,'

'Where?' interrupted Rose.

'Gods, you two are impatient, aren't you.' He loaded his fork and stuffed his mouth full of cutlets. He chewed and grinned at the same time while Rose and Frankie held on to their footlongs, not daring to start. He swallowed and then continued. 'A little later Kintersbury went out, and guess what, he went to the same address, and what's more it was the same address that he sent a note to the night before.'

'And?' said Frankie and Rose together.

'They went home.' Algernon dived into his food again as if he had now finished all he had to say.

Frankie and Rose looked at each other in the silence, and then Frankie leant forward and grabbed Algernon by the throat. 'Algie, this is not funny.'

Algernon had a full mouth at the time, and Frankie's hand

around his throat was not conducive to good digestion. He coughed and sent splatterings of pork flying across the pub's patio.

'If you don't carry on telling us the story, I'll be ramming this footlong somewhere where the sun don't shine, closely followed by the one that Rose is holding.'

'Frankie,' exclaimed Rose, letting her dinner fall to the plate. 'I was just looking forward to eating that.'

'Well?'

Algernon nodded and Frankie let go. He coughed again and then swallowed, rubbing his neck at the same time. 'I was just getting to that Frankie, honest. They went to Havelock Crescent. Dumchuck went first, but left before Kintersbury got there, so they weren't there at the same time.'

Frankie held on to Algernon's hand to stop him eating and indicated that he should continue.

'I then made some enquiries about the place, and what came back was quite interesting. It would seem that your two friends share the same sort of recreational activities. The place is a brothel.'

'A brothel?' queried Rose. 'You mean that they were both…' and she made a circle with her thumb and forefinger and used the finger on the other hand to indicate a time honoured gesture. '… doing it in the same place?'

'Not only the same place, but the same woman. It's a one woman operation, and she only caters for the rich and powerful. She is by all accounts very picky about her customers. Apparently, amongst other things, she's a dominatrix.'

Frankie grinned from ear to ear and leant back in his seat. 'Oh, that's beautiful is that — our two little friends are whipping boys.'

CHAPTER 14

'Oh, it's you, Mr Cornwallis.' Mrs Gridlington turned as the door swung open.

Cornwallis strode through with a grin on his face, despite just coming back from a visit to the Bagman. She looked a bit surprised to see him.

'Yes, it is, Mrs Gridlington. Or it was the last time I looked.' He grimaced as he heard himself speak; it wasn't even half a joke. Mrs Gridlington seemed to do that to him. He tried this morning to force a light-hearted comment, but again it seemed to come out as the utterings of a moron.

'Well, it certainly looks like you, Mr Cornwallis, though I didn't expect to see you until later, what with all your running around.'

'Yes, I thought I'd pop back to see how you're getting on, and I must say you've made an improvement. I see the desk came.'

'Yes, thank you, Mr Cornwallis.' She turned away from his desk and smiled. 'Just been tidying all this up. I'm going to put all your current paperwork into the cupboard in this box file; you really need to get a lock on that, even when you've knocked through to the other room.'

'I will, though you've done wonders with all the old files. Where did you put them?'

'Next door, but I've locked the door. It makes the whole place look brighter, don't you think?'

'It certainly does, Mrs Gridlington.'

She had placed her new desk opposite his, just under where the old files were. She turned back to finish putting the paperwork away and he sat on the edge of her desk and watched as she bent down to the cupboard. His mind went back to the morning when they were on the floor in each other's arms, and the glint he had seen in her eye. He studied her a little more closely. He thought she couldn't be much older than him, but she wore no make-up and had a severe hairstyle; but the hair had lustre to it, a rich dark nut brown. Her clothes were very plain and frumpy and covered everything, including her legs. Cornwallis mused on his thoughts, and decided that if she took more care of her appearance, dressed a little differently, and slapped on a bit of make-up, then with what he found this morning, she would turn into quite a good looking woman; and if circumstances were different...

'Is there something wrong?' asked Mrs Gridlington, as she stood up and turned around.

'Uh?' replied Cornwallis.

'Only you seemed to be staring at me, is there something not to your liking?'

Cornwallis felt a flush coming. 'Oh no, not at all. I was just thinking. Miles away, sorry,' he finished lamely.

She smiled, and held her arms demurely in front of her, clasping her hands. 'I'm glad. I think I will like working here. Are your two colleagues coming back today?'

'Er, probably. I sent them to see someone, so I expect they will.' He stood up, paced a little, and then came to a decision. 'You can finish early if you like, Mrs Gridlington, you've been very busy and I want to go through some things before I go out again.' There was something a little school-girlish in the way she stood, and a couple of things were definitely being squeezed together.

'Why thank you, Mr Cornwallis, in that case I will leave you to it. Where are you off to, if I may ask?'

The thought of Miss Thrape entered his mind and he found himself grinning. 'Just out. Having an evening at the Jerkey Turkey actually, Mrs Gridlington.'

She moved over to her desk and picked up her bag, she brushed herself down and then looked at Cornwallis. 'In that case I hope you and the young lady have a very nice time.'

Cornwallis' eyebrows shot up.

Mrs Gridlington grinned back and she winked. 'Can't pull the wool over my eyes young man,' she said, walking past and tapping him on the arm. 'See you in the morning.'

Cornwallis stared at her back as she went through the door, replaying the conversation in his mind; at no point did he mention going to see anyone, or doing anything — so how did she know? He sniffed and shook his head slowly before grinning to himself. He hoped that he had read Miss Isabella Thrape, just as well as the astute Mrs Gridlington had read him.

He busied himself while waiting for Frankie and Rose by going through the events of the day. He poured himself a coffee as he ordered his thoughts and gazed out of the window. He saw Mrs Gridlington hurrying down the street and he thought he really should have found out a little more about her, like where she lived and what her husband did for a living; all the things a good employer should know about a member of his staff. He would have to address that the next time he had a few minutes with her, and he made a note in his mind. He definitely had the feeling that she would become an asset to the team, and he wouldn't put it beyond possibility that at some time she might even be good enough for some minor investigating on her own. The future looked very rosy indeed.

He turned away from the window and went over to his desk and pulled out his chair, he sat down and swung his feet up, squirming around in an attempt to get comfortable. He took another slurp of the strong black concoction and felt his senses being stimulated. Now, he thought, the fog had lifted and it had become very clear. He went over it all in his mind again and came to the same conclusion. It was obvious when you pieced everything together, but he still needed proof, and he suspected that that would be hard to come by. Knowing and proving were two totally different things, but at least he could start with the knowing.

Frankie and Rose came noisily up the stairs and he realised that he had been sitting there thinking for quite some time, the light had faded, and it began to get dark outside, but he hadn't even noticed.

'There you are, Jack.' Frankie and Rose burst into the room laughing. 'You are going to love what we have to tell you.'

Cornwallis looked up and smiled. 'In that case you'd better tell me before you do yourself an injury, Frankie.'

Rose went around lighting the lamps and then checked the coffee pot; she poured three mugs and then brought them over before inspecting Mrs Gridlington's new desk. She tried the chair and found that it was one of the new swivel ones that spun around. Frankie, having seen Rose revolve, decided he wanted a go as well. Cornwallis waited patiently while the children played.

'That's enough now, you two,' announced Cornwallis with exasperation. 'You said you had to tell me something.'

'We did at that,' replied Frankie, as he tipped over and fell to the floor; he had spun the seat right off the pedestal. 'Oh bugger, I've broke it.'

Cornwallis sighed.

'It's all right,' said Rose. 'Those things just screw back again;

the secret is to remember not to spin too much.' She helped Frankie replace the seat and then hand-spun it back to its original position. 'There, all better now.'

'Well, I'm glad you're happy now,' said Cornwallis.

Frankie grinned and looked at Rose. 'Shall I tell him or do you want to?'

'You can Frankie; you seem to be enjoying repeating it all so much I'm loath to stop you now.' She turned to Cornwallis. 'He must have said it to me at least twenty times by now, and I was there when he first heard it.'

'Frankie does that,' agreed Cornwallis. 'Hears a good story; then flogs it to death, everyone's bored rigid by the time he's finished.'

'But this one's worth it,' said Frankie, aggrieved.

'Well, bloody well tell me then.'

Frankie got himself comfortable and then took a drink to wet his throat. 'Algernon,' he began, 'kept an eye on our two friends. Nothing much to report about yesterday and today, but last night they went out into the bad old world of Gornstock. First Dumchuck and then Kintersbury, and they went to the same place, but not at the same time.'

'Go on,' encouraged Cornwallis.

'Well, Algie followed them and then made some enquiries, and as luck would have it he found out a bit about the place. Kintersbury and Dumchuck have interesting little habits; this house they went to is, and wait for it... '

'A brothel,' interjected Rose laughing.

'Oi, Rose, that's not fair. I was telling the story.'

'A brothel?' queried Cornwallis, smiling. 'You mean they're paying for it?'

Frankie shot Rose a look. 'Yes, but not only that; this brothel specialises in a particular quirk.' He raised his eyebrows a little and then broke into a broad grin. He then mimed a whip being cracked whilst at the same time clicking his tongue. 'I think our friends are bondage boys.'

Cornwallis' feet slid off the table in surprise. When he righted himself, he leant forward eagerly. 'Really?'

'Oh yes, no doubt about it. The place is a one woman business and she only caters for the likes of you.'

'What do you mean?' exclaimed Cornwallis, horrified at the implication.

'I mean rich people,' adjusted Frankie, quickly. 'Nobs and such like. Apparently, it reminds them of when they were at school.'

'Must have been some strange schools around in those days then,' added Rose, thoughtfully.

Cornwallis laughed. 'Not really, you should have seen what went on in mine. Thankfully, I emerged untouched and unaffected, but some of the things that went on... Hang on,' his mind snapped to attention, 'Tell me, where is this place?'

'Havelock Crescent,' answered Frankie. 'Why? Are you thinking of making an appointment?'

A triumphant look came over Cornwallis. 'Havelock Crescent,' he repeated. 'I heard today that Bertram Radstock goes to the same place. Now, what do you make of that, eh?'

Rose and Frankie looked at each other. 'I don't know,' answered Frankie. 'What are we to make of it?'

'Radstock is the Bagman's informer,' sighed Rose, picking the point up straight away. 'That's two high ranking government officials and the head of the Bank. Are they connected in all this though?'

'There must be something, too much of a coincidence otherwise,' said Cornwallis, thinking it through. 'The Bagman always seems to know just a little bit more than us.'

'So we will have to keep a watch on the place then,' said Frankie, stating the obvious.

'I think so, but Kintersbury and Dumchuck won't be there tonight as they have a prior engagement.' Cornwallis explained about the call to the Assembly and the meeting with the Warden that would be happening later tonight, and then he voiced his suspicions about the whole thing so far and what he thought was involved. Frankie, a bit slower on the uptake than Rose, listened slightly bemused at first, but eventually got the drift.

They agreed that the three of them would go to Havelock Crescent in the morning to cast an enquiring eye over the place, and if necessary would then get Algernon to put a man on it. Cornwallis checked his watch and decided that time had come to get ready for his nocturnal appointment, so he ushered out Rose and Frankie, then hurried upstairs.

He showered, shaved, and changed into clean clothes and then inspected himself in the mirror. Satisfied with what he saw, he brushed himself down again before skipping out of his apartment and heading down the stairs. He knocked on Miss Thrape's door and waited patiently. He knocked again and waited a bit longer; he then began to get a little concerned. He tapped his foot and then looked down, only to see a little piece of paper with his name on it. He bent down and picked it up and saw that it had been attached to the door with a little bit of sticky, but this bit obviously wasn't up to the job. He unfolded the paper and found that Miss Thrape had gone on ahead, as she put it, to get things ready. He smiled to himself as he headed off down the road in the direction of the Jerkey Turkey; with the promise of an evening of fun and frolics on the cards — the emphasis, hopefully being on the frolics.

It took about twenty minutes to get to the Jerkey Turkey, which was next to Trotters Field, where the city held its livestock market. The Turkey catered for the more wealthy farmers who came to the city and in consequence sold good beer, good food and kept clean rooms.

He had a lively step as he entered Poulterer's Way and he grinned as his eyes alighted on the swinging sign above the pub, a turkey with a hand around its neck and about to be throttled; the sign writer had the look of dismay on the face of the turkey just about right.

Cornwallis pushed at the door and it swung open, revealing the early evening punters and a small group of farmers supping beer and bemoaning the prices currently on offer for their goods. He stepped up to the bar, nodding greetings and sympathising with the farmers, until the landlord came through with a large plate of pork scratchings, which he laid ceremoniously on the bar in front of the customers.

'Good evening, sir, and what can I get you?'

Cornwallis was just about to say that he was here for the ghost, when it occurred to him that perhaps that might not be the best thing to say in the circumstances. 'Er, I'm really here to help Miss Thrape,' he said instead. 'Is she here yet?'

'Miss Thrape? Oh, yes indeed. She did say she expected someone, come this way.' He drew Cornwallis hurriedly through a side door in the bar and over towards the stairs. 'Thank you for not mentioning our little problem,' he confided. 'Only some of my customers get a little nervy at the mention of the, er, departed.'

'No problem at all, landlord, we like to be discreet. Now has Miss Thrape ordered any sustenance for our vigil?'

'Er, no, sir.'

'Well in that case, a nice little buffet with a couple bottles of wine and a crate of beer, if you please. It could be a long night you understand, and we can't allow our concentration to waver now, can we?'

'No, sir, right you are, sir. I'll get one of the girls to sort it. Do you think you will be staying *all* night, sir?'

'Quite possibly. In these circumstances who can tell, but once we start we can't be disturbed, you know. Any disturbance could spoil everything.'

The landlord nodded his understanding. 'I just want rid of the thing. Can't let the room out until he's gone, scares the life out of me every time I see him. Now this is the room, sir,' said the landlord as they turned a corner, he pointed down the corridor to the very end room. 'The best room in the house as well; I do hope you have a successful night.'

'So do I, landlord, so do I,' agreed Cornwallis.

Cornwallis waited while the landlord made his way back downstairs before taking a deep breath and stepping towards the door. He tapped quietly, then turned the handle and entered the room. It took him a few brief seconds to adjust his eyes to the gloom inside, as only a weak light came from a partially covered candle sitting on the chest on the far side of the room, and when he did, he could see Miss Thrape languishing on the bed seductively. She lay on her side, with her head resting on her hand, and the sight quite took his breath away. She had changed from earlier, now wearing a loose blouse with a good few buttons undone. The skirt was long and dark and split right up to the thigh, a leg provocatively peeping out.

'Jack,' she breathed huskily. 'I'm so glad you came.'

'How could I not, Isabella,' replied Cornwallis, giving a silent whoop of delight. She moved over a little to allow him room and patted the place she'd just vacated. 'I took the liberty of instructing the landlord to bring us something to eat and drink,' he added as he sat down. 'That should come quite soon, and then he's promised to leave us well alone. I assume you need to be undisturbed to achieve what you need to achieve?'

'Oh yes, Jack, I'm sure that just you and I can manage.' She reached out with her hand and traced a finger down his arm. 'Why don't you take your jacket off? I think it's going to get very hot in here soon.'

Cornwallis didn't need a second invitation. He cast off his jacket, kicked off his boots and joined Isabella on the bed. She turned over and lay flat on her back, with a lazy arm stretched out above her head, one knee bent showing a shapely leg right up to the thigh. He now lay propped on his elbow and looked down on her. Her hair fanned out behind her head and she smiled as she looked up at him. He took a deep breath and placed his hand gently on her waist, and then leant forward, bringing his head close to hers.

She stopped him with a finger placed on his lips just as they were about to make contact with hers. 'I have a job to do first, Jack, we must wait for the ghost; but once he's gone, we'll have the rest of the night to ourselves.'

Cornwallis sighed, mentally hammering it back down; he just hoped that the bloody ghost wouldn't be too long in appearing, then they could get down to the real business of the evening.

'Mee, ow.'

Miss Thrape sat up, all her senses quivering. 'What was that? They told me a man haunted in here.'

Cornwallis had heard it too. 'Sounds like a cat to me, ignore it, it must be outside.'

Miss Thrape settled herself back down to wait; she snuggled up to Cornwallis who had put a pillow behind his head and now lay with her head on his chest. She breathed deeply and relaxed as his hand gently stroked her shoulder. She thought for a moment, and then suddenly sat back up. 'Jack, we're on the third floor.'

'So?'

'So how can a cat be outside?'

Cornwallis had a feeling of dismay, and as if to compound his misery he heard a reply to Isabella's question.

'Yeah, how can's I be outside, I ain't on a bungy, youse knows.'

Cornwallis jumped off the bed and scrambled on the floor; he thrust his arm under the bed and grabbed hold of a big ball of fur. He dragged it out and stared into its eyes. 'What the hell are you doing here, Fluffy?'

The cat grinned. 'Looking fer work, what are youse doing?'

Cornwallis grimaced. 'Never mind me, how did you get in?'

Fluffy twisted in his grip and broke free. He shook himself, then sat down and licked his paw. 'Followed youse in, didn't I. Saw's youse in the street coming in 'ere and I fought's there has to be mice in a pub, so I might's get a little employment. When youse opens this 'ere door, I sort o' skittles by.'

'Ah bless,' purred Isabella. 'Isn't he sweet?'

'No, Isabella, this cat is anything but sweet. You can get out now, Fluffy; there is no work for you here.'

He went to move over to the door, just as the cat jumped onto the bed, padded up between Isabella's legs, and then curled up between her thighs. Fluffy regarded Cornwallis with a look of utter contentment as he nestled down, his head burrowing deep into the area that Cornwallis planned to explore.

'Out,' ordered Cornwallis.

'Oh no, Jack, let him stay, he's doing no harm,' defended Isabella, stroking its head.

'No harm?' exclaimed Cornwallis aghast. 'How the hell are we going to…? Well, you know, with the cat here?'

She smiled as Fluffy rolled over onto his back and stretched out. 'It's only a cat, I'm sure he won't take any notice.'

'Isabella, this cat will hold up a bloody score card.'

Fluffy seemed to chuckle. 'Can't do that, no thumbs, see.'

'Besides,' continued Isabella, taking no notice. 'Talking cats are so rare nowadays; I might ask him to be my companion. They're very sensitive to the spiritual, you know. Would you like to be my companion?' she asked, directing her question to the cat.

Cornwallis' shoulders slumped and he held out his hands as if pleading, he opened his mouth to say that the whole evening will be ruined when he heard a knock on the door, closely followed by a girl's voice announcing that room service had arrived. He shook his head in resignation and then stepped over to the door; at least he would now be able to drink himself into oblivion.

As he opened the door, a figure barged past him, and with the light being so poor, the figure just about registered in his subconscious as being a bit big for a girl. Another large figure entered, and he suddenly had a feeling of dread; they had cornered him with no means of escape, perhaps this would be the successful attempt on his life. He only hoped they would leave Isabella alone, she didn't deserve to be part of all this.

'Evening, Jack,' said the first figure.

'Wha... wha...?' stammered Cornwallis.

'Evening, Jack,' said the second.

'Frankie, Jethro,' replied Cornwallis. 'What the...?

Frankie grinned. 'Don't forget Rose, she's got the grub. Come on, Rose, don't worry, there's nothing untoward going on.'

Rose now entered carrying a big tray laden with food, while Frankie and Jethro had hold of the wine and the beer. 'Evening, Jack. I hope we're not disturbing you?'

Cornwallis sighed. 'No, you're not disturbing us. Nothing at all happening here; and neither is anything likely to happen, not now,' he added, almost silently to himself.

'Evening, Miss Thrape,' said Frankie and Jethro together.

Rose just looked at her and smiled, and immediately an understanding passed between them.

'Good evening,' replied Isabella politely. 'So kind of you to bring the food with you.'

'Well, well, well. If it isn't Fluffy,' said Frankie innocently. 'Look you two, it's the cat.'

Both the cat and Isabella jumped off the bed. She then quickly buttoned up her blouse and skirt, once again looking the prim and proper medium. She brushed herself down and watched as Frankie went over to the window and peeked behind the curtain, retrieving the two chairs that she had hidden earlier. Rose put the tray down and started fussing the cat.

'All right, all right. What's this all about?' asked Cornwallis, now exasperated.

Frankie plonked a chair down and sat. 'All about, Jack? You told us you were ghost hunting. When I told Jethro here, he said he'd never seen a ghost hunt, so we got it into our heads to pop down here to have a look. You don't mind, do you? I mean, it's not as if you were getting up to anything you shouldn't have, is it?'

Cornwallis' mouth moved, but to start with, nothing came out, but then he rallied a little, and in a quiet but slightly menacing voice said. 'I think we'll have a chat about all this another time, Frankie.'

MacGillicudy offered the other chair to Rose, but she declined, preferring to sit on the end of the bed. The cat jumped up next to her, and eventually Isabella sat down next to her with the cat in-between. Fluffy was in his element as two hands were stroking him at once.

Frankie and MacGillicudy began to open the bottles and pass the drinks around, both taking mouthfuls of the food at the same time. Cornwallis pulled his boots back on and stood up, morosely, with his hands in his pockets; until MacGillicudy thrust a beer bottle at him and he had no choice but to take it.

Within a few short minutes, Rose and Isabella had their heads together and were talking quietly so that the others couldn't hear. Frankie talked loudly about what he hoped to see to MacGillicudy, while Cornwallis just sat at the top of the bed dejectedly and drank his beer. Eventually his sense of disappointment dissipated; he decided that it wouldn't do to carry on being peeved at them all, so he joined in with the conversation with Frankie and Jethro and learnt that Dewdrop had been re-christened Lord Dick, and that there were loads of little cartoons doing the rounds of the Yard.

As the beer began to run out, Frankie had to pop out to get some more, he came back up shortly with a handful, saying that the landlord will send some more up in a bit; so the little private twosome that Cornwallis had expected, turned into a jolly little private party.

Rose and Isabella were getting on famously, as their frequent laughter indicated, while Fluffy lay there, curled up in a ball. MacGillicudy entertained them with his impression of ex Senior Sergeant Grinde as he heard he was being reduced in rank, which left Frankie in hysterics, and even Cornwallis couldn't help but laugh along too, when suddenly the hackles on Fluffy's coat rose. The cat half stirred but then quickly went back to sleep, then there came a knock.

Frankie half turned mid-guffaw and waved a hand at the chest. 'Shove it all there will you mate, and shut the door, it's a bit nippy, all of a sudden.'

'Er... sorry?'

'The beer, the wine. I told you to send some more up.'

'No,' said the man thoughtfully. 'No, I don't believe you did.'

Frankie sighed noisily. 'Yes I did... 'ang on, who are you? You're not the landlord.'

The man shook his head. 'No, I'm afraid I'm not.'

'Then who...? Ah!'

The man smiled bashfully before reaching into his pocket to pull out a piece of paper. He looked at it then put it away again. 'Whhhhooooooooooh,' he said, raising his arms half-heartedly.

Cornwallis and MacGillicudy turned to look and lapsed into silence. Rose and Isabella did likewise, until Isabella suddenly remembered why she was there.

'Oh, so you're the ghost?' she asked hesitantly.

The ghost nodded. 'Whhhooooh,' he said again. He appeared to be a man in his sixties with grey wavy hair, wearing light-tan coloured trousers with a matching waistcoat and a darker jacket, a dainty white cravat at his throat.

'Very scary,' observed Frankie wryly. 'Aren't you meant to sort of pounce at the same time?'

'Er, I don't think so. I'll just check,' and he pulled the piece of paper out again. He read it for a few moments and then shook his head. 'Doesn't say anything about pouncing here.'

'What have you got there?' asked Frankie, holding out his hand. 'Let's have a look.'

The ghost shrugged his shoulders and offered over the paper. Frankie reached out for it, but found that his hand just passed straight through.

'Ooooh,' said the ghost, 'that tickled.'

Frankie tried again and suffered the same effect. 'This ain't gonna work; tip it around so I can read it.'

The ghost unfolded the paper and held it out while Frankie peered at it; he had to concentrate hard to see the vague writing, but at last managed to read the words.

'These are instructions on how to haunt,' said Frankie, feeling innately pleased with himself. 'The heading says G.A.P.S, what's that?'

'It's the Ghosts, Apparitions and Poltergeist Society. They're taking care of me.'

Frankie turned to Isabella. 'Have you heard of this crowd?'

Isabella shook her head. 'No, I haven't. Perhaps the ghost will tell us all about it.' She stepped towards the ghost. 'Erm, excuse me, but what's your name?'

The ghost smiled. 'I'm Greyson De Garcy, at your service ma'am.' He held out his hand as if to shake, but then withdrew it awkwardly when he remembered a ghost couldn't.

Isabella smiled warmly. 'Now, Greyson. May I call you that?'

Greyson nodded.

'Good, now who are these, er, people?'

'Ah well, now I can tell you that. They are what you might call the ghosts' union. They give us legal protection and the power of a body united. That's their motto, that is: The power of the body united. Good, eh?'

'Very nice, I'm sure. Now, Greyson, how did you meet these people?'

Cornwallis and the rest looked on with interest as Isabella started to get into her stride. They were now in her territory, and somewhat lost in how to deal with all this. Fluffy sat up, then jumped off the bed and sauntered over to Greyson, he sniffed and walked through him, turned, and walked back. He shook himself, and then jumped back up on the bed. 'Call that a ghost,' he huffed, dismissively. 'Seen scarier kittens.'

'Greyson turned to the cat apologetically. 'Look, it's not my fault, I'm new to all this. It's a fine art, this haunting; I've got to learn the ropes. Come back in a hundred years or so and I should have got the hang of it by then.'

Isabella cast Fluffy a glance and then returned her attention to Greyson. 'These G.A.P.S people, you were just about to tell me all about them.'

Greyson looked a little downcast at the cat's comment and seemed to be about to burst into tears. 'Yes, well. S'not my fault, I'm doing my best.'

'I'm sure you are, Greyson. Now, could you tell me please?'

The ghost sniffed and then stood up straight. 'All right,' he said, stiffening what used to be his backbone. 'When I passed over a few weeks ago, in this very room, I'll have you know; bit unfortunate that, as I hadn't quite planned to pop my clogs just yet. Had a lovely meal and came up to rest for an hour or two, when suddenly, whumph: I got poleaxed. The old ticker, don't you know, couldn't take the strain anymore, I suppose. Always planned to shuffle off this mortal coil in bed with a lovely young thing, in flagrante delicto, alas though, it never came to pass. Anyway, there's me looking down on me and I feel a tap on my shoulder. There's a fella standing there urging me to come with him, a guide, you know, so I start to follow him. Up or down? I ask, and he grins. Ho, ho, I says to myself, I'm going down. So I decide to come back and stay here.'

'That's not right,' said Isabella. 'If fact there is no heaven or hell, or up or down; just across. I'm told you get a choice; you could even come back as a person again. If you don't, then it's a bit like being on holiday, you can do what you want.'

'Oh. Really?' he sounded disappointed.

Isabella nodded. 'So what happened when you came back here?'

'Erm, another ghost met me. He said he was the G.A.P.S representative, gave me a book of rules and welcomed me to the brother and sisterhood of the departed. Told me we were a minority and we should all stick together, after all, we have rights too, you know. We have meetings and all sorts of things. It's rather fun actually.'

'I'm sure you do, Greyson. The problem though, is that Mr Jacobs, the landlord here, can't let this room out to guests. So I'm afraid that you'll have to go.'

Greyson shook his head. 'No, that's not exactly right.' He pulled a thick book out of his other pocket and began to read. 'It says here, "a spirit has the right of occupancy, that when there is a conflict between the departed and the pre-departed then mediation should be sought from the appropriate authorities." We have branch negotiators you know, but nobody wants to listen. At some point, we may have to all go out on strike and then where will you be, eh? Income from us ghosts will dry up, people will lose money; you'll want to listen then, won't you.'

Isabella sighed. 'I'm sorry, Greyson, but you leave me no choice.' She turned back to the others. 'I'm afraid that I'm going to have to have some help here, he's been indoctrinated and he's going to be stubborn. I will call down one of the supervisors.'

Cornwallis raised his eyebrows. 'Oh, and how are you going to do that?'

'Ectoplasm, I'm afraid. It won't look very nice so I would prefer it if you would look away.'

'Ecto what?' interjected Frankie.

'Plasm,' explained Isabella. 'Life force. A spirit needs a life force to manifest, and I supply that. Green gunge, as it's commonly known. It sort of comes out of my body's orifices, so it's not pleasant to look at. Rose can look, as she might be able to help.'

Rose nodded. 'Of course I will, just tell me what to do.'

Isabella smiled. 'If it seems to be getting out of control then just give me a slap. It should be a nice steady stream which coalesces into the shape of a figure. If it seems to be turning into anything else, then give me a slap, it will jolt me out of the trance. It will only be a slight trance and I will be able to answer questions.'

Rose nodded again.

'Good, now the rest of you can turn your backs please, this won't take long.'

Cornwallis, Frankie, and Jethro reluctantly huddled into a group and turned away from Isabella as she began to go into her trance state to summon the supervisor.

Rose looked on fascinated as tiny little tendrils of vivid green luminescence began to emerge from Isabella's mouth, eyes, nose and ears. She looked down, and even saw two tendrils seep out from the bottom of her skirt.

'Oh my,' exclaimed Rose. 'It's coming out from under your skirt.'

Isabella slightly turned her head. 'It will, Rose. It's lucky that I'm not wearing any underwear, otherwise the pressure can really build up.'

Cornwallis opened his mouth and rolled his eyes. No underwear! She just said she wasn't wearing underwear! He felt like crying.

'Yuk,' said Fluffy, watching the ectoplasm get thicker.

Rose looked on as the green gunge began to morph into a man; it sort of swirled around getting faster and faster until it began to solidify and change colour. Her eyes widened as he began to take more of a shape and she could see that he was going to turn out rather handsome and well dressed. Then she heard a clicking sound and the ectoplasm began to dry up.

Suddenly a man stood there, solid, whole, and she wanted to reach out and touch him.

'You can turn back now,' said Isabella to the others. 'It's all done.'

They turned, and Cornwallis saw another man now in the room. 'Who's that?' he asked, amazed.

'He's a sort of policeman from the other side,' explained Isabella. 'He's harmless to us, but he's going to help Greyson here.'

'No he's not,' snorted Greyson. 'I'm a member of the union. I told you, I have rights.'

The celestial policeman slowly shook his head. 'Not here, you don't, my lad. You are now part of the deceased majority, and as such you have to leave the minority to muck up their lives as best they can.'

Greyson looked panicked. This haunting lark had seemed a pleasant way to spend eternity, and now this ghost planned to whisk him off to wherever and whenever and whatever, if what his union man said was true.

'Come on son, let's go quietly and leave these good people to their mean existence.' He pulled what looked like a handcuff attached to a long piece of string from out of his pocket when Greyson refused to go. 'Oh well, I tried.'

The cuff snapped on. The policeman threw the other end into the air which then snapped tight, and then Greyson was suddenly yanked away, the protest in his throat fading away to silence as his image disappeared into the ether.

The celestial policeman nodded his thanks to Isabella before looking at the rest of them. 'Be seeing you, then,' he said by way of parting, and giving a brief salute, he too then faded away.

The room went silent, and it took a good few moments before anyone found enough effort to speak.

'Is that it?' asked Fluffy, breaking the tension. 'No fireworks, no sparks, no screaming?'

'No,' answered Isabella. 'It's all very subdued.'

'Well, I'm impressed,' said Frankie admiringly.

'So am I,' agreed MacGillicudy. 'I just wish I could do that to a good few people I know.'

'I suppose we'd better break up this little gathering of ours and tell the landlord he can have his room back,' said Cornwallis. He cast his eyes over to Isabella and hoped that she would contradict him. Unfortunately for him, she didn't.

'Yes, I agree, it's been quite a tiring time all in all.'

Frankie and MacGillicudy finished the beers they were holding and put them down in the by now quite full tray of empties. Isabella sorted herself out and looked over at Cornwallis, smiling sadly. He smiled ruefully back and sighed, the night for him had gone entirely against plan — and no underwear! She waited for a moment as the others left the room, holding Cornwallis back with a gentle tug on his arm. She blessed him with that wicked smile of hers, and then lowered her eyes. 'Sorry, Jack, but I think it might be for the best. We would only get embarrassed next time I had to pay the rent.'

'I wouldn't have minded a bit of embarrassment,' he responded, a little hope rising. 'All we have to do is to turn around and then lock the door.'

She shook her head. 'No, we'll leave it as it is. Anyway, I saw how you looked at Rose when she came in, and however much fun it would have been, I wouldn't want to be second best. I can't compete with that.'

Cornwallis wanted to deny it, but he hesitated, and then she knew she was right.

'However, you can let me hold on to your arm as we walk back home.'

He smiled wryly and kissed her on the cheek, then arm in arm they headed down the stairs.

Isabella had a brief word with Mr Jacobs the landlord before they left and relief flooded his face, with the ghost gone, he had his pub back. He bit his lip as he hesitated to broach the subject of the drinks that had gone up to keep them refreshed.

'Er, there were quite a few bottles consumed,' he ventured at last.

Cornwallis held up his hand and put his mind at rest. 'Don't worry, Mr Jacobs; we will pay for it all.'

'Frankie, Rose, Jethro,' yelled Cornwallis. They turned back from the front door. 'You can settle up with Mr Jacobs for all you've been drinking, think of it as your contribution to the evening's entertainment. Isabella and I will wait outside for you.'

'Wha...?' groaned Frankie.

Cornwallis and Isabella brushed past them and stepped out into the late evening air. They shared a look and she patted him on the arm. They walked a few steps down the street and turned to wait for the others to come out, while the cat sat down and huffed. Even though it was late, there were still people about, carriages trundled by and they could hear the clip-clop of horses as folk made their way home, the only thing to interrupt the peace. In any other circumstances, it would have been romantic, but fate had intervened, and waggled its fingers at him derisively.

A battered coach clattered to a halt just in front of them, an unfortunate occurrence, because the noise hid the footsteps that were coming up from behind.

Cornwallis stared into the distance and pondered what might have been, when Isabella gave a scream of outrage. He turned to her, and found that a man had one arm around her waist and the other clamped around her mouth. From the corner of his eye, he noticed another man reaching towards him and he saw a glint of steel in his hand. Cornwallis whipped around and chopped down on to the hand holding the knife, then punched the man with all his force. He caught the attacker neatly on the nose and blood spurted out, but the hand that held the knife kept on coming. He managed to twist his body somehow in that fraction of a second, the point of the knife passing a hairsbreadth from his ribs. He snapped down on the hand carrying the knife again, and he twisted with all his strength. He heard the bones creak at first, and then a snap. All the time he could hear Isabella's muffled screaming and he took a moment to look up. Someone flung the door of the coach open as the other man dragged her towards it, then hands reached out and grabbed her, pulling her unceremoniously inside. Cornwallis rent the air with a yell of fury.

Frankie, Rose, and Jethro, came storming out of the pub, just in time to see the coach pulling away. Cornwallis screamed at them that someone had taken Isabella and they began to run after. Cornwallis had to stay put as he still had hold of his assailant who now writhed in his grip. A head appeared from out of the window of the coach, followed by an arm carrying something. He ignored the three pursuers and aimed a crossbow directly at Cornwallis. As the man triggered the catch, a bolt came searing through the air, and Cornwallis had snapped the assailants head up and turned him to face the coach, a microsecond later the bolt hit home, right into the assailant's chest. The coach gathered speed, and with a crack of a whip, it disappeared around the corner into Trotters Field, with the three pursuers trailing in its wake.

Cornwallis lay his assailant down, and he noticed that he looked a little like a sundial with the bolt sticking out of his chest. The man coughed and a trickle of blood seeped out from the corner of his mouth.

'Why? Who ordered this?' demanded Cornwallis, shaking him by the shoulders.

The man grinned, he knew he hadn't much time left and he didn't seem to care. 'You'll never find her,' he croaked. 'She'll be a willy warmer to some eastern fat boy before you know it.' He coughed again and the trickle turned into a flood. He gasped and then grinned again. 'Just think, your girl, on her back, and it will be your fault for sticking your nose in where it weren't wanted.' His breath became ragged and Cornwallis shook him again. 'Strange though, why did you make her wear a dark wig?'

'What?'

'They said she was blonde.'

Cornwallis screwed up his face in puzzlement for a moment and then clarity entered his mind. He wasn't sure how to react, but he knew what they'd done. 'You got the wrong girl, you bastard, that's why.'

'Uh…? Oh no,' and he died.

'That's a shame,' said a disappointed voice behind him.

Cornwallis turned and vaguely recognised the man standing there. Then it came to him, he had only seen him fleetingly, but he had a good memory for faces. 'You're Magpie, aren't you?' he growled.

Mr Magpie nodded. 'A bit late with this one,' and he tapped the body with his toe, 'but it looks like it's been sorted. No harm done, eh?' he said lightly.

Cornwallis breathed deeply and then stood up; his eyes narrowed in anger as he grabbed Mr Magpie by the throat. 'No bloody harm done?' he screamed into his face.

Frankie and the others returned exhausted, they were all out of breath from the chase and they had only given up when the coach had disappeared from sight. 'Who's this then?' he asked, pointing at Mr Magpie whose face now took on the colour of a blueberry with the constriction around his throat, 'another one of them?'

Cornwallis shook his head. 'No, this little toe-rag is Magpie, my protector.'

'Oh,' sneered Frankie.

'The bastards got away,' explained Jethro. 'I'll get the Yard on to it straight away. Is he dead?' he asked, pointing to the corpse.

Cornwallis nodded. 'Yes, and he wouldn't tell me who sent him. He indicated that the plan is to sell her out east.'

'Oh Gods, that's awful,' exclaimed Rose.

Cornwallis looked at her and nodded. 'That's not all, Rose. I'm wondering what they will do to her now when they realise they've made a mistake. I'm sorry, but they were after you.'

Rose's eyes widened to resemble two big saucers. 'Me?' she gasped.

'I'm afraid so,' confirmed Cornwallis. 'He thought Isabella wore a wig.'

MacGillicudy put the whistle to his mouth and gave three long blasts. The sound was piercing, the call to summon every feeler in the vicinity who should come running to give assistance.

'You going to let him breathe?' asked Frankie, pointing again at Magpie.

Cornwallis still had hold of him around the throat, and when he looked, the purple colour hadn't gone away. Magpie's arms were weakening as he tried to pull Cornwallis' hands away from his throat. 'I shouldn't, but I suppose I will.' His gripped lessened, and Magpie's colour began to return.

As the constriction became lighter Magpie gasped with relief, and then he bent double, drawing in great deep breaths as soon as Cornwallis released his grip. 'Wh... why did you do that?' he gasped.

'They've taken Isabella, you moron,' informed Frankie, angrily.

People began to take notice of the little group standing around a corpse and came over to look. Cornwallis gave then short shrift and growled at them, making them change their minds quickly and hurry away. Rose looked around for the cat.

'Must have decided to bugger off when it all kicked off,' concluded Frankie. 'I'm a bit surprised, thought he had more in him than that.'

MacGillicudy's whistle had had its effect and feelers were hurrying from all directions. At least something was now going right, thought Cornwallis dejectedly.

CHAPTER 15

Fluffy grimly hung on to the coach, desperately trying to get a better grip before being added to the mess in the streets. He had his paws wrapped around the suspension arm and looked like a little furry trapeze artist as he swung from side to side. He'd noticed a little platform just at the back of the coach on the underside and he tried to ease his way towards it. A toolbox sat in there, but Fluffy decided that it wouldn't be there for long. Just above him he could see a wooden support, so he unsheathed his claws, reached up, and dug them deep into the wood. He had a purchase now, and he swung towards the platform catching his foot claws on the border. Arm over arm he traversed the support, and then dived into the tool platform with a squeal of triumph. He kicked at the tool box and pushed it to the edge; he then got his claws underneath and flipped it out and over, he had space, and now he could breathe easier.

When Isabella and Cornwallis were attacked the cat was ready to fight too, but when the man had grabbed hold of Isabella and dragged her off towards the coach he knew that she would disappear into the city, perhaps never to be found. She had said she wanted a companion and he had envisaged a life of pampering and luxury. If he didn't find out where they were taking her, that dream would go the way of all the others — plus the fact that he quite liked helping the investigators.

The coach slewed around a corner and came to an abrupt stop, the wheels screeching as the driver applied the handbrake.

The horses were blown from their exertion and lathered in sweat. Fluffy took a peek and saw the driver jump down and fling open the door to the coach.

'Keep hold of her,' ordered the driver.

'You try and keep hold of her; the bitch has nails like talons.'

Fluffy saw the driver jump in and then the coach rocked wildly as the three men fought to keep hold of Isabella. A male voice yelled in pain followed by a cry of triumph from Isabella's.

'Get your hands off me you malicious evil bastard,' cried Isabella, as she fought the attackers.

'See what I mean,' said one of the men who had been inside with her.

'Don't you dare touch me there,' she yelled indignantly.

'Ow! Grab her hands; she's got hold of me gonads!'

Fluffy had a problem; did he go to Isabella's help now, or wait for a better opportunity? It looked to him as if they were inside a yard with a stable block. He wouldn't have a problem in getting away, but he doubted that it would be as easy for her. Fluffy knew he had to wait and see what they were going to do.

He heard a thump, and then everything began to get quiet. The motion of the coach slowed until a little bit of peace descended. Fluffy heard the men breathing hard, and then a click as the door opened.

'Let's get her out now, then she's gonna be her problem and not ours,' said one of the men.

The others obviously agreed, as shortly after there came a scraping noise, and then a grunt, and then they carried an unconscious Isabella out of the coach and across the yard to the back entrance of a house. Fluffy waited for a few seconds and then jumped down to follow.

They'd left the back door open as they went through, but

that didn't matter, as they were obviously cat lovers in the house as the door had a flap built into it. Fluffy grinned and knew he had an escape route. He tentatively edged his way into the house and saw the men carrying Isabella go around the corner of the corridor and then into another room. He ran forward and watched as they kicked open a door and went through. Fluffy saw there were steps leading down and he waited, and then they took Isabella through yet another door, which unfortunately this time banged shut. Fluffy waited for a few seconds before padding down the steps to the bottom. He sat down and licked his paws.

A crash startled the cat as something hit the wall. 'Who do you call this, then?' screamed a voice. Another crash came, followed by lots of tinkling noises. 'I told you to get the girl he was with, not this one.' Then a thwack, as something solid hit something squidgy.

'Ow! That hurt!'

'It'll hurt a bloody sight more in a minute, can't you do anything right?'

'Gordon got killed; Cornwallis did it. This girl was with him. Ow! Don't do that!'

Fluffy grinned to himself.

'You are all bloody useless; if we still had Maxwell here, he'd use your sodding heads as doorstops. I've lost count of how many times you've managed to bugger it all up.'

Another crash and something else disintegrated, quickly followed by another thwack and then a low groan. 'Get out all of you; I now have another problem to sort out, thanks to you.'

Fluffy dived up the stairs and skidded around the corner, just as the basement door flew open and the men inside rushed up, covering their heads from the missiles that followed after. The door below banged shut and the men at last slowed to a halt.

'Could have been worse,' observed one of the men after they got their breath back.

*

They had searched all night. MacGillicudy had got half the Yard looking as well, but they couldn't find any sign of the coach, and even worse, no sign of Isabella. The trail had quickly gone cold. They had checked with Algernon and his band of watchers, but there had been no movement at any of the locations under watch. Everything had drawn a blank. They had even checked the warehouses, and took a quick look at the brothel, but all appeared silent. As they trudged forlornly back to the office all three were in despair.

Rose stoked up the fire and brewed a fresh cup of coffee. All of them tired out from searching and they needed to take a few minutes to think. They were getting nowhere running around the city like headless chickens, they had to stop, work it all out and come up with a plan; unfortunately, at the moment, nobody could come up with one.

'If what that man said was true,' reasoned Rose, as she set the mugs down on the table, 'then at some point they are going to have to get her out of the city. If the plan is to sell her out east then they will need a ship.'

Frankie nodded. 'And that means the docks.'

Cornwallis looked at the two of them through eyes full of remorse, he blamed himself for the situation and the guilt weighed heavy. 'You're just forgetting one thing, Rose, I don't really want to point this out, but they weren't after Isabella; they were after you. As soon as they realise they haven't got you, what will they do?'

If Cornwallis felt guilty, then Rose felt the guilt equally so. She had inadvertently escaped being kidnapped, and should therefore feel relieved. But she didn't. She felt as if it was her fault that Isabella had ended up in the hands of these evil greedy people, and possibly faced a fate far worse than she would have done. 'Thanks, Jack, it's not as though this is easy for me. I know what should have happened; perhaps you'd have felt better if they had taken me instead.'

'You're being silly now, Rose. Of course I wouldn't feel better, but if I hadn't kept hold of that man who tried to kill me, then I could have stopped it.'

'Or have been killed in the process.'

Frankie tried to inject some semblance of reason into the proceedings, a novelty for him. 'It don't matter who did what or who didn't do this, we can't do nothing about it now, apart from trying our best to find Isabella. At the moment all I hear is you two competing to see who is feeling worse about it. I say forget guilt, 'cause that ain't gonna help anybody now. We're sure it's all tied up with Kintersbury, so I say, let's go grab the bastard and squeeze him 'til he squeaks.'

Cornwallis and Rose stared at Frankie for a moment because he'd hit the nail on the head; they were each trying to outdo the other in the guilt department, and in so doing were forgetting what they should in fact be doing. Cornwallis held up his hands. 'You're right, Frankie.' He turned back to Rose and apologised. 'I'm sorry, Rose, I know we both feel like shit about this, but feeling shit is not helping matters. It's not our fault; the fault lies with the bastards who grabbed Isabella.'

From somewhere Rose found a smile, the first one since they had left the Jerkey Turkey late last night. 'It's all right, Jack, I think we're all tired and worn out and our tempers are a bit frayed; that's not really helping much.'

'Good morning,' trilled Mrs Gridlington, as she breezed into the office. 'My, my. Look at you all, anyone would think that you've been up all night.'

Cornwallis snapped his head up and painted on a smile of welcome. 'Good morning, Mrs Gridlington, I didn't realise that was the time,' he responded, checking his pocket watch. 'We haven't had a very successful night, I'm afraid, so are not looking our best. You're a bit early aren't you?'

'Tch, tch. Never mind I'm sure. Yes, I am a little; I thought I'd pop in first to see if you need me to do anything. Mr Gridlington is a bit unwell this morning, but this being only my second day, you know, what would it look like if I didn't turn up? I told him I'd pop back a little later, if that was all right with you?'

'Unwell, you say?' said Cornwallis.

Mrs Gridlington nodded.

'Then I suggest you go home and look after him. There's nothing here that can't wait a day or two.'

Mrs Gridlington looked surprised. 'Are you sure, Mr Cornwallis? It looks like you three could do with a little looking after, I'm sure he won't mind.'

'No, no. You go. We have a lot to think about, and to be frank, we would be better off thinking without you here. We don't want to burden you with our little problems.'

'Oh dear, you do sound very depressed. Incidentally, a gentleman handed me this letter to give to you as I came in.' She fished out the letter from her pocket and handed it over.

Cornwallis took the letter and slid his fingernail down the edge; he pulled out the contents and then began to read. Suddenly all his weariness drained away and he sat up in attention. He read the note again and then handed it to Rose. 'Who gave you this?' he demanded.

'Oh, a gentleman downstairs, but he's gone now. He tapped me on the shoulder and said to give it to you. Is it important?'

'Yes, Mrs Gridlington, it is. What did he look like?'

'Oh, I didn't really get to look at him. Just an average sort of man, I suppose.'

Cornwallis sighed as Rose gave Frankie the note to read.

'You go and look after your husband. We'll be all right here,' said Cornwallis sombrely.

'Well, if you insist. Toodle pip then, and thank you.' Mrs Gridlington blessed them all with a smile and then departed.

When the door closed, Cornwallis reached for the note again. 'Ten thousand dollars ransom they want. Gornstock Bridge, tonight.'

'At least we know she's still alive,' said Rose, with a little relief. 'What are we going to do?'

'Pretend to pay it of course, unless we find out where she is before then. We have all day to work it out.' Cornwallis' face took on a steely expression. 'The bridge is the worst place for them for an exchange; we can seal off both ends.'

'Bastards,' exclaimed Frankie vehemently. 'If they harm her, I'll rip them apart with my bare hands.'

For the next few minutes, they went over all the possibilities and ramifications of the ransom demand. The act of receiving it had nudged them back into positive thinking and suggestions were coming thick and fast. They were so engrossed in contriving a workable action plan that nobody heard the scratching at the door, and it wasn't until a howl like a banshee assaulted their senses that they realised that something out there wanted to get in.

Rose jumped up and flung the door back on its hinges to reveal Fluffy sitting outside. The cat regarded Rose with a look of utter contempt before standing up and striding in with his tail stuck up high in the air.

'Well, look what the ca…' began Frankie, before realising that the cat actually brought itself in.

Fluffy looked disdainfully at Frankie before turning his attention to Cornwallis. He jumped up on the desk and sat down with a superior look on his face. 'Youse wondering where I got to, ain't youse?'

'I expect some back alley somewhere,' replied Frankie with a sneer. 'Hiding perhaps?'

'That's not fair, Frankie,' replied Rose, regaining her chair. 'You can hardly expect a cat to tackle a man with a knife.'

'It doesn't matter,' said Cornwallis calmly to Frankie, 'Fluffy owes us nothing; he's already been more than helpful.'

Fluffy lay down and purred. 'I can be even more helpful now, if youse wants to know.'

'Really? How?'

'Because while youse lot were scrapping and running, I got on the coach.'

'What?' exclaimed Cornwallis, his head snapping up.

The cat had everybody's attention now.

'How?' 'Where did it go?' 'What happened to Isabella?' The questions were suddenly pouring out of them, while Fluffy lay there cleaning his whiskers and enjoying the attention.

Fluffy explained what had happened and how someone decided to lock the cat flap, trapping him in the house, however, the wait was worth it, as he overheard that they planned to send Isabella overseas, where she would be auctioned off to the highest bidder. Fluffy didn't know when they were to do this, but he assumed it would be soon. In the meantime, they held her in the cellar at the house, but he couldn't get in to see her as they kept the door locked. There were five men and a woman guarding her, and the woman screamed the place down when the men turned up with the wrong girl. She eventually recovered and decided to make as much money as she could out of the failure. It wasn't until this morning that anyone in the house ventured outside, giving Fluffy the opportunity to escape. Rose had shown him the office when she brought him back the other day and again last night to meet up with MacGillicudy, but Fluffy still had to find it. It took a lot of going up blind alleys until he eventually came across somewhere he recognised and could make his way here. Of course, he didn't relate everything to Cornwallis, as that would have given the game away about how they had all followed him last night.

'That settles it then, the ransom note is a ruse,' deducted Cornwallis, when Fluffy had finished. 'They just sent it to buy some time. They don't want us digging around and finding out where they are, which means they plan to move her on today. They're hoping that we won't do anything until after the deadline.' He grinned mirthlessly. 'But they are going to be wrong.'

'And you think you can find this place again?' asked Rose.

The cat grinned. 'Of course I cans, what do youse take me for?'

'In that case,' said Cornwallis. 'What are we waiting for?'

The cat's information had galvanised them into action, renewing their energy straight away.

Cornwallis and Frankie made sure they were well armed, but Rose made do with just a small dagger. They would have to inform MacGillicudy as they might need a few more men to help storm the address. Fluffy described the layout of the house the best he could, adding that it had a communal stable and a yard out back. Cornwallis listened attentively, being thankful that because of the cat's quick thinking they would soon be able to save Isabella. Anything else they might find out would be a bonus.

Fluffy led, and the three people followed frustratingly behind. The cat had eventually found them in Hupplemere Mews but he'd taken a lot of detours on the way; and by retracing his steps, he did the same, because he followed his scent trail. Fluffy had sprayed at virtually every street corner and the cat now admitted that it began to get a little confusing, as his scent had got mixed up with all the other cats that had passed by.

'We's a getting closer now,' Fluffy confirmed, as he sniffed at a particularly rank piece of boarding. He twitched his whiskers and headed off down a fetid alley. 'Definitely came this way, recognise this bit.'

'We're going in circles,' observed Frankie, his frustration increasing. 'This is a cut through back to Buryshaft Lane. We've already been down there.'

Rose was more understanding. 'He's got to go the way he came, it might take us a while, but he'll get us there in the end.'

'Yeah, but will the end be too late?'

Cornwallis set his face hard as they followed the cat; he kept his impatience more in check than Frankie did, but that didn't stop his mind from screaming at the cat to hurry up. Then half way down the alley the cat stopped, his hackles rose and he went into stalking mode. Behind him, the three investigators stopped and waited for a moment; as Cornwallis opened his mouth to say something, Fluffy shot off beneath a railing and into an old building. Cornwallis, Rose and Frankie looked at each other; in the end, Rose ventured the question.

'Do you think we're there? This doesn't look like the terrace house he described.'

Frankie shook his head slowly. 'Why-oh-why are we following a bloody cat?'

'Because the cat's the only one who knows where they're holding Isabella,' replied Cornwallis, tight-lipped.

Fluffy crept out from under the railings looking as sheepish as a cat ever could. 'Sorry, saw a mouse,' he said by way of an excuse. 'Difficult to stop the old urges youse knows.'

Frankie sighed. 'Any more of that and I can assure you, I'll find a way,' and then he mimed wringing a neck.

'No needs fer that, a cats gotta do what a cats gotta do,' he said indignantly.

'Let's get going,' interjected Cornwallis, seeing that the two of them could keep this up for hours. 'Time is passing and we don't need arguments.'

'Not arguing,' said Fluffy, huffily, before running to the end of the alley and taking a sniff.

Fortunately, there were no more cat excursions after mice or rats or any other edible small rodent, and the rest of the journey passed without incident.

Nearly an hour after they set off they came close to the House of the Assembly, and for the first time in an age they just waved to Frankie's mum instead of taking a break and eating a free lunch. As they crossed the road, Fluffy seemed to be more confident in his location and now set out with a determination born of knowledge. He stopped sniffing the scent trail, and with his tail held high, he confidently walked down the Trand. They dodged all the people and traffic then turned into a side street, then another turn into a side street, and Cornwallis felt a sense of foreboding descend. If they turned left at the bottom of this street, it would confirm what had just gone through his mind.

They turned left.

Cornwallis swore to himself as they stood at the corner and looked over towards Havelock Crescent. Last night there had been no sign of anyone in the building, no lights, no nothing, just deathly quiet. They had been so close, but they hadn't realised it, and here they were again. A brothel of all places; they should have realised that a brothel should have customers coming in and out of the place. Fluffy confirmed that they had been aiming here all along, and he indicated the house that held Isabella by running over and sitting outside. It confirmed it all.

'We are definitely going to need some more bodies,' decided Cornwallis, thinking the situation through. 'We are going to have to be patient for a while longer.'

Frankie went for reinforcements while Cornwallis and Rose kept an eye on the place, hoping against hope that they weren't too late. Rose stayed on the street corner watching the front of the house, while Cornwallis made his way to the back with the cat. He strained at the leash as he desperately wanted to go ahead himself and force a rescue, but with the probability of there being at least six of them inside, he reckoned his chances were remote. Better to wait just a little while longer and be certain of success.

Fluffy brought him around to the stables and showed him the back gate into the house, which appeared firmly shut; but whether locked or not, he couldn't take the risk to find out. The stable block looked like a good vantage point as a little hayloft overlooked the yard. He pushed open the door and poked his head inside. The heads of five horses stared back at him from the neat row of stalls; they regarded him with interest to start with, but that soon wained, as if to say if you haven't brought any titbits, then you can just sod off. Cornwallis ignored them and looked for the ladder to take him up to the hayloft. The horses snickered one by one as he walked past them with Fluffy; the cat looking up at them disdainfully as if to say you're banged up, but I'm not. The horses looked back at Fluffy as if to say that if you came in here we might change our mind about being vegetarian.

Cornwallis came to where the ladder leant against the loft. The stable block was shaped like the letter "F", and there in the first "-" of the "F", they found the battered coach from last night. He gave himself a wry grin, then climbed the ladder and kicked a path through the loose hay to the loft door. He knelt down to look through the slats, and found he had a good view of the houses opposite, being able to see over the wall and into the garden, where he could observe both the back door and the privy, and he could see who would use it. A technicality entered his mind, and he decided that it was a long drop, old technology but still useful; it just meant that some unfortunate servant would have to go down periodically and clean off the pebble dash. He had a much better one, up to date and inside the house too. It had a water cistern fed from the tank on the roof, and a u-bend just after the pan which stopped it from smelling. Strange what entered the mind when a long quiet wait beckoned, he thought. He sent Fluffy back to Rose to tell her he had found a good position, and then settled down to wait, hoping that Frankie wouldn't be too long in bringing the reinforcements.

Rose found it a little more difficult to be inconspicuous, the street corner being not perhaps the best place to stand when observing a brothel. A few people passed by giving her curious glances, but her own imagination did the rest. Street corner. Brothel. Girl standing nonchalantly. How many of them *know* there's a brothel here, she wondered? That would be the second time in a matter of days that someone had mistaken her for a lady of easy virtue. She decided to move around a bit, always keeping the house under observation. The park seemed a nice place to take a stroll, but would that be worse? Virtually all the other girls she has seen around this residential district wore long dresses, and most had a hat. She wore trousers and a jacket, which definitely placed her in the working fraternity, and as the trousers weren't far off being of the painted on variety, her standing near a brothel might have indicated what work she did. So perhaps she could understand the looks she received. And, she continued thinking, if it wasn't for her spurning Jack, then Isabella wouldn't have been kidnapped, because Jack wouldn't have gone to the Inn to see the ghost and hope to indulge in the afters. She still felt guilty, not only because Isabella had been kidnapped, but because after they had spoken for a while she found she actually liked her, and thought that they would be friends. Isabella had told her that one look from her, and how Jack had looked at her when they'd come in, was enough to know that whatever might have happened would definitely not happen now, and besides, she quite liked Frankie too.

She sighed, and Fluffy sighed. Rose looked down at the cat, who she had not noticed come back, and bent down to ruffle his neck.

'He's in the hay loft out back, he sent me to sees if youse is all right,' purred Fluffy.

'I am. It's just a matter of waiting now.'

Cornwallis watched the door and the windows through the slats, hoping that they wouldn't move just yet. He piled up some hay to make it more comfortable and settled back down. He cast his eyes along the windows of all the houses and noticed that he could see inside relatively easily. Little dramas were being played out, and here he sat, watching it all. It reminded him of working on suspected adultery cases, but with more of an edge to it. A movement took his eye along the row and he could see a maid at the window polishing. He counted the hands and made it four. He screwed up his brow in thought and then watched as two of the hands began to wrap around her waist. She began to giggle, and part of him wished he'd bought one of those new-fangled seeing-up-close devices that had just come on the market in order to see better. He slapped his wrist and returned his attention back to where it should be. A curtain twitched in the upstairs window and he concentrated, trying hard to see who twitched it; but he just saw a shadow, so he put away the information that someone was up there. The back door flew open and a man hurried to the privy with a rolled up newspaper tucked under his arm. That looked like it could be a long one, he thought, hoping the seat was full of splinters. The back door opened again and this time two more men came out, but this time they went past the privy, but took the opportunity to bang on the door and laugh. They then headed for the back gate, opened it, and walked through; with a degree of concern, he then saw them come towards the stables.

He hunkered down low as they opened the big double doors, listening intently to hear what they were up to as they came in; they swore profusely and headed straight for the coach to drag it outside.

'Haven't long put the buggering thing away and she wants it bloody out again,' says one of them.

'Aye,' agrees the other. 'She's never sodding happy. This should be the last time for a while though, gonna take her guest down to the docks to wait in the warehouse for the ship to come in.'

Cornwallis snapped to attention.

'Oh right, well thank the Gods fer that. You gonna drive?'

'Hmmm,' affirmed the driver.

'That old git Kintersbury didn't stay long, where'd he go?'

'I overheard him saying he had to go to the bank; then him and Dumchuck were going to the Collider later, what a waste of money, eh? I could retire in luxury for just a fraction of what they charge for that thing.'

'Probably getting the bank to pay for it. As long as it don't come out of our money, eh?'

Cornwallis couldn't believe his luck, Dumchuck and Kintersbury, neatly wrapped.

They dragged the coach out and then returned for the two horses. Cornwallis wracked his brain trying to think of a way to nobble the coach, as he knew that he and Rose had little chance of taken them on their own.

He watched through the slats as they harnessed the horses to the coach and then they tied up the reins to a hook on the post. They then started laughing at some joke as they headed back inside the house.

Cornwallis didn't have much time. He jumped down and moved to the door and pulled out his knife, he checked to make sure they hadn't come back and crept out. The horses looked at him suspiciously and backed off a bit as they saw the knife, but he patted one of them on the haunches and they settled back down. He then proceeded to cut the traces, leaving just a thread between the halves. The horses seemed to know what he planned to do and he could have sworn they were grinning. He dived back inside the stables just in time, as the gate opened and one of the men came back out. Cornwallis prayed that he wouldn't notice the sabotage.

Fluffy appeared again just as he began to climb up the ladder, he paused, and then took the couple of steps back down. 'Go and tell Rose they're trying to take Isabella to the warehouse on the docks. I've done my best to stop them, so if she sees two horses going hell-for-leather then I have, if she sees a coach still attached then I haven't. Got that?'

'Fer…!' whined Fluffy. 'Yer gonna wear me legs out.'

He watched the cat disappear and then began to climb the ladder again. He got to his vantage point just at the right time as four men marched out of the door, pulling Isabella with them. They looked quickly as they got to the gate and then hurried to the coach. The man who'd come out first, flung open the door and the four pushed and pulled her in. Isabella didn't make it easy for them as she fought like a tiger, kicking out and twisting this way and that. The door slammed shut and the driver climbed up to his seat and took a deep breath.

Cornwallis crossed his fingers as the driver picked up the reins and then let off the handbrake; he adjusted himself a little to get comfortable and then snapped the reins, shouting 'Gee, ah.' The horses didn't move, so he swore and snapped the reins again, still nothing happened so he fished down the side and came up with a whip. He tightened his grip and shouted at the same time as cracking the thing. The horses snorted, and then took off like a ferret after a rabbit.

There were two problems for the driver. The first of which were Cornwallis' doctoring of the traces, which had the effect of at first a slight movement of the coach, closely followed by a loud snap as the traces parted company, and hence a gentle roll forward a few feet before coming to a stop. The second problem was that the driver had looped the reins around his wrist which tightened into a knot the moment the horses took off. The drivers face contorted in pain as the reins gripped, and then he realised that he would shortly become airborne, only to stop being airborne at some point within the next few seconds, which would undoubtedly hurt; a lot. His mouth opened in a scream, but it shut off pretty quickly as the ground rushed up to meet him, which resulted in an oomph noise followed by a rasping sound, and then his mouth found the scream that he'd lost and he wailed in pain. The horses were enjoying themselves; they went from standing still to a gallop in just a few short yards, and by the time the driver had made contact with the ground they were going at full pelt. They hammered out of the yard and then turned into the street, sensing a freedom that they could only have dreamt about; the time had come to pay back all those whippings they'd got in the past. The driver's ordeal lasted for just a few short seconds, for after the third long bounce he lapsed into unconsciousness as his head hit the ground. He had a moment's lucidity before oblivion took over, and he wished he'd listened to his mother after all and had taken that job in the funeral parlour.

Cornwallis grinned in satisfaction as the horseless coach ground to a halt. A head poked out of the window to see what had happened and spat an expletive. The first head dipped back inside and then another head appeared momentarily before it too disappeared. The door on the far side crashed open and all the occupants, including Isabella, poured out and hurried back to the house. None of them even thought about going after the hapless driver.

Rose listened to Fluffy and watched the well-dressed distinguished man, who had just walked past her, knock at the house. The door opened, just as a noise diverted her attention. At first, she heard the thundering of hooves, before looking around and seeing the two horses come hammering down the Crescent and then turn into the street towards her. She then noticed a bundle of rags dragged behind before identifying it as a person as it sped past. Her gaze followed the tableau, and as she raised her eyes, she saw Frankie come hurrying around the corner. He had a group in tow, and from that group she saw two figures detach themselves and step into the street; one looked like Big George and the other looked like Chalkie from the docks. The horses took one look at the two bears and skidded abruptly to a stop, panting and snorting from their exertion. Rose dare not think what the facial expression of one of the horses would have been, because the driver, bouncing along behind them, was still in mid-air as the horses stopped, their tails high in the air. The momentum carried him through the air until his head entered a horse, just below the raised tail, and even from that distance, Rose could hear the squelch. The aim was perfect! The horse reared at the unwanted attention in its back passage and began to dance around in order to get rid of the obstacle. The drivers knees bounced on the ground, before at long last his head slipped out and the hapless driver's ordeal came to an end. She couldn't take her eyes away from the drama for a few moments, and when she finally managed to drag her eyes back up to the house, the man had disappeared inside.

Frankie pulled up puffing from all his running. 'What's that all about?' he asked, pointing at the driver lying unconscious on the ground.

She explained it was probably one of the men holding Isabella.

Frankie grinned evilly. 'Well, he ain't dead, unfortunately, but he's definitely full of horse shit.'

MacGillicudy turned up with a bunch of feelers in tow, including Dewdrop. He told them that he had a hurry-up wagon on its way and it should be there shortly. Gerald and a few of his heavies also made an appearance, because as he put it, "Someone had gone and shat on his turf, so he would go and have a shit on theirs."

Fluffy then rushed back to Cornwallis with the news of the man at the door and the arrival of Frankie with the additional man/bearpower, and what did he want them to do?

It all began to happen now; Rose could hardly keep pace

with events.

*

Mrs Fitchley opened the door and saw Bertram Radstock standing there with a smile on his face.

'Oh, Mr Radstock. What, er, a surprise.'

'Yes, Mrs Fitchley, it's me. I know I don't as a rule come during the day, but I've had a particularly torrid time in the House, and the mistress did say to call anytime.'

'Oh… er, yes, but…'

Just then, she heard the thunder of the horses and saw the coach-less equines come haring out from behind. Her eyes widened for just a moment and then she pulled Radstock inside. Something had gone wrong. She hurriedly ushered Radstock into the parlour and closed the door behind her.

'I don't think it's very convenient at the moment, Mr Radstock, the mistress is somewhat busy, I'm afraid,' she explained, agitatedly.

'Oh, I don't mind waiting, anticipation is half of it, you know,' beamed back Radstock.

'Right, erm… Just wait here a moment.' A kerfuffle came from the hall and she whipped her head around at the noise, 'I'll just go and see…'

She smiled thinly, yanked the door open, and quickly stepped into the hall. She took a moment for a breath then hurried through to the back door where the little entourage that should have been on the way to the docks stood around looking confused.

'What happened?' she barked.

'Sommat went wrong wiv the 'orses and coach,' explained one of them. 'It all broke. It weren't our fault; it was Broddy, 'e were meant to be driving.'

Mrs Fitchley swore and then gathered her thoughts. 'Upstairs, and take her with you. Keep your hands off her and make sure she doesn't get away; and keep her quiet. Now off with you quick, I'll deal with it all later.'

The four of them dragged Isabella towards the stairs and then up, all trying to go upstairs at once, jamming it, like a cork in a bottle. Mrs Fitchley watched and then slowly shook her head as the jam cleared and they managed to disappear around the bend in the stairs. Without giving them another thought, she hurried to the back room and down the stairs to the basement, quickly tidying up after Isabella's incarceration. When she'd done that, she rushed back up the stairs and then stood outside the parlour to get her breath back. She calmed herself and then opened the door.

She smiled at Mr Radstock. 'The Mistress has agreed to see you, but the price will be double as you have no appointment. I'm afraid she wants payment in advance today.'

Radstock nodded agreement; he considered the money well spent. He counted it out and handed it over. 'Thank you, Mrs Fitchley, I'm sure she'll treat me that extra bit special, she does so like a willing customer.' He waited a moment, hoping for a cup of tea and biscuits, but it seemed that today he would be disappointed, tea appeared off the menu.

Mrs Fitchley ushered him out and down the corridor; she had a quick look upstairs and listened briefly, but it seemed as if they were at last doing as they were told. She showed Radstock into the back room and opened the door to the basement, smiled at him as she reminded him about the bottom step, and then shut the door. Radstock descended the stairs and went into his favourite room to wait.

As normal, Radstock began without being told. He picked

up a cloth and began to polish all the ornaments in the basement. It seemed quite a while later, when he had gone through nearly half of them, that the door opened and Miss Lena came in. She carried a particularly nasty looking three thronged leather punisher in one hand and a long whip in the other; Radstock felt his heart quicken.

'You started before I told you again, Radstock.' She cracked the long whip. 'That means you will be punished. Everything off. *Now*,' she ordered.

Radstock obliged, feeling his excitement increase.

*

Cornwallis felt confident that they had more than enough assistance to deal with anything they would find in the house and to free Isabella unharmed. He decided a cordon of feelers outside the front of the house should prevent anyone from running away, while everyone else, including the bears, would go in through the back and then pass out to the feelers everyone they caught. MacGillicudy insisted on going in with the rest, and Dewdrop pleaded to go too. Rose, still feeling sorry for his embarrassment on the docks, persuaded Cornwallis to agree to Dewdrop's request.

Frankie, Rose, MacGillicudy and Dewdrop, plus two other feelers, stood in the yard waiting to go in the gate. Gerald and two of his men, Snuffler and Conk, along with Cornwallis, Fluffy and the two bears, waited too. Cornwallis told Big George and Chalkie to wait outside the back door, because they were far too big to go marauding through a house without getting in the way, and grab anyone they didn't recognise. The rest of them were to go in and methodically search.

MacGillicudy, Dewdrop and the two feelers were to do the

ground floor, Gerald and his men to do the first floor. The top two floors were for himself, Rose, Frankie and Fluffy. He checked that everyone knew what they were doing and then grinned. He felt he should give a little speech to get them in the mood, but a look at all their faces told him that if he did they wouldn't be responsible for their actions. He kicked open the back gate and they all went in.

Something jogged Cornwallis' memory as they went through in a rush, he stopped and spoke quickly to Big George and Chalkie and then carried on. Frankie kicked the back door open and they stormed in.

George and Chalkie grinned at one another and then turned to the door of the privy. Cornwallis had remembered he had seen one man go in, but he hadn't seen him come out again. George knocked politely on the door and received a reply.

'Sod off, I ain't finished yet.'

Chalkie yanked on the door and pulled it open.

The man inside sat comfortably with his trousers around his ankles reading the back page of the paper. He looked up and opened his mouth to issue a response to the intrusion when he abruptly changed his mind. Chalkie reached inside with his paw and flicked out his claws one by one. The man stared dumbstruck at the deadly talons as they each appeared in sequence. Chalkie issued a low growl and bared his teeth, then swiped down at the paper, shredding it in one fell swoop. Having already finished what he had gone in there to do and now just bided his time to finish the paper, the appearance of the two bears and the shredding of his paper had the remarkable effect of inducing another urge, which dissipated remarkable quickly as he fell forward in a faint. George craned his neck through the door and sighed in disappointment. Chalkie reached down, grabbed the man by the ankles, and dragged him outside, still with his trousers at half-mast.

As the rest of them went in, a door in the corridor came open. A head appeared, but it took too long to compute what was going on. Dewdrop, closest to the head, held his trusty truncheon in his hand; whether a reflex or a reaction to his humiliation on the docks, he couldn't have said, because where normally he would have turned tail and run, this time he didn't. He raised the weapon and brought it crashing down on the top of the man's head with a thwack sound, a grunt followed, and then the man collapsed. Cornwallis grinned and patted Dewdrop on the back before rushing up stairs.

Gerald and his men dived into the corridor on the first floor and began to kick open the doors one by one, while Cornwallis and Rose headed further up with Fluffy. A scream came from the first floor and Frankie stopped, a female scream, more than likely Isabella's, so he yelled to Cornwallis that he intended staying there. Cornwallis called back his agreement and carried on up.

They found the second floor empty as they quickly searched the rooms, then Fluffy ran up the next flight of stairs, closely followed by Rose. At the top, she began to peer into all the rooms before finding one that had an incumbent. She stopped, and stared, and the man inside smiled back.

'Jack,' she yelled down. 'Jack, I think you should come up.' She then noticed an arm on the sill of the window.

Fluffy saw it too and leapt. His claws sprang out and he raked the arm, then sunk his teeth into the flesh and bit down hard; a yell came from outside and the arm was yanked away. Fluffy very nearly went with it, but just managed to jump down in time. Rose hurried over to the window and saw a man sliding down the drainpipe.

'George,' she yelled, and the big brown bear looked up.

The man had got half way down when Rose yelled, and he made the mistake of twisting his head to look below, swallowing hard as he realised that two bears and an unconscious looking colleague awaited him. His choices were limited. He looked up as Rose looked down and she blessed him with a knowing smile, his chances of getting away were somewhere between nil and none. He decided to risk it and jumped. Chalkie still had the first man in his hand, and as the escapee jumped, he began to swing his arm. A polar bear is perhaps one of the strongest animals around, and the man in his hand felt as light as a feather, so he swung hard. As the man landed he came head to head with his friend at a particularly rapid speed of knots, and the sickening crunch of head meeting head set Rose's teeth on edge.

Cornwallis dived into the room and abruptly stopped, sitting on the bed he saw a man they had been looking for — Roland Goup.

A couple of floors down, Gerald and Frankie had found Isabella. They had also found two more men, one of whom pointed a crossbow at the door, while the other held a knife to Isabella's throat.

They backed off into the corridor and waited a moment before Gerald shook his head. 'No point in waitin'. Let's go get 'em,' he said, rubbing his hands.

Frankie nodded. 'I'll take the one holding Isabella, you can have the other.'

'Suits me,' agreed Gerald. 'I wonder if 'e knows about me?' He then stepped into the door frame and grinned at them. 'Shall I introduce meself? My name is Gerald, an' I come from the Brews. What do I call you, dead an' deader perhaps?'

They had obviously heard of the King of the Brews as they quickly looked at each other with a worried glance.

'Well, my boys, are we going to do this the easy way, or are yer going to make it difficult? I'd like you to choose the difficult way because then I won't feel guilty about what I'm about to do. Now tell me, which o' you buggers went treading on my territory, eh?'

Frankie stood behind Gerald, and Snuffler and Conk stood behind him. The two men failed to respond to Gerald's polite enquiry, they just looked two very confused and scared individuals; they didn't expect all this to happen.

The crossbow wavered and wobbled a bit and then as Gerald stepped in, it fired. The bolt hurtled straight towards Gerald's chest, but to the amazement of the firer, it went straight through and thudded into the wall.

Gerald grinned.

Frankie had only a moment to act as the man holding the knife dropped his jaw in astonishment. Gerald stepped further in as Frankie stepped towards the knife holder, just as the one holding the crossbow rushed at Gerald. He made a mistake in thinking he would just bowl him over, but instead found that going through Gerald was like wading through treacle. When he emerged from the other side he went straight into the arms of Snuffler and Conk, who gleefully dispensed instant justice. Frankie saw that his man was still open-mouthed; with the knife held against Isabella's throat, but as the crossbow fired, the knife dropped a little and then fell away completely as he watched his friend dive straight through Gerald. Before he could recover, the man looked up, just as Frankie's fist came towards his face.

Cornwallis met a grinning Frankie on the landing as he made his way down, a safe and unharmed Isabella clinging onto his arm. He sighed in relief, all had gone to plan, and no one had been hurt; well, none of the good guys anyway.

On the ground floor MacGillicudy called up. 'You done up there, Jack? Only we've just found the cellar.'

They all stood in the back room of the house and listened at the door to the sounds that came up from below. MacGillicudy winced at the thwacking noises, closely followed by cries of pain and a pitiful whimpering moan. 'If he's paying for that then he wants his head examined,' he opined, to everyone's agreement.

Cornwallis decided they had to clear the house once and for all. He began to descend the stairs, followed by Rose and MacGillicudy and then Dewdrop and Gerald. Frankie held back until last, as Isabella still clung onto his arm and he got to like it. The bottom step creaked and then splintered, and Cornwallis had to move quickly before it gave way. He listened for a few moments, concerned that the noise of the step had given away their presence; but he needn't have worried, as another thwack came and then a moan. The moan turned to a whimper and he decided that the time to finish had arrived; he then slowly turned the door handle.

The door opened and everybody began to pile through. Once inside, they all looked at a sight that none of them had ever seen before. The woman wore high-heeled thigh-high leather boots, a leather thong, and a tiny leather support for her chest; there was absolutely no doubt that she was superbly built.

'Wow,' said Dewdrop, his tongue hanging out.

She wore a leather mask and had long dark hair down to her waist. Her elbow length gloves held two whips, both directed at a naked man standing on a little turntable. Above his head, he had his arms tied to a similar turntable, and the whole seemed to spin around. They had come through the door at the same time as the woman struck, and the man moaned again. Rose's eyes widened as he obviously enjoyed the experience.

The woman spun her head at the intrusion. She hesitated for just a moment, and then struck out at Cornwallis with the long whip, cracking the air. He just managed to get his arm up in time, but felt the sting as the end whipped around his wrist, but then he yanked back with his arm and the whip flew out of her hand. Dewdrop had obviously found his courage a little earlier when he had smacked the man on the head, because now he raised his truncheon and stepped towards the woman.

'I am arresting y—' He never got any further as the woman grabbed hold of his truncheon and pulled him towards her. She expertly spun him, wrapping her arm around his throat and pulling him tight in against her. His legs buckled, and his head nestled between two very interesting looking earmuffs.

The man spun and then came to a stop facing Cornwallis and the others.

'Oh, Gods,' he whined, as his excitement waned.

'Radstock!' exclaimed Cornwallis, recognising the man. 'It's Bertram bloody Radstock!'

'Oh, Gods,' he whined again.

The woman dragged Dewdrop over to the side and grabbed a silver toasting fork off the table, she held it out towards Cornwallis and began to manoeuvre her way to the door. As she edged closer she kept everyone away with repeated stabs of the fork, but then Dewdrop excelled himself. He turned his head until he had the left one in reach of his mouth and bit down hard. The woman screamed, dropping Dewdrop like a hot coal. Cornwallis took his chance and pounced.

Cornwallis had the sensation of feeling soft warm flesh as he flung himself onto her. They clattered to the floor and he heard the rush of air as it gushed out of her lungs. He reached for the fork and managed to dislodge it from her grip, just as Rose and MacGillicudy dived on top. The short fight was over quickly as her arms were now pinned to the side. Cornwallis breathed, relaxed, and then remembered what and whom he was lying on top of; he then scrambled to get up.

Dewdrop had regained his footing and stood looking at the woman with a mixture of admiration, desire, and distaste. She had been perspiring with the effort of using the whip and he could still taste her salt in his mouth. He licked his lips, his mind full of "what if's?"

As Rose and MacGillicudy dragged her to her feet, she seemed to sag, as it now dawned on her that the game had finished.

Cornwallis stepped closer, and then reached out to grab her mask. 'Let's see who we are, shall we?' he said, prising the mask up.

He stood back, and he stared in shock.

'Mrs Fitchley,' exclaimed Radstock, from his upright spit.

'No, it isn't,' replied Cornwallis, shaking his head. 'It's Mrs Gridlington!'

From somewhere she found a smile and held her head up high. 'That's the second handful you've had off me, Jack Cornwallis, but if you let me go, I'll let you have as many handfuls as you like.'

Cornwallis chuckled wryly and shook his head. 'Thank you for the offer, but I don't think I'll take it up, but you could tell me why.'

She chewed her lip for a moment, and part of him felt gratified to see that she seemed a little disappointed. 'Why what? If you mean why did I come to work for you? It's so that I could know what you were up to and where you were going. You were getting to be quite a nuisance. It's just a pity that I got saddled with amateurs who couldn't do their jobs properly.'

'No, not that. I mean Isabella.'

She laughed. 'It wasn't meant to be her, only the boys got it wrong. It should have been this one,' and she tilted her head towards Rose. 'A pity, as she would have made some good money for me; mind, Miss Thrape would have brought in a bob or two too.'

'You had no intention of releasing her then, you sent that ransom note just to give you time to get away?'

'Release her? Of course not, we would have been well away by then.'

'On the ship? The Greyhawk?'

Mrs Gridlington stared at Cornwallis, her composure beginning to slip; she looked a bit worried now.

'It wouldn't have arrived; it's currently in the hands of... Well, let's just say we have it safe,' he continued.

Her eyes widened and Cornwallis grinned.

'You have the gold then,' she replied deflated. It was a statement, not a question, and Cornwallis remembered that the Bagman had said they'd found nothing. He didn't think the Bagman would lie about that, so where had it gone?

'And to think I actually liked you,' said Rose with a sad shake of the head.

Cornwallis decided to change tack. 'Kintersbury and Dumchuck were taking their orders from you, weren't they?'

Miss Lena/Mrs Fitchley/Mrs Gridlington nodded. 'Of course they were; they're customers of mine. I just persuaded them to take their subservience a little bit further.'

Gerald peered closer at her. 'Hmmmm,' he said, thoughtfully. He then snapped his fingers. 'I know yer, don't I? Yer Glenda Pilchard, a tuppeny tom from the Brews, ain't ya?'

She looked at Gerald with loathing. 'And you would know, wouldn't you, seeing as you used to take advantage. It's men like you who made me what I am today. Just use me and discard me, eh? Good for nothing else, eh? A quick knee trembler to clear out the custard, eh? What a man, eh? I probably told you how good you were, that you were a real man, eh? I was just a young girl with no money doing the only thing I could to get by. I got the bruises too, got knocked about a bit. But you wouldn't have worried about that, no, just whip it out, shove it in, and give it a wiggle. That's why I decided to do this, time for me to get my own back,' she spat, contemptuously.

At least Gerald had the decency to look ashamed, and he nodded as if he agreed with her. 'I wondered where you 'ad gone,' he said lamely.

'But why?' asked Rose aghast. 'You would have sent Isabella or me to that sort of life, why?'

She turned her head to look at Rose. 'Simple. You have it too easy.'

All those arrested were led out of the front door to the waiting feelers. Big George and Chalkie dragged their prisoners through the house and chucked them into the hurry-up, which now had got quite full. They released Radstock, though they were tempted to leave him in situ for quite a while longer.

As they filled up the wagon, a man approached. 'You've done well, Mr Cornwallis,' said Sparrow. 'Mr Hawk is going to be pleased. However, you still have the other two to find.'

Cornwallis whipped his head around and regarded the man with distaste. 'You, Sparrow. Go away. Now.'

He smiled back. 'I don't think so. I'll take care of these fine looking people you have here, thank you.'

Frankie and Rose came and stood either side of Cornwallis. 'You won't,' growled Frankie, 'they're all ours.'

Sparrow chuckled. 'No, I... nuh!' He didn't get any further.

Cornwallis stepped forward and let fly with his fist. Sparrow's head snapped back and the nose sort of collapsed in on itself. Before he hit the ground, he was unconscious.

Cornwallis shook his hand. 'Ow, that hurt. But by the Gods

was it worth it.'

'What are we going to do with him?' asked Rose, looking down on Sparrow.

'Throw him in with the others. Let the Bagman sort it out,' replied Cornwallis, indifferently. 'And it's my guess it will take quite some while. In the meantime we have to go and pick up Kintersbury and Dumchuck, and I know where they are.'

*

They found Algernon at the Collider, still being diligent, following Kintersbury and Dumchuck out from the bank and into the countryside to the Universal Collider. They were just debating what to do when Cornwallis happened upon them.

MacGillicudy had commandeered a wagon and they'd hurried out with Gerald and Isabella as well, so all in all there were six of them. Rose had been very subdued on the journey out, and Cornwallis could only think it had something to do with Glenda Pilchard. He had tried to break through the barrier, but she had steadfastly refused to let him get inside. Isabella on the other hand hadn't let it worry her one little bit, and she laughed easily at Frankie's jokes, a little disconcerting because they were never funny. Even Gerald was unusually quiet, and a polite enquiry just elicited a grunt in reply. So it just left Cornwallis and MacGillicudy to talk between themselves for a while.

They now stared at the edifice built into the hillside as they discussed the best way forward.

'Why don't we just wait until they come back out?' suggested Rose, coming back a little to her normal self. 'It's not as though they can get lost in the streets.'

Cornwallis nodded. 'But they have horses tethered in the compound, and I don't fancy chasing them all the way back to

Gornstock. No, I think we will go in and catch them; they'll be trapped inside. Algernon here can wait outside, just in case. How many have you with you Algie?'

'Three and me,' replied Algernon.

Cornwallis nodded again. 'Good. If they come out without us then do what you like with them, only don't let them get away.'

The wagon rolled forward into the entrance to the Universal Collider. Cornwallis had never been here before, as he'd never really seen the point. Why spend all that money trying to find out your future, when the really interesting part of it was to let it all happen without knowing what was going to happen. To his mind, if you found out was going to happen and decided to do something about what you had learnt, then whatever was going to happen wouldn't happen, so in effect something else would happen, and then where would you be? Having to go back to the Collider to find out what would happen. You would just go around in circles all the time, and nothing would happen except what should happen. So he saw no point in trying to find out what was going to happen in the first place. It seemed simple to him.

They left the wagon tied up in a line of coaches, and the six of them made their way to the entrance. It would be MacGillicudy's warrant card that would get them in, otherwise it would have be Cornwallis' pocket, which he was loathed to do, as he knew how deep it would have to be. However, the jobsworth in the Collider wouldn't let anyone in, not without a paper signed by the Justice, who at that moment probably wondered how his basting experience on the spit had come to an abrupt stop in the cellar. They should have brought Radstock with them. Frustrated they turned tail and walked back outside.

Cornwallis tried to think, and then an idea came into his

mind. 'Gerald,' he began. 'Can you remember how you got in all those years ago?'

'Uh?' replied Gerald, still in his reflective mood. 'Oh, right. Erm, yes, I think so. Why?'

'Because that's the way we're going to get in.'

Gerald took them around the back of the Collider to where it looked for all intents and purposes just a hill in the landscape, but as they began to climb up the slope, they saw small vents cut into the hillside.

'Where's all the security?' asked Rose.

'They don't think they need it,' replied Gerald. 'The vents are locked, so as far as they're concerned the Collider is secure. This one'll do.' They gathered around a small vent with a side opening, and Gerald dug into his pocket. 'I know I gotta key here somewhere,' and he smiled at them as he produced the lock-pick.

It didn't take long with an expert like Gerald. The little lock began to grate, and then it clicked. The bars on the vent swung open slowly, and then all of them looked deep inside.

'Now the way to get down is to keep pressure on the sides, if yer don't, it will be like going down one o' them kiddy slides. An' keep quiet, as the sound will travel. It's downhill all the way, so I'll lead, an' I'll try an' remember the way.'

One by one, they all started to climb in. Cornwallis followed Gerald and then came Rose and MacGillicudy with Isabella behind him. Frankie brought up the rear, making sure he pulled the vent to, but it missed the catch and swung open a bit as he moved on down.

A bit like a caterpillar, the awkward little procession crawled along. There were times when the vent got a little steep, but with care, they slowly made their way into the inner depths of the Collider. Gerald had to think hard at several junctions, but in time, they began to hear the noises of people talking. They were getting close now, and Cornwallis could only hope they were in the right area.

The vent then began to go horizontal, with gaps where short extensions branched down into a room. As they passed over, they looked down, trying to figure out where they were. But as the only person who had been in there before was Gerald, they just had to trust to his memory and judgement.

Soon there came the unmistakable hum of the Collider itself, and everyone knew where they were. Gerald dipped his head down the offshoot and took stock of his bearings. There were a few people about, but he wanted to find an unoccupied room where they could all get down unobserved. He pulled himself back up and pointed along the vent a bit, then slid over and dipped his head down once more. This time he came up satisfied, giving them all a thumbs-up.

He flicked the little catch on the grille and let it drop down gently, stuck his head through to check again and dropped through, then one by one, they all tumbled out. They were in a store room, and Cornwallis walked over to the door and opened it a crack to peer out into the Collider chamber.

It was just as Gerald had described, a big room with what looked like a large mirror on the far wall with desks in front of it lined with toggle like things. There were a few people walking around, but more were sitting at the desks, fiddling with the toggles and looking at the screen. Cornwallis supposed they were trying to focus on something or other, but he couldn't see either Dumchuck or Kintersbury amongst them.

'We've missed them, they're not here,' he said dejectedly, as he shut the door and turned.

Isabella came over and opened the door a crack. 'I hear there are some private rooms where they link the feed in, so that you can view it undisturbed. Perhaps that's where they are.'

Cornwallis nodded. 'Perhaps, but how do we know which one and where it is? It's not like we can go in there and walk around searching for them.'

'Why not? Look.' She backed off and Cornwallis took her place. A group had entered the chamber, and it looked like a guided tour. One of them, presumably the tour leader, began to gesticulate, explaining everything. There seemed to be quite a few of them, so it was possible one or two more wouldn't be noticed. He beckoned Gerald over and together they slipped out as the group passed the door and joined in at the back. Gerald at least had the advantage of being able to walk through a door, or at least sticking his head through without having to open it first.

The guided tour leader, obviously knowledgeable but far too nerdy for Cornwallis' liking, dragged the group around, spouting facts in a patronising manner, as if to say, look how clever I am. Each door they passed, Gerald quickly poked his head through, the idea being that even if someone on the other side saw him, they just wouldn't believe what they were seeing.

The guide then began to tell the group about how all the universes exist at the same time in the same place, albeit in a parallel plane, and that here everything became connected through a fault in the time/space configuration, and that by careful manipulation, someone who knew what they were doing could focus in on a particular moment within a chosen universe, basically, as he put it, to have a good nose at what was happening on the other side. Cornwallis looked up at the big screen and saw the tour group looking back, all of them, including him; except for Gerald, who stood right next to him. He turned his head to look and then turned back to the screen.

Gerald just smiled, because he knew he didn't exist.

Cornwallis felt a chill go down his back. Although he knew

Gerald's story, here in the Collider it brought it home to him in no uncertain way. There on the screen in front of them — was not Gerald.

He had an urge to ask the guide and see how he dealt with it, but they were here to look for Kintersbury and Dumchuck, so he would have to leave that pleasure for another time. Gerald shoved his head through yet another door, and this time came back with a grin on his face. He twitched his head in the door's direction, indicating that they had found who they were looking for.

The guide started to look perplexed. He kept looking at the screen and then looking at the crowd of tourists. He scratched his head and then began to count. Cornwallis smiled as he saw him. He nudged Gerald, thankful that his arm didn't go through him, and cocked his head towards the guide. They didn't need to panic, instead Cornwallis looked to the store room where the others were peeping out and beckoned them over. The time had come to act, and there would be now something else for the guide to comment on — the arrest of two felons.

MacGillicudy, Frankie, Rose and Isabella poured out of the storeroom to the consternation of everyone in the Collider, and then hurried across the room. The guide watched bemused, not sure what to do, as this had never happened before. MacGillicudy pulled out his warrant card and held it aloft.

'Police,' he yelled, above the hum of concern. 'Please all stay calm and stay exactly where you are.'

The conversations became an excited buzz, much like a swarm of wasps when an idiot with a stick decided to poke the nest. The buzz then settled down as they all waited to see the next instalment in their exciting day.

'Your key please, Frankie,' ordered Cornwallis, as the hush descended.

Frankie stepped up and shook his shoulders before bracing himself to kick out. Rose got in first and turned the handle, it clicked and the door swung open.

'You have a habit of not checking, haven't you?' she said sweetly.

Cornwallis coughed and had the decency to look a little contrite, while Frankie just shrugged his shoulders. They quickly regained their composure and piled through the door.

The room was just a smaller version of the main Collider chamber, a big screen dominating the far wall with a bank of controls in front. There a man in a white coat pulled levers behind a protective shield, which stopped him viewing the screen to give the customers total privacy. Standing next to him, and looking up at the screen, were Kintersbury and Dumchuck, both wearing a look of consternation as they saw everyone come through. Gerald caught hold of Isabella and held her back to guard the door, the only door into the room.

'What's this?' demanded the man on the desk, his head whipping around at the sound of the door coming fully open. 'This is a private viewing.'

'It was,' replied Cornwallis easily. 'But now it's on general release.' He looked up at the screen and saw himself staring back, and like a mirror, so were everyone else — apart from Gerald. 'Did you see this in your viewing?' he asked Kintersbury, taking a step towards him. 'Did you know we were coming through? Did you see that you were about to get arrested?

Kintersbury took the momentary look of confusion off his face and replaced it with a knowing grin. 'Actually, yes, we've just seen what happens, Mr Cornwallis, and you are going to be very disappointed.'

'And pray tell, why is that?'

Kintersbury's grin widened. 'Because in a few seconds time

you will wish you hadn't stepped foot inside this building. We are not on our own you know.'

'Cornwallis,' warned Gerald. 'He may be right. Sum o' them tourist out there are starting to look a little mean.'

'How many?' enquired Frankie, coming over to look.

'Six,' replied Gerald. 'Oh dear, it looks like they may be armed.'

Kintersbury could hardly contain himself with the excitement that foreknowledge had brought. 'Give up now, Cornwallis, and you may actually survive all this.'

Cornwallis looked hard at Kintersbury. 'Is that what you saw then, me giving up?'

Kintersbury shook his head. 'Actually, no, you died.'

Rose's hands went straight to her mouth and she gasped.

'You too, Miss Morant, in fact none of you will come out of this room alive,' added Kintersbury, gleefully rubbing his hands. 'Oh, this is wonderful.'

'Er, Pelegrew.' Dumchuck spoke up for the first time. 'That gentleman there,' and he pointed towards Gerald. 'I don't remember seeing *him* on the screen.'

'Of course he was,' replied Kintersbury dismissively. 'The Collider never lies.'

Frankie quickly pulled Isabella out of the way and together he and Gerald barred the door.

'No,' countered Dumchuck with a little more certainty. 'I'm sure he wasn't, in fact I *know* he wasn't.'

'Then you weren't looking properly, Abraham.'

MacGillicudy pulled out two pairs of handcuffs and handed one over to Cornwallis. 'I don't know about you, Jack, but I have no intention of dying just yet, I've only just been promoted.'

A commotion began at the door, and Cornwallis fought the

temptation to look around, instead he stared up at the screen. Frankie had already suffered from a knife wound to the chest and the six men were rushing through the door. One of them grabbed Isabella, while two others ran towards Rose. Cornwallis couldn't look at it anymore and spun around to confront the knife that headed towards his ribs. When he turned, he found no knife coming towards him, in fact, Gerald and Frankie were not only holding their own, but had already downed two of the tourists.

He turned back around and grinned at Kintersbury, who now had a look of utter confusion on his face. 'You should have listened to Dumchuck, Gerald is an anomaly, he ain't really there.'

Rose watched the screen too and saw the way Isabella and she had been grabbed, not altogether very gentlemanly. It made her feel violated, even though nothing had actually happened. It was though she could see things through a different pair of eyes, but a part of her knew that she looked at things that were actually happening somewhere else, in some other universe, at some point in time. She looked at a reality, and she willed herself to fight back as the men grabbed her. Mesmerised, she just couldn't take her eyes away from the screen as she saw herself fight off the men. She could also see how Cornwallis had turned, just as the knife had entered his ribs. He staggered, clutched at the knife, and then fell to his knees, a hand held out towards the other Rose. Having fought off her attackers, she rushed over to him and took him in her arms. Then she saw a man throw a knife at her, hitting her in the back, and she slumped forward on top of Cornwallis. She gave a long shudder, and then both of them went still.

Frankie had knocked out another of the tourists, and Gerald had his hands around the throat of yet another. Rose finally managed to drag her eyes away from the screen and back to the events in *her* reality; she then stepped determinedly towards Kintersbury, wanting to exact her revenge for the other Rose, for the other Cornwallis, for the other all of them, to do to Kintersbury what he and his men were doing to her and her friends.

Cornwallis stepped in front of Rose just as she reached Kintersbury. 'No, Rose, don't do it.'

'But, Jack, didn't you see what happened up there?' she said, angrily pointing towards the screen.

'I did, Rose, but that is not how it ends: *this* is how it ends.'

'But, the screen shows what happens — at least somewhere.'

'Everything happens somewhere, but not here. In some places we aren't even born, some places we don't even exist, have never existed and won't exist. Here is the only reality that we know. The dangers of the Collider are just this; looking at something other than what is, does not mean that it will in reality happen.'

'But the Collider shows the other universes.'

'But not here. If the operator plays with his toggle, we go to some other place at some other time. There are infinite places anyone can go, but here, now, is the only place that matters to us. This is all we will ever know.' Her eyes were wide and frightened and she panted as her heart raced. Cornwallis reached out and held her arms; he pulled her forward, forcing her to look at him. '*That...*' and he indicated the screen with his head, '... did not happen here. *They*...were not us. *It*...did not happen.'

Gerald downed the last of the attackers and peace finally descended. There followed a round of applause from the genuine tourists who thought that their money had been well spent, considering all the entertainment they were getting. The big screen showed the other reality, and the guide desperately tried to explain it all in a way that did not become detrimental to the income of the Collider. He knew now that Gerald had caused it all, because he still did not show on the screen, but he couldn't explain how.

The operator now decided that discretion would be the better part of valour and pushed back his chair and ran for the door. Bugger his boss's instructions to stay whatever happened, he intended to make sure that whatever happened didn't happen to him. Frankie and Gerald smiled as they stepped out of the way to let him pass.

MacGillicudy took a step towards Dumchuck, slapping on the bracelets before the banker could even move. 'You are being arrested for murder, kidnapping, and I believe theft of a substantial amount of money. Anything else you can think of, Jack?'

'Not at the moment, Jethro, though I'm sure we will find something.'

'It's finished, Pelegrew,' sighed Dumchuck, looking over towards Kintersbury. 'And quite frankly I'm glad. This has all been such a strain. Mrs Dumchuck has been wondering why I've been so tense.'

'Abraham, this is far from finished. We are men of power with powerful friends; nobody will convict us as there is very little evidence for anything.'

'I think there is, Kintersbury,' replied Cornwallis. 'You thought you would get away with it, but you haven't. You stole all the money that the bank received from the Assembly, didn't you? You put it into Gornstock Trust and Holdings and then bankrupted the business. I know now that you intended to get it out of the country, but you didn't. You see, the Bagman intercepted the ship and he has it safe. All the gold you stole is still sitting in that ship, it's going nowhere, Kintersbury, and neither are you.'

'You have to prove it, and you won't be able to. You're dealing with a banker and the Treasury Secretary here, you know. Don't you think we would have found a way to hide everything? The ship means nothing, so go ahead, that was just small change.'

'That won't be my problem. Somebody else will go through all the books, somebody who knows far more than me; and quite probably, far more than you too.'

Cornwallis let go of Rose and advanced towards Kintersbury to slap the handcuffs on, when suddenly the screen flickered and the picture broke up. It went blank for a few seconds, then another picture came up, and this one showed everyone alive and well — only…

Rose stared at it, even more confused now. Kintersbury cast a look over his shoulder and saw the new image. He winced; he just couldn't understand it at all. As Cornwallis stepped forward, Kintersbury sprinted away, and he moved pretty quickly, but he could only move towards the screen. He stopped in front of it and turned, and then pulled a knife from his pocket and started waving it menacingly in front of him.

'No closer,' he growled. 'This is not over yet.'

'I think it is,' replied Cornwallis patiently.

'You're wrong. I checked the Collider, it confirmed everything.'

'We have your mistress too, you know that. Your Miss Lena is under lock and key and has told us all about it.'

Kintersbury turned and looked up at the Collider screen, and saw himself looking back; but his clothes were different, and so too were everybody else's. Cornwallis wore some sort of uniform with a flat type of hat, and so too did Rose and Frankie.

MacGillicudy wore a kind of suit and stood there with his hands in his pockets. Isabella wore a short skirt that showed quite a lot of thigh. All of them stared at Kintersbury, both on screen and off.

He backed away from them until he could hardly go any further; the screen being right behind him; then in through the door came Fluffy.

'Where d'you come from?' asked Frankie, looking down.

'Come wiv yer, didn't I. I were under the cart as youse told me I couldn't come. So when youse went down that pipe thingy, I came too. So here I is. That's the one I's scratched,' he said, indicating Kintersbury. 'Still sees the marks, see, did 'im good and proper, like.' He sauntered over and jumped up on the desk in front of the screen.

Rose looked at herself on screen in that strange uniform and wondered what it all meant. She peered closer and saw the words "Police" on a thick padded waistcoat and she sort of felt better inside as it confirmed that she was still on the side of the law. She stepped closer to Kintersbury just as Cornwallis did too. Fluffy meowed and then spat, and then arched his back just as Kintersbury began to wave the knife again. The cat took exception to the knife whistling just past his head, so with a growl, jumped off, and sank his teeth into Kintersbury's leg.

Kintersbury kicked out, and the cat went flying across the room. But the action left him unbalanced and he stumbled backwards towards the screen. He threw out his arm to counter the imbalance, but he just wind-milled and continued to fall. Cornwallis suddenly realised what was going to happen, and leapt forward.

Everything happened, but it seemed to happen in slow motion, but so quickly at the same time. Kintersbury fell into the screen, and as he touched it, it sort of sparked. It then dragged him in, further and further, and Cornwallis watched in fascination as the two images in front of him sort of merged into one. He leapt forward to grab hold, but it seemed like something held him back. Try as he might he just couldn't break away from whatever anchored him. Kintersbury screamed, and then came a sort of sucking sound, and then suddenly Kintersbury had disappeared.

Everyone stared at the screen, and those on the screen stared back, their expressions were exactly the same. They were horrified.

'Well,' said Gerald, breaking the silence that followed. 'I've been there, got the shirt with the logo on, even. So I can tell yer this; 'e ain't coming back!'

CHAPTER 16

'Well?' asked Rose, as Cornwallis walked through the door.

He smiled at them and walked over to take his seat. Frankie picked up a beer and knocked off the top, then handed it over to him before relaxing back into his chair. MacGillicudy had only just arrived after having dealt with everything at the Yard and perched on Mrs Gridlington's desk, swinging a leg impatiently.

When they all got back to Scooters Yard with Dumchuck and the six accomplices, Cornwallis had been nabbed by the Bagman; that had been some hours ago and he had spent all that time incarcerated with the man. Gerald had waited for a while, but eventually he'd had enough and decided to go back to the Brews and find out the story later. Isabella too had waited, but her exhaustion took hold and she had retired to her room downstairs to sleep. Rose and Frankie found time to go to the Stoat and pick up some celebratory crates of beer, and for Rose to freshen up and grab a few other things. Fluffy went off somewhere, probably after something, and no one had any idea when or whether they were likely to see him again; however, the cat did indicate that he might well be relocating to the neighbourhood.

'Well, indeed,' replied Cornwallis impishly. 'Well, well, well indeed.' He tipped up the beer and took a long pull. He smiled again and then regarded them all, each in turn, finally fixing on MacGillicudy. 'I take it due process is still taking place?'

MacGillicudy nodded. 'All banged up and no place to go.

Bough is enjoying himself immensely and has even notified the press. Your name is going to be plastered across the front pages of all the papers tomorrow.' Frankie gave him a hurt look. 'You too, Frankie, and Rose,' he added with a smile. 'I will just have to content myself with a pat on the back from Bough.'

'Oh, that's a shame. You've done just as much as the rest of us,' sympathised Rose.

'I'm a feeler, Rose, and feelers do what feelers do.'

'Well, you're one feeler who did an awful lot.'

'That goes without saying,' interjected Cornwallis. 'We couldn't have done it without you; and you had the pleasure of seeing Grinde take a walk down the road.'

MacGillicudy's grin broadened at the thought. 'Gods, yes, now that *is* a bonus.'

Frankie grabbed another beer. 'Bugger Grinde, Jack, come on, what happened?'

'I'd rather not have to bugger Grinde, thank you,' replied Cornwallis with distaste. 'But I can tell you what it was all about.'

'Go on then,' they all urged.

'Now, where shall I start?'

It took a while, but eventually Cornwallis told the story.

'Glenda Pilchard was the architect of it all, and it began when her hatred for her life became too much to bear. Her clientele were all influential men, and then she got the idea that if she used some of them, she could start a new life somewhere else, and leave her present one far behind. But she overreached herself when she decided to get her own back on the city.

'Kintersbury and Dumchuck were clients of hers. The foremost banker in Gornstock, and a member of the Assembly who had responsibility in the treasury department, and they were too good an opportunity to waste. She began to squeeze them, until eventually with promises of untold wealth they became willing accomplices.

'She persuaded Kintersbury to enter the drugs trade, and with the profits from that, he bought Gornstock Trust and Holdings. His ship had been bringing all the drugs in for a while now and had cornered the market; they put Maxwell in charge of all the drug smuggling and forced most of the other traffickers out of business. All the profits from the drugs went through Goup, who sent it on in a roundabout route to Kintersbury, who then used the firm to extort money from any place they could. It started with buying up debts from the bank, and they did that with the help of Dumchuck. They would then use strong arm tactics to get the debtors' money into the firm's accounts. That went well until Glenda got the idea that she could use the bank as well.

'With Kintersbury's contacts overseas she began to set up bogus investment companies, and Dumchuck used his influence to persuade investors to invest in these off shore companies with the promise of high returns, little knowing that these companies were nothing but a fraud. Information kept coming back on how well these companies were doing, and they were issuing guaranteed bonds, which were in effect worthless, for the investments and returns. This encouraged others to follow suit. Dumchuck persuaded the bank itself to invest long term, and then began to divert the money over. The bank's resources began to dwindle, so the move to get the government to bail them out short term came into play. The same promises of a high return for the short term loan persuaded the Assembly to grant the loan, which they immediately invested into Gornstock Trust and Holdings, which then converted the money into solid gold. They melted the gold down and cast it into small fragments which they placed on Kintersbury ship, the Greyhawk, as ballast, which was why the Bagman had such difficulty in finding it.

'The overseas companies are still in place, and the difficulty now is to try and follow the trail to get at the money that had already been converted. Fortunately, it's going to be the job of the investigators from the treasury department to follow everything up, as they were partly to blame for not picking it all up to start with.

'Kintersbury's ship, Greyhawk, was due to dock today and the three of them were to board it and be spirited away to a life of luxury. For them the icing on the cake came after last night's meeting with the Warden, which resulted in yet another loan from the Assembly in the form of guaranteed bonds. These were found in Dumchuck's briefcase, so if nothing else, we've got Dumchuck bang to rights.'

'So where did Radstock and Goup come into things?' asked Rose.

Cornwallis sighed. 'Some time ago, the Bagman recruited Radstock as his eyes and ears within the Assembly. The Bagman had heard of his "preferences" and had used the information to coerce Radstock into doing what he wanted. The Bagman had then instructed him on ways to find out hidden information. Then one day, while speaking to Kintersbury in his office in the house, Kintersbury went out for a few moments, and so Radstock decided to practise looking. He found a little more than he bargained for as he unearthed a letter from Dumchuck explaining that his wife had sent the wrong information to Goup and asking what he should do about it. He found a note written on the letter saying that Kintersbury would deal with it. Radstock became worried and told the Bagman all about it, so he placed his agent into Goup's office. Glenda had used Goup as her accountant for some time and they had got close, so close that they actually fell for each other, so when Kintersbury told her what had happened, she got Kintersbury to spirit Goup away

411

and hide him in the dwarf tunnels. She then arranged the deception on the ship, just in case they were being watched, which they were; by us, in actual fact. But they had a few problems. They had drugged him to make him more malleable, but overdid it a little. A couple of her men had earlier been planted on the ship and took him off, just as the ship was about to leave, when we were distracted by Sparrow. They took him to Havelock Crescent, where they were to run away together when she had got all the money; but he had no idea that his Glenda was a master criminal and a prostitute. The presence of Radstock at Havelock Crescent when we raided was pure coincidence, but what a beautiful one it was.'

By now Frankie's head reeled, he could hardly keep up with the chain of events. 'So how did we get involved?' he asked, shaking his head.

'Because the Bagman thought that potentially, it would be politically explosive. If his department investigated, then it would probably be swept under the carpet. He wanted it spread out so all could see. He used us, that is for certain, and he omitted to tell us that he knew it involved Kintersbury from the start; his argument being that we had already started to find out about him, so he wanted to see how all the strands were going to come together. Besides, he said he didn't want to compromise Radstock at that moment, I assume because he's got something else going on. He knew that Kintersbury was involved in the murder of Miss Knutt all along.'

'What about Freddie the Weasel?'

'Maxwell hired him, and Kintersbury gave him an old suit so that he would at least look the part. Unfortunately, when he had done his work; end of Freddie.'

'They nearly got away with it,' said MacGillicudy. 'If it wasn't for Dumchuck's wife, then they would have.'

'Yes, but she didn't know anything about it. Dumchuck meant to leave her and set sail into the sunset with all his ill-gotten gains.'

'What a nasty bunch of people,' observed Rose.

'Politicians and Bankers: in all honesty, what do you expect? They were going to bleed the city dry and to hell with everyone else, but at least the money should be recoverable now.'

'Except for the little people like Brownlow, they will never get their money back,' said Rose. 'It's always the little people who have to pay, and they're the ones who can't afford it.'

Cornwallis nodded. 'But at least they can rest easily at night knowing that their elders and betters are taking such good care of them,' he replied, ironically.

MacGillicudy laughed. 'You are so right, Jack, you are so right.' He slapped his thigh and stood up.

'You off somewhere, Jethro?' asked Cornwallis.

'Back to the Yard. I only popped around to see what happened with the Bagman, still got tons of paperwork to do, thanks to you.'

'That's a shame. I was about to suggest we hit the pub.'

MacGillicudy pulled a face.

'We'll do it tomorrow then instead,' conceded Cornwallis, looking at the disappointment on Jethro's face. 'It's late anyway; we'll only get a couple of hours in.'

As the door closed behind MacGillicudy, Frankie sighed. 'Shame that, but that still leaves us three, and I'm sure we can do some damage in a couple of hours.'

Cornwallis grinned. 'That sounds like a good idea, but I want to shower first.' He stood up and headed for the door. 'Keep yourselves amused while I'm gone. I won't be long.'

The door closed and Rose stood up. 'I'm just going to change, Frankie; I'll use the cupboard next door.' She picked up the bag she had brought with her from the Stoat, and she too headed for the door.

Frankie took a long slow deep breath. A minute ago, there were four of them, and now only one. He finished the beer in his hand and thought about opening another when he decided to wait. He screwed up some scrap paper which he began to flick at the bin on the other side of the office, just to waste some time while his mind went through everything that had happened over the last few days, and he smiled; all in all it had been a good few days and he wouldn't have missed it for the world. He stood up and thrust his hands deep in his pockets and paced, Rose seemed to be taking a bit of a while, he thought. He heard the cupboard door close next door and decided that he would have a stern word with her now, before Jack came back down. The investigation had finished and Jack would likely be a bugger to work with unless she got her finger out.

His head spun around as Rose opened the door and came back in. Frankie took one look and stood transfixed.

'Do you think this will do?' she asked innocently, coyly biting her bottom lip. She took a slow spin around and then raised a questioning eyebrow.

Frankie couldn't find the words; in fact, at that moment, he couldn't find anything.

'I'll just go and see if Jack is managing all right, if that's okay with you?' she said when he didn't reply.

Frankie just stared, and then nodded slowly.

Cornwallis stepped out of his shower and wrapped a towel around his waist and then another around his head. He hummed to himself as he walked out into the hall and through to his bedroom; all in all, he felt pleased with the outcome, with the only really unfortunate incident being when Kintersbury disappeared into the Collider. He wondered if Kintersbury would be aware of what had happened, whether his conscious self hovered somewhere between worlds, or if he had somehow popped out into another? As the Collider people said, the chances are that he now just didn't exist, not died, but just stopped existing, like Gerald, but not like him. It was a strange concept to consider, and he wondered what the ramifications were going to be.

He took the towel from around his head, wiped his face and shook out his hair, then threw the towel into the corner and used his fingers to comb through the tangles. He turned to his cupboard and selected some clean clothes and put them on the bed, he turned back around — and then stopped.

Rose stood in the doorway.

He looked at her, and she looked back at him.

'I just thought I'd better say thank you for buying this and all the other clothes from the Elves,' she said with a smile. She wore the purple dress that had made such an impression on him the other day. The one that seemed like a second skin, the fluid one, the one that moulded to her body in such a way as to defy the senses, the one that she couldn't wear any underwear with! 'Does it look all right?'

Cornwallis closed his mouth and nodded. 'Yes,' he managed to say in the end, but it came out a little strangled.

She smiled, and looked down to his towel. 'I'm so glad, because otherwise I would have to take it off again, and I really shouldn't do that when it's all that I'm wearing.' She stepped up to him, wrapped her arms around his neck and pressed her body up against his. The response from down below was only natural, and she looked down and giggled. 'On the other hand…'

Cornwallis' towel fell to the floor.

'…ooh, if that's for me, then I suppose you'd better help

me take it off, after all.'

He kissed her and held her tight. 'In that case, I suppose I'd better,' he said breathlessly. A few moments later, the dress slid to the floor in a whispered sigh.

Frankie opened another beer while he waited, and he was still waiting when he'd finished drinking it. He knew that up above was Cornwallis' bedroom, and he sat there with a grin on his face. Soon he heard what he expected to hear, a little creak of the springs. His grin widened as he heard a few more creaks, and then lots of creaks — and then lots more creaks. He thought that one day he would tell Cornwallis to get a new bed, but maybe not tonight.

He closed the door slowly and quietly and then headed down the stairs. He had a spring in his step, thankful that at long last, the two of them had come to their senses; life in the investigation business probably wouldn't be the same again. He stopped outside Isabella's rooms and thought for a moment, she'd had quite an ordeal over the last twenty four hours and he wondered how she was coping. He knocked and waited, and soon the door opened and Isabella stood there in her dressing gown.

'I just thought I'd check to see if you were all right,' ventured Frankie, with a touch of concern.

She smiled back at him. 'Thank you, but I'm fine. I've had a few hours sleep now and feel a lot better.'

'That's good. We'll have a drink tomorrow to celebrate, and I'm sure you can come too. Incidentally, you shouldn't answer the door wearing that at this time of night. Get a little chain so you can see who it is first.'

Isabella nodded, and then thought, and then looked at Frankie. 'Hang on a second.' She closed the door and left him standing there for a few moments. He wondered whether he should just leave her be when the door opened again and she stood there once more, right in front of him. 'Is this any better?' she asked sweetly, and this time she wasn't wearing her dressing gown.

Frankie thought that he had died and gone to heaven as she pulled him inside; someone up there must really, really, like him.

end

Visit my website at
www.clivemullis.com
Where you can join the Black Stoat VIP Club for my latest news
and the occasional bit from Eddie, landlord of our favourite
pub.

Also by Clive Mullis

Scooters Yard
Under Gornstock

ABOUT THE AUTHOR

Clive Mullis was a paramedic for thirty years until deciding that
there must be another way of making a living. He lives in
Bedfordshire with his wife, son and two dogs.

Made in the USA
Middletown, DE
14 May 2023